"Science fiction meets Ebenezer Scrooge in this intoxicating, modern update of *A Christmas Carol*. Only this time, the rich man's rants and unkindness can bring down his entire society. Well-crafted and thought-provoking."

    - Heather Redmond, author of *A Dickens of a Crime* series

"Ransom Stephens densely packs the pages of his latest fast-paced story with elements of Dickens, warnings of technocracy, and an addiction redemption narrative. With great care, he weaves a complex story that will leave a reader shaken by dire warnings about the repetitive cycles of history and humanity. Stephens has written an ambitious, page-turning epic that is a love story, a social commentary and a dystopian fantasy all in one."

    - Amber Cowie, author of *Rapid Falls*

"Deliciously complex and steeped in the apocrypha of Silicon Valley, *Too Rich to Die* delivers a tale of the worst possible outcome barely diverted by humanity's better impulses. What if you not only had the power to see alternate timelines, but you had the technological prowess to pick and choose between them? *Too Rich to Die* is a delightful sequel to the fast-paced and complex time-bending of *The 99% Solution*. Stephen's trio of Timeweavers has localized a moment in time when everything changes for the worse. Now they must pull off the difficult task of changing the way a trillionaire sees the world."

    - Kimberly Unger, author of *The Gophers of High Charity*

Other books by Ransom Stephens

Novels:
The 99% Solution, a Time Weavers Novel
The Sensory Deception
The God Patent

Popular Science:
The Left Brain Speaks The Right Brain Laughs: A Look at the Neuroscience of Innovation & Creativity in Art, Science, and Life

Check them out at: www.theintoxicatingpage.com

TOO RICH TO DIE

A NOVEL

By Ransom Stephens

STRANGE FUSE

an imprint of Short Fuse Publishing,
a division of Fuse Literary, Inc., www.fuseliterary.com

Text Copyright © 2019 by Ransom Stephens

Thank you for buying the authorized, official, licensed version of this book. We'd like to remind you that it is illegal to reproduce this work in any form, printed, electronic, smoke signals, broadcast, etc, without the author's written permission. Well, smoke signals are okay. If, however, you finagled a pirated or stolen version, you should send the author beer money; he's trying to make a living.

Cover design and graphics
Copyright © 2019 by Heather Stephens
Check her out: www.designseed.nl

ISBN: 9781937791773

This is a work of fiction! Names, characters, places, and incidents are used fictitiously and/or facetiously and/or are the product of the author's imagination and/or delusions, and any resemblance to actual persons, living or dead, business establishments, events, or locales is entirely coincidental. Further, the political views and senses of humor expressed herein are those of the characters and in no way reflect the modest views of the publisher or the author, his friends, or family.

No beagles were harmed in the writing of this book.

Mystery, Thriller, & Suspense > Technothrillers
Mystery, Thriller, & Suspense > Historical
Mystery, Thriller, & Suspense > Psychological Thrillers
Mystery, Thriller, & Suspense > Suspense
Science Fiction > Time Travel
Science Fiction > Alternate History (prevented)
Literature & Fiction > Political
Literature & Fiction > Coming of Age

for you

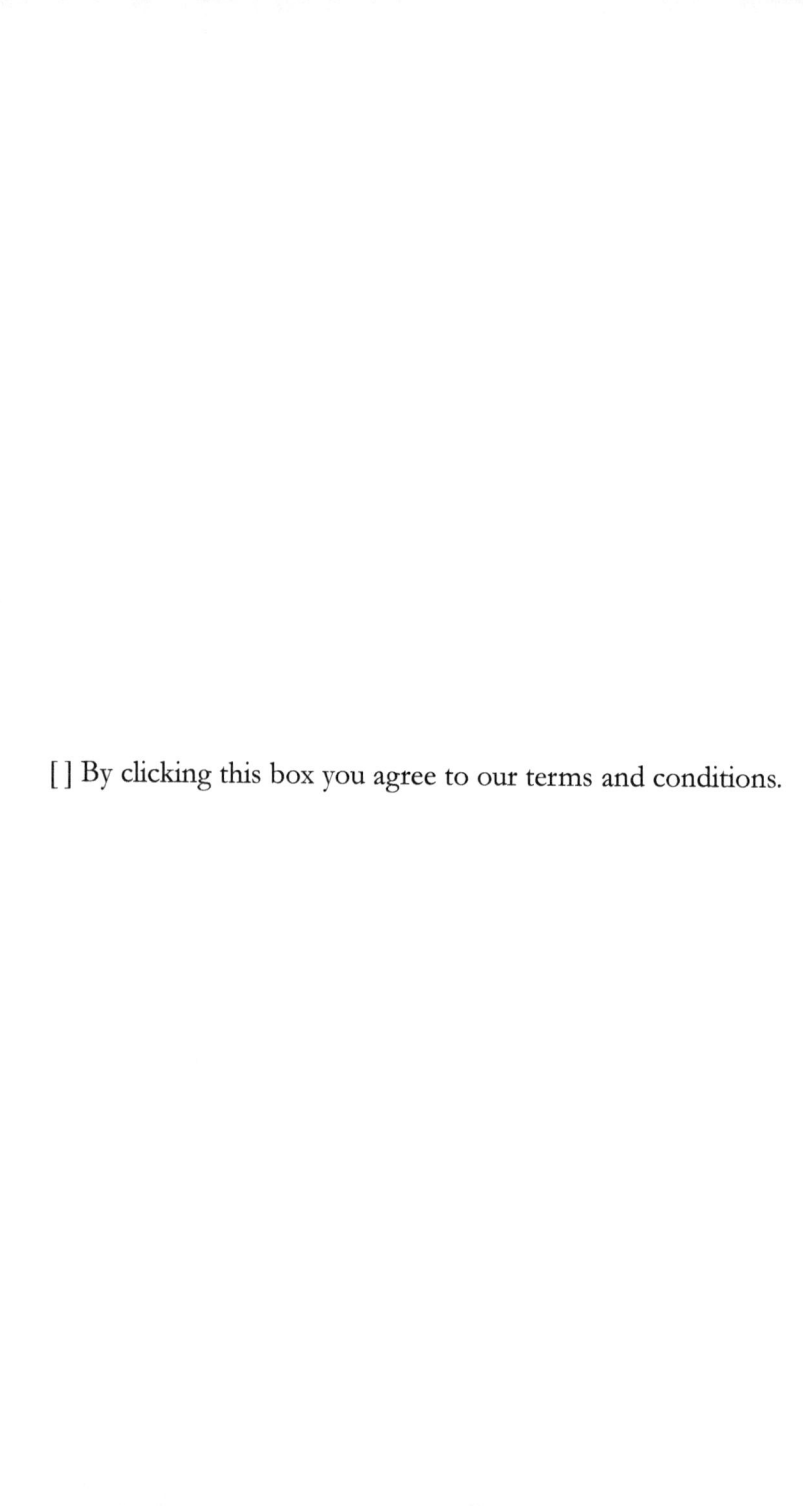

[ ] By clicking this box you agree to our terms and conditions.

I. The Pivot

"Give me a hundred, you techie bastard!" A woman in rags reaches out to a twenty-something man with perfectly parted hair.

His eyes lock on the woman as though she poses a mortal threat.

My beagle companion, Winter, stretches his leash toward the woman. With his ears perked and tail wagging, he seems to have taken her side in the conflict. As a techie myself, though not a bastard to the best of my knowledge, I empathize with the young man, but the woman—wrapped in a filthy jacket, her skin grimy and dark hair hanging like twine—merits far more compassion than the man dressed techie-chic with his immaculate white hoodie and jeans creased the way that my suit pants ought to be.

"How's your app, Scratch?" the woman sneers. "Have you made your fuck you money yet?"

The man tries to leap aside, but she grabs him by the hood and whines, "Come on, Eben, give me five dollars. Help me out."

With her arm outstretched, she exposes a tattoo of excellent quality: A planet on her right shoulder with two arrows emerging from opposite sides of its equator curving down her arm and colliding on her bicep with a starburst at the point where they meet.

The man twists under her arm. She loses her grip and falls. He leaps away, adjusts his glasses, straightens his hoodie, and rushes across Market Street.

The woman moans, her moan becomes a sob and she cries out: "Fuck you." She folds into herself, sinking into a puddle on the sidewalk, and her voice grows softer with each word: "Fuck you, you tool, just FU."

My stroll along Market Street is not purely for physical fitness or to greet the Summer Solstice, though this splendid cool day is wrapped in the formality of San Francisco's trademark fog. Nineteen days ago my colleagues and I predicted that a pivot point of historical significance would occur right here and now.

I put my hand to my ear to check the status of my earbug—still installed and functioning—and say, "Was that it?"

My dear friend and colleague, Fiona Black, who you will soon meet if you haven't already, is connected by our earbug tech. "Right," she says, "we're now in the rapids of the river of time." She speaks with a delightful vowel-amplifying Australian accent.

Then I hear my friend Volodya Kazimir's sharp Russian accent through my earbug: "Mm. I confirm that a pivot point has occurred. It is a problem." His accent makes everything he says sound like a debate point. He uses the word "problem" often and runs the two syllables together like "prubl'm."

Fiona, Volodya, and I, not to mention Winter, are in almost constant contact either in person or through technology. We are in the business of calculating the probabilities of possible future timelines. While the possibilities are indeed infinite, the probabilities are quite finite. The timelines combine to form an inter-dependent weave that follows a more or less stable path from the past into the future, but immediately following a pivot point, the timeweave unravels into a spray of possible destinies—what Fiona refers to as the rapids of time.

Winter tugs his leash from my wrist and rushes to the poor woman. Her pants wick moisture from the puddle and tears run down her face. Winter dismisses all etiquette and muscles his way onto her lap. Her lips attempt a smile as Winter kisses away her tears. Winter is a friendly little fellow, but I've never seen him lavish affection so boisterously on a stranger.

I walk over and take his leash. "Terribly sorry, ma'am, he's normally more reserved."

She looks at me, then Winter, then back at me. I lean down and offer a hand. She grips my arm and pulls herself up. Winter delivers a final kiss as she rises. Her lips finally manage a smile but it disappears when she looks across the street at the techie. "I hate that bastard."

I offer my hanky and she takes it. I say, "Is there anything I can do?"

She starts to shake her head but stops and says, "Twenty bucks?"

I take my wallet from my coat pocket. "I only have seven dollars and 32 cents."

She takes it.

The two of us watch the accosted techie on the other side of Market Street. He's bent over as though he has osteoporosis, but straightens to jump out of the way of a young woman riding a skateboard who yells, "Out of my way, Glass-hole!" He continues down New Montgomery Street. With his bent-over posture, he looks like he's monitoring the sidewalk to avoid stepping on cracks.

A wisp of fog passes between the woman and me. I turn away because—oh no—I feel it coming on. It starts with overwhelming vertigo, that feeling you get when you stand on a bridge, hoping that you won't jump or fall. You have no intention of jumping and don't expect to fall, but it sure is a long way down. That niggling possibility can gnaw at your gut. The vertigo builds until you feel dizzy and what started as an absurd fear emerges as possible, and then probable.

I pull my suit jacket tight against the chill, but it's not the cold that makes me shiver, it's something internal, something I don't understand, perhaps a talent, maybe an illness, certainly a curse.

A seam forms. The seams resemble the green edges of sheets of glass, like windows separating inside from outside, one world from another. The vertigo draws me to the boundary and I fall.

The hustle and bustle of Market Street shifts in focus. An executive waits in line for a cable car. As the tinted seam passes through him, his fine pin-striped suit shifts from contemporary elegant to depression-era destitute. The line for the cable car evolves into a soup line and what remains of his executive stature floats away on a foggy gust. His black fedora fades to gray and droops over his eyes, his skin weathers, his lips turn down, and his calloused hands reach for a bowl. I don't know if the world has spun off of its axis, but I have surely spun off of mine. I lean through the different seams and each timeline induces sensations from trepidation to contentment, dread to hope, and anger to calm. Cars dial back their makes and models from hybrids to V8s to fins to horseless and then to horse-drawn carriages. The earth seems to quake as it must have when the big one hit in 1906, but these people of the past don't notice. A panel van tugged by horses and labeled "Bank of Italy" shifts out of focus under a cascade of green-tinted fog and emerges as a bright red Bank of America automatic teller machine.

I struggle under a 30 pound weight that wriggles on my chest and licks my face from chin to forehead: Winter, my service dog, performing his service. As I rise to a sitting position, he squirms away and sits facing me with his white chest out and brown ears folded at attention. I look around, hoping that I haven't distressed anyone. Seven other people recline on the pavement of this block of Market Street, each a case of misfortune. Among them, my episode is not worth noticing, though the distraught woman seems to be monitoring me.

I check my earbug and say, "How long was I gone?"

Fiona replies, "Simon, dear Simon—these episodes are growing more frequent!"

I say, "No, they aren't," and wish I believed it.

"Less than fifteen seconds," Volodya says. "And you lie, my friend, you lie."

"Reality must be growing less stable," Fiona says. "You had episodes less than once a year when I first met you."

"I didn't." I lie a second time.

Volodya growls like a suspicious bloodhound. Volodya's growl indicates three things: first, his disagreement with Fiona's belief that it is reality that has grown less stable rather than my psyche; second, his impatience with my lie; and third, the unique ability he has to convey several bullet points with what barely qualifies as a syllable. "Please, they are not 'episodes,'" he says. "Simon, you experience delusions."

"Delusions, my fine ass." Fiona's voice ramps up. "Delusions don't give 100% accurate insights into how the future emerges from the past." I still haven't found a journal article that describes my curse, though I've been accused of schizophrenia, paranoia, psychosis, grandiosity, epilepsy, and even alcoholism, none of the symptoms add up.

1. The Post

Eben glances back at the woman who just accosted him and shudders. He watches a man in a rumpled gray suit with a beagle help her up.

A girl on a skateboard wipes in front of him. He adjusts his eyewear and rushes past the understated awnings of the Palace Hotel and turns onto Mission Street. He steps ahead of three women into a crisp stainless steel office tower, enters the elevator, and presses the button for the seventh floor. From behind him, one of the women asks him to hold the door. He has no time for such nonsense and ignores her.

The elevator rises too slowly for his taste. He uses the time to polish the ScratchCo logo. The elevator doors open and a tall, thin, impeccably dressed man named Yao Wo greets him with a wide, toothy smile: "Good morning, sir! Your call with the Punjab office has been delayed so you'll have extra time to review accounts—I know how you love to mull over a nice profit-loss statement. Absolutely kick ass way to begin summer, sir, though I do regret that—"

"Seriously?" Eben steps past Wo and strides between cubicles on the way to his office. Eben's company is a reflection of his own finely-tuned efficiency. With only 42 employees, ScratchCo's revenue is seven times that of the world's largest bank but with 1/7000 the payroll.

"Sir, I regret that—"

"I regret you."

"I do what I can, sir." Wo rushes ahead of Eben, carefully threading his way between cubicles to avoid encroaching on Eben's path. He barely makes it to Eben's office in time to open the door before he arrives and offer him a tablet computer. Eben stops at the door to clear his sinuses; he bobs his head and swallows three times, each with a high-pitched whine. Eben takes the tablet and examines the list of his morning appointments. The day prior to a business trip is always extra busy.

Something doesn't feel right in his office. It's not just the lights, which everyone on the seventh floor knows must be set as dim as possible to reduce costs. He looks up and sees a man and a woman rise from plastic chairs opposite his desk.

The woman says, "Are you Eben?"

To Wo, Eben says, "Who are these people?"

"Yes sir, I regret that—"

"How did they get in here?"

"As I was saying, sir, I fear that—"

"Fears and regrets. Get them out of here."

The woman taps the chair with her knuckles—the sort of absent-minded nervous twitch that annoys Eben—and says, "Would it be more convenient for us to speak to Allison?"

Eben says, "Allison is dead." He settles into the high-backed leather chair and sets the tablet on his desk. "You're not on my schedule. Run along."

The man clears his throat.

Eben takes off his Glass and sets them in their charging dock. Rubbing his eyes, he says, "Time is money. My money. You have something to say? Get it out."

"Eben." The man coughs up his name but can't seem to get any further.

"Mr. Scratch," the woman says, "we are from the Human Trafficking and Slave Liberation Fund collecting donations from San Francisco's generous tech executives. Every $50 we collect liberates a slave—"

"Are you slaves?"

"Well, no, but—"

"Then you have no problem. Buh bye."

The man looks befuddled, which nearly gives Eben cause to smile.

The woman says, "Every thousand dollars you contribute can stop the abduction and sale of twenty children." She leans forward as she speaks and her chair scuffs the floor. "Think of the burdens you can lift from thousands of people. With just a bit of compassion you can—"

Eben shakes his head at the scraping sound. "They can earn their freedom in weeks or months or however long, I don't care."

"If only it worked that way," the man says. "No, these people are ensnared in debt. Their captors charge more for room and board than they are capable of earning in the salt fields, sweatshops, and, well, as you can imagine, far worse."

"If I buy a slave's freedom, when will he or she pay me back and at what interest rate?"

"My gosh." The woman shakes her head as though trying to dislodge the concept. "Pay you back?"

"Gosh? Gosh isn't even a word."

Her mouth opens, but she contributes no sound to the conversation.

"Yes, pay me back. Don't you think they want genuine liberty—the real thing—instead of some gifted version?"

She steps forward and puts her fists on the opposite edge of Eben's desk, pushing up to increase her height. "Fifty dollars is nothing to you, but to them it's a life!"

Eben reaches down and presses the lever at his chair's base. The hydraulic action slowly elevates him. When he is eye-to-eye with the woman, he says, "You don't get to judge the value of fifty dollars to me."

"What? You're one of the richest men in the world! You make more than fifty dollars every minute."

"Not in these minutes, I haven't. Buh bye."

Still trembling, the woman says, "All of the major high tech executives South of Market are contributing. We just met with Marc Benioff and he pledged a million. Mark Zuckerberg and Jack Dorsey both pledged a hundred thousand, surely I can mark you down for—"

"Null. Mark me down for the whole null set." Eben lowers the chair back to desk-level. "Let laborers labor. Let them pay their debts. Let them earn their freedom just as I have, or at least give them the dignity of dying trying." He turns to his computer and the tasks required before the business trip. He opens the profit-loss database, and commences analysis of the revenue streams from the CurrentSea app, ScratchCo's original and still primary product. He forces himself to focus on his cherished database and watches it update the way that a parent watches a child on a swing.

The next time he looks up, his office is empty.

He turns to the list of scheduled software updates and discovers a bug in the latest release. He sends email to the hacking circle to find and fix it. Then he realizes that it wasn't a bug at all, it was a feature that he had requested. It's the beggars, he realizes. They've put him off his game; the charity beggars and that panhandler on Market Street. He's not sure whether he's more annoyed that she recognized him or that she had the nerve to touch him.

He checks the calendar and is reminded that the first leg of his business trip will be a frivolous party in a forest—oh how he hates it when the unimportant becomes urgent. Leaning forward, he tries to pull all the details into the big picture. Above software releases, P & L databases, and networking, he pictures himself walking into a magnificent 14th century Paris boardroom to give the most important pitch of his life. On that day, in just three weeks, he'll win the greatest victory and experience the greatest glory of his life. And then, Eben tells himself, no one will impose on his time. He'll wash his hands of the beggars, losers, and quitters forever.

At 11:15, Wo sets a fresh cup of coffee on the saucer at the corner of the desk, but instead of leaving, Wo lingers.

Eben looks up slowly, intentionally.

"Sir?" Wo says.

For the most part, Wo speaks the same English as any other third generation Californian, but now he speaks with a slight Chinese accent. The 'r' in sir comes out with no ring at all, not quite the clichéd sound of an 'l', but enough to trip Eben's suspicions.

"What do you need?" Eben asks, but he inflects in such a way as to discourage Wo from answering.

"Will there be anything else, sir?"

"You're clocking out early the day before we travel?"

"It's my son, sir."

Eben looks back at him but doesn't say anything.

"It's cool, sir," Wo says. "I assembled the itinerary and everything is ready to roll."

Eben let's several seconds pass before saying, "Another trip to the hospital?"

"Yes, sir. You approved my request." He leans over and taps an icon on the display of Eben's calendar that displays a virtual seal of approval.

"I suppose you'll want to use my car?"

"You did approve it, sir. And taking Muni can be dangerous for a child with—"

"So I won't be able to rely on you until you're bankrupted by these treatments?" He turns back to his computer, applies a series of commands and then turns the monitor toward Wo. "My car's GPS automatically updates this form." He turns the monitor back. "Will you charge these hours to your flex-time or do you prefer your pay docked?"

"I'm sorry sir, I've spent both weeks of this years' flex-time."

"Be here at end of business."

"Thank you, sir."

Eben leans back and watches Wo scurry away. A mirth-free chuckle dribbles through his vocal chords. Wo's title is Executive Administrative Assistant, though his role at ScratchCo is closer to Chief Operating Officer. Yao Wo would be the most difficult employee to replace, but rather than pay him accordingly, Eben keeps him unsettled and unaware of his negotiating position.

Another hour passes. Eben settles into exchange rate analysis. The feeling brought on by the beggar fades behind the keyboard clattering and hushed discussions in the cubicles beyond his office door—the rhythm of corporate efficiency.

His landline interrupts the calm of analysis. The caller-ID shows that it's his older sister, Sally. He grumbles at the realization that Wo isn't present to deflect the call.

He lifts the handset and says, "Yes."

"Eben?"

"I said, yes."

"Happy Birthday, Husker!"

"You know I hate that nickname."

"The big three-oh!"

"You're still capable of arithmetic."

"Seriously, Eben, how are you doing?"

"Too busy to chat, thank you."

"How's the weather up there?" Sally lives in Santa Barbara near one of Eben's properties.

"Foggy and cold, just the way I like it."

"There's a beach in Cabo with clear skies, hot sun, and gorgeous waves. Break away for a weekend and come with us. If you don't feel like celebrating your birthday then we'll celebrate summer like we did when we were kids. Come on, Husker!"

"I have responsibilities."

"Eben," Sally's voice turns serious, "you're too young to be such a curmudgeon."

"You can only get to my beach by boat."

"What?"

"The law says that the beach at my central coast vacation home is public property, but I won't be there to open the gate, so if you want to use my beach, you'll have to travel by sea like anyone else."

"You think I'm only inviting you—"

"Yes, because you want to have your party on my beach."

"Oh Husker, what's happened to you?"

"I've made some money. Kinda successful. And please, I've outgrown that nickname."

"You haven't outgrown it, you've just forgotten who you are." She sighs. "Everyone would love to see you. Evan is fourteen already, can you believe it? You won't even recognize him—but he still talks about you. He's started programming and he's such a formal kid, thoughtful and patient just like his Uncle Husker. Okay, Uncle Eben."

Eben tries to focus on exchange rates.

"How are you, Eben? Is there anyone in your life?"

Eben remains silent.

"Husker, I'm not giving up on you—even though you're an old man of thirty now. I'm going to invite you every summer and hope that someday you'll accept, but if you don't, well, it's your life."

Eben stares at the phone as Sally disconnects. His knuckles are white and he realizes that his shoulders are tense. When did everyone on earth decide that he owed them something? He's sick of it and this time he's not going to just sit by and let the quitters, moochers, and low-lifes sap his energy. No, this time, he'll tell the world what he really thinks of them.

He opens a social networking web site. He gets an extra twinge of ire at his 5000 "friends;" just another 5000 people who want a favor. He starts typing:

> "Market Street is disgusting. The heart of this rich city is teeming with drug abusers, failures, and the criminally insane—losers of every stripe, human trash. They act like they belong here, like they have a right to our streets. It's unacceptable. In truly great cities, the lowlifes keep to themselves; they sell trinkets, they beg quietly and with well earned shame, and they realize the privilege of spending time in the sophisticated parts of the city. We can practice compassion and preach about liberty, equality, and fraternity, but the degenerates and the working class should know their place and stay in it. Look, if they offered a penny's worth of value, I'd welcome them. But as it is, they're a liability. As productive citizens, we should install them where they belong and keep them there."

2. The Intoxicating Page

The bell on the door tinkles as Winter pulls me into The Intoxicating Page, Fiona's bookstore-saloon-café which also serves as our US business center, research lab, and software development hub.

It's toasty warm inside. I rub my hands together and inhale the scents of dried ink on paper and dried beer on concrete under the pervading aroma of fresh brewed coffee, sourdough bagels, and blueberry scones. Fiona pairs beverages with literature. The deeper you wander into the store, the more concentrated the alcohol-literature experience. The recessed spot lighting provides perfect illumination for reading, the requisite dimness of a bar, and the diffuse lighting of a café, and it's complemented by acoustic guitar instrumentals. I liberate Winter from his leash. He shakes from nose to tail and then trots through the juice box and Dr. Seuss section to the bar that occupies the store's center. It's an oval-shaped counter of polished walnut centered around a column modeled after a Greek temple that bears much of the weight of this three story building. Fiona tends the bar from within the oval.

She calls out, "Simon, we're short on time."

Fiona and I met in college, two years after she lost her leg. In the interim, she has determined myriad ways to compensate. She furnished The Intoxicating Page so that she could navigate through the store without using her prostheses—difficult technology when the leg is lost at the hip—or her ridiculously clichéd duck-handle cane. Her short, dark brown hair is parted on the side and shows the first hints of gray. Her blue eyes twinkle with her every thought and her cute little nose contradicts her rather strong jaw line. A tattoo adorns her chest, a crescent moon suspended from her clavicle with a witch mounted on its tip dangling high heels at her sparse cleavage, but it is her smile that captures your attention as you enter The Intoxicating Page. Today, her smile is tempered by tension and doubt, which is not at all her default.

Winter hops onto a barstool.

Fiona maneuvers over. "Bloody hell," she says, "I can never get him his biscuit before the drooling starts." Winter accepts his treat and shuffles off to the loveseat in the romance and pink champagne nook for his late-morning nap. Fiona runs a cloth over two small dots of drool, emerges from the bar, and guides me to my other cohort.

Volodya, whose name rhymes with melodious, makes a guttural sound of discontent in a Russian accent. He sits at a table with laptop and tablet computers in what Fiona refers to as the high-brow literature and single malt scotch ghetto. I met Volodya in 1983 at a conference in Sarajevo. He represented Moscow State and I represented the University of California. We argued at length but built a friendship on our shared passion for the capital-T truths of physics. To continue our arguments, we had to hack into the telecommunications infrastructures of the Soviet Union and the United States: our first collaboration.

Fiona pulls me past tables populated by people with their noses in books, laptops, or cell phones. Her remarkable gait betrays the challenge of flourishing with just the one leg but in no way diminishes her ability to deliver me to Volodya. He is a tall, sharp, athletic man with a straight-sloped nose, thin lips, and gray eyes that cut a path straight to your soul. We are both in the early stages of our second half-century, though his taut cable-like arms, firm triangle-shaped physique, and ability to sprint all-out for every second of fifteen minutes gives him the physical prowess of a twenty-year-old. My physique represents men of our age far more accurately.

Volodya wears tight fitting but flexible clothes; I prefer flannel suits that have visited the dry cleaners enough times to have developed the texture of your favorite blanket. I'm neither a tall nor a short man and, having grown up next to a river, I seem to have acquired its characteristics: my skin is a sort of pale gray like river rocks and my hair and eyes are the color of the muddy river bottom. Winter, on the other hand, is a striking creature with a coat composed of contrasting patches of black, orange, brown, and nearly fluorescent white; the very definition of beagleness.

I sit in the chair next to Volodya, take my laptop from my satchel, and say, "How much time do we have?"

"Timing resolution is weeks, not months; could be days, hours, or maybe is already too late," Volodya says, without looking away from his monitor. "It is a problem."

"Until what?"

"Onset of hundred year dark age. Hundred years if we're lucky; unlucky, maybe a thousand."

"A dark age?" Fiona says. "A bit cliché, even for you."

"Since a beggar asked Eben Scratch for five dollars, every strand of the unraveling timeweave leads to different type of dark age." He examines the timeweave graphic on his monitor. "Dark ages have happened over course of human history and will happen again. Why not now? The hegemony of the United States is in question with no one to step in. Europe on edge of disintegration, the Middle East in turmoil …"

Fiona leans over me. She smells spicy, like sandalwood. "Simon, what did you see?"

I say, "It was very mild. I'm fine," but she rolls her eyes so I describe the mishmash of visions—the transformation of an executive into a pauper, the cable car queue turning into a soup line, and the evolution of the Bank of Italy into a Bank of America ATM.

Volodya says, "You don't believe prediction derived from data, but you believe Simon's delusions?"

"Is it consistent with the timeweave?" Fiona asks.

"Much easier to predict past than future."

"You know what I mean." She perches on the table next to him.

His eyes rise from his laptop to her tattoo and when they reach her eyes he says, "History doesn't repeat."

"But if it did …"

"Simon's delusions are not specific, not predictive."

Where most people see their lives as a single image in time, during my episodes I perceive a collage of overlapping, interrelated, entangled shadows and intersections of possible timelines. As if that weren't disconcerting enough, I can shift from one reality to another and when I do, I bring you and the rest of the world with me. While I hold this as a visceral truth, the way that you're aware of night and day without giving it a thought, I have never assembled enough evidence to convince Volodya.

Fiona says, "Eben Scratch used to work for us. Do you remember him?"

Me: "No."

Volodya: "Yes, of course."

Me: "No you don't—you saw it in his timeline."

Volodya taps his monitor. "Okay. It is true. I have his timeline."

Fiona: "He worked on the Watergate app."

Me: "The one that follows the money?"

Fiona: "Right."

Our timeweave prediction engine consists of a huge library of programs that runs on a fleet of computer servers in our lab in Vienna. Volodya and I design our software but contract freelance programmers to write much of it. Since our work is quite sensitive, not just because of its dubious legality, but because the power of our predictions could easily be used for personal profit at the expense of humanity's wayward path in the general direction of civilization, we lead our contractors to believe that they are producing components for smartphone apps. Most of our employees leverage their experience into employment in the tech sector. Eben started his career here at The Intoxicating Page coding for us. We call our company TLA, which stands for Time Line Associates in Vienna where Volodya files our taxes and Three Letter Acronym here in San Francisco where Fiona files them.

"And, as you might expect in this epoch of history," Volodya says, "this dark age begins with a Facebook post." He orients his monitor so that the three of us can read the post.

Fiona is the first to speak. "It's horrible—he calls homeless people human trash." Her voice rises in both pitch and volume: "Privilege of spending time in the sophisticated parts of the city? Install them where they belong?"

Me: "How could 1093 people 'Like' this?"

Fiona: "He pisses off half the world and validates the other half."

Volodya scrolls through the comments, an unfolding debate on the value of desperate, downtrodden, and disaffected human beings.

I say, "The polarization of sympathy and antipathy fertilize suspicion and misunderstanding and revolution is the inevitable result."

Fiona: "And even the most idealistic revolutions cause as much suffering as blatant power grabs."

Volodya: "Bolsheviks could not have been more idealistic."

Me: "Or the French."

Fiona: "Something has gone off. The Eben who worked for us would never say this. We need to find out what happened to him."

Volodya: "You're siding with someone who disparages the weak and poor?"

Fiona: "No historical pivot occurs in a vacuum."

Me: "Look at this comment from one of our other protégés."

Volodya: "Owen Lockett?"

I read Owen's comment out loud: "We're not like this guy! Techies are good, caring people. We like figuring out puzzles and sometimes we get carried away, but we're not greedy assholes like Eben Scratch."

Fiona: "We did well by Owen."

Volodya: "He made fuck you money with video game."

Me: "How does one 'fuck you' with money?"

Volodya: "FU money is level of savings people target for early retirement."

Fiona: "He comes in now and then." She motions to the science fiction and absinthe section. "He's working on a game that uses gadgets like Google Glass to augment reality."

Me: "Eben wears Glass."

Volodya: "He does?"

Me: "Yes. Rims with no lenses, just a microprocessor that projects images onto one eye, web access, video, messaging, maps."

Volodya: "Ability to see through Eben's Glass could provide key perspective on this pivot point."

Fiona: "You haven't hacked Google Glass yet?"

Me: "Haven't needed to. No one uses it."

Volodya: "No one but Eben, our only clue to this pivot point."

Fiona: "I'll ask Owen to stop by, maybe he'll help. But right now, we need to identify the woman."

Volodya: "Homeless woman? A pawn."

"Right. The poor woman couldn't possibly be as important to history as the rich man," Fiona says. "It's the lack of prejudice with which Volodya approaches data that has made us so successful."

Volodya shrugs and I nod. Volodya and I have worked together for so long that his shrug and my nod divvy up the tasks at hand. I prepare timeline calculations as he initiates facial recognition software. We launch the code and it crawls through the feeds of hundreds of surveillance cameras on and around Market Street, mostly private security cameras monitoring building entrances, ATMs, and when necessary, smartphone cameras.

Fiona sits at the table with us and Winter hops on her lap. She scratches behind his ears.

"There we are leaving the Ferry building."

"And there's Eben," Fiona says, "Rotten posture, bent over like an old man."

Me: "Sill, it's a purposeful stride."

Fiona: "Nose to the grindstone."

Volodya: "Now woman approaches." The feed shows her reaching for Eben. Volodya pauses the feed with a clear view of her face and says, "Face recognition should return identity in a few seconds."

Fiona: "That's Allison!"

Three seconds later, the name Allison Anatolia appears on the screen with her social security number, birth date, and blank fields that would normally be filled with her current address, cell number, and login usernames.

Me: "She's twentynine? She looks much older."

Fiona: "She worked for us. Eben must have recognized her. The shock of seeing a former colleague in that state—he must have lost it and gone online to vent his guilt. A right tosser."

Me: "She wrote excellent code—she even commented it."

Fiona: "I wonder what happened."

Volodya pushes back his chair and stands. "It is one question we will ask her."

Switching windows, I configure a search. The servers in our Vienna lab hack into surveillance cameras at ever larger circles centered on that point of Market Street.

Volodya steps to the coat rack near the noir fiction and cheap bourbon bookcase. He puts on his jacket and sets his earbug so that we're in constant contact.

When he's halfway to the door, I say, "She's at the corner of Geary and Polk."

3. Allison

Allison leans against a wall between a liquor store and a bar. She pulls her green canvas jacket tight. A pigeon rises from the pavement as though looking over her. She smiles at the bird, takes a breath to steady herself, and then steps into the path of a middle-aged couple who are dressed in shorts and sandals with fleece jackets zipped to their necks.

She says, "Where are you from?"

The stout man says, "Just in from Chicago."

"Can I help you find anything?"

The woman looks Allison up and down.

Allison says, "Don't worry ma'am, I won't bite you." Then she winks and adds, "Well, maybe, but that costs extra."

The woman steps back but smiles as she does so.

The man takes a map from his back pocket. "Is it too far to walk to Grace Cathedral?"

"Take a cable car." Allison points to a spot on the map. "If you jump on here you won't have to wait in line." As the man puts the map back in his pocket, Allison holds out a plastic cup and jostles the coins in it. "Maybe a contribution to my next meal?"

The man digs into his pocket and puts a few quarters in her cup.

Allison leans back against the wall. A cat rubs against her leg and the pigeon perches on the awning above her. She makes a soft nasal sound that emanates from the back of her throat and conveys delight and affection with a hint of melancholy. She cradles her arms and the cat leaps up and purrs.

An elderly man walking a tiny dog and struggling with a full bag of groceries passes in front of her. She slips her cup of change into her coat and says, "Can I help you with that?" The man shakes his head. He hesitates at a crosswalk, looks both ways, and then steps into traffic. His dog lunges forward. A car turns onto the block and accelerates.

Allison lets the cat down and rushes into the narrowing gap between the old man and the car. She pulls the man back. The dog screams. The car skids to a stop where the man had been standing. He drops his bag of groceries. The driver of the car jumps out—a twenty-something business woman who begs forgiveness.

Allison drops to the ground and peers under the car. The dog is curled into a lump whining.

The old man says, "Glenda! Where is Glenda?" He can't quite bend down far enough to see under the car. His eyes are wide and face is white. "It's my dog, my friend. Is she all right? Is she dead? Glenda!"

Allison takes the leash from the man and reaches under the car. She makes that same sound. As it works through her vocal chords it becomes the comfortable whine that puppies make when they curl up next to their mothers. She gives the leash a gentle tug and the little dog scurries into her arms.

She stands with the dog tight against her chest. "I think she's okay. The car went right over her, drove over the leash but didn't touch her." She hands the little dog to the man who is still shaking.

Allison and the driver assemble the fallen groceries back into the bag.

The man sets the dog on the ground and makes certain the leash is wrapped around his wrist. Allison hands him the groceries, he reaches into his coat.

"I don't have much," he says. "But you saved my Glenda." He holds his wallet out to her. "You can have everything in it."

"No," Allison says. "No, no, you'd have done the same for

me. I'm just happy to see you safe and sound." She points at the ground and adds, "Except for that head of lettuce."

It makes him laugh and he squeezes her shoulder. She hugs him and asks him to be careful and he continues across the street.

She watches him cross and then scans the block. A large man with a shaved head motions to her from down the block. She walks to him. A tattoo of a rattle snake wraps around his neck, rising onto his face so that the snake's mouth coincides with his own.

He says, "You got somethin' for me?"

She bumps him with her hip and says, "I always have somethin' for you."

The two of them step into a doorway. Allison hands him a wad of cash. He licks his thumb and straightens each bill and organizes them by value as he counts. Allison stands with her back to him, blocking him from passersby. A seagull dips down to her eye level and she hands it a little piece of bread. Rattler mumbles something about feeding flying rats and she ignores him. A tall wiry man walks up and shows a toothless smile. She says, "John boy!"

He says, "Is the store open?"

"Wait for me down the street and I'll bring you a nice surprise."

The man nods and walks away.

Then three people approach.

A woman wearing a short, tight red dress, torn fishnet stockings, and heels so high they're practically stilts says, "Bitch, you stylin' in those kickers."

"You like these?" Allison raises one leg as though her torn jeans and duct-taped combat boots were an evening gown and pumps.

From behind her, Rattler says, "Get them outa here."

"I'll meet you behind Edinburgh Castle." She refers to a bar less than a block away.

Allison turns to Rattler. He looks both ways and she holds her jacket open. He puts a gallon-sized plastic bag in her interior pocket. She reaches in and runs her hand along it. "Do I detect a little extra?"

"You're employee of the month."

"And right when I need it the most." She hugs him as he turns to go. "You're a lot nicer than my last boss."

Allison crosses the street to deliver the promised dime bag to John boy. As she walks along Geary, she thinks of that other "boss" and a wave of ire pushes her appetites to the side. Seeing Eben this morning stirred up too many emotions, emotions that she will soon tamp back down where they belong.

As she passes Edinburgh Castle, two men step out. They're both wearing polo shirts and staring at their phones. She says, "Fuckin' geeks."

Neither of them looks up.

She says, "Give me a twenty."

One stops, the other steps around her. She sticks out a leg as though to trip him. "There's a toll here, techie."

"Come on, Russ," one says and motions away from Allison.

She grabs the phone out of Russ's hand and runs down the block. The two chase her. She stops and turns to face them with the phone now in one of her jacket's many pockets and a knife in her right hand.

They step back. One says to the other, "It's not worth it, just buy another phone."

"Funny you should mention that," Allison says, "I have a phone for sale."

"Twenty bucks?"

"Sure."

He steps farther back and pulls out his wallet.

She takes out his phone, the latest Samsung Droid. "You should password protect this." She checks the installed apps. There it is, CurrentSea. She opens it, scans the totals and says, "You're currently worth nearly ten million dollars. Give me a Benjamin."

"How did you get in that app?"

"When I wrote it, I put in a backdoor." She closes the interface and exchanges the phone for a hundred dollar bill. "Nice doing business with you."

A few minutes later she sits on a curb in an alley with her three closest friends—the woman in the tight dress and crazy heels calls herself Lexus, a man named Jerry with a gray beard and a T-shirt that doesn't quite cover his belly, and a young man named Candy, a boy really, he just turned 19, in a tight T-shirt and Capri jeans and sneakers. As she sits, an orange cat scurries down a fire escape and climbs onto her lap.

"Look," She says and waves the hundred dollar bill. "I'll give this to rattler tomorrow, but tonight we party." She takes the cellophane bag from her pocket and counts out twelve tiny baggies, six have small white rocks and the other six have dark brown chunks about the size of pencil erasers. She distributes them to the others and keeps one with white pebbles and two with brown chunks. The cat noses her baggies. "None for you sweetie." She kisses the cat on its head.

Jerry takes out a pipe and Candy pulls a syringe from his shoe.

Allison rolls up a sleeve. "I fuckin' need this."

Lexus leaps up and says, "Narc!"

The baggies and paraphernalia disappear in seamless motions.

A man walks up the alley. He takes long, fluid strides, wears dark pants and has his hands in the pockets of a short black jacket. Allison can see his gray eyes from here. He's sharp, the way he wears his clothes, the way he moves, his chin and cheek bones, everything about him is sharp.

"Allison." Even his accent is sharp. "Come with me."

She says, "For a price you can have all of us."

Jerry stands and takes a step back. Candy lights a cigarette. Lexus leers at the man and says, "He's not a cop, too good lookin'."

"Only you, Allison—what will you require to come with me?"

"What do you want to do?"

He's now standing a few feet from them. He looks down at Allison, ignoring her friends. He says, "You have changed."

"That's life Igor, people change."

"Igor," Jerry says, "he needs a hump on his back."

Candy adds, "I'll give him a hump."

Lexus snorts.

"Do you not remember me? I am Volodya."

Allison does recognize him. And that makes her angry because it brings back memories of Eben and app writing and the world that she lost. "Fuck you."

Jerry steps forward and says, "You should be on your way."

Volodya reaches out to Allison. "Come with me."

The cat hisses at him. He barely pulls his hand away from its claws.

Jerry grabs Volodya's retracting arm and pulls, applying leverage that should drop Volodya to the pavement. Allison has seen Jerry use this motion before, but this time it doesn't work. Instead, Volodya increases his momentum in the direction Jerry pulls. Rather than falling over Jerry's leg, Volodya hops over it, pops his forearm into Jerry's mouth, and throws him to the curb.

Volodya wipes his hands on his trousers. "Allison, you will come with me. Please, I will pay you reasonable amount for your time. Maybe you even like to return to Intoxicating Page? You remember Fiona, you know she will help you."

"Three hundred up front."

Volodya squints as though puzzled. He looks at her shoes and then at her arms. She pulls down her sleeves, self-conscious of her needle tracks. He shakes his head and holds a hand to his ear. She spots a small earpiece that looks like a hearing aid.

He says, "She wants money." He shakes his head a few times, obviously listening to someone. He reaches up and taps the device in his ear. He grunts and it reminds her of the hours she spent writing software in the camaraderie of the Intoxicating Page.

"Allison, you put me in awkward position. Your desires don't benefit you." He looks at her friends and rubs his hands together. "I must deliver you, conscious or not, to my friend's bookstore."

The statement stops Allison. She remembers him as the meticulous Russian who once guided her through the nuances of memory management.

He grabs her arm with one hand and the back of her jeans with the other. He pushes her out of the alley.

"You don't have to be an asshole about it."

"It seems that I do."

4. Eben's Home on the Hill

Eben looks at his watch again. Five to ten and Wo hasn't returned. He works by the light of a single desk lamp and four monitors. The seconds tick by, two minutes to go. Well, Eben thinks, Yao Wo should have found a way to go to college; he should take advantage of the resources at his disposal right here on the seventh floor; he should dedicate himself and persevere like—

But the train of thought derails with the familiar tap on the door.

Eben checks the system backup just to be sure—he knows better than to trust the IT department—shuts off the monitors and takes his hoodie and knapsack. The door opens and he steps out.

Wo says, "Whuz up, Sir?"

"Seriously?"

Wo holds the hoodie for his boss who slips his arms into the sleeves.

Eben marches to the elevator, but the doors are closed.

The two stand silently. The elevator finally arrives and they descend. They're silent all the way down, through the lobby, and out the door where Eben's car waits at the curb. Eben senses tension in Wo's silence and furtive glances.

Eben gets into the back seat of the three-year-old Prius. He blinks his Glass to a menu and settles into a TechGuy podcast. That is, he tries to settle, but Wo keeps looking at him in the rearview mirror.

Wo maneuvers the car around the block but turns into a traffic tumor. A current of orange and black clad humanity flows in the opposite direction. Eben says, "You managed to overlook the fact that the Giants played this evening?"

"We won, sir! Beat the Dodgers."

Eben starts a stopwatch on his phone so he knows how many minutes to charge Wo for wasting his time.

"Sir?"

"What now?"

"Nothing, sir. Sorry to bother you."

Thirty minutes later, they arrive at the summit of Nob Hill, less than three miles from where they started. Wo jumps out and open's Eben's door. Eben steps onto the sidewalk. On clear nights you can see the Transamerica Pyramid and the Bay Bridge from this spot, but tonight the city lights scatter within the mist of the cloud that enshrouds them, providing no more than a hint of city life on the streets below.

Eben says, "Be here at seven tomorrow morning prepared to drive me to The Bohemian Grove."

"Yes, sir."

Eben walks up the stairs to his building. Wo trots ahead to the door, but instead of opening it, he stops and says, "Sir, could you please do me a big favor?"

"Can I ask you a favor?"

Wo lights up. "Anything sir, what can I do for you?"

"Open the door."

"Oh." The tense look returns. He opens the door and Eben steps through.

Wo clears his throat and says, "I need a loan, sir."

Eben takes a breath of the cool night air. He wonders why beggars can't resist him today.

Wo's smile doesn't waver but it's accompanied by a nervous titter. "Everyone in our building is helping, but it's not enough."

"You've read my terms and conditions."

"I'm sorry, sir?"

"The Ts and Cs of our most profitable product, you're familiar with them."

Wo swallows his smile. "I am. But sir, the collateral—I can't risk …"

"Click agree or not."

The elevator finally arrives.

Wo says, "Is there any other way?"

Eben steps into the elevator but holds the doors open. Now that Wo's enthusiasm has been properly stowed, Eben has a few words for him. "Wo, you come to me for a loan. I tell you that I'll grant you the loan and you don't thank me. Run along."

He watches Wo step away from the building and then passes his key-fob across the panel so the elevator will override other signals on its way to the 49th floor.

The elevator doors open and he trudges into his apartment. It covers the entire floor but he rarely wanders from the three rooms closest to the elevator: den, kitchen, bedroom, and the hallway that joins them.

Entering the kitchen, he reaches for a light switch. A pattern on the ceiling brings him to an abrupt halt. Fog-filtered light scatters through windows from streetlights below and moonlight above. Eben has followed this precise routine at this precise time for two years and has never encountered this phenomenon.

The light and shadows have conspired to form a pattern on the floor before him: a circle shaded so as to give the dimensionality of a sphere. Lines emerge from the sphere's equator and curve out, around, and below the sphere. Each line ends with an arrow and a point of bright light emanates from where they meet.

"Seriously?" he says out loud. It's much like the tattoo on his right arm.

He turns on the lights and the apparition disappears. He turns them off again to check, and the symbol doesn't reappear.

He uses his Glass to confirm that his dinner will arrive soon. He sets one place at an oak table that could comfortably accommodate a dozen and then carries his backpack into the den. He passes a row of photos in the hallway. One shows his sister, Sally, and her family at the beach. He does a double take—three kids? He thought there were just two.

The den has bookcases on two walls and floor-to-ceiling windows opposite the door. It smells of lemon furniture polish which Eben finds cheap and tawdry—can he hire no one competent? He scans the room for any symbols before turning on the light. The light comes on and he sees a stack of paper resting on a bookcase next to his autographed copy of Kernighan and Ritchie's *The C Programming Language*. The printout is a trophy of sorts. He steps over and flips through it: source code from Watergate, his very first app. Of course, the first thing he sees is a bug. He marks it with a pen. He sets the printout back on the shelf and once again stops cold. He ruffles the pages and it's unmistakable: Allison. The smell of Allison is on these pages.

The elevator doors open down the hall and the lemon scent is replaced by that of curry. The elevator closes and he sees the white bag where it is placed every night. At the table, he dips naan into the vindaloo, but the naan is burnt. Burnt naan? How could she burn the naan? He grabs his phone to pop off a one-star review but stops. Burn marks on the next piece of naan, faint but certain: a circle with a slash through it—an icon for nothingness, nil, irrelevance.

He gasps out the words: "I am not irrelevant."

He shoves the food aside. Leaving the dishes where they sit, he steps back into the den to check his interests in Asia where it's now midmorning.

He wipes sweat from his brow. Has he come down with something? Could his ventilation system, guaranteed to eliminate every allergen that aggravates him, have failed? The thought makes Eben clear his sinuses. The nasal whine is followed by three deep swallows that include clicking his tongue against the roof of his mouth to produce the pressure difference necessary to clear his ears.

Back in the den, he takes a keyboard and gets to work. The maid seems to have left a window open. It feels like the fog has reached in and tapped him. He crosses the room to close the window. A breeze blows an opening in the fog below. The city looks like it's covered in a thick blanket. He imagines the people below him shuffling through their lives, falling in and out of love, laughing and living and having babies, and children excited for their summer vacations. He remembers riding the bus home on the last day of school singing the "no more pencils no more books" song on his birthday. He marches back to his desk, but in turning from the window, he knocks a memento from an end table: a 24 karat gold corncob engraved with: "Son, don't forget how you got here."

"Give me a break!"

He stomps out of the den, down the hall, and into the huge living room straight to a wall covered in framed photos. He screams at one of them, "Leave me alone!" Taken from a first generation camera phone, the photo is pixilated and really has no place being framed and set on the walnut panel of a Nob Hill Penthouse; it shows seven people sitting around a table at The Intoxicating Page. There he is, five years ago, broke and happy, one arm around Allison and the other around Fiona with a big smile lighting up his eyes for the camera.

He takes down the frame, opens a window and throws it like a Frisbee in the general direction of Market Street. He collapses on one of the couches fighting unwelcome emotions.

Five hours later Eben awakes to Wo calling from the elevator, "Sir?"

His phone indicates that it's 7am. "In here, Wo." He stands and stretches. "Help me pack while I shower. I had a tough night."

Wo scans the room. "Of course, sir, happy to. What does one wear at the Bohemian Grove?"

"Clothes for drinking wine and smoking cigars with the most powerful men on earth—I should look my part, though: shorts, T-shirts, my Vans and Stanford hoodie. Make certain they're pressed," Eben says. "A ridiculous play tomorrow night and some bands and speeches. The whole thing is a ludicrous networking exercise." He waits for Wo to look up and adds, "but I am looking forward to the old-school industrialists' response to Fortune Magazine's announcement."

"Oh, that'll be hella killer, sir! I'd love to see George Schultz and Jack Welch, not to mention Sean Parker and Peter Thiele give you your due."

Wo carries his bag and Eben checks market updates through the internet connection of his Glass.

Eben sits in the front seat and Wo says, "Very nice to have you up here, sir. Go for it, take over the radio." Eben surprises himself by connecting his phone to the car stereo and sharing his favorite play list.

Wo bops his head to the mix of jazz, reggae, hip-hop, and old-school grunge for the 75 miles north to the Bohemian Grove, a redwood forest near the town of Monte Rio. Once they're across the bridge and through Marin County, Eben's egalitarian mood wanes and he finds Wo's enthusiasm for the playlist embarrassing.

5. ThievesWorld

I'm sitting in the light beer and sports section of The Intoxicating Page listening to a poetry event and working through possible futures. I'm trying to divine those seemingly insignificant instants of serendipity that nudge fate in ways that completely alter history the way that the flaps of butterfly wings can create or prevent storms. If we can determine these ostensibly irrelevant events, then we can influence them in ways that point humanity away from catastrophe. The responsibility weighs heavily on the three of us, though Winter takes it quite lightly. Fiona believes that my episodes afford me a peculiar talent for recognizing these fateful instants. Volodya credits my obsessive approach to debugging software. One thing they both agree on is that I'm good at identifying butterfly wings.

Winter cocks his head and scampers to the front door seconds before it opens. The brass bell hanging from the door handle tinkles. Volodya guides Allison inside. She looks apprehensive, as though she's waiting for her eyes to adjust to the light, but the illumination inside is hardly 11 lumens brighter than out. No, that's not it.

She stands rigid just inside the door. Winter sniffs a particular fold of her jeans as though he's convinced a squirrel has taken residence. Her gaze passes right over me and then zeros in on Fiona. Fiona is mixing a whiskey-cosmo-sour for a poet wearing plaid shorts.

Volodya guides Allison around the poets to the back of the store—which is just as well because I'm feeling a bit embarrassed by the current reader's series of erotic Haikus. Fiona maneuvers out from behind the bar to a mostly private section next to addiction recovery memoirs and herbal tea.

Fiona reaches Allison with arms open for a hug. An instant of uncertainty passes between the two women.

Allison says, "Don't try to make nice."

Fiona pulls out a chair and offers her a seat.

Up close, I detect a greenish tint to her pale skin. Her brown hair has settled into a series of tangles that remind me of dread locks with ample dread but very little lock.

Still standing behind her, Volodya says, "Sit." She doesn't move until he rests a hand on her shoulder. Fiona takes a chair on one side and Volodya on the other, I am across from her. She holds her hands together, fingers interlocked and knuckles tense. Three separate lines of tiny puncture-scars highlight the path of veins on her right arm. That she does nothing to conceal her track marks adds to her rebellious presentation.

As Fiona appraises Allison, her brow furrows until six lines converge above the bridge of her nose. "My god, Allison, what happened?"

Allison responds by blowing air between her lips resulting in a pffft sound.

Fiona emits separate syllables as though searching for a word. She reaches out and puts her hands on the sides of Allison's face and leans in until their eyes are separated by three inches. Her chin folds in on itself and her eyes water. Winter works himself between the two women, pushing his muzzle into the gap. He licks Fiona and breaks the spell.

Fiona lets her hands fall to Allison's shoulders and says. "I'm so sorry. I don't know what to say, Allison. If I'd only known, I would have—but, and—we're going to help you."

Allison scowls. "By kidnapping me?"

"No," Fiona says. "We're going to find a way to get you out of this mess." She turns to Volodya and then to me. "Right?"

Allison pulls away from Fiona. She scratches Winter's favorite spot and he licks her neck. It occurs to me that Winter has not left her side since she entered.

I am a man of generous temperament, not so much because I'm generous as because most social situations elude me. In my lack of understanding, I am fascinated into a state that gives the impression of immense tolerance, but right now I feel a hint of jealousy. He is, after all, my service dog. I tap my knee but Winter ignores me.

Fiona says, "Please tell us what happened."

Allison rubs her eyes, they're a pale shade of green. "Well, my startup didn't make me a billion dollars."

Volodya says, "What do you know about Eben Scratch."

"I know that he stole everything from me. Everything." Her eyes defocus for an instant and she shakes her head. "Look, I'm not in a position to give anything away. If you want me to talk to you, you need to provide some compensation."

Fiona rises from her chair. "I'll get you something. Earl Grey tea, right?" She goes back to the bar.

Despite Winter's continued adoration, beads of sweat have accumulated on Allison's forehead.

Fiona returns in roughly 47 seconds with a cup of tea.

Volodya says, "You wrote apps for us a few years ago?"

"Years, lifetimes." Allison pushes the tea away. "I had something a little more existential in mind."

Fiona says, "When did you last eat?"

Allison rubs her arms, scratching the area around her tracks and pushing her shirt sleeve above her tattoo.

A young man with a long beard wearing a miniskirt sets a bowl of chili next to Allison's abandoned cup of tea. Allison pushes it away.

"Your tattoo has remarkably sharp lines," I say. "What is it?"

Allison tugs her sleeves back down. "If I ever have enough money, I'm getting it removed."

"It's an interesting symbol, what does it mean?"

"It's a stupid symbol from a video game, ThievesWorld, not even our own code."

Fiona reaches over and touches the sphere and runs her fingers along the lines that come together in a spark below it.

"He's got it too. We got them when we worked for you, burned a whole paycheck on them." She speaks quietly to avoid interrupting the poets and I have to lean in to hear. "He obsessed over the symbols. One time he saw the symbol for 'avoid this area' in the clouds and cancelled a software launch." She's talking so fast that her words run together. "The market window was perfect for a launch, but he sat on it for weeks," her voice drops in pitch, imitating a man, 'because the signs aren't right.' I mean, it was so stupid. Then, one day, in a stain on the stairs at Union Square he saw the symbol for 'all free'—

in the game it means the police have been paid off—and that's when he decided to launch the app." A bead of sweat rolls down her forehead onto Winter's tongue. "This is exactly what I did not want to talk about."

Volodya says, "He's obsessive? Superstitious?" He makes eye contact with Fiona. She nods in response. I feel left out.

Fiona pushes the chili back and offers Allison a fork.

"Food is not going to satisfy this appetite." She points a shaky finger at Volodya. "Can I have my stuff back?"

Volodya takes a plastic bag from his coat. He says, "Maybe we give her half a dose? Enough to prevent withdrawal?"

Fiona says, "Not in my bookstore, you don't."

Volodya: "Upstairs then? Outside, we risk arrest and then we get no information."

"Oh Allison," Fiona says, "I don't want you to suffer." She turns to Volodya and says, "Why do they arrest people who are sick?"

Volodya: "She's breaking the law."

Fiona: "She's medicating herself, it's pain relief, pain that we need to understand so that we can help her."

Allison: "Can I please have my stuff?"

Fiona: "You need rehab, not a fix. We'll pay for it, too."

"I need to go." She starts to stand but Volodya holds her down.

"We're not abandoning you again."

I say, "Let her have some cocaine, we want her to talk, don't we? Allison, do you need the heroin? Will cocaine suffice?"

Fiona looks at me across the table. "What do you know about cocaine and heroin?"

"I'm familiar with the stoners," I say. "I grew up in California."

Allison's eyes defocus again, nearly cross, and she seems to struggle for breath. "Okay, I'll do rehab, just let me have my stuff."

Volodya takes Allison's wrist. He says, "For your pulse." And she doesn't jerk away.

Fiona holds Allison's bag below the level of the table, removes individual packets, and sets them on the table, sticky brown chunks and white pebbles. "You're dealing crack and heroin."

"It's that or hooking, and I don't like hooking."

"You're a software ace!"

"Yuppie-techies can have it." I notice a subtle shift in her bearing, starting with the tiniest cant of her head, a shiver works down her neck, into her arms and body but stops when she clenches her hands into fists. "I'd rather have this life than that one; inauthentic, insincere, asshole haters." She grimaces and pulls Winter against her belly. I've never seen a dog purr before. "Look, I really need a little help here or it's not going to be pretty."

"I'm taking you to a rehab center tomorrow morning."

Volodya begins assembling the individual packets of drugs back into the bag and moves to put it back in his coat pocket. Allison grabs the bag out of his hand. She pulls back but not before Volodya seizes her forearm.

"That's mine!"

He relaxes his grip without letting go. He looks in her eyes and says, "I understand."

Fiona says, "You're not going to let her have it."

"Some of it," he says. "Is not our place to subject her to withdrawal." He reaches in and takes out a packet with a brown chunk. "You carry this. I carry that." She makes the exchange. He returns the bag of drugs to his coat pocket. Then he pulls Allison's chair out. The wooden legs complain as they scrape the floor. He says, "Her pulse approaches 200." He bends down and lifts her up, one hand under each arm. "You can walk?"

Volodya guides Allison to the rear of the store, behind the end of life advice books and old vine zinfandel and the stairs up to our apartments.

Fiona's temperament usually varies from positive to absurdly optimistic but now, her face turns crimson. I wonder if rage can produce flames that might shoot out of her ears. She says, "I want timelines for every person who has ever worked for us and if any of them, *any of our family*, needs our help, we're going to find them and help them. Do you understand?"

Though her eyes seem to be focused far away, I suspect that her mind is pointed at Volodya and me. Still, her use of the pronoun "you" isn't well defined.

Desiring clarification, I ask, "To whom—"

"Find them." She glares at me. A glare that I so rarely see that it fairly manipulates my arms to open my laptop, engage a database of our employees and, perhaps most of all, lowers my head below the angle of that glare.

6. Addictions

The list of people who have composed software for us nearly provides a Who's Who of software engineering. A few of the people on this list are here tonight: Penelope Rafferty, Stepan Petrov, and Alina Romanov share a table. And Owen Lockett, the man who responded to Eben's post with such vehemence, sits with Fiona at a table next to mine. They're discussing the game that Allison described as the origin of her tattoo, ThievesWorld. Fiona sketches symbols in the notebook she carries in her jeans pocket.

When I finish queuing up timeline calculations for everyone who has ever helped us, I join Fiona and Owen and ask him about Google Glass software and his augmented reality game.

By the time Allison and Volodya enter the front door, he has delivered an excellent and enthusiastic tutorial.

Color has returned to Allison's face. Volodya also looks relaxed.

I had expected them to return from our apartments through the back. I also find it odd that 97 minutes have passed since they went upstairs to satisfy her illegal appetite.

Fiona rises from Owen's table. "Where've you been?" Fiona's maternal nature waxes and wanes with the behavior of her subjects. I'm not as fond of her stern matriarch as I am her indulgent protector.

Volodya says, "We took walk to encourage blood flow."

Allison leans against Volodya and adds, "Old Russian tradition." She trills the 'r', imitating Volodya, "One hit smack for me, two shots wahtka for Volodya; one hit crack for me, two shots wahtka for each of us—is balance."

I wonder why they felt the need to go to a bar for drinks when The Intoxicating Page has such a complete and well-paired collection of liquor. The answer comes to me as Fiona points to a vacant table and says, "Sit." Winter obeys immediately.

"Vodka supplements drugs," Volodya says, "reduces necessary dose for desired effect." He sounds defensive. "Standard Russian treatment."

Volodya joins me at the table, but Allison dances to Fiona and hugs her.

Fiona holds her shoulders and says, "We have an appointment at Spirit Stone Detox Center tomorrow morning." She describes the facility, the doctor who will guide her treatment, and the view of Mount Tamalpais from her room. "Allison, please, you have so much promise. Your world can be fulfilling and you can dream again."

Allison looks slightly less euphoric.

"When you get cleaned up, you can work with Owen on an augmented reality project—remember him?" Fiona indicates the thin black man and he smiles back. "Right now, you need support. Where are your parents? Do you have brothers and sisters?"

"Please don't tell my aunt," Allison says. "She's a nice old lady and she can't do anything anyway. It would just upset her. Please don't tell her."

"Okay," Fiona says, "we'll protect your aunt, do you have anyone else?"

"No. I'm an only child. My parents died in a car wreck when I was ten and my aunt took me in."

"You have us." Fiona motions to Volodya and me. Winter's tail whacks her chair.

"Right now," Volodya says, "we need you to answer questions about Eben."

As he speaks, Allison let's loose a long sigh that gives the appearance of melting her into the chair and, before he asks a question, she starts talking.

"Our CurrentSea app just took off. We didn't even promote it." She speaks with a lazy tempo. "It's like the right guy downloaded it and told his friends or something. And once the money started rolling in we devised a plan. A really awesome, righteous, decent plan—that's why I hate him so much—our plan was so good and he was so rotten."

Fiona says, "Current?"

"We built it from the Watergate app we wrote for you guys. Instead of just following the money invested by corporations, unions, and all of them, CurrentSea follows the money between all of the users' accounts. When you buy something or invest in something or get a paycheck—any income or outgo—the app manages where the money comes from and where it goes. It manages your bank accounts, your credit cards, brokerage, mutual funds, 401k, everyway that you spend or earn. It optimizes your finances with the state of the economy, inflation, tax rates, stock prices, exchange rates, everything. When you pay for something, the app determines the best place to take the money. Instead of transferring money from checking, savings, or investments, the app chooses the best currency, maybe dollars are weak when you buy your boat, so it transfers funds in Yen or Euros or BitCoin whatever is best *at that instant.*" She laughs and adds, "I can't believe I managed to say that in one breath. Did it make any sense?"

Her eyes have relaxed. While I had recalled the fact of her having worked with us, only now do I begin to remember the delightful energy she provided, always witty and warm if not cheerful—and now I also recall that Winter adored her.

"Yeah, it went viral among rich people—they all use it now. One way or another all the money spent by the wealthiest people in the world goes through Eben's hands first."

Volodya says, "Fuck." Spoken with his accent, this single syllable usually bursts forth like a vocal bullet, but this time, he stretches out the vowel. He turns to me, and then Fiona. "With control of so much capital, Eben can influence stock prices, the values of companies; he can alter exchange rates almost at will. This one man can dictate success and failure." He frowns and looks into my eyes. "I begin to understand the problem."

"That's not the point," Allison says. "The CurrentSea app was supposed to fund our real project. You see? We were going to help people. We were going to make the world a better place. We were going to fix things." She speaks softer and softer.

Volodya stares at the table. I don't think he's listening.

"We were going to use all that money to make microloans. For a woman in Sudan who needed five dollars to make water filters from straw and a special culture of algae. For a farmer in Afghanistan who needs ten dollars of seeds to start a crop other than opium. A guy in Bangalore who needs $100 to make payroll for his software startup. All automated through smartphones. We were going to build cell phone base stations and hand out cheap smartphones to people in different regions, we were going to call them AllisonZones, places where—" She takes a breath as though inhaling dreams from a forgotten past. "Where Eben said love could grow. We were going to help people with that money."

Fiona says, "What happened?"

"I remember him saying it. We were walking in Crissy Field looking at the ocean from under the Golden Gate Bridge. He said that we could fund the world out of poverty. But it all went to shit. Eben got addicted to money and I got addicted to heroin."

* * *

Fiona owns the third floor of the building that houses The Intoxicating Page. She maintains rooms for Volodya and me when we're in San Francisco, just as Volodya's apartments in Vienna have plenty of living space for all of us. The distinction between her bookstore and her living quarters consists primarily of carpeting. Bookcases line the walls and every third shelf is a mini bar with literary motivated drinks. Even the kitchen has bookcases and booze.

I pass through the nook between my room and the kitchen and see Allison either sleeping or passed out on a couch. My curiosity about her form of unconsciousness is outweighed by my respect for her right to it. Winter has no such respect. As I tiptoe past, he glorches a kiss across her oblivious visage. She sits up, squints at Winter and me, and then settles back down. I whisper to Winter, "Well done old chum, she's just sleeping."

I continue into my room and set up at my antique roll top desk. My analysis of our previous employees' socioeconomic conditions has populated a ranked list of people who, save for

Allison, clearly don't need our help. It occurs to me that Fiona, Volodya, and I might do well to seek contract employment from our former contractors.

I climb into my cold and lonely bed; Winter has forsaken me for Allison. Not quite seven hours later, Fiona shakes me back to consciousness.

"Have you seen Allison?"

Winter sits up, evidently he joined me in the night. He emits a beagle howl, hops off the bed and trots to the nook where Allison had been sleeping.

"Fiona," I say, "surely you didn't expect her to keep her word."

"I'd hoped." She sits on the bed. "We have to find her, find a way to bring her back to life—she's one of ours. We're responsible, do you see that?"

"The essential symptom of addiction is hijacked self-control." I put my arm around Fiona. "You can't help her over that hurdle."

"Simon," she says, "you really do get it, don't you?"

"What?" I ask. "Get what?"

She pushes off of me and maneuvers out of my room.

I rise, put on my robe, take my satchel, and follow. Winter rolls around on the couch where Allison slept. I follow the scent of coffee into the kitchen. Volodya sits at a table with black coffee, his phone, laptop, and tablet.

I arrange a bowl of kibble for Winter.

Fiona says, "I'm calling the rehab center and setting up a standing appointment for Allison." Then she turns to me and says, "Allison mentioned an aunt. Please fetch her contact info for me."

I sit at the table next to Volodya, take out my laptop. It takes me an additional 41 seconds to identify and locate Allison's Aunt Lydia. I forward the woman's email and phone number to

Fiona. "She lives in San Diego."

Fiona starts to tap in the number but stops when Volodya says, "Allison is back in the Tenderloin explaining to her employer that his drugs were stolen."

I say, "You should probably return them."

They both look at me. Fiona pats my head and Volodya offers a very rare smile.

Winter devours his kibble in the time it takes me to pour cream and four sugars in a cup of coffee.

Fiona puts on her coat and grabs her car keys. Volodya steps in front of her and says, "She will get treatment only when she desires it."

Fiona looks at the ceiling for two seconds and then relaxes into the chair at the table next to me and calls the rehab clinic.

Volodya sits back down and positions his tablet so that Fiona and I can both see its display: Eben's timeline from two years ago to the present. Volodya's furrowed chin conveys that he's displeased by our ability to resolve Eben's activities over the past two years. Instead of a single timeline trunk linking the pivotal events of his past to the present where it then branches into future possibilities—each tagged with a probability—Eben's past is more like a system of vines that wind around each other and lead from an uncertain past up to yesterday where it solidifies at the point when our systems began keying on him.

He says, "Insane to think that this man, this ultimate techie, could leave so sparse a trail."

Me: "This is the timeline of someone who has been disconnected."

Volodya: "But he is the most connected. The man wears Glass!"

I say, "We have his calendar."

"Any hacker could get his calendar. Let me show you something." He clicks on a link within Eben's timeline and it brings up a web browser with the Fortune Magazine web page that will be posted and go into circulation tomorrow. "You see the headline?"

I say, "That is unprecedented"

"But even CurrentSea app cannot account for so much wealth."

Fiona: "Can't you just check ScratchCo's finances?"

"You think I have not done this? Really? I have tax returns and all financial statements that have ever emerged from ScratchCo, but we cannot—that is have not yet—been able to penetrate his system."

The two of us bury our faces in our laptops. Fiona relaxes with the San Francisco Chronicle, the genuine paper version.

Thirty-four minutes later, Volodya looks up from his analysis.

Fiona says, "The whole techie culture is taking it on the chin in the press for Eben's post. It's so distressing that he's one of ours." She folds the paper.

Me: "Quite a firewall."

Volodya: "And very nice encryption.

Me: "He appears to be a man of little trust."

Fiona: "People who don't trust others can't be trusted."

Volodya: "I don't trust others."

Fiona: "I know."

Me: "Volodya's the exception to the rule."

Volodya: "I have half our computing power searching for weaknesses in his system."

I say, "He's spending next week in my hometown at The Bohemian Grove."

Volodya: "Followed by trips to India, Mexico, and Paris—this timeline, I cannot look at it! We need information! It is the grist of our mill."

Me: "ScratchCo tax forms indicate substantial income from India and Mexico as well as from Somalia, Brazil, Mongolia, Angola, and the Philippines."

Volodya: "Sweatshops?"

Fiona: "Microloans?"

Volodya chortles. "I do not think so." Fiona moves to the other side of the table, behind Volodya, and rubs his shoulders as he speaks—alternating arguments with fawning seems to be the essence of their friendship. It bothers Winter.

Fiona: "Does ScratchCo manufacture cheap crap? Cell phone cases? Shoes?"

Me: "Financial instruments are the only products indicated—and since it's all new tech, he hasn't had to deal with brick-and-mortar banking regulations."

Volodya: "It will be worse than sweatshops. Eben Scratch is a bad man, rotten excuse for human being."

Me: "He used to be quite meticulous and polite."

Volodya: "He's the only clue we have. We know embarrassingly little about him. We must monitor his every move, every word, every breath."

Me: "Millions of lines of code, the best pattern recognition algorithms in the world, AI, analytics, and we can't connect the dots from his job to his income. It is embarrassing."

Fiona: "Look, Allison is a junkie, her life is ruined but so is Eben's. Don't confuse his bank balance for contentment. Allison is out on the street, but we'll find a way to save her. We have to do the same for Eben."

"Fiona," I say, "How do you redeem a rich man?"

Volodya stands. "This Eben Scratch has tremendous power." He speaks three decibels louder: "And we have no idea how much power." He increases his volume another decibel. "All we know is that he is driven by greed. And you think we should help him?" He cranks it up another two decibels. "Help him?"

Fiona looks up at Volodya and speaks in a polite fashion. "I have something in mind."

"You are strange woman." Volodya drops back in his chair and his voice drops six decibels. "But we agree: in order to act we need more information."

Fiona turns to me and says, "Simon, fancy a trip to the Grove?"

"Of course," I say, "We'll compose a list of what we'd like to know. I'll take it to the Grove and ask him." While I'm hardly the sort of statesman or corporate icon serviced by San Francisco's Bohemian Club and the extravaganza they hold each summer in Monte Rio, I am a member. My status as a noteworthy if not particularly famous scientist, combined with the fact that I spent summers working at The Bohemian Grove during my youth, plus endorsements from my mentors, generated an invitation to join at a reduced rate.

Fiona and Volodya look at each other. Fiona's eyebrows rise. Volodya frowns. It is their telepathy.

After several seconds, I say, "Well?"

Fiona says, "I have an idea for how you can acquire the information we need and perhaps even help Eben see beyond his own nose."

Fiona motions me into her living room.

Volodya says, "I will go downstairs and alert your staff that you will not be in today."

We were in college the first time Fiona trained me on matters of social grace, including but hardly limited to subtle manipulation of the other humans. Had she taken me under her wing just a week sooner, I'd have had a chance to spend my life in the arms of Gwinnie, the most brilliant, charming, and beautiful woman in the world.

The two of us sit on a couch. Sunlight streams through a

picture window with a view of Valencia Street. Today's weather might actually resemble summer.

Filling me in on her plan includes showing me the notes she's been taking in the tiny notebook she carries. We finish in 56 minutes, but she insists that we practice the social subtleties of the plan through role playing.

II. The Making of a Tyrant

Winter and I cross the bay by ferry and then take a sequence of three buses 75 miles north to the redwood forested hills of Monte Rio, the town where I grew up. The bus drops me nearly a mile from the Grove entrance on a gravel and redwood-needle carpeted roadside. The other men who make this annual pilgrimage are more apt to travel by personal jet. It's hot in the sun, but the ocean breezes and the sound of the river offer that special welcome that only home can provide.

The Bohemian Grove consists of 2712 forested acres in a gorge along the Russian River. We're greeted at the entrance by a hundred year-old gate adorned with a welded web of steel embedded with the phrase: "weaving spiders come not here." The phrase is meant to deter the male-dominated economic and political power structure of the United States from negotiating deals beyond these gates, but the exclusivity of The Bohemian Club draws suspicious protestors.

The protestors take little notice of Winter and me until I tap on the gate and he pees on it.

A voice calls from the other side, "Can I help you?" and then, "Oh for Christ's sake, not a dog."

The speaker is a man named Rod who I've known since kindergarten.

Fortunately, Winter wears his "Service Dog" vest.

"Hi Rod."

"Simon?"

I bow.

"It figures." He scrolls a tablet computer and seems disappointed when he finds my name. I smile for a surveillance camera.

Sixty-six minutes later, dressed in a sport coat, khakis, and sneakers, I follow a path from my assigned cabin to the meadow that serves as The Grove's central meeting area. It's nearly cocktail hour when Winter and I join the other members.

Rows of tables form successive arcs facing a stage across a river-fed pond. A thirty-foot tall statue of an Owl stands behind the stage. The owl is carved of weathered redwood and nestles into the scenery so well that his presence is likely to slip your mind the way that we forget about security cameras. It's clearly a male owl since women are not allowed in The Bohemian Grove after 6pm.

Groups of men mill about laughing and drinking but not emulating weaving spiders. There are plenty of men in their 50s and 40s, very few in their 30s, but a large fraction in their twenties. I've never seen so many young men at the Grove and I first worked here when I was 15.

A valet presents a tray of cocktails. I accept a tumbler of fine scotch and suggest that Winter might like a dash of hoppy ale.

I pass a covey of politicians that includes a mix of state and national representatives and a flock of CEOs. Former President Bush scratches Winter's ears as we pass.

Scanning the crowd for my mark—since I am here on a covert mission, I feel comfortable using caper-jargon—I approach a loud group of young men down by the pond. Passing a row of tables, I see Eben among the Silicon Valley new money—a term I hear in passing spoken by Bert Deck, the CEO of a chain of stores that purvey dry goods.

At the new money center, Jean-Claude Nguyen, a trader of cyber currencies, holds up a magazine. The others crowd around and exclaim amazement and adoration tempered with envy. Standing with his back hunched, Eben looks embarrassed.

It's the cover of the new issue of Fortune with a photo of Eben above two-inch letters. "World's First Trillionaire."

Another app writer and occasional venture capitalist asks leading questions without quite querying "How did you do it?" The oldest gentleman among the new money upstarts, Internet pioneer Marc Andreeson, makes the bawdy suggestion that Eben may have acquired his wealth through ill-means. Eben appears genuinely offended.

In his iconic blue hoodie, Mark Zuckerberg pats Eben's shoulder and says, "You're too rich to fail." The crowd boils in laughter and Eben looks even more uncomfortable. Nguyen says, "No, that's not it, he's too rich to die." He says this without humor, though the other fellows' laughter intensifies along with their good-natured jibes. Nguyen and I make eye contact and I see that he's serious.

Eben looks as though he'd relish being rescued from his peers. I'll have to work quickly. The valet returns with Winter's saucer and two choices of beer, a local IPA or a more local IPA. Winter begins drooling and I suggest the latter. As he sets down the saucer of beer, I ask him to bring me four bottles of wine and a five pound bag of flour. He notes my request on a pad of paper and asks, "How many goblets? Perhaps a corkscrew?" I picture the setting I'm after and say, "Corkscrew, no goblets."

Winter slurps the few teaspoons of beer. A man waves to me from a clique upstream from the new money. These gentleman are three decades older than the upstarts, and their money is at least three centuries older. They wear fine plaid pants, colorful shorts, and white tennis shoes or polished leather loafers. Guy Bourbon, a Frenchman whose lineage can be traced to Renaissance Paris waves me over. Winter finishes his beer and we approach.

We pass the son of the owner of a local football franchise who yells at the new money: "No Glass at the Grove, you classless idiot!"

I see Eben remove his Google Glass. The Bohemians ban Internet access and scramble cell service so the only way Eben could be connected is with some sort of satellite link. My earbug, for example, connects through a Blue Tooth connection to my phone which has a satellite transceiver.

When I finally make it to his table, Guy Bourbon bobs his bald head and clinks his cognac snifter against my tumbler.

"Simon," he says in the expansive way of royalty, "we have some work for you, nothing extraordinary, mere currency projections." His French accent is so perfect that a sidewalk café clouds my vision and I hesitate. This would be a bad time for an episode. I take a deep breath and hang onto this reality but get a contact nicotine rush from his cigarette smoke.

My earbug makes a buzzing sound. The satellite routing causes poor quality and an annoying delay. Volodya says, "We need the work."

The waiter returns with my requests in a grocery bag.

An Englishman to my right takes my arm and leans into my face. "Are you all right, Wentworth?"

"Oh, Richard," I say, "how nice to see you." Richard Womersley has the driest sense of humor you can imagine. Sometimes it takes months for one of his jokes to work its way through my brain. "Yes, I'm fine. Thank you. Stepped on a twig. The dog pulled me over." I hope Winter won't mind carrying the burden of my social ineptitude.

Fiona interrupts my thoughts through the earbug: "Skip the

gig, we need information from Eben." Volodya: "We must pay our bills!" Fiona: "Civilization is careening toward a dark age and you're worried about making rent?"

Bourbon encourages me to sit next to him.

I adjust my earbug so that it transmits to Volodya and Fiona but doesn't receive. This way they can argue to their hearts' content and I can think straight; straight being an exaggeration, of course.

Bourbon and Womersley describe a project that truly is our specialty, projecting the relative value of the Euro against other major currencies and under different assumptions of economic performance, specifically the performance of France, Germany, the United Kingdom, and Russia. Volodya can configure the analysis faster than it will take Fiona to create a six-figure invoice.

The conversation worries me on two accounts: By weaving a business web, Bourbon and I are breaking the primary rule of Grove policy; I wonder if we could be arrested. Second, his request reminds me of John Law, the 18th century millionaire, gambler, and murderer who set up a bank that issued some of the first paper currency and created one of the first economic bubbles.

As that second worry absorbs my consciousness I feel myself receding from the "conversation". Another breath of cigarette smoke accelerates the process. I pull Winter with me into distinct but wavering green boundaries. The shadows of the men flicker and their voices are out of synch. Winter hops onto the bench between Bourbon and me. On this side of the green edge, Bourbon wears a black vest with gold watch-fob. Through the greenish pane he has a yellow sweater vest over a white tennis costume.

The John Law currency bubble spread from Mississippi across French colonies to Paris and ultimately resulted in the

Bourbons acquiring the most expensive acre in Europe, the Place Vendome, where Bourbons have lived for 294 years.

Winter licks my face, nibbles on my nose, and, just as he begins barking directly into my face, I manage to climb above the green-edged realities, back to the Bohemian Grove and this now.

Bourbon concludes his extensive monologue with, "... we French have very long financial memories and have not trusted paper money since."

An outburst of laughter emanates from the new money group down by the river. Guy Bourbon, speaking to Richard Womersley, says, "They don't know what they're doing." And Womersley says, "It will be a problem." Even in his polished English accent it reminds me of Volodya's response to nearly every stimulus, I'm tempted to enable my earbug's receiver just to hear Fiona laugh. He has lit yet another cigarette so I lean away from the smoke and excuse myself.

Winter and I hike up the ridge and sprinkle flour along the way in preparation for my caper with Eben. When we have everything in place, I return to the valley floor and find Eben at a table now populated by politicians. I sit at the end of the row. A glorious serving of lobster tail garnished with New York steak is set before me. I set to work on the baked potato and wonder why this 57 cent tuber stars on the stage of my plate. Chives, I think to myself, butter and chives.

After supper, waiters distribute cigars, cordials, coffees, and port. I see Eben rise from his table. Following him brings a delightfully sinister feeling. In the tradition of The Grove, he chooses a tree to urinate on. I follow suit several trees away. When I finish, Winter sniffs the trickle I've left, raises his leg extra high, and then proceeds to direct a stream of urine as high as he can to cover the entire pattern I produced. I say, "It's your providence, I suppose."

"What?" Eben says, zipping up.

"I was talking to the dog."

He steps away and I follow at least ten paces behind.

Concentrating on the lack of chalance with which I follow, it takes the better part of six minutes for me to realize that he's not returning to his table. My entire plan depends on intercepting him in the commotion following the play. Mentally reviewing Fiona's instructions, I am at a loss.

Eben stops at a fork in the path and examines the small wooden sign. One tong leads to the Ridgeline Trail and the other to a campground. The flour sprinkled on the one path fairly glows in the scattered light of dusk. Winter and I position ourselves to block the campground path.

Eben says, "How did that get here?"

Lying is hardly my forte and with the flour diagram looking so nice in this particular light I'd normally boast of my own creativity. Instead, Fiona's training takes hold. "Oh, that's just Sequoia sempervirens pollen."

"Tree pollen? In that precise configuration?"

"Eben? Eben Scratch?" I lie. "Do you remember me? Simon Wentworth. You used to write apps for TLA?" He keeps staring at the symbol.

He finally looks up and says, "Dr. Wentworth?"

Up until this point I have recalled Eben within the category of app writers we employ, but now the details of his character surface. Eben distinguished himself in his formality. He used titles in addressing us when no one else did. His software had a tidy look to it with uniform indentation that made his programs look elegant.

I say, "Yes," and reach out to hug him. I'm not a hugger, but having seen the error of Eben's ways and heard Allison's description of his fall, I'm taken by Fiona's affection.

Eben holds out a hand. Apparently he's not a hugger either.

We exchange firm, manly handshakes.

He asks, "Where does this path go?"

"It leads up to the ridge."

He kneels down and examines my flour diagram. "The trees made this pattern?"

I wonder how actors manage to lie so proficiently. "What else could have? They must have dribbled it out with intention. That very symbol."

I fear I've gone too far, but Eben steps past the flour onto the Ridgeline Trail just as Fiona said he would. Winter and I follow. He stops at the next break in the trail and examines the next flour pattern. I can't conceive how anyone could think that tree pollen could form such a perfect shape; I should have added a signature to my artwork.

Eben says, "It looks a lot like the danger sign from ThievesWorld."

"Sort of?" I say. "What do you mean? It looks exactly like—" I catch myself in time to reel in my indignation, "—a random configuration of pollen, what else could it be?"

"Seriously," he says, "there's nothing random about it."

He moves farther up the hill and away from the danger sign.

I disconnect Winter's leash and he runs ahead. The next symbol marks the junction of three paths. Two are well-trod trails leading to different highlights of The Grove. I marked the third with a symbol that, in the context of ThievesWorld, indicates a risky high value target. Twigs, branches, and grass across the path show how rarely people follow it.

"Is there any reason to believe that something, umm, something unique might lie up this path?"

Winter gallops up the trail—he knows the way.

I execute the strangest component of Fiona's script: "Maybe we should head back."

"What?" He says.

"I don't know, Eben, it's kind of scary." This line comes out flat. After all, my favorite place on earth lies at the end of this trail, but it works anyway. He chases Winter up the hill.

A step ahead of me, he stops and puts a hand on my chest. He whispers, "What's that?"

We're now 981 feet above the valley floor and deep in the forest. The sun has set and the moon has yet to rise, but the bleached-white flour symbol ahead of us fluoresces in the starlight.

I say. "What do you make of it?"

"It's a sign that powerful wizards use to warn passersby. Come on." He runs the rest of the way up to the ridge. Winter breaks into a sprint to stay ahead. When I make it to the clearing, I find him crouched in front of the small stack of kindling that I placed there.

He says, "Why have I been drawn here?" and I'm tempted to answer.

Spring's clearing forms a circle within the forest where granite lies beneath a carpet of redwood needles.

"Are those matches?" I say, knowing full well that they are.

He picks them up. I sit on the ground in front of the kindling.

"Won't we start the whole hill on fire?"

I say, "You better check."

He lowers to his knees and feels around the fire pit that I built as a teenager: a plain of granite surrounded by a four foot circle of rocks.

Eben says, "It seems safe enough." He lights a match, holds it under the twigs, and gets a flame going. I hand him some logs and he sets them over the rapidly burning kindling in a pyramid shape. The logs quell the flames at first and the two of us blow on the embers until they start to catch.

I settle against the rock where I placed the corkscrew and

wine 77 minutes ago and open a local Pinot Noir. "No stemware," I say and drink from the bottle.

Eben takes the bottle and sits with his back against a tree trunk. He takes a languorous drink. Winter curls up between us. Eben hands me the bottle, I accept it, and he scratches Winter behind the ears, making a friend for life.

"Trillionaire," I whisper.

Staring into the still-struggling flames, he sighs. He takes the bottle and drinks. I can see from the angle he holds it that he's making good progress.

"A measure of wealth beyond any other, ever," I say. "More than most nations."

"You wouldn't believe how hard I worked for it."

"Of course." I open the second bottle, this one's a Zinfandel.

"It's just points." He holds his hands up to the fire. The bottle rests against his thigh.

"Money as points," I say. "Who are you playing against?"

He faces me. "Why don't you, Dr. Kazimir, and Ms. Black do a better job monetizing your work? That's all I've done."

"Yes," I say, now with genuine feeling: "That is all you've done."

"You three can hack into any system, you could write your own rules."

It's true, our timeweave engine could produce a vast fortune, but that would alter the system of human progression and render our technology impotent for our true mission. Winter puts his muzzle on my knee. I look down at his closed eyes and realize that my beagle possesses more wisdom than a trillionaire.

Eben finishes the first bottle. I hand him the Zinfandel and open the third, a 23 year-old cabernet. "Success is easy to lose so I follow the symbols and work hard. If I let up, even a little, it will all fade away."

He's hunched over staring into the flames, speaking ever faster, and I think his vision is clearing. At night in a forest, ghost stories are easy to tell and easy to believe. You can see them in the flames.

He turns to me as though he'd forgotten I was there. "The weak steal from the strong. They have no sense of self-responsibility, self-respect."

"Some people just don't get it. Going on vacation, avoiding risk, getting sick …"

"They're all jealous quitters who want to use me."

We each take long drinks from our wine bottles.

Staring in the fire again, he says, "I own some oceanfront property—good investment real estate, private property—and people think they have a right to my beach."

"People only respect their own private property. We're a very subjective species."

"The majority doesn't own a beach, so they want mine. They don't want to work as hard as me or risk what I've risked, so they just vote for it. Democracy needs to be debugged." He sips again. "Even my sister. Every summer she *invites me* to spend a week with her family at the beach. I guarantee that if I didn't own that beach, she'd never call."

"You do and you do for people and they just want to use you."

"That's right."

"Older or younger sister?"

"Older."

"And she's never done anything for you. Pathetic."

"Well, when we were kids—"

"She risked nothing when you were children. Now look at you. She just wants to use your beach, probably expects you to put her kids through college, or pay their medical bills if they get sick or—"

He drinks and stares into the flames. "Well, there was one time, one summer …"

7. Cornfields of Nebraska

On the last day of school, which was also the first day of summer, the temperature and humidity both leveled off at 99. Deep in the cornfields of Nebraska, the school district felt that air conditioning wouldn't grow the character that this rural community wanted for its children.

Eben sat alone in the classroom. It was his tenth birthday. The plastic seat drew sweat from every pore. Hunched over the desk, Eben wrote the same sentence over and over, page after page: "I will respect school property and will never commit vandalism again." When his pencil encountered a drop of sweat, it tore the paper and he had to start that sheet over. He had 700 more sentences to repeat before his summer could start. He took a breath and wiped his brow. Thoughts of the fun everyone else was having tortured him: his friends, his sister, the whole school was at the pool eating ice cream, racing laps, and playing Marco Polo. Eben loved Marco Polo and this summer, he intended to go undefeated. On offense, the trick was to take a deep breath, drop under water, and lash out in every direction, eventually you had to bump into someone—others opened their eyes but getting caught cheating meant defeat. On defense, all you had to do was sink underwater and wait. Eben had terrific confidence in his ability to out swim his peers.

Another page full of that sentence, he looked up at the clock, 3pm, there was no way he could finish before the pool closed. He started another sheet. A few more sentences later, he heard a sound behind him. He didn't bother to look back, probably just the wind.

"Pssst."

He turned in time to see his sister Sally climb through a window.

"Husker, come on," she whispered. "Everyone's at the pool."

"Don't you think I know that?"

"School's out. He can't do anything to you."

A few minutes ago Eben could have rolled out a thousand horrible things that Mr. Abernathy could do to him, but with Sally staring at him he couldn't think of anything. "You don't even know."

Sally picked up the pages he'd already filled out. "Doesn't your wrist hurt?"

"Just go back to the pool, why are you even here?"

"I'm here to rescue you! We just started playing your favorite game." And then Sally dropped his pages. They floated to the floor.

Eben turned and saw the puffy, enraged face of his teacher.

Sally started backing away.

Mr. Abernathy jabbed at her, catching her by the arm. She screamed. He twisted her around and took her by the back of the neck. Eben knew the feeling well, thumb and middle finger pinching the skin of the neck as the forefinger poked into the top of the spine. He also knew what would come next, though he'd never seen Mr. Abernathy do this to a girl.

"What are you doing here, young lady?"

Sally couldn't respond. With so much pressure on her neck, she could barely breathe.

"Well!?!"

Eben stood. "It was me, Mr. Abernathy, I made her come help me so I could leave early."

"You think I wouldn't know the difference in your handwriting?" As he spoke, Mr. Abernathy lifted Sally from the floor by her neck, the same way that Eben's father lifted lambs on the farm.

"Please put her down, she didn't do anything!"

"Happy to." He let go and, even though he'd only held Sally a foot above the ground, she fell in a heap and started to cry. "Now you will both write a thousand times: I will show Mr. Abernathy proper respect and follow his rules." As he said this, he collected all the sheets that Eben had filled and tore them in half.

"But, sir, it's the last day of school."

He yelled, "Sit" at Sally and her sobs grew louder.

Eben stood. "Sir, please, she didn't—"

"Get back to that desk!"

Now facing the rear of the classroom, he could see the window that Sally had climbed through. He'd never realized they opened that far. Sally was twelve and a little bigger than Eben. He'd never seen her so cowed. Everything seemed wrong to Eben. The first day of summer was the best day of the year. He couldn't let Sally suffer like this, for him.

He stepped between Mr. Abernathy and Sally. "Sally, go. Now! Go for it!"

In one smooth motion, she ran across the classroom, dove out the window, landed on the lawn outside, rolled twice, and got up running.

Mr. Abernathy reached for Eben's arm and neck at the same time, but Eben knew that move. Instead of ducking, which had never worked, Eben jumped straight up and out of Mr. Abernathy's grasp. Eben sprinted for the window. His was no single smooth motion, but he managed to get through and onto the grass outside. As he took off running, he heard Sally laughing ahead of him and Mr. Abernathy hollering behind.

"He's coming!" Eben yelled. "Go through Nelson's field."

Ahead of him, Sally cut to the left into the cornfield that bordered the schoolyard. Eben followed her. In late June the corn was already six to ten feet tall and covered 500 acres. Five hundred acres that every kid who grew up here could navigate but almost no one else could.

Fifty yards into the cornfield, Eben caught up with Sally. They looked back and saw Mr. Abernathy following. Eben and Sally led him deep into the cornfield, turned left then right, then right again, and so on. Then they ran back to the schoolyard.

"You did it, Husker!" Sally laughed. "He'll be lost in that maze for an hour."

Eben said, "Maybe I should go find him."

"It's summer time! Let's go to the pool."

* * *

Looking at Eben as he finishes the story, I realize that it's the first time I've seen him smile.

"When we got to the pool everyone cheered. They were happy to see me and when Sally told them what we'd done to Mr. Abernathy they made us take a bow—the whole hip-hip-hurrah treatment." He spills some wine down his mouth and wipes it with his shirt. "I couldn't believe she'd do that for me. It was *summer* after all. That night, Sally told me how scared she was when that old bastard picked her up by the neck. We made a pact to always look out for each other."

He stares into the flames at who he was those two decades ago. His smile fades and he turns to me, quite serious. "Getting lost in a cornfield can be dangerous." He takes another drink. "After a couple of runs at Marco Polo, I went back to the cornfield and found Mr. Abernathy lost and panicked, but when he saw me, he yelled and came after me. I led him out of the cornfield."

"And you went back to the pool."

"No, I finished my sentences." He chuckles. "I wasn't the one who wrote on the bathroom wall. I don't know who did it, but I wrote 2000 sentences promising I'd never do it again."

I scratch Winter behind the ears and he stretches out. Eben puts another log on the fire. When he settles back in place he mumbles something.

"What was that?" I ask.

"Nothing."

Winter rolls onto his back so I can rub his belly.

"Vacations are for children," Eben says, and then, "I love my work."

Winter and I make eye contact, he's not convinced. Of course, if your life consists of six to ten naps a day interrupted by walks, frolics, and barking opportunities, it would be hard to imagine anything resembling work; service dog, indeed.

"I worked for you during the recession. We were buried in student loans." He picks up a redwood twig and pokes it into an ember. "Ms. Black pretended to loan us money. She told us that she kept track of our debt. She once announced that the ability to pay your bar tab should be a citizen's minimum aspiration." His twig has caught a flame. Winter's ears perk. "But I checked her books." He turns to me, but I'm preoccupied by the flame climbing his twig. "Instead of recording our debts, she was writing notes about our conversations, goals, and friendships."

He tosses the twig into the fire. Winter sets his head on Eben's leg, presumably so that he can more easily monitor Eben's pyromaniac propensity.

"She is the best of us," I say.

"But it was a sad business plan."

The latest log produces a higher flame and, in its light, I can see Eben quite clearly. The tension he carries in his facial muscles has relaxed. His cheeks have a red wine glow and his frown lines—that's it, that's the primary difference between this man of 30 and the lad I once knew—the frown lines have evaporated.

I say, "Fiona would give you the shirt off her back in a blizzard."

"Not much of a sense of self-preservation."

"No, really, I've seen her do so."

The moon has just now climbed over the eastern ridge and lit the river valley.

"One morning at the Intoxicating Page, we were working on our apps. It was one of those cold summer days in San Francisco and the furnace failed. Ms. Black got really mad and gathered us together. I thought she was going to call in our debts or fire us, but she said, 'I declare a road trip.' She closed the store, rented a van and drove us south to a beach just this side of Santa Barbara."

The dancing flames reflect from his eyes as he unravels his youth.

"It was the finest day of my life. Second to none." He says this in a voice that sounds as though it hasn't experienced joy since. "We camped on the beach, surfed, drank beer, smoked pot, cooked all kinds of food. Pretty awesome."

He's quiet for several seconds. Winter makes his harrumph sound.

He finishes the zinfandel. I hand him the cabernet and open a blood-thick syrah.

In a softer voice, Eben says, "People came and went—which seemed to be your employment model."

"We don't have a model," I say. "If someone brings a skill, we …" I don't bother to finish because Eben's staring in the flames again.

"That was the day you hired Allison."

8. Husker's Cove

Fiona crammed fifteen of them into the van. They tied ice chests, sleeping bags, surf boards, and boxes of food to the roof. Eben sat on the floor in back of the van and tried to sing along, but he didn't know the songs. The others told jokes and bawdy stories and he listened. When they got to the beach, they unpacked like a well lubed machine—which they were, having spent weeks collaborating on software projects. Fiona insisted that they lather on sunscreen. "No lobsters on my team."

Eben had never been to a beach just for fun. He wasn't so keen on swimming with sharks and God knows what else. The Pacific Ocean didn't look like the best Marco Polo stadium. Several of the others went surfing, but it looked too difficult, hardly a sport he could win without a summer of practice.

He helped put up a volleyball net and played four-on-four. The new girl was on his team and he tried not to ogle her. She was stout and strong, with what his mother would call childbearing hips. He exchanged only game-related communication with her. He found her inner strength and confidence almost as attractive as her smile. He realized she wasn't the sort of beauty that most men fell for and that gave him just the bit of courage he needed to believe that she might tolerate a skinny, pale man.

After volleyball, she went surfing and Eben walked along the beach, knee deep in salty froth, pretending to look for shells but actually spying on her.

The wind picked up, the waves got choppy, and the temperature dropped. He watched Allison walk up from the water, her dark hair flashed shades of brown, red, and gold in the sun, her skin suffered goose flesh, and she'd acquired a splotchy sunburn. Eben did a quick inventory, but of course, he'd applied a methodically even layer of sunscreen and remained as pasty as ever.

She sat right on the sand. Eben took a deep breath, grabbed a towel, and sat next to her. He handed her the towel and she said "thanks" as though it were expected. With his courage spent on the effort to sit next to her, he had little to say. She talked to the others about waves and wipeouts. The more she talked, the more he struggled to think of some way to join the conversation. He finally decided to give up. He stood with the intent of helping Fiona distribute the food, and Allison reached up and took his hand.

She said, "I'll save your place," and dove right back into the conversation.

He came back with hamburgers, chips, a half-gallon of sangria, and another towel. He said, "Can I put this down for you?"

"How gallant of you."

He could feel his face flush but bowed anyway. "M'lady."

He sat next to her and the conversation finally turned to technology. When someone described an idea that impressed him, he dove in and explained why it was such a sharp idea and listed a dozen new applications. As he spoke, he saw her beaming at him.

As the sun started to fade into what he'd thought was the southern but must obviously be the western horizon, she stood and said, "Come on." She walked down the beach with the jug of sangria.

He said, "Should I bring a towel? Would you like some fruit?" He puzzled over the merits of wearing shoes, bringing food, or putting on a shirt.

Fiona appeared next to him and, in a voice only he could hear, said, "Eben, she's interested in you. No worries, mate, relax and enjoy."

The two of them walked up the coast. The tide rolled out as the sun set, leaving tide pools exposed. They climbed across a reef into an isolated cove. Allison set the sangria down and said, "Bet you can't catch me!" And ran into the water.

When Eben caught her she kissed his cheek but squirmed away, swimming into the breaking waves. He followed and, when he paused at the point where the next step would put him in water too deep to stand, she swam beside him and hummed the Jaws theme.

He treaded until the trough of a wave flowed by. He tried to touch the bottom but couldn't. As he came up, a wave crashed into his face and he inhaled a pint of foam. Allison ducked below the waves as they broke and surfaced behind them. Eben coughed and treaded but the waves conspired to crash over him every time he took a breath. A wave approached, curling fifteen feet from trough to crest. It broke and crushed him with the force of thousands of gallons of water. Panic pushed aside everything he knew about swimming and he thrashed for the surface, inhaling salt water just as another huge wave broke and pushed him to the sea floor.

Fighting for his life, he felt something touch him. Certain it was a shark, he pushed away but it seized him and pulled him up. He thrashed to the surface and sucked in another lungful of froth.

A voice behind him said, "Try not to fight it."

Another wave curled in front of him and he couldn't help but struggle.

She said, "Take a breath and then we'll go under it."

He did and she pulled him underwater. The wave broke and they jostled about but then popped above the surface behind the wave and he finally managed a full breath. He turned and Allison hugged him. He started to apologize, to shrink in humiliation, to explain that he'd never swum in the ocean before, but she kissed the words away and when the next wave broke, he knew the rhythm.

They stayed in the water long enough for Eben to recover his dignity. When they returned to the beach, the tide had come in. To get back to the others they'd have to swim past the breakers and negotiate around the reef they had walked across on the way here.

"You were right," she said.

"I was?"

She shivered and stood very close to him. "About the towels, we could use them now."

"Maybe we can get back by walking inland, up to the road."

"We're not climbing that cliff in moonlight, silly."

"Oh," he said, his teeth rattling the single syllable into two.

She put her hands on his waist and said, "Warm me."

And he did.

They woke in full sun, covered in sweat and sand, and ran into the water. She taught him how to body surf. Eben found tremendous gratification back floating feet first into the waves.

They swam down the beach and rejoined the others. No one commented on their absence, other than Fiona's covert wink.

The next night, they brought a sleeping bag to the cove and were enmeshed in each other's affection as the tide came in and sealed their privacy. As they looked at the stars, they talked. She told him how she'd come to San Francisco to make her fortune in technology but couldn't get a job. He had the same essential story, though he came from Wood River and she from San Diego.

She asked, "What are your greatest hopes and grandest plans?"

He rambled on for hours, listing every big idea he'd ever

had. She closed her eyes for a while, but her smile told him she was listening. She was very straightforward, honest, and seemed to believe his every boast. He said, "I want to start a business that will solve the biggest problems on earth."

She opened her eyes and told him that she believed he could do it and, just like that, something clicked in Eben, and he believed it too.

The next morning, they shook the sand out of their sleeping bag and headed back down the beach. As they ventured out on the treacherous footing of the reef at low tide, he stopped and put his arms around her. He motioned to their cove and said, "Someday I'm going to buy this beach for us."

* * *

Staring into the flames, I do believe that I can see the beach Eben has described. "That was Allison?" I ask. "The woman who accosted you?"

"It was," he says. "Was and never will be."

"She saved your life and you wouldn't give her five dollars?" Eben doesn't seem to have heard me.

"We fell in love and we were partners—partners in everything we did." He rolls up his sleeve and holds his arm in the firelight. "We got matching tattoos that summer and spent all our free time making love or playing ThievesWorld—that's where all these symbols come from; which is why it's so weird that the tree pollen formed them. It's a very powerful night. Very powerful." He takes another drink and when he swallows, the frown lines return.

Following Fiona's instructions, I say, "Isn't she the human trash? Shouldn't she just keep to herself?"

"Well, yes, it was her, but …"

"Surely you don't think she deserves anything from you."

"No, she made her choices. But I shouldn't have been such a dick."

"But she's a degenerate. She should sell small trinkets, and beg quietly with well-earned shame."

Eben nods and frowns and hunches over into that position that I'm certain will ultimately result in a fierce case of osteoporosis.

He says, "I own that beach now."

"That's your beach?"

"That's the one. My private property that everyone thinks they have the right to trespass."

"Such a nice place, you must spend a lot of time there."

"Well, not so much anymore." He exhales into the fire and a few sparks dance into the sky. "Actually, I've only been there once since that night."

9. Humiliation

Eben took his seat at the end of a long conference table with Allison on his right. "This is it!"

The CurrentSea spending-investment-tax optimization app was bringing in $10,000 a month, far more than most apps getting angel investment. Eben came here to the SomaAngel venture capital investment firm to pitch a social-network based financial management app.

A SomaAngel executive leaned in the conference room and said, "We're a bit late, just sit tight for a few more minutes."

Allison tapped the table. Eben ran the zipper of his hoodie up and down.

"Look at us," Allison said. "We have our own startup and we're going to get funded. We're actually here, Eben!"

The conference room had floor-to-ceiling windows overlooking Harrison Street. The concrete floors, exposed I-beams, and ductwork fit the industrial chic motif as well as T-shirts and jeans. Eben wondered how the investors would react if he wore his father's work clothes: overalls, boots, and a baseball cap. He chuckled to himself, dad made millions in that uniform, but Eben would make billions in this one.

The musing settled his heart and he communicated that calm to Allison by leaning over and kissing her on the neck, right where she liked it. He took a deep breath of the flowery musky scent of Allison and her Charlie perfume. It settled him down and she stopped tapping. Then he heard a familiar sound, like someone in heels walking on concrete but with an extra tap. The sounds stopped at the door.

A woman leaned in and said, "Hey kids!"

Eben said, "Ms. Black?"

Allison said, "Fiona!"

"The VCs asked me to consult on your next generation app."

Eben felt a surge of glorious victory rise from the floor through his legs and torso to his heart and mind. Of all the high tech gurus that SomaAngel could have brought in as their independent consultant: Fiona Black, the most positive person Eben had ever known and his all-time favorite boss. He felt like dancing. Instead, he stood and took Fiona in his arms.

Fiona said, "You're getting affectionate in your old age, what are you, almost 28?"

Allison said, "We've been kind of nervous about this meeting."

"No, no," Eben said, "We have a killer proposal."

Three men came in. Two wearing Converse All Stars, jeans, and sport coats, and one in a black turtleneck sweater, jeans, and sandals. One of them brought a light cloud of Polo cologne.

SomaAngel CEO, Peter Delvin said, "Let's get started." The other two men checked their watches. "Go ahead, Eben, what have you got for us?"

Eben's nerves settled halfway through his first Power Point slide. He suspected that the CurrentSea app would be the only already profitable product SomaAngel would see from a startup all year. Plus, Fiona was there. Like a good luck charm, he'd never failed at anything he'd done in proximity to Ms. Black, Allison was proof of that.

"The CurrentSea app solves the problem of money-optimization in real time, but the market for CurrentSea consists of just the highest wealth percentile. Today, I'm going to propose a money management app for everyone." He pointed at a graph of the app market with a key ring laser. Switching to a chart of the average wealth of CurrentSea users, he said, "Of course, the nature of CurrentSea is that this graph isn't an estimate, we *know* the net worth of every user."

Delvin said, "You *know* it? You *know my net worth?*"

"Of course," Eben said. "We can hardly optimize your purchases, investments, and tax liability, if we don't have your numbers." Then he smiled and cocked his head. "Surely you read the terms and conditions before clicking 'agree.'"

The others laughed.

Delvin said, "Solid."

Eben moved to another slide. "CurrentSea4Evr1 will be an all new platform integrated with Facebook, Twitter, Pinterest, Instagram, Reddit, Match.com, eHarmony, all the social and dating networks. With this app people can 'like' their values and the values of others. The app will—"

Fiona interrupted, "What? You want people to *share* and *like* their bank balances?"

"Yes, of course, being able to share your net worth in a dating application provides actionable information—a man or woman becomes far more attractive with a high balance than low. In addition, it's as natural for people to share the news when they make an investment or take a profit as they do for other life-events."

Fiona held up a hand. "Let me sort this out. You would encourage people to brag about their wealth?"

"Well, yes." Eben could feel the muscles in his back tighten up, felt himself hunching over.

Seated a few feet from Eben, the other executives laughed at him, not with him. Eben tightened his jaw and concentrated on their faces. He would remember them, remember who laughed at him. He took a deep breath, but it was infected by Polo cologne.

Delvin said, "Do you expect people to do something online that is social taboo offline?"

"The online experience has opened many types of behavior."

"No, not really."

One of the other executives jumped in, still smiling. "Where did you get that idea? Dude, you've got it all backward." He laughed again. "Let me explain how the internet economy works."

"I know how client-server technology works. I understand e-commerce. I designed the most successful app you will see this—"

"No, apparently you don't." The smile was glued to his face. "Online behavior mirrors cultural social behavior. E-Bay is a meta-flea market, Amazon is a meta-shopping mall, Facebook is a meta-town square. What you're suggesting is ludicrous."

Eben's rage built. His face burned and he choked on that tainted smell.

"Have you ever heard of such a lame app?"

"And he pitched it to us."

"He thought we'd be impressed by his ten-grand monthly revenue."

"It's like, the lamest app ever."

"I know, right?"

Allison looked to him as confused by the response and as he was.

Fiona was his last hope. She watched the three men laughing and carrying on with her brow furrowed. Surely she got it; surely she could convey the obvious value of CurrentSea4evr1.

Fiona finally spoke. "You think people want to *Like* each other according to their net value? Well, let me tell you something, I don't 'Like' you." She rose with the help of her cane and walked out without looking back or saying another word.

Advancing to the next slide, Eben said, "My approach is streamlined and integrates optimization, like the original CurrentSea app. Loans of any value are processed automatically based on the state of the users entire—"

"Sorry, Eben. That's not a direction we want to go." Devlin stood and walked around the table.

The man who smiled as he'd dashed Eben's dream stopped at the door. Still wearing that infernal, insincere, condescending grin, he said, "You should bone up on your cultural studies and economics."

The room emptied. The silence gnawed at Eben. He examined the shiny, concrete floor. Allison tried to put her arms around him. He pushed her away. "Please, Allison, let me have some dignity."

"Eben, we don't need those guys."

He looked at her. His heart ached to impress her. She hugged him and he buried his face in her hair.

"It's okay. We have lots of app ideas. It's just one hurdle in a long race."

"I'd like to leave now."

"How about we go to the beach? Our beach."

"Soon," he said, "I need to do some work first."

"Let's just go, put this behind us. We'll come back refreshed."

"Maybe next week." He put his laptop in his backpack. The two of them walked to the tiny apartment they shared on South Van Ness above a restaurant and Eben got to work and continued working all night at the desk next to their bed. He worked at that desk constantly for weeks that grew into months and then years.

Allison worked at a table in the restaurant downstairs, but Eben rejected her software modules. He said, "This app has to be perfect," which seemed to mean that he had to create it himself.

As he perfected it, the CurrentSea app monthly revenue grew to $20,000. Allison stopped offering software for Eben to reject and Eben stopped updating her on his progress. When revenue hit $50,000 per month, Eben was ready to rent office space and hire a staff. He composed a budget and went through their accounts, but there was a problem.

He rose from his desk one day. His back felt hunched and it took several minutes of stretching to stand up straight. He looked around their studio and felt like he was emerging from a cloud. Dirty clothes littered the floor, dishes piled in the sink and on the counter, and the bed sheets hadn't been changed in months.

That night, Allison came home in the wee hours. Eben sat next to a window where he'd been watching for her.

"What's wrong?" she said. "Why aren't you working? Or sleeping?"

"Where have you been?"

"Out." She set down her purse. "Does it matter? I've been out."

"You've been spending my money?"

"I've been living life, Eben. What does it matter to you?"

"Our bank balance should exceed $300,000, but it's barely

$200,000."

"Good for you. You've scored a lot of points, have you won yet?"

"It's enough for office space and a staff. It's enough to pursue business without being beholden to stupid investors."

"You just don't get it, do you?"

"Allison, we can't stop now. We only barely escaped."

"Escaped what?"

"Failure. We had no funding, but I've pulled us through."

"Us? You stopped having any 'us' a year ago."

"We were losing. It took a year to fight our way back. If we stop now—"

"You're afraid of the world." Allison stepped to the kitchenette, took a plate from the counter, and wiped it off. "One by one, all of your goals have faded behind a single number." She took a folded piece of paper from her pocket. "Do you even remember what our profits were going to finance?" She unfolded the paper and sprinkled white powder onto the plate. Using a credit card, she arranged it into a single long line. "Eben, we haven't shared our lives in a year. The lease is in my name." She leaned over the plate with a rolled up dollar bill and inhaled the line. Sitting up and squeezing her nostrils together, she added, "I don't want you around here anymore. You take up too much space."

"But Allison." He rushed toward her. "What about our plans? How can you quit now?"

"Your only plan is to be as rich as you can possibly be. But you don't want me along for the ride and I don't really want to ride along with you."

"But Allison, I love you."

"No, Eben, no you don't. Back when we had ideals and aspirations, we loved each other. We're no longer those people." She scraped the credit card on the plate, trying to assemble another line of powder from the dregs. When she realized the futility of her effort, she licked the plate. "Time for you to fuck off and die. I want you out of here tomorrow. Someone else is moving in so FU."

* * *

"Wow, I thought I had it hard with Gwinnie." I refer to the mostly unrequited love of my life.

Eben drinks the last of our fourth bottle of wine. "I'd almost forgotten that."

"What? You know Gwinnie?"

"Why did your partner, Ms. Black, turn on me? If they'd funded us, everything could have been different. We could have earned our ten million in FU money, Allison wouldn't have given up on me, I wouldn't have gotten so obsessed, she wouldn't have become an addict. I thought Ms. Black was my mentor, my friend, why did she ruin me?"

He starts to set the bottle to the side of the campfire, but even though he's sitting, he loses his balance. Winter pulls away. "Ruined. I suppose you are."

"Those bastards mocked me, but I showed them, I'm the trillionaire, now. Sure it was a crappy idea, but if they'd shown any respect they'd have gotten a piece of my trillionaire app."

"You mean the banking app with auto-processed loans and collections?"

"Yes, loans at any time for anyone, similar to what Allison and I designed that first night on our beach—my beach. It's huge now, an entire empire. Are you familiar with Eben-Notes?"

"Sorry?"

"EbenNotes." Eben narrows his eyes, focusing on me. "To work in countries with weak currencies you have to be creative. I'm creative." Then he laughs the solitary laugh of the self-impressed.

He hunches over and stares into the embers. "That's another thing I forgot," he says. "All this time I thought that I had broken up with her—she threw me out."

Few processes of human behavior are more pathetic than a drunk crying over the loss of a love that he willingly destroyed. "Allison? I can't believe you're crying over a drug abuser, a failure, a lowlife."

"You're right." He wipes his eyes with his sleeve. "Sentimentality gets in the way of good business practices. I even bought the building where we lived, the whole block. I convinced myself that she needed a place to live. She never knew. And she still owes me for the rent." He tries to drink from the empty bottle. "You don't understand how difficult it is to have this much money. If I don't keep pushing, I'll lose it." He sets the bottle down with an air of finality. "And I am unfinished. Are you aware that there exists less than a couple of hundred trillion dollars in the entire world?"

"That's a lot of dollars."

"No, that's the total value of all the money; all of it, the sum of Euros, Yuan, Pounds, Pesos, Rubles, Reals, Yen—all the money. I set my goal the day that those fools humiliated me: I want all of it!"

"All of it? You want *all* the money?"

"Sure, why not?"

"Allison was right, you got addicted to money and she got addicted to drugs."

"What?"

"Never mind."

10. Medication

Allison stands at the corner of O'Farrell and Leavenworth. Her friend Candy works the corner of the next block and

Lexus leans against the window of a smoke shop behind her. Candy opens his fist, a covert signal that he's spotted a customer for Allison. She starts up the block, scanning every direction for police, competition, or thieves. She passes a Turkish restaurant and something catches her eye. She gets that tenuous feeling that her world is just slightly askew. She looks back at the restaurant but there's nothing there. Allison tries to shake off the feeling but it won't budge.

Candy's chatting with a kid in a thrift-store tuxedo jacket. The kid asks for a gram of blow and she exchanges a small folded bindle for a hundred dollars. She says, "Some brown sugar would go nice with that, or maybe you want to—" but she stops mid upsell. Her eyes fix on a newspaper in a rack behind him.

She says, "No way," drops to a knee, eye level with the front page of the San Francisco Chronicle. It's the image of Eben that tingled her annoyance and it's accompanied by a headline: "World's First Trillionaire."

"No." Her fists tighten. "No, no, no."

Allison is an intelligent woman; valedictorian of Mesa High School, a Regents scholar at UCLA, and winner of the undergraduate innovation award. Allison has always been sharp, sharp enough to realize that her desire to get high and stay high is her way of staying insulated from the harshness of reality.

The swell of disappointment breaks on the beach of her failures and leaves a backwash of regret and the desire for retribution. But retribution? How much more can she hate Eben than she already does? She shakes the newspaper rack and tries to kick it over, but it's chained to a street light. She kicks it again and again. Candy urges her on. Lexus runs up and tells her to chill, but she keeps kicking and crying. "Eben, you stole my life. You ruined me, ruined everything, fuck you, just FU already!" She curls into a fetal ball on the sidewalk. Her friends stand over her. Candy tells her to "get the bastard" and Lexus says, "Just try to get by and live your life."

Allison lets the tears flow. A stray dog curls up next to her. She sits on the curb with her head in her hands but can feel the newspaper rack staring at her back. When the last sob escapes her lungs and the final tear drips down her nose, she looks up into the fog and it offers the same answers that it always does. Candy's gone now. She vaguely remembers him walking away with a mark. Lexus is gone too. Everyone's just trying to get by, no harm in that. She looks at the newspaper rack again and thinks, "Except Eben who believes that more is always better than enough."

She stands and that hollow, shaky feeling engulfs her. She walks down Eddy Street and turns into a familiar alley, sits in a comfortable doorway, and sets about making the world a softer place.

Hours later, a police officer walking his beat glances down the alley. He sees a dog sitting next to a body. The cop recognizes her and calls her name. The dog leans over and licks her face, but she doesn't rouse. The cop kneels down and the dog bares its teeth. Her eyes are cracked open, unfocused and unresponsive and she's drooling. He calls an ambulance. He sits with her and after a few minutes the dog lets him monitor her pulse.

Allison feels safe here in the deadened euphoric haze of heroin and cocaine. The world turns on a tenuous state of semi consciousness at the apex of in here and out there and not at all. She's not hungry or cold or unhappy anymore and at least for the moment she doesn't remember Eben Scratch. She barely remembers Allison Anatolia. No, she's just here, zooming along to nowhere.

Someone else is with her. For a second she wonders if she's turning a trick. She sees him looking down at her. No. It's not a trick. Minutes pass, maybe hours, maybe days, and now she smells bleach. It reminds her of laundry and clean sheets. She's stretched out straight and jostling along. Lights and noises flash here and there and she doesn't care. And the not-caring brings a veil of melancholy bliss, bliss made of sadness, bliss because she doesn't have to worry or fear or blame or hate ever again.

11. Fiona's Guilt

The extent to which red wine hangovers belie the sophistication of Sonoma County grapes can't be overestimated. I awaken in a Grove cabin with a Roman Legion camping on my tongue. I move slowly from a state of rot to one of showered fester to the front gate where the sun casts its hellish rays onto my face. The walk, the bus rides, even the ferry offers no respite. Winter laughs at my misery.

Dragging my corpse through the doors of The Intoxicating Page brings the tainted ringing of the bell on the door. With my hands squeezing my temples, I work my way into the bar/bookstore avoiding eye contact with the satanic distillations that ornament shelves of otherwise innocuous literature.

Fiona, ever generous and compassionate, has Alka-Seltzer fizzing at a table in the Remedy Section. I inhale and then drink this effervescent nectar of the gods and it lends hope to the dismal future.

She sets a bowl before me of what looks like vomit. Nausea works its way up my throat. She says, "Don't look at it, eat it." The first bite is tenuous—an egg scramble with sausage, cheddar and gouda, tomatoes, olives, and bacon. The second bite is ambrosia. Minutes later, I've consumed Winter's weight in fat and protein.

Across the room, Volodya snickers in a Russian accent, indicting my decadence. I attempt a glower in response and discover that Fiona's treatments have returned me to the finer side of society. With my satchel now comfortable over my shoulder and if not a spring, at least a step in my step, I join Volodya in the western and American whiskey section where he's set up with a full-size monitor, tablet, and laptop. Fiona's laptop is across the table. She serves a customer cappuccino and then joins us.

I notice dark shadows below her eyes and that her hair is mussed. In a downtrodden voice, she says, "Two people can watch the same events and come away with utterly different perceptions of what occurred." She leans on the Louis L'Amour bookcase. "But I remember. Eben pitched an idea and they laughed in his face. And I, sod it all, I shot him down and walked out. They humiliated him and then …" her voice goes soft. "And I shamed him."

Volodya says, "It was very bad product concept."

"Yes," Fiona says, "but I shouldn't have shamed him. And now look …"

I reach around her waist and Volodya takes her hand, and she leans into us. I hope she doesn't cry. The whole world looks hopeless when Fiona cries.

She takes a few deep breaths and says, "He's my responsibility. I have to fix him."

Volodya and I both say, "You can't fix another human."

"I made him, I have to fix him."

I have no idea how to respond to this statement.

Volodya purses his lips and says, "There is more. Now I speak anecdotally not analytically." He takes a breath as though he's about to confess a sin. "Maybe unrelated, but you are my friends." He looks at Fiona, and then me, and finally Winter. "I received message from my cousins in St. Petersburg. It could be evidence of cracks in the economy."

"Just say it, mate," Fiona says. "You don't have to confirm

every thought with a calculation."

"Russian government—President Putin—has increased prices of heat, water, electricity, internet access for people like my family who he thinks unfriendly to Mother Russia. By unfriendly, he means people who speak out, who protest, who don't vote for his candidates. Shortages, preferential treatment, it is much like old days."

Fiona: "Send them money."

Volodya: "Our finances could be stronger."

Fiona and I both say, "Send them money."

Volodya: "I performed analysis for Guy Bourbon last night during Simon's binge with Eben. If we can invoice him our finances will be much stronger."

"We can't deliver the results this fast. We must at least give the illusion that we had to work for it."

"Yes, I expected this answer," Volodya says.

Fiona steps away from the table. She alternates between leaning on her cane and swiveling around it; this is her form of pacing. She stands between our chairs and says, "It's my fault. The whole thing, it's my fault."

Without looking up, Volodya says, "Of course, but to the point." Perhaps if he looked at her, he wouldn't be so callous.

Fiona sags against me.

Volodya clears his throat. It sounds like the winch of an ancient drawbridge. He motions to his monitor. It shows the updated timeweave.

"It has hardly changed?" I say. "Even with the data Eben shared last night?"

"The prediction of economic chaos and repercussions has not changed," Volodya says. "We already saw from tax data that Eben has substantial income from seven poor countries: India, Mexico, Brazil, Mongolia, Somalia, Angola, and Philippines. Further analysis indicates that he generates this income by somehow leveraging capital of CurrentSea app users."

Me: "He's *spending* other people's money?"

Fiona: "It's what banks do."

Volodya: "CurrentSea offers loans, of course. A user can be granted a loan in seconds. CurrentSea automatically acquires the investment collateral of the user and grants the loan. Payments and interest are deducted automatically." He puffs through his lips like a French flight steward conveying the pointlessness of pursuing lost luggage. "Inconceivable that loans in these poor countries could generate hundreds of billions." He turns to me, or rather, he turns on me. "Simon, why you didn't ask about this business and—what he said? EbenNotes? There is no reference to these on any network. It is a problem."

Fiona: "Do we have any idea what we're up against?"

Volodya: "We see hints. Analysis for Bourbon shows marked shift in wealth. Techies, what the French once called the *nouveau riche*, encroach on economic power of European aristocracy."

Fiona: "Are Eben and Allison at the pivot point of a battle between new money and old money? And everyone else loses?"

Volodya: "Is essence of disruption. Has happened before, will happen again."

Me: "It happens in every epoch of wealth creation: agriculture, railroads, automobile and oil, electricity, and again during the Internet boom. But a dark age?"

"Is in the details," Volodya says, "small causes leading to big effects." He opens a software development environment and brings up source code. "Recall the gaps in Eben's timeline?"

Me: "We can't even predict his past!"

"Of course, a man like Eben Scratch is never out of network contact. Never. Even if he took vacation, he would be connected—he is this sort of person. But when he travels to business interests in any of those seven countries, he goes dark."

Volodya's gray eyes have zeroed into my river-bottom brown eyes. He says nothing.

"Oh, I see," I say, and, remarkably, I do see. "Eben must use a standalone network that doesn't follow industry standards."

He hits the little green arrow in the top of the software editor and the program runs until it reaches a breakpoint in our most adept automated hacking program. "See? Ethernet packet but no TCP/IP header." This means that Eben uses standard networks but with signals that don't make sense to any devices but his. Volodya hits the green arrow again and the code stops in another routine. "Is gibberish in any protocol we've ever seen."

I rub my hands together. "Oh boy," I say, "it's going to take some real old-school hacking to get in."

Volodya: "A tremendous amount of work for you."

Me: "Me?"

Volodya: "I will be with Eben in India. We must obtain information."

Me: "You're going to India?"

Volodya: "We cannot, absolutely cannot risk ignorance of his actions when he is off the grid. Just as you acquired data at Bohemian Grove, so I will in India."

Me: "I should go back to Vienna—having the full lab at my disposal will speed up my hacking project."

Fiona: "No, Simon, I want you to stay here."

Me: "Much as I love the Intoxicating Page, it's easier to work in the privacy of our lab with my six monitors and peace and solitude."

Volodya: "You had another episode yesterday."

"That doesn't count." I can hear myself whining. "The cigarette smoke triggered it!"

"I'm worried about you," Fiona says. "I don't want you and Winter so far away."

"All right, we'll stay, but I'm not going back to that quack."

"Simon," Volodya speaks in his most annoying tone. "She is a Nobel Prize winning psychiatrist."

12. Is this the Bottom?

As the day rolls into night, Fiona finds rhythm in working the bar of The Intoxicating Page. Her thoughts revolve around how shaming Eben years ago led him to the pivot point and she grows more determined to heal the wounds that she's caused.

A customer sets down a Pulitzer Prize winning novel by a local author. She says, "Cointreau and soda with an orange rind."

The customer says, "What?"

"The perfect drink for *The Amazing Adventures of Kavalier and Clay*, or maybe Canadian Club and grapefruit soda—it depends, do you fancy yourself more like Kavalier or Clay?"

"Oh, of course," he says, "the Cointreau mix sounds nice." He opens the book to the title page; it's a signed first edition.

Fiona says, "Chabon thinks it would go best with a Manhattan, but that's rubbish, it's a book about cartoonists, after all." She scoops ice into a highball, leans back, grabs the Cointreau bottle, falls forward, pulls the soda gun, and mixes equal parts of the citrusy liqueur and bubbly water. "Do you like cherries?"

"I do."

The landline rings—the archaic ringtone always throws her—and she falls to her right, grabs the phone, pushes off, says, "Just a sec," puts the receiver in her pocket, adds a maraschino cherry to the glass and slides the drink over. "I reckon you'll fancy this with the first chapter."

"This is the weirdest bookstore on earth."

"Thank you." She runs the customer's credit card.

Finally, she takes the handset from her pocket and says, "The Intoxicating Page, can I mix you a drink of words?"

A woman replies over a background cacophony, "I'm calling from the Emergency Room at San Francisco General Hospital. We have a patient here that you may know."

Fiona scans her store, sees Simon and Volodya safe at a table in the bourbon and noir fiction section with Winter asleep at Simon's feet. "Who is it?"

"An unconscious woman with no identification. She had a piece of paper with the phone number of Spirit Stone Rehab in her pocket. I called and the nurse said it might be someone you made reservations for."

"Oh no."

"She overdosed on a drug cocktail with so many impurities that we're not sure what her state will be when she comes around."

Fiona says, "I'll be there in ten minutes." She takes her cane from its peg and walks to Simon and Volodya. To Volodya, she says, "Engage surveillance cameras at San Francisco General." To Simon, she says, "Prepare face recognition," and then she describes the phone call.

Volodya shows her a still image of Allison on a stretcher passing through the doors of the emergency room. He says, "From two hours ago."

Fiona sighs. "Oh Allison, why would you do this to yourself?"

Simon says, "The images from the video feed match Allison Anatolia with over 99% confidence."

Fiona says, "I'm off to the ER, then."

It takes longer than she'd expected to get across town and longer still to park. She walks into the ER half an hour after receiving the phone call. She signs in and a few minutes later the nurse who phoned guides her into a room lined with beds separated by curtains.

Allison looks surprised to see her.

Fiona leans on her cane with one hand and reaches for Allison's hand with her other. "You silly girl."

Allison pulls away.

"Are you ready to get better?"

The nurse says, "She's still groggy."

"This is as sober as I've been in two years," Allison says. "What are you doing here?"

"I have to release her as soon as she can walk."

"Then I'm ready to go."

Fiona catches Allison's hand. "I'm here because I care for you. You're so talented, you don't need to—"

Allison's voice hardens. "Did you know that Eben is a trillionaire?"

"You resent him so much you'd do this to yourself? Is your heart so broken?"

"Hearts have nothing to do with it. It's just business, even Eben could see that."

"Injecting poison is bad business." Fiona taps her cane for emphasis. "Eben never stopped caring for you."

"Caring? The only thing Eben cares about is his bank balance. Except for you. He hates you more than he hates me."

"I suppose he does." The reinforcement of her fears derails her argument.

Allison laughs through a frown. "I have a right to half of every dollar he's made, to every product, every patent—I wrote that code!" Her eyes start to well up. She looks around the room, at the curtain, the equipment, and the bed. She clenches her teeth and manages to stave off the tears.

"You wrote the software backbone to a trillion dollar enterprise. You're that good. You can do it again and I'll set you up."

"Just what I need, another lecture from Fiona Black."

"This is the bottom. Please let me help you up."

Allison looks past Fiona at the closed curtain. "You think he still cares about me?"

"I know he does."

Fiona spins her cane between her hands, trying to shake the notion that Eben hates her. She doesn't see how Allison shakes her head at the idea of Eben still caring for her and doesn't notice the hint of a smile or her eyes focusing as she rubs her chin.

Minutes pass and then Fiona says, "Where will you go tonight?"

"Got nowhere to go."

"Yes you do."

"Well, if there's a free bed for me to sleep in, I guess it beats Eddy Street." Allison sighs. "But no more lectures."

Nearly an hour later, Fiona guides Allison to her car, an aging Honda Element. They're quiet on the drive through the city, but when Fiona drives toward the Golden Gate Bridge, Allison says, "Where are you taking me?"

"Rehab."

"Let me out right now."

"It's a free bed, free food, and there's no way I'm letting you out right here, at the most popular place in the world to commit suicide. No. Way."

Allison looks around as though dizzy, as if the act of jolting upright and the rush of anger was too much for her. She goes silent and they cross the bridge.

"I talked to your aunt," Fiona says.

"No! I asked you not to."

"She loves you and cares. You need all the support you can get."

"She's ninety years old. The worry could kill her."

Fiona rests a hand on Allison's. "She's tougher than you think."

Allison shakes the hand off and covers her eyes. "She doesn't even know Eben and I broke up. She really liked him. How can I explain this to her?"

"You don't have to explain anything. Just let her back into your life. She'll help you."

"I seriously wish you would stay out of my business."

By the time they enter the Robin Williams Tunnel, Allison's asleep. They continue into a valley dotted with increasingly smaller and less affluent towns. On a windy road through rolling hills, Allison says, "Even like this, he still cares for me?"

"Yes, he does. Try to remember who he was before."

"Then I can still break his heart."

"Allison, you're sick, you need to take care of yourself before worrying about other people. You have to go forward."

The road curves along a rocky hillside with a steep drop on one side. A few minutes later, Fiona turns on a one lane street that twists up a hill and farther away from civilization, Allison says, "I'll try it. If that bastard is a trillionaire then I can be a multi-trillionaire."

The one lane road leads to a parking lot below a series of wooden buildings nestled into the hillside. Fiona parks and looks at Allison. Allison looks back, calm now.

Fiona is a woman of intuition and she's not convinced. In the three musketeer-like friendship she shares with Simon and Volodya, her instincts provide clarity as often as the calculations of their timeweave prediction engine, but this time her instinct sits on the cusp between truth and bullshit. She taps her earbug twice and Volodya says, "Projections give coin-flip odds that she is sincere."

"Allison," Fiona says. "Just make it through the program so that you can decide what you want to do without heroin choosing for you. If you want, you can write code or work in the store, or move on. Just get through the program."

Allison says, "Okee-dokey," and steps out of the car.

Fiona checks Allison into the facility. Allison fills out forms and gives every appearance of being ready to move on with her life. Fiona feels unconvinced.

When everything is set, the two of them stand in Allison's room. Two beds with a view of a wooded valley. Her roommate sits on one of the beds with her legs curled under her as though meditating.

Allison smiles a grin of dubious serenity. "Do you have a PC I can use? My coding skills are a bit rusty."

Allison's request for a tool hits Fiona square in her desire to do something tangible. She lights up and says, "There's a laptop in the back seat and it's loaded with compilers for different programming languages!" She goes out to the car and when she gets back, Allison sits on the bed next to an open window where a mocking bird has perched. She rubs its back with one finger.

Fiona says, "Download the Google Glass development kit. We have a project coming up with Owen Lockett—you can still make your fuck you money."

Allison takes the PC as though it's a fix and mumbles, "I am not going to make another asshole rich."

III. The Tyrant

Yao Wo drives to the pick up area of the Bohemian Grove, leaps out of the Prius, rushes to his boss's luggage, and as he passes Eben, holds up his hand for a high five. "Up here, boss. First Trillionaire—word!"

Yao went in for his first high five two years ago when Eben promoted him to personal executive assistant. Eben frowned and told him to "grow up." Yao managed to hold back the high fives, the fist bumps, the low fives, the soul-brother handshakes, and all the rest for nearly a week. In these two years, Yao has come to believe that stern, hunched-over Eben Scratch secretly enjoys the enthusiasm. So, as Yao passes Eben with hand held high, he expects no response, but this time the hint of a smile appears on Eben's face for well under a second.

"Sir! You give me such a fright with that behavior."

"That's enough, Wo." Eben gets in the backseat and shuts the door.

Yao assembles the luggage in the trunk, gets in the car, and begins driving to the San Francisco Airport. He steals glances at Eben and wonders if he imagined the smile.

With Yao on business travel for the next four weeks, his wife, Shu, will have to manage without him. His paycheck will be deposited two days before the rent is due and he hopes she won't forget. She works full time in her uncle's restaurant. She doesn't drive and he wonders how she'll get Tam, their youngest, to his treatments. Plus, their oldest daughter just turned 15 and a neighbor told him this morning that she's dating a boy who is in a gang.

At SFO, he checks their bags to Punjab and sits next to Eben at the gate; all the other executives wait for their flights in the Admiral's Club. Yao figures that such prudence must be part of how Eben became the richest man in the world. When they board the plane, they pass through business class to economy and sit in an emergency exit row.

Yao puts his boss's suitcase in the overhead compartment and then offers Eben a plastic container. "Would you like some soup? I'm sure it's better than anything they'll serve." He waits for a response but gets none. "Hot and sour, my daughter made it, quite delicious."

Eben holds up a hand. "Stop pestering me. There is nothing wrong with me that a miserable dose of reality won't fix!" He motions at the seats behind them and adds, "These people breathe through their mouths—it's seriously irritating. And the menu; why would anyone eat cheese made from non-cow milk? It's disgusting. Yes, I'll have that soup."

Yao settles in and texts his cousin, who lives in the apartment next door to the Wo's, asking if she can drive Shu and Tam to his treatments.

Thirty hours and two connections later, they land at Sri Guru Ram Das Jee International Airport in Amritsar, Punjab India. The airport is crowded and dusty but resonates with sitar background muzak that Yao finds quite pleasant.

A short man in a bright yellow turban rushes through the crowd to greet them. Rishi Raji received the first small loan that Eben ever offered and has made the most of it. He's dressed a cut above the other men in Punjab—white Oxford shirt, linen trousers, and leather sandals. The first time they came, Rishi lathered Eben in false praise that left Yao unimpressed, but since then he's worked up the ranks to lead the

India EbenZone.

Five men follow Rishi, two at each flank and one behind him. Eben accepts Rishi's enthusiastic greeting by barraging him with questions about margins, overhead, debts, collectables, and the status of every one of the thousands of loans that have been granted to inhabitants of the EbenZone in the last quarter.

Outside the terminal, the eight of them climb into a Land Rover. Yao feels cramped, but notices that their car carries fewer people than a three-wheeled vehicle next to them. He watches the famous Indian street dogs trotting along the roadways rummaging through trash and rubble. They cross rivers, circumnavigate lakes, and pass villages assembled from what looks to Yao like spare parts: soot-covered tin, decaying plywood, blue tarps, broken cinderblocks, and corrugated sheets of plastic. The road takes a broad turn along a huge fenced area past a gate where Yao sees a sign in English as well as Hindi identifying it as the Harike Bird Sanctuary.

Finally, they arrive in Makhu. Yao looks up at the three base stations that manage communications among the EbenZone's nearly 70,000 inhabitants.

13. The Zone

Volodya spent last week with Simon trying to hack into the ScratchCo systems, but every time they penetrated a firewall they hit a mine that chased them back to the TLA servers. Pile that frustration onto thirty hours on airplanes and Volodya is a bit crankier than usual when he lands in Punjab.

A small woman with a huge smile waves to him from a fifty year-old VW microbus. The rusty side of the old bus is marked as property of the Harike Bird Sanctuary. She introduces herself as Shalini and expresses enthusiasm and gratitude for the job. Volodya takes a deep breath of hot wet air and vehicle exhaust. His shirt is glued to his torso and his pants feel two sizes smaller than they did on the plane. Shalini turns the key; the microbus coughs and backfires. Volodya climbs in. It sputters forward, she cuts in front of a moped that has a refrigerator perched across its handlebars. The clutch grinds and Volodya wipes sweat from his brow and notices how cool Shalini looks in her orange and red paisley sari and headscarf. She threads between cows, a bicycle-powered rickshaw navigating in the wrong direction, and a herd of goats.

Through the mayhem, Shalini provides an introductory lecture on Punjab sociology: The region is about 80% Sikh, a monotheistic but low-dogma religious culture built on strong family-oriented communities; the neighboring Pakistan border presents political, religious, and economic problems that include opium smuggling through India to Europe; and, though the economy lags behind tech-driven Delhi and Bangalore, Punjabi citizens are enthusiastic about their future. Volodya says, "Yes, ideal environment for high expectations and low returns."

Nearly an hour later, the old microbus passes through the gates of Harike Bird Sanctuary along a muddy road to a bungalow hidden by trees, brush, and vines. The foliage is dense over creeks and ponds, birds, insects, and frogs play a wetland symphony, and the shade does nothing to quell the heat.

Carrying a canvas suitcase that surely outweighs her, Shalini attempts to hold the door at the entrance to their bungalow. Volodya tries to help with the suitcase, but she pulls it away from him and its momentum carries her through the door. Her sociology lecture shifts to delight with the luxury of the furnishings, the food in the cupboards, the caretaker's decorating prowess, and on and on.

Shalini takes two khaki-colored cotton shirts from the suitcase, hands one to Volodya and puts one on over her sari. The shirts mark them as Harike officials. Shalini's hangs down to her knees. She removes her headscarf—the same orange and red as her sari and Binde—and ties it around her waist so that the shirt becomes a dress. When she expresses joy at her fashion statement, Volodya's gruff façade takes a hit.

Pulling a long piece of blue fabric from the suitcase, Shalini says, "Your turban!" She finally stops talking while wrapping it on Volodya's head. He listens to the song of the bird refuge as she walks around him, concentrating on each fold. He hopes that their work won't endanger her.

When Shalini deems them prepared, they drive between the fenced-off bird sanctuary and an area concealed by dusty bushes, trees, and creeks with well worn dirt roads that funnel into a steel gate. They park in the roadside dust. The bird sanctuary's smell of hot grass, blossoms, and steaming mud on one side of the road is overwhelmed on this side by the smells of diesel fumes, sewage, wood smoke, and sweat with just traces of incense and curry. They can hear crowds, engines, and equipment but can't see much more from here than the outskirts of a shanty town with looming cell phone base towers.

Shalini insists on unloading the equipment they'll use to hack into Eben's communication system. It's about the size of a microwave oven and fits nicely among the bushes. Volodya identifies the cell transmission band with a radio frequency scanner and then configures the satellite linked repeater.

With the equipment in place, they return to the bungalow. Volodya sets up his laptop and connects to the satellite transmitter. "Shalini, please, if you could be quiet for few minutes." She goes silent but seems offended. He asks for a cup of tea and her smile returns.

Within seconds he can hear Simon at the Intoxicating Page. He says, "Simon, I'm transmitting high resolution recording from Eben's base station."

"Fiona and I have taught Winter to balance a biscuit on his nose."

"Please, Simon, I'm tired."

"The data's coming now. It's a modified GSM transmission operating on an offset frequency spectrum."

"Good night, Simon."

"Good morning, Volodya."

Volodya wakes ten hours later and checks his laptop. Not only has Simon solved Eben's base station protocol, but he's set up a private network. Volodya activates his earbug.

"Simon?"

"After six days trying to break into ScratchCo servers, I needed this," Simon says. "I've integrated the live traffic into our system. We can activate surveillance cameras and microphones but with the usual risk."

Volodya says, "What do we risk by leaving a footprint?"

Simon says, "That they shut it down or trace it back to us."

"Lads," Fiona says, "if we get caught then we'll confront Eben, we're going to do that anyway."

Over the next few days, Volodya and Shalini disguise themselves as ornithologist researchers and tour the outskirts of what ScratchCo calls an EbenZone. Every person carries a white smartphone and every square meter is monitored by surveillance equipment. At night, the two of them watch the feeds from surveillance cameras and smartphones and listen in on conversations. Shalini fills the gaps in the translation software.

Volodya assembles a report on the evening of his third day in India. He sits on a rug with his laptop and initiates a video conference call to the Intoxicating Page where it's morning. Shalini brings him mint yogurt, fennel seeds, and tea. He starts to decline but realizes he would either lose the argument or cause her to carry everything back to the kitchen. She sits next to him and waves at the images of Simon and Fiona on the PC. They wave back.

Shalini says, "It's a whole city."

"More like a refugee camp," Volodya says. "But unlike refugee camp, this slum has been assembled next to three new industrial-scale warehouses. On the high ground, well separated from the slum, is small mansion complete with a large fountain and courtyard that faintly resembles the White House. Looks like a Silicon Valley McMansion."

Fiona asks, "In this country of 50% literacy, how do they use these phones?"

Simon puts up the display of a phone and says, "They use graphic interfaces—illustrations instead of words. But look at this, every phone has a weird version of the CurrentSea app with a constantly updating debt."

Volodya then shows surveillance footage of people standing in line at a warehouse. "They enter and then emerge with packages and board buses headed for Delhi, some to the Amritsu airport, some to Bangalore, Calcutta, or Mumbai." He switches to a surveillance camera inside the warehouse. "These are drugs, of course, packages of powders and bags of pills. The pills are manufactured in this lab."

Fiona says, "It looks more like a meth kitchen then a pharmaceutical plant."

"The pills are packaged and labeled with trademarks of Merck, Glaxo-Klein, and Pfizer. Here is inside of another warehouse." The video shows people crammed together on benches hunched over PCs. "There are five floors packed with 28,000 young women, men, and children. I thought it was maybe a phishing operation, identity theft. No, it is a BitCoin mine. Each operator tries different software tricks to solve peculiar mathematical equations that generate BitCoins. Results per person are pathetic, but returns for Eben are immense.

"Here we see people exchanging clothes, food, cigarettes, alcohol, and drugs—even blood. Blood transfusions are quite profitable business. You can see here in the slum, in the shade between dwellings, men gamble, smoke hash and opium, inject heroin, drink, and argue."

"And now we know how Eben generates wealth."

"At least in this EbenZone," Simon says. "That is what he calls these places, he also has EbenZones in the other six countries we identified. Notice the multiples of seven in everything he does."

Volodya: "Eben is suspicious, superstitious, bad man. Is bad place. A problem."

"Eben uses the smartphones to lend money to anyone for anything, as long as they click agree—microloans."

Fiona: "Microloans? No. Microloans are small loans that give poor people a chance to excel."

Volodya rubs his eyes. "He does not lend money, he buys human beings."

Shalini says, "In all of these transactions, no one exchanged money, not a single rupee."

"EbenNotes," Simon says. "They pay for everything in Eben's own currency through phone apps. It's required in the terms and conditions."

Volodya says, "Eben is evil."

Fiona: "Other than a few minutes in the BitCoin mine, Eben hasn't interacted with anyone but Rishi Raji. Maybe he just lends money and collects debts without knowing what the loans are for."

Volodya guffaws. "Please, Fiona. Is ludicrous thought that he would loan money for drugs to junkies. If he gave a diabetic a candy cane would you agree he is evil?"

Simon: "The whole system is automated, there's really no need for him to know."

Fiona: "How does he control the people who owe him money?"

Simon: "The terms and conditions—"

Fiona: "No one reads terms and conditions—and half these people couldn't read them if they wanted to. We're missing something."

Volodya: "Loans require collateral and these people have no collateral. We don't know what keeps debtors from walking away."

Fiona: "Whether Eben knows what he's doing or not, it's time to rub his nose in the consequences of his actions."

Volodya: "Then we agree."

Fiona: "Be careful, Eben may be superstitious but he is not stupid."

Eben's Mind

Eben loses track of the debts, interest rates, profits, and losses that Rishi rattles off. It's not Rishi's accent that cripples Eben's natural talent for memorizing figures, it's the accumulating sense of unease. Even now, as they approach the new manor, he sees another one.

Eben started the tour of Rishi's computing mine with an instant of pride: young men and women digging through the cyber mine for BitCoin veins; thousands of poor people getting a chance to generate wealth according to their abilities. In the dim light of the warehouse, their skin shone the same shade of green as his when he analyzes billing and accounts receivable. Rishi introduced seven who had mined enough BitCoin wealth to advance a level.

Then Eben saw the symbol. Rishi leaned forward and the wrinkles in his shirt formed the unmistakable insignia of the con artist guild in ThievesWorld. If he hadn't seen the shape of a victim sign scratched out in the mud an hour before, he might not have even noticed it.

And now this.

The rains create thousands of puddles, but this one at the manor's entrance has bright green algae in the shape of an upright triangle with a slash through it: no exit. His breath catches in his throat. He tries to scrub the symbol away with the soles of his shoes.

"Mr. Scratch," Rishi asks in what sounds to Eben like a mocking tone, "is something wrong?"

Eben looks up at the small mansion built of stone with marble columns and, at the entrance, a concrete statue of the Khanda symbol of the Sikh faith, a Khanda sword upright with a chakkar circle around its blade, all framed by two kirpan swords crossed at their handles. Marble! He rubs one of the columns and quizzes Rishi on the cost of the construction, every stone and brick, the plaster façade, and then the marble. At first, Rishi spouts the prices in both rupees and EbenNotes, but Eben demands details that Rishi can't provide and when Rishi stumbles, it confirms Eben's suspicions.

Eben goes to his room where Wo meets him with an independent asset report. Eben concentrates on the report, but doubt itches at the back of his neck.

They're called to a seven course meal; more of Rishi's wasteful decadence and, worse, they serve Lipton tea rather than Assam. Worse still, the air conditioning aggravates his allergies.

"The best tea in the world is grown in this country and you pay extra for Lipton?" He clears his sinuses. "Seriously?"

"Mr. Scratch," Rishi says, "we imported Lipton from America to suit your tastes."

Prior to retiring to his room, Eben asks Wo to add the cost of the meal to Rishi's debt.

He settles into bed with his laptop. His accounts show exponential returns, but even profits don't bring contentment. He sets the computer next to his Glass, turns out the light, and tries to relax on three feather pillows, another extravagance that kindles his temper.

A tapping sound, like someone opening or closing a cupboard, pulls him upright only to see a shadow on the curtain. It forms that symbol: no exit. He rushes to the window and pulls aside the curtain. Something rattles the armoire and a floorboard creaks. He starts for the light switch on the other side of the room but stops. He sees that damn symbol out the window glowing in the evaporated puddle.

He opens the window and hot, wet air blows in the Zone's smell; substantial and real. He returns to bed. The shadow-symbol is gone now. He tries to sleep, but his heart still races.

He takes his laptop from the nightstand. It's morning in Mexico, the perfect time to check the numbers from the Mexico EbenZone. He sees that the population of the Durango Zone has reached 140,000, time for a split. The algorithms will reward Alejandro, the Durango Baron, for his success. Eben trusts the algorithms, he wrote them after all, but is not comfortable with the increasing power of his barons. He pulls up Alejandro's debts.

That is, he tries to pull up Alejandro's debts, but the laptop display shows a Chinese woman and he hears the voice of Yao Wo: "Are things better at the restaurant?"

"Same," she says. "No, not same." Her voice cracks. "He only gave me three shifts."

"Why? Xi knows we can't miss a paycheck."

Eben hits the keyboard, clicks the mouse, even holds control-alt-delete for ten seconds, but his assistant's personal Skype call is stuck on his display.

"He said that I miss too many shifts."

Wo says, "Can't he schedule you around Tam's treatments?"

A ball flies past the screen, a child screams, another erupts in laughter.

"He does schedule me around Tam's treatments, but he can't schedule me around trips to the emergency room." A cat steps across Mrs. Wo's keyboard.

"Did you tell him about the trial? The stem cells?"

She whispers, "The insurance company sent this notice." She holds a sheet up to the camera with the health insurer's logo: a form letter explaining that the stem cell trial for Tam's leukemia has not been approved by the FDA so it's considered optional treatment.

"But that's the point of the trial—to get FDA approval!"

"They say it's optional! They won't cover it and without it …" Her voice quivers to a stop.

Eben pushes away from the laptop and the video pauses with an image of Mrs. Wo wiping her tears.

He hears a voice say, "Yao Wo is your friend." It's a man's voice with a Russian accent and it stirs memories. He looks around the room, not sure if it came from behind him or the laptop's speakers. Moonbeams filter through tree branches that shift in the breeze and create dancing shadows from the floor to the ceiling. "Only friend you have."

Eben is now certain that it comes from the laptop. He says, "He's just an employee."

"He spends ten hours at your side every day while his son dies of blood cancer."

"I pay him. I provide medical insurance and a 401k plan."

"If Yao Wo is not your friend, who is?"

"My colleagues, my sister, my family."

"Your colleagues despise you. When did you last see your sister?"

He sits on the bed, the laptop to his side. From here the voice could be coming from anywhere. He no longer cares. "I just saw her, well, it must have been, umm, last—"

"You had lunch with her two years ago and split the bill. Yao Wo is your only friend. But you are no friend to him."

The feed resumes and Eben can't pull himself away.

Mrs. Wo finishes wiping away her tears.

Wo says, "He's in the trial, though."

"Not if our payments are late."

A girl leans into the frame. "Daddy, I got a job at the Ferry Building selling cheese. My commission is almost as much as mom used to make in tips."

"Used to?" Wo says. "I thought you just lost a few shifts."

The woman looks away from the camera.

Another child, a boy, leans into the frame. "Dad, I'm sitting out baseball this year—doing dishes and food prep at the restaurant."

"Yao, everyone is pulling together," Her voice quivers, "but it's not enough. When will you be home?"

"Maybe two weeks, we go to Mexico next and then Paris, perhaps Hong Kong after that."

Then a young woman with a striking resemblance to Mrs. Wo leans into the frame. "Hi Daddy!" Her wet hair drips on her mother's shoulder. "I got the lifeguard job, it only pays minimum wage but I get a free hamburger from the snack bar so everything I make can go to Tam's bills."

The young woman and her mother both look to the side and a soft, high pitched voice says, "Let me tell him about my Kickstarter."

Mrs. Wo looks back into the camera, swallows, and forces a smile. "Yes, Tam, tell Daddy what you're doing."

Every other child in the house has shiny black hair, but this smallest of them all is bald with only traces of eyebrows. Tam's face fills the screen. A gentle looking boy with twinkling almond eyes, a full lipped smile, and cheeks that reward you with dimples when he laughs, but his skin is rough, pale, and creased.

Eben says, "He's a duplicate of Wo, except for the hair."

"Yes, ten years old and looks forty."

Tam coughs until he chokes, and then speaks slowly. "I put my trial on Kickstarter and people are donating. I called it stem cell research and promised that if I get through the trial, that I'll give everyone a T-shirt." He pauses for breath. "We've gotten fifty-two dollars already. Doctor Thall said he'd contribute too and one of the nurses is helping me design the T-shirts." He coughs again, now out of control. When he recovers, his mother carries his emaciated form out of the frame.

Mrs. Wo returns and whispers, "The trial will cost almost a million dollars. Can you borrow it from Mr. Scratch?"

Eben hears Wo breathing and can picture his companion for the last two years biting his lips.

Eben says, "He's in the trial, why doesn't the insurance cover it?"

The feed pauses. "You do not expect insurance to pay for every desperate attempt. You would run a business that way? Without balancing your books?"

"But if he doesn't get the trial ..."

"He will die." A text document with the UCSF Cancer Center logo appears on the screen. "Is from Tam Wo's medical records." The document says that there is a 95% chance that Tam will die within one month without the trial. With the treatment, his odds of surviving twelve months are 20%. "Twenty percent chance of survival for a million dollars? Would you make this investment?"

Eben says, "It's his only chance."

"Then you will lend him the money."

Eben says, "I don't even know this boy."

Back on the Skype call, Mrs. Wo says, "Scratch won't help. That rotten man has been misleading you since you were hired.

You'd be better off working for a Tong—the Wo Foo To would pay for information about Eben Scratch."

"Sell out Mr. Scratch? Never," Wo says. "We'll be okay. Mr. Scratch promised me shares when his company goes public. We'll find a way to get by until he comes through. He will, too. He's not a bad man. He's not."

"Are you trying to convince me or yourself?"

"Please, I ..." Wo takes a breath. "Tam's in the trial. He's going to be okay, stem cells are the future of medicine. We'll find the money somehow. Don't worry! I am the executive assistant to the richest man on earth, a million dollars to him is like a penny to us."

Mrs. Wo sighs.

"It really is. We have almost ten thousand dollars in our savings. A penny is one millionth of our savings and a million dollars is one millionth of a trillion. Mr. Scratch will surely let us borrow a penny."

The monitor goes blank.

The breeze settles, the moon has risen above the trees and the sound of a million insects fills the silence.

"Do you intend to go public?"

Eben doesn't answer.

"Will you lend him a penny?"

"It's not that simple."

The laptop goes dim and unresponsive. He steps past the armoire and looks out the window. The puddle is in the shadows now. "It's just mud, algae, and pebbles. Nothing there, nothing at all." But his heart still feels like it's pounding through his rib cage. The curtain catches a breeze. He looks away and, on the floor at his feet, carved in moonlight: the symbol for immediate danger. He jerks back to the window trying to figure out how that combination of light and shadow could form so precisely. Moonlight reflects from every surface, anything could form the pattern. He looks back at the floor and isn't surprised that the symbol has disappeared. That symbol, immediate danger, never lasts for long.

Sweat beads down his nose and his thoughts tangle. The walls close in. He pulls the window farther open, climbs out, and perches on the sill, dangling about ten feet over the ground.

As he works up the courage to jump, he sees a willow tree and is amazed that the graceful boughs could form the silhouette of wings. He drops from the window, lands on his feet with bent knees, does a shoulder roll, and comes up in a crouch. The ground is soft and damp but not muddy. The front of the manor is well lit and well guarded. At this point, Eben trusts nothing. Staying crouched, he runs to the symbol of escape and freedom.

* * *

Volodya waits for the guards to pass before dropping from the window. He works his way along the building until he's clear of the entrance and then runs to the willow tree.

Eben turns just as Volodya covers his mouth and forces him to the ground. "I will make you one of them."

Eben squirms.

"In life," Volodya speaks in a monotone, "you get opportunities to learn lessons. Each time you fail to learn lesson, stakes increase. I will give you one more chance to learn lesson about profit and loss." With one hand covering Eben's mouth, he grabs Eben's throat with the other. "You promise to be quiet so that I can be civil?"

Eben struggles for several seconds until Volodya realizes that he's trying to nod. "If you make noise, I will kill you."

Eben coughs and trembles from his Twitter T-shirt down to his loafers. "Whatever you want, I can pay—"

Volodya says, "Unfortunately for both of us, money does

not motivate me." He guides Eben on a path that circles the Zone. They see a few people out in the moonlight: the homeless, the hopeless, and those whose skills are most effective while others sleep.

At the Zone boundary, Volodya pushes Eben through thick brush. They cross the street and walk to the VW bus which is parked just inside the bird sanctuary. The van door is open and the dome light is on. Eben looks at Shalini. She smiles at him. He turns around and Volodya pushes him inside.

Eben says, "You?"

"You remember me."

"What universe is this? You used to, in a past life, I—what are you doing here?"

"Helping you learn important lesson."

14. Allison's Friends

The first time in over three years that Allison's brain has been clear of opiates, speed, and cocaine results in a rebound effect: she's never been so clear of mind. Sure, the first five days were a bitch and the monkey clinging to her back is offended by espresso and cigarettes. If it weren't for the center's therapy dogs and the desire for revenge, she wouldn't be sitting here in a room next to a window. Her raven friend sits a few feet away on a redwood branch. With the computer in her lap, she staves off the cravings the old fashioned way: by hacking into her nemesis's system.

The code that defines ScratchCo's firewall reads like Eben's psycho-biography. His passwords at every level of administrative access combine Eben's superstitions, ThievesWorld symbolism, and places where they had sex. It's more like a trip down memory lane than hacking. Instead of a password, the top level requires both hand drawn and biometric signatures.

She knows this page because she created it. She uses the mouse to sketch a silhouette of wings on the blank screen and then she leans close to the camera so it catches the retina of her left eye and, voila, she's in.

She laughs out loud. He never changed the security sequence? Why would Eben be so stupid? No, he's absent-minded, not stupid. He's always been like that. There was a time when she found it endearing. Now she finds it convenient. The raven opens its beak and makes his funny sound, like gargling nuts.

It takes another hour to confirm that there are no new traps at this level, just the ThievesWorld landmines she put in place in a previous life. She watches other hackers and sees a few dumb bots that don't have a chance, a hacker who she chases back to a Latvian host, and one that she recognizes from New Zealand. One has made it passed the first firewall but is stuck several layers below the top.

When she's convinced that she's the only person other than Eben himself who can access the top level and see the whole breadth of his empire, the first pieces of a plan come into focus. The information is organized in databases and software. She works through links to his assistant's files, itineraries, and presentations. His fastidious nature enflames greater resentment; it's just Eben being Eben and she wants him to suffer.

She goes back to his personal directory and finds a protected version of his business plan. Her jaw drops. The raven turns to her and goes silent. She whispers, "I didn't believe him when he said it. How can someone be so greedy? He wants all of it." She turns to the big black bird and asks, "When did he go insane?" It opens its wings, drops from the branch, and soars over the valley.

She lights a cigarette and drinks the rest of her espresso. That persistent hacker starts to get on her nerves. Not because she cares whether they destroy Eben's business, though it would interfere with her plan, but because she takes offense that they think they can get through the wall that she built. She waits for them to try again and then chases them down a chain of routers until she gets lost. She tries again. Her competitive juices keep her focused and she waits for them to make a mistake. She watches them open the calendar and the notes of Eben's assistant. She manages to insert a tag in the file just before they copy it. She chases the tag back to servers in Europe. At first glance, the firewall looks simple, and it is: simple like a brick wall. Her first attempt to break in brings up a message: "We see you!" and explains that they use a bit counter so that, if she does hack in, the system will automatically shut down. She's never tried to hack a system that comes right out and says why it's impossible.

She surrenders but waits long enough to catch a few packets of data transmission. The headers in those packets include both the source and destination of the hackers. Oh, they're anonymized, of course, but it only takes another hour to discover that they came from an internet connection in a San Francisco bookstore.

15. Correlations

Fiona sets a third cup of coffee in front of me and says, "This one's decaf."

"Decaf? What's the point?" I sip it anyway,

"The rehab clinic called to tell me that Allison checked out."

As she says this, Winter rises from beneath my table and trots over to the bar as if he can't bear any more bad news.

"Look at this," I indicate a graphic. "I've integrated all the data from the EbenZone cell system into the timeweave."

"Nothing?"

"There are 8847 new timelines plus many more that are so unstable that they come and go every time someone performs a Google search. Each one describes a unique way for humanity to destroy civilization. We're truly a creative species."

"So many means but just the one end, bugger all. Any indication of when and where, or perhaps how?"

"Eben and Allison are the pivotal who. Whos? Perhaps whose?" I stir four sugars into the decaf.

"Right," she says, glaring at my mug. "How about when?"

"The different timelines that make up the timeweave resolve at different times. They're quite frayed right now, but most continue into various futures for weeks, the most probable 'when' is 13 days from today."

"But nothing on where?" She watches me pour milk into the decaf until the meniscus rises above the rim of the mug.

"A hint." Of course, stirring is out of the questions so I slurp the milky layer from the top. "You'll recall that Eben's next meeting is in Mexico and then he goes to Paris. The theory of a battle between old and new money would fit Paris. Not only does the timing fit that calendar, but Eben and Guy Bourbon both have meetings scheduled at the Paris City Hall on the same day."

"At l'Hôtel de Ville? Quite swanky."

"And of tremendous historical significance." I can now successfully stir the milk and sugar into the decaf, though I become so fascinated by the vortex that some splashes over the top. "When is Bastille Day?"

"July fourteenth."

"The peak probability for the timeweave to resolve is that very day and Eben will be in that very city."

"Are you sure?"

"It's just an average and I still have 8847 timelines to investigate." I sip from my mug and wonder why the milky ring is still on the table. "Where's my dog?"

"He was with Owen a minute ago."

I look at the next table. Music leaks from Owen's ear buds. The tidy, bald fellow offers me a quick grin and dives back into his augmented reality Glass game. I'm embarrassed to admit that I envy his progress.

"Bloody hell," Fiona says, "look who's here?"

Following her gaze, I see Allison sitting at the bar, leaning down from her chair scratching Winter behind the ears.

Fiona hops up and walks to the bar, fixes a cappuccino, and takes it to her. "Hello Allison, aren't you supposed to be recovering in the beautiful foothills of Mount Tamalpais?"

Allison responds with a large grin and describes her experience waking up after years on drugs. She explains that she is unique, that she has always been capable of shifting gears in a heartbeat, and that Fiona shouldn't worry about her addictions, they're all in the past, "… and thanks to you my heart's still beating. I'm ready to earn my FU money." She laughs and adds, "Can I have my old job back?"

Allison reaches out and wraps her arms around Fiona.

Now I'm not a cynic, though perhaps I feel compelled to fill that role due to Volodya's absence, but I don't recall Allison ever being a grinning and hugging sort of woman. She has a fine sense of humor, an excellent laugh, and a warm demeanor, but hers is a dry temperament.

I catch Fiona's eye and offer a subtle shake of my head.

She holds Allison by the shoulders and appraises her. "Your eyes are clear, like the green of leaves in springtime. Your hair looks wonderful, but it hasn't even been two weeks and you think you've beaten it?"

"I know how it sounds—I just want to get on with my life."

"You have to finish the program."

"But I'm clean, what more can they do?"

"You have no desire for drugs?"

"Desire? I suppose, but no. I'm done with that and there's no point in going back to rehab."

They argue for another 18 minutes, Fiona offers to take her back to rehab eight times and Allison, wearing that uncharacteristic smile, insists that she's fine nine times. Fiona then offers to drive her to her drug dealer for some heroin. In the instant it takes me to realize that Fiona is being sarcastic, I wonder where she would shelve heroin. Allison's smile gets larger and she declines the offer.

"It's like this," Allison says and her smile dims. She looks at Fiona and then at me. Winter appears jealous. "My life got off track when I stopped working for you. I just want to start over where I left off. Even if I never make my FU money, I like it here."

I say, "Owen could use her help with the Glass app." Since I haven't been able to get into his servers, our need to hack Eben's Glass grows ever more acute.

Owen looks over and removes his earbuds.

"Please!" Allison says. "Give me a really tough problem to solve, something that will take over my mind."

"It's a complicated game," Owen says. "It allows for almost anything you can do in real life, but you have to—"

"We need people we can rely on," Fiona says, but I can tell that she's already decided.

Owen shrugs and puts his earbuds back in.

Fiona and Allison stare at each other long enough for me to entice Winter back to my side with a treat. Fiona's eyes well up. "Allison, I'm so sorry for everything, if I'd known …" Then they start chatting again and the personal details both elude and bore me until Fiona says, "Simon? Simon!"

"What?"

"Allison can work with Owen on the Glass project, but she

can't stay clean with her dealer and druggie friends a mile away. We've got to get her out of San Francisco."

"Of course," I say but have no idea what she wants of me. She continues looking at me. I add, "Oakland?"

"No," Fiona says, obviously upset that I haven't read her mind. "Vienna."

"Can we afford to take her to Vienna? And Owen, too?"

"Volodya's not here to count the pennies."

"Are you coming with us?"

"I'll come later. There are some pieces to the puzzle that I can't solve from Vienna," Fiona says. "You and Allison can look after each other and Owen can look after both of you."

16. No Translation Necessary

Volodya sits in the cab of the old VW checking the timeweaves of different countries on his laptop. Eben spends most of the night hunched over, pacing with his hands in the pockets of his hoodie and kicking rocks. Shalini plays a wooden bansuri flute and the night goes on. When the moon sinks behind the trees Volodya tosses Eben some clothes and says, "Change into these."

"Why?"

"Lifelong learning."

"These clothes are stained."

Shalini says, "Stained but not soiled."

Eben crosses his arms against his chest.

Volodya grabs his wrist and pulls. The motion unwinds Eben's crossed arms and spins him through a half circle. Volodya grips the neck of his T-shirt and pulls it over his head. Shalini offers a long sleeved, collarless, off-white shirt. "Or would you rather dress yourself?"

"I'd rather leave."

"I don't think you would." Volodya releases him. "Eben, you have not yet learned this lesson." Volodya looks away from Eben and taps his earbug. "Suggestion?"

Fiona says, "Do it your way."

Volodya wraps an arm across Eben's chest and flips him to the ground. "I will restrain him and you will dress him."

Shalini holds up a pair of thin linen pants that match the shirt.

"All right!" Eben says. "Tell me what you're doing and I'll put on the clothes."

"I'm offering you altered perspective."

"But why?"

Volodya lets a closed-mouth smile stretch his lips.

Eben kicks off his loafers and drops his skinny jeans. He pulls the shirt over his head, tugs up the trousers and fumbles with their rope-tie, and then sits on the ground and puts on the well-worn rope sandals.

Volodya says, "Is he too light skinned?"

Shalini begins wrapping his hair in a drab turban. "As long as you say nothing and avoid direct attention, everything will be fine."

They walk into the maze of hovels assembled from tarps, charred wood, and cast off pieces of sheet metal. They blend into the knot of humanity streaming in every direction. Children kick a ball made of wound rags. People line up at outhouses set directly over a stream. Those at the front of the line stand back from the splashing shit and urine. The rag-ball bounces to Eben. A boy rushes up and kicks it over a row of hovels. The boy lets out a hoot and, along with a dozen others, runs through the crowded labyrinth after the ball.

* * *

Eben looks at Volodya, grimy and unshaved in the blue turban. Volodya glares back.

He watches the kids chase their ball. He remembers what it was like to belong somewhere, to play and compete, win and lose. These kids know this slum as well as he knew the cornfields. They know their place.

Shalini leads them between homes. Volodya presses on Eben's lower back, but it's not necessary. He won't admit it, of course, but Eben sees the value of surveying his investment from within.

The rag-ball flies over the corridor and the sound of that pack of children approaches again—laughter, frustration, exuberance—all the ingredients of childhood pass by them. Even a limping boy using a stick for a cane joins the chase.

The child brings Tam Wo to mind. Tam doesn't know if the next day will come, but he still seemed happy.

They reach the road that separates the shiny new warehouses from the residential slum. Hundreds of people crowd around a bus stop. Eben can see the manor between two warehouses with its columns and statuary. The contrast of wealth and slum fits his design. Though he studied almost no history, he knows how important it is to know your place.

He sees Wo walk out of the manor and down the steps. Wo stands in the shade and waits. Eben suspects that Wo will wait for him in that spot all day.

Rishi steps out of a warehouse with seven guards. Volodya nudges Eben into a corner. With so many people moving in so many directions, it's unlikely that Rishi or his men will notice the three of them.

Rishi continues into the slum and Shalini leads Eben and Volodya several steps behind.

People shuffle out of Rishi's way. An old man struggles on two sticks that substitute for crutches. For an instant Eben fears that Rishi's guards will trample him, but the old man manages to fall out of the way and catch himself on the corrugated tin wall of a hut.

The sound of the boys closes in. The ball clangs off a wall. Two older boys turn into the corridor at full speed, pushing against one another, they don't see Rishi or his men until it's too late. One of Rishi's guards strikes the taller boy in the head. The boy's legs fly out from under him and he lands on his back. The other boy manages to get away. A guard picks up the rag-ball, looks at it for a second and then tosses it into the stream that runs below the outhouses.

Rishi stops at one of the hovels and checks his phone. He speaks to a guard who pulls the blue tarp open. Another guard rushes inside. Seconds later, he pulls a thin man out.

Rishi scans the crowd, his eyes pass right over Eben, Volodya, and Shalini. Eben realizes that Rishi wants as many people as possible to witness this exchange.

Rishi yells at the man. The guard who destroyed the tarp door pulls the rusted sheet metal roof away from the structure. The other guards peel away the mess of cardboard and wood. Rishi continues berating the man as his guards destroy the home.

A woman and two children crawl into the light and stand up.

Eben looks around, expecting a crowd to form, but it doesn't. People continue as though nothing out of the ordinary is happening. The word ordinary echoes through Eben's mind.

Rishi tears the shirt from the man and a shard of empathy hits Eben's heart as he recalls how Volodya tore off his own shirt.

The man's arms have rows of blisters. His ribs and stomach are covered in blotchy welts. Rishi lowers his voice and holds out an open palm. The man puts a grimy white phone with a cracked display in Rishi's hand. Rishi taps it twice. He looks at the man and shakes his head in false disappointment.

No translation is necessary. The man is overdue on his debts and Rishi is here to collect. Eben wonders how much the man borrowed and what for. As though to answer the question, Rishi's guard kicks a box out of the man's home. A couple of empty vials and an oily, brown syringe fall at Rishi's feet.

Rishi points at the woman and children. The boy is about the same age as Iam Wo. His eyes shift between the guards, his mother, and his father. The girl, who appears to be in the age range from 10 to 12, stares straight down as though trying to block the scene from her mind.

Rishi lets go of the man and he falls. The woman and children step away from him, right into a guard.

The corridor goes silent. The passersby have stopped to watch and Rishi makes a show of it.

The man struggles to his feet, steps over to his family and speaks to his wife. Tears drip from her eyes and fall in the dirt, but she doesn't make a sound. Rishi indicates the man's son and says something. The man objects and Rishi shakes it off. It looks more like haggling than arguing. Finally, the man takes his daughter by the hand and leads her to Rishi. Rishi cups the girls chin, forcing her to look up at him. He stands back and looks her up and down and then passes her to a guard. The guard takes the girl's arm. She screams, cries, and struggles to get out of his grasp. He drags her away.

Rishi nods to the man, takes out his white smartphone, opens an app, and types into it.

Eben's heart stops. He knows exactly what Rishi is typing: The value of the girl is being credited to the man's debt, credited in EbenNotes.

Eben can't breathe. He wants to do something, anything to stop this, but he can't move.

Volodya steps in front of him. Eben silently begs for the powerful Russian to rescue the child. He wishes he could do it himself, but he does software not hardware and certainly not wetware; he's not armed; he's never been in a fight.

The muscles in Volodya's shoulders tense, he sinks into a crouch with his arms out and biceps taut. But then he puts a hand over his ear and cocks his head to the side. He spits on the ground and rises face-to-face with Eben, his back to Rishi.

Eben watches as the girl is dragged to a warehouse. In the opposite direction, Rishi and the other guards walk to another hovel to collect from another debtor.

Shalini leads them out of the slum. Eben is still swallowing air instead of breathing. Volodya grips his arm and shoves him forward, across a field, and into the shade of the willow tree whose branches are still arranged in the shape of wings. The symbol for escape and freedom opens Eben's lungs and he sucks in air.

Eben says, "Why didn't you stop him?"

"Me?" Volodya says, "No. No, no, no. You own this. It is yours." His chin tightens. Eben cowers, certain that Volodya will strike him. Instead, Volodya shakes his head. "The man owed you money—why did you not grant him bankruptcy protection?"

"You can't just let him take that girl."

Volodya speaks slowly, "The man clicked agree."

Shalini says, "It would have been worse for the boy."

Volodya and Eben both turn to her.

"Rishi gave the man a choice," she says. "His son has healthy blood, healthy organs, was worth enough to pay the debt. It will take longer for the girl to generate the necessary income, but at least she will live." And then she walks away.

"For money," Volodya says. "You have done all of this for money."

"He didn't have to borrow from me." Rather than meet Volodya's eyes, Eben watches Shalini walk away.

"You will lend money to anyone for anything?"

"It's supposed to be a free market—I never thought that—"

"But you are not lending, are you? You are buying."

"No, it's just that—opportunity, it's about opportunity."

"Opportunity to live in a slum, to create tyrants who have the authority to steal a mother's children."

"It wasn't supposed to be this way."

Eben looks up in the tree. A gust of wind blows the branches apart, removing the symbolism. When he looks back, he sees Volodya walking away. Eben shakes off the turban and throws it against the tree where it unravels and falls to the ground.

Wo runs to him. "Mr. Scratch! Where have you been?"

Eben watches the drooping willows dance in the wind and recalls how things were when he and Allison started this business. It really wasn't supposed to be like this.

17. The Tax

I sip my morning coffee, the wonderful taste of Vienna. Mrs. Gorkum, our neighbor who runs a Turkish deli in the Naschmarkt downstairs made it extra muddy for me and gave Winter a slice of cheese. I'm careful to lock the door behind me. Winter curls on his pillow below my desk.

Connecting, I see email from Gwinnie, the woman I've doted on since my first day of high school. Her note lacks the warmth for which I yearn, but I forgive her within the first sentence. She has been laid off. She doesn't answer my call so I send her a text. It's 7:37 in the morning here in Vienna and 4:37 in her first unemployed afternoon. I offer her some money, nothing untoward, just enough to get by for a month. She texts back, thanking me but rejecting my offer. She's moving to a less expensive area in California's central valley. I release another in a long series of sighs over Gwinnie; farther away, Gwinnie just keeps getting farther away.

As I have done so many times before, I let her go and try to focus on whatever it is I have to focus on. Yesterday I finally managed to hack deep into the ScratchCo computing system, but the accomplishment drowns under my heartbreak. Besides, I couldn't get all the way in. What appears to be Eben's personal directory sits at the top layer of security and requires two biometric signatures for access. Still, I accessed the ScratchCo databases, all but the 103 gigabytes in that top directory, and connected them to our timeweave prediction engine. Eben's timeline will now be complete and the latest timeweave calculation should be much more accurate.

"It was a huge accomplishment," I say. Winter opens one eye for just a second, still upset about Gwinnie's job. "You should be very impressed." He's not.

I sigh again and pull up the timeweave.

"Holy shit," I say. Winter sits up, ears perked. "This can't be right."

Yesterday the timeweave still looked like a spray of unraveling possibilities, but it has resolved into a single thick cable with an overwhelming 99% certain destiny: not just economic chaos plunging humanity into a dark age—I'm at least accustomed to that—but with it the death of Eben Scratch in less than 49 hours in Durango Mexico.

Winter hops up on my lap and stares at me. My heart is racing and I feel perspiration on my forehead. With Winter sitting on me I find it difficult to remove my coat.

I zoom in on the weave to examine the timeline threads that fluctuate around that all-but-certain cable. They have one thing in common.

Then, from my earbug I hear Volodya say, "I could have saved the girl." I can hear the sounds of the airport behind him, he's leaving India.

Fiona's earbug is on too. I picture her sipping a late night crème de mint in the Danielle Steel section of The Intoxicating Page. She says, "What would you have done with her?"

Volodya: "I'd take her back to the US with me, or Vienna, or fucking Pakistan, anywhere would be better than the fucking EbenZone."

Fiona: "They would have killed you and I'd have lost my friend."

Volodya: "I'd have died doing the right thing. Instead we live with this knowledge."

I say, "I finally breeched the ScratchCo central servers, except for one top-level firewall, but there's a problem."

Volodya: "If we access surveillance systems across Punjab we can still find her."

Fiona: "You know what would happen."

Volodya: "What? Maybe I rescue more than one such child from assured destruction? Maybe I rescue them all?"

Fiona: "I'm not sure they'd all fit in my apartment."

Volodya: "Why do people stay in these EbenZones? The people are free to come and go. It is poor country, yes, but poverty is worse in these EbenZones. Everything is worse near Eben."

Fiona: "That poor girl was collateral for loans spent on heroin."

Volodya: "They could have walked away the day before. We know very little."

Me: "We know that algorithms control everything—interest rates, maximum allowed loans, promotions and demotions—all according to one criterion: a person's point total, their balance. The leaders of the EbenZones, people like Rishi Raji and the man he's meeting with in Mexico, are called Barons and Dukes just like in ThievesWorld. Have you played this game? It's quite addictive."

Fiona: "He just wrote the code, right?"

Me: "Yes, he wrote the optimization software and may not have had any idea what would emerge from it."

Volodya makes the sound of a bear who has been duped out of a cub. He adds, "I have to board plane."

Fiona: "We can hear the announcements; they're boarding first class, you have at least 20 minutes."

"Wait!" I say. "Eben is going to die and the world is going to die with him." Winter leaps off of me.

Volodya says, "Simon?"

Fiona says, "You all right, mate?"

"Pull up my screen and look for yourself." I wait an agonizing 19 seconds so that they can see the cord-like timeweave. "Eben is going to die in Mexico and when he does it's all over."

Fiona: "How will he die?"

"I don't know." I manage to catch my breath.

"Trillions of tiny effects go into these calculations." Volodya sounds calm now, as though he finds certain disaster soothing. "They combine into this timeweave—this cable of destiny. But Simon, have you analyzed character of low probability threads?"

Me: "None of them are stable, still popping up and disappearing, but they all have one thing in common."

Fiona: "What is it?"

Me: "We have to get Eben to that meeting in Paris."

"You should just say so," Volodya speaks in a clear, certain tone. "I will go to Durango and make sure that he gets to Paris."

"But he's going to die."

"I will get him to Paris."

Volodya's confidence soothes me until I recall another detail. "On Bastille Day."

"I don't like that," Volodya says. "Consider if French Revolution occurred now. World is tightly linked, borders can no longer contain revolutions. This result, it is a problem." He makes a sound that recalls an economist facing the guillotine. "But first Eben must survive Durango."

Fiona says, "I'll meet you there."

"Not necessary," Volodya says. "You are more effective support from San Francisco where you have high bandwidth connection."

"Maybe," she says, "but if Eben survives I have a lesson to teach him and if he doesn't …"

I can hear Volodya shuffling down the boarding ramp. "Is one other thing. I have email from Russia. My family is being harassed by police. My cousin Boris was in oil workers' strike, was arrested and fined. Russian police suggested his 'rich American cousin' pay fine. Is almost hundred thousand dollars—we must invoice Guy Bourbon for currency project."

Fiona says, "Already taken care of."

Volodya: "Simon, find a timeline that can get us out of this mess."

Me: "After I get Allison set up with Owen, I'll work through every thread in the weave."

Volodya says, "Do not let Allison near our labs."

Me: "I'm going to ask Frau Feuerstein to arrange a corner of her café in such a fashion that Owen will be comfortable."

Volodya: "You will pay the tax?"

Me: "What? Tax?"

Volodya chuckles. "You will understand when bill comes due."

* * *

The trick is to find the right metaphorical flap of figurative butterfly wings; a skill that Fiona claims I uniquely possess. I refresh the timeweave and begin the arduous task of tracking different scenarios to see what small actions can budge reality onto a timeline where Eben doesn't die and or civilization doesn't decay, or that exposes the logical flaw that would indicate a bug. I'm in neck deep when I realize that I haven't done my chores. Owen and Allison need a workspace.

I swivel toward the door. Winter hops up from his spot beneath my desk, leaps for the coat rack, and pulls his leash down. I catch the falling rack. Thirteen minutes later, we walk into the Café Feuerkessel.

The proprietress, Frau Feuerstein, is a gentle widow and the café Feuerkessel has been in the Feuerstein family for 197 years. She greets me with a plate of strudel. I explain my need for a favor and that I'm in a hurry, behind on an important project with a looming deadline, and in fear of imminent failure.

She takes my hand and says, "You should relax. Calm down, enjoy some strudel." She turns to an employee behind the counter. My German is good enough to catch that she's planning an hour respite from running the café.

I say, "The world will sink into a dark age if I can't get this done by tomorrow morning!"

"Simon," she says, guiding me through a rear door and upstairs, "nothing is that bad."

"But it is!" I swallow the rest of the strudel.

"Come with me and I'll make it all better." She tucks my arm against her body. We enter her modest apartment and she commences preparation of coffee drinks which makes no sense given the café downstairs.

Winter sniffs about her apartment.

"I have two colleagues who need a place to work. I was wondering if you might have space, of course I can hire an office for them, but it's so much more pleasant here with you."

"Of course, Simon. I'll partition work space for them." She

pours schnapps into our coffees, tops them with whipped cream, and directs me to the sofa in a room where we can see the Danube River.

I take the suggested seat and she hands me my drink. The mixture is delicious, though flammable. Frau Feuerstein sits next to me, facing me with one leg curled beneath her and the other stretched out to the coffee table at an angle that denies me the ability to disengage.

Maintaining my cultured nonchalance, I sip this delicious cocktail. The warmth, sweetness, and alcohol-heat consume my senses. The urgency of Eben Scratch's foibles seem less imminent. I should have checked his flight schedule to determine my actual deadline.

Frau Feuerstein reaches over and wipes a bit of whipped cream from my nose. She smiles and looks into my eyes, leans toward me, and licks the cream from her finger. I hear Winter exhale a sigh.

Why am I the last to realize the obvious?

Just over an hour later—a duration that I intend to share with Fiona and Volodya at the earliest convenience—Winter and I walk out of the café.

Frau Feuerstein was right, I feel much less stress. We walk with a purposeful but not measured stride. The route back to the lab takes us to the far-end of the Naschmarkt. Near home, the market has fixed stalls manned by permanent businesses. At this end, it's more like a flea market. A young man sells skateboards, another T-shirts, and a woman sells flowers. One gentleman, dressed in a long leather coat on this warm summer afternoon, seems to have no wares whatsoever, though he doesn't lack customers—mostly youths in varying states of disarray. I find it odd. Winter finds him fascinating, sniffing about his boots and torn dungarees. The man pushes Winter aside with one boot, not quite a kick, but sufficiently aggressive to arouse my ire. We rush home.

I knock on the door of Fiona's apartment and Allison steps out. Winter leaps into her arms. I must admit that Winter's affection for Allison ratchets up my respect for her. I say, "Let's get Owen and I'll guide you to the Café Feuerkessel where Frau Feuerstein will provide you workspace, beverages, and pastries."

"Pastries?"

"Oh yes." I offer a conspiratorial smile. "Strudel! But we need to hurry, I've got a huge debug job."

The three of us walk through the Naschmarkt to Owen's apartment giving the cruel bastard in the long coat a wide berth. At the Café Feuerkessel I introduce them to Frau Feuerstein and she serves us venison goulash that Owen and Allison fairly launch into. I look at my watch and attempt to deflect the invitation, but Frau Feuerstein references how I "must have built up quite an appetite." Turning down a meal seems utterly ungentlemanly. We each consume at least three thousand calories of Eastern Europe's heaviest cuisine.

Frau Feurestein provides Allison and Owen a well lit, isolated corner of the café. Owen sits across from Allison and describes their project. He's a quiet, solitary man, sleight of build—though not for long if Frau Feuerstein continues to feed him—he wears glasses and is easy to overlook, except here in Vienna where so few people of African heritage live. His enthusiasm grows with each detail: his grand plan is to shift videogames from computers, couches, and living rooms to cities, mountains, rivers, and beaches. Using Glass to impose visual overlays based on GPS positioning, his game will merge reality and fantasy. In exchange for helping him, he'll let us access his source code. From there it's a simple task to connect our hacking spiders—the heart of our timeweave prediction engine—to any set of networked Glass.

IV. Does it Matter Whether You Win or Lose?

Yao Wo usually loves stepping onto real ground and tasting fresh air after a transcontinental flight but not today. He can't stop worrying about Tam. The suffering is horrible and Tam's positive outlook through the pain almost makes it worse. He's not sure that his wife could handle losing her youngest. He can't stand to see Shu suffer and he wonders if their marriage will survive if or when.

The air is thin up here on the steppes of the Sierra Madre Mountains. He looks up at the ridge but can't see the Eben-Zone. With twice as many people as the one in India, Mr. Scratch plans to split it. Being part of a fast-growing international corporation can be exciting, but today he has to fake it. He steps into the airport.

Mr. Scratch leans against a wall writing in a notebook that he bought before their flight—a paper notebook. Yao has never seen Eben write on anything but a laptop. Even weirder than writing longhand on paper, his shirt hangs out of his waistband as though he started to tuck it in but got distracted.

He collects their luggage and heads for the exit. Mr. Scratch tucks the notebook in a pocket and walks alongside. Yao notices another alarming detail: rather than his usual long strides, hunched over as though examining each step, Mr. Scratch stands nearly straight and looks around the room as he walks.

"Everything all right, sir?"

"Not bad, thanks."

Mr. Scratch has never thanked Yao for anything. "How is your back, Sir?"

"My back?"

"You're standing straighter than usual."

"I am? No, I'm good." Scratch turns and looks at him. Looks him up and down and the examination frightens Yao. "How's your son?"

"Sorry sir?"

"Your son, his name is Tam, right?"

"My son? You're asking about my family?" Yao steps back. "You know his name?"

Then the weird becomes bizarre. Not only does Mr. Scratch smile, but he reaches out and puts a hand on Yao's shoulder. "Yes, I'm asking about your family. How is Tam's treatment going?"

Yao wonders if asking Mr. Scratch for a loan was a mistake. Is Mr. Scratch going to fire him? Yao takes his tablet computer from his blazer pocket and zips through emails and memos; he asked for the loan in person, so it's not documented, but Mr. Scratch never forgets money. He looks deeper but can't find any organizational mistakes. "Sir, I sent you the list of questions you dictated for our meeting with Mr. De Vegas last night, have you received them?"

"Tam's okay, then? Improving?"

"He's fine, sir." Yao swallows the lie and adds, "He's awesome," because it's not a lie.

Two men in loose fitting black suits and sunglasses meet them next to a black SUV. One of them holds the door and another man steps out. Though he's never seen him, Yao recognizes Alejandro Gustavo Mauricio De Vegas. Taller than Yao by several inches, De Vegas has thick wavy hair parted in the middle and feathered back. He wears a black shirt with mother of pearl buttons, blue jeans, and snakeskin boots. He eyes Mr. Scratch and smoothes his mustache. The man who held the door takes Mr. Scratch's laptop which upsets Mr. Scratch, though he doesn't say anything.

The driver takes the luggage. Yao thanks him and starts to step into the car behind Mr. Scratch. One of the men who greeted them steps in front of Yao. The man frowns and stands with his feet shoulder width apart. Yao smiles and starts to maneuver to the other door. The man grabs Yao by the forearm and twists.

Unlike his eldest son, Yao Wo never showed much competence in the martial arts, but like his sons and all the boys in his neighborhood, he took lessons for years.

Yao rotates with the twisting motion so that he ends up face-to-face with the man, a simple defense to an arm lock. Yao falls back and pulls the man with him. The man lets go of Yao's arm. Yao drops into his kung fu stance. The other man uncoils a kick where his head had been.

Yao rotates so that his arm wraps around the leg. As the man pulls back his kick, Yao catches his foot and continues rotating, taking the leg just under the knee. It's an obvious white-belt level move.

Had the move progressed as Yao expected, he could have thrown the man to the floor and taken a position of control with one arm holding the leg and the other poised to chop the throat. But before Yao can complete the flip, the man kicks Yao's kidney with his other leg. Yao tries to hang on. The man lands on his hands, jerks back both legs, and springs to his feet. The man chops the back of Yao's neck, jabs him in the solar plexus, and Yao hits the ground gasping, immobile.

The man gets in the SUV and it takes off.

18. Collateralized Death

The timeweave has not veered from its dire course.

I update Eben's timeline and see that 17 minutes ago Yao Wo reported to the Durango police that Eben Scratch has been abducted. I swivel to another monitor, dig back into the ScratchCo system, and launch network spiders into the Durango EbenZone system. The spiders search through surveillance systems, cell phones, everything connected to the network using face recognition software to find him. It takes six minutes to locate him. I sip my Turkish coffee and spend an instant wondering if this task requires more or less caffeine.

Our software impresses me to the extent that I waste the better part of a minute before I notice that it's devouring so much bandwidth that it must be obvious to anyone on the network that I've joined them. I reduce the network load to the cameras and microphones of the PCs in the room where Eben sits. One camera shows Eben sitting at a table staring at a laptop monitor. The other two show young men seated at the table working at similar laptops. An angry looking giant of a man stands behind Eben. Our software tags him as Alejandro De Vegas—a shockingly handsome fellow who would be the ideal lead for a production of *The Mark of Zorro*.

I hear De Vegas tell Eben to transfer some accounts. Eben opens a database and selects a group of 15 digit numbers. As Eben digs into his system, I rub my hands together. Eben's not working on his own laptop; it's one of De Vegas's and lacks Eben's biometric security measures. Since Eben is connected to that impenetrable top level, I can piggyback in through this machine.

I finally get behind the executive-level firewall.

He has accounts in banks all over the world with concentrations of money in the currencies where his zones are located, a veritable cash cache. Among dozens of such accounts, I see one with exactly ten million dollars in a Cayman islands bank. It's the smallest balance of all the accounts and the only one with such a precise sum. Something strikes me about the account number. I type it into a simple decryption program and it reports that the number spells "ourfuckyoumoney" when typed on a phone number pad.

Eben appears to copy the Durango account numbers from one database and paste them into another, but the account numbers float back to their original positions; a simple trick with graphics.

De Vegas slaps him and says, "Die now as a trillionaire or live your life as a millionaire. It seems like a simple choice to me." He taps a piece of paper on the table next to the PC. "Transfer the money to this account."

"Something's preventing me from making the transfer," Eben says. "I'll figure it out in a minute."

De Vegas motions to one of the others. "Hector?"

A short, heavyset young man types a flurry of commands and says something in Spanish that seems to indicate a not so confident "no."

De Vegas strikes Eben's jaw with an open palm. His Glass fly across the table. De Vegas catches and crushes them in his fist. "You will transfer the funds now or you will die."

Eben keeps his eyes on the PC and says, "I'll try another approach."

Despite everything I've learned about Eben, I find myself stunned by this level of greed. Does he really believe that he can take it with him?

* * *

Eben stares at the laptop. De Vegas stands behind him talking to his software experts, Hector and Jose. Eben tested them with a few feints and misdirections shortly after he logged on. Hector caught the simplest one but neither of them could detect any sophisticated hacks. Hector is older than Jose and might be a better programmer, but Jose is more curious and less concerned with impressing De Vegas. Eben knows that he'll have to be careful but is confident.

His nerves have settled now. It helps to keep in mind that he's still the most successful man on earth, still a winner as long as he's alive. Yet here he sits, captured by a debtor, an employee, and his allergies are going crazy.

Eben believed that he'd accounted for every possible contingency. EbenZone systems acquire vast amounts of personal data; EbenPhones catch every sound and vision. Phone data is correlated to EbenZone surveillance systems. Pattern recognition algorithms tag, store, and reconstruct embarrassing data—it's a simple formula: man with a woman who's not his wife? Correlate the times, the conversations, identify lies and deception. Performing illegal, immoral, or ill-advised business transactions? It's in the database. Appear somewhere you're not supposed to be? Break a promise? Violate a religious mandate? It's in the database. Every embarrassment, every betrayal, every cheat and lie, every act of treachery is loaded and ready to be released in a way that maximally assassinates a debtor's character.

If Eben disappears for three full days, it will all be released: mass character assassination. A million lives will be ruined unless someone rescues him. It seemed like the perfect safeguard: a dead man's switch of certain, total destruction: Worldwide exposure of the corruption, depravity, and deceit of the world's most powerful people, and its weakest. But Eben overlooked a crucial piece: What if his debtors hated him more than they feared exposure?

He overlooked something else, too: he doesn't want to ruin a million lives. Eben doesn't want to ruin anyone.

It wasn't supposed to be this way.

Eben was supposed to have friends and family who cared for him. People who would notice he was missing, people who would look for him if he disappeared. People who would care.

The feeling rises slowly in a shiver up his spine. He fights off a sneeze but it aggravates his post nasal drip. He tries to clear his sinuses.

Volodya was right. Eben has no friends. Yao Wo is not his friend. How could he be? Mr. Wo lives in a building surrounded by people who love him. No one has loved Eben in almost three years. No one will be rescuing him, either.

De Vegas put a blindfold on him back in Durango and didn't take it off until they set him in this chair. He tries to recall the warehouse design. The same design was used for all warehouses in every EbenZone; why pay an architect more than once? He writes a little script that will find and copy the design onto this PC along with all the other Durango Zone designs and maps.

"What are you doing? Hector, what is he doing?"

Eben says, "I'm doing what you asked. I told you it would take a while." He says it without looking up and tries to sound just a bit frustrated, anything but scared.

Jose says something in Spanish.

Eben can't open the warehouse design with Hector and Jose watching and De Vegas sitting behind him. His eyes itch and run, he can picture mold growing in the ventilation system. The sigh escapes his lungs before he realizes it's coming.

De Vegas says, "*Señor*, now maybe you see how I feel?"

"I have allergies," Eben says.

"Oh no," De Vegas says, "trillionaires don't cry." And then he laughs.

Eben increases pressure through his sinuses. It generates the sound of a honking goose but it's the only way to clear them out. He says, "I didn't design the system to make it easy to splinter off large fractions of the organization. I told you, it's going to take a while." He leans back in his chair, surprised by a growing confidence in his ability to keep cool. "This database has the coordinates of different CurrentSea accounts." He continues talking, making up ever more arcane tech-sounding gibberish—"relational vectors between arrays combine bit descrambling and Gray coding to alter symbolic relationships"—and concludes with: "The longer you leave me alone, the faster I can fulfill your request. Jose and Hector are welcome to help." He swivels the chair around to De Vegas and adds, "Given the growth rate of this manor, I was going to give you more authority anyway. I came here to promote you."

De Vegas jabs a fist into Eben's stomach. "I am not a fool."

Eben doubles over and falls off the chair. The pain keeps him in a fetal position, but it's not so bad that he can't take in details of the room. The ventilation grates are at floor level. He lets loose three body-shaking sneezes and then climbs back into his chair.

Eben operates computers like jockeys ride horses. Within a few minutes of logging on, he knew the machine's memory and processing power and the network bandwidth. This PC is less a thoroughbred than a pinto, but it should be more powerful than this. The drag on the processor could just be Jose and Hector monitoring him. Bringing up the task manager would raise suspicion, so he writes a script that puts the names of all processes in the account database and then he scrolls through it.

He finds Jose and Hector's processes first, but there are two others. One is a system-level process that's a big bandwidth hog. He doesn't recognize it but the other process is named

ThievesWorld.

He feels a flash of hope, someone is out there!

Hector says, "Why do you stop?"

De Vegas wraps his hands around Eben's neck. Eben looks across the table at Jose who looks away. Hector, on the other hand, grins back at him.

Eben opens another data array to cover his tracks. The familiar manipulation of keyboard, the connection he feels between the processor, the interconnects, the disks, and his network, *his* network. Whatever game they're playing, it's on Eben's turf and if there's one thing Eben does well, it's score more points than his opposition.

Who could the ThievesWorld process be but Allison? Process of elimination is easy when there's no one to eliminate. But Allison? How could Allison be on this system? And why? None of it makes sense. Doubts move in. He stops and looks at the screen: columns of numbers and an old-school DOS prompt.

The hands around his neck tighten.

"Cutting off the supply of blood to my brain won't help me concentrate." The hands loosen and De Vegas delivers a short lecture in Spanish to Hector and Jose. Eben starts a translation program that writes a text file of whatever they're saying. Maybe he'll have a chance to look at it later.

De Vegas leaves the room. As the door closes, Eben sees at least two guards standing in the hallway, including the one who assaulted Mr. Wo.

Hector moves to the chair next to Eben and watches his screen, but Eben's not using a graphical interface. He does everything with control sequences and prompt commands so that onlookers can't follow what he's doing. He types in coordinates to draw the ThievesWorld symbol that means "you're being watched" and then sends a text message to the ThievesWorld process: "Help?"

Within seconds a two letter acronym appears on his screen: "FU." It was the last thing Allison said to him when she threw him out and the last thing she said when he saw her on Market Street. That shred of hope blows away. Eben covers his face with his hands. The temptation to surrender forms a lump in his throat. And then he laughs at his own misery.

"What's funny?" Hector says.

He yields to the coughing fit and concludes with a loud sneeze. "May I have a cup of coffee or tea? Something hot to drink, please. The ducts in this building need to be cleaned."

Jose leaves the room.

Eben puts his fingers back on the keyboard. When he gets out of here—yes, *when* he gets out—he's going to buy himself some happiness, one way or another, no matter how much it costs; but before that, he's going to clean the ducts in every building he owns. He stomps the ground in frustration. He can feel Hector's discomfort behind him, so he says, "It's frustrating. I designed efficient firewalls. If you think you can do this, go ahead."

19. Just a Game

Allison sits in the Café Feuerkessel working with Owen, her laptop on a table, her ass on a bench, her fingers blazing across the keyboard. Owen dozes now and then. His keys, wallet, and smartphone lie in a heap next to his laptop.

She doesn't mind Owen. He's easy going, quirky, quiet, funny in the way of hermit-geeks; the techie-opposite of Eben's hyper-drive tunnel vision. In a different world she might even like him. But she's not going to make him rich.

Now neck deep in Eben's executive partition of the ScratchCo system, she sees a folder packed with images, videos, emails, texts—it's like a character assassination treasure trove. She sees the dead man switch too. That Eben would even think of a system so evil depresses her. People change. Her hatred climbs into her throat like bile. She digs deeper and sees accounts in banks around the world, absurd sums of money, except for one that has a simple tidy sum.

There it is.

Their fuck you money sits in one account waiting for her. She's going to take it too, just what is rightfully hers. She's not going to sink into Eben's pit of greed, but she is going to destroy him. And then she's going to buy as much land as she can out in the middle of nowhere and live with the animals in peace and harmony.

She pulls herself out of the daydream when a message appears on her screen: "Help?" What a bizarre thing for a trillionaire to say. She replies, "FU," and continues her search for the key to his destruction.

And then she sees another process. Nothing obvious like her ThievesWorld process, so blatant that it shows up in the task manager, it's a quiet, system level process—the same one she saw a few days ago while she was working with her raven friend at the rehab clinic. It's not hard to guess why Simon, Volodya, and Fiona would be so interested in the world's first trillionaire, and hence, the reason they're supporting her recovery. Everyone wants something.

She leaves ThievesWorld running on Eben's PC, opens another window on her laptop and does a few pedestrian web searches on her new sponsors. TLA doesn't have a website and doesn't operate out in the open but she finds plenty of references to their app development business plus a few hints that they also perform consulting services.

She tries to hack into the TLA servers but now the greeting says, "We see you, again!" along with the description of their brick firewall.

Frau Feuerstein leans in and says that she's closing the café. Owen awakens and looks at the clock on his phone. He says, "You shouldn't work so hard—it's just a game." The way he says it gets to her a little bit, like he really means it, really cares. It must be nice to be rich.

She walks groggy, good-natured Owen back to the room he's rented. She stops at an ATM along the way and uses his card to get a hundred Euro. He waits for her, as unaware that she's using his card as he was when she watched his fingers type in his PIN at the airport ATM. He keeps talking about the game they're writing, how augmented reality can be used in every aspect of human life, how it will transform tourism, blah blah blah. He thanks her at his door and goes on in.

It's not yet midnight and there's just one vendor left at the Naschmarkt. She doesn't know the language, but she knows the protocol. She even knows the prices. A few simple gestures convey her desires. Five minutes later, she types the code that Simon gave her and heads upstairs to the third floor. Walking along the hallway, she smiles at Winter's nose print a foot below the knob of Simon's door.

She slips inside Fiona's apartment. She turns on the light over the range and settles at the kitchen table where she mixes the brown paste with the white powder into the bowl of an immaculate glass pipe. The buzz comes on like a trusted lover, soft and satisfying. She leans back and notices the crown molding and intricate designs on the ceiling. The buzz displaces a lot of the noise she lives with, the doubts, the fears, and even most of the anger, but here and now, this time, it doesn't displace her ambition.

She ponders her situation, her goals, and the greater plan. Except for a few pieces, it feels like it's coming together. She smiles and chops up some blow. A sound jars the silence. She recognizes the exhaust fans from the refrigerator vents of the supermarket on the ground floor. She leans over to snort the coke and that's when it comes to her.

Back in San Francisco, before it was legal, she knew pot growers who got busted because of their heat-footprint. The cops use infrared tech to find grow rooms from the heat of the lamps that burn for 16 hours a day. When those growers posted bond, they set up a grow room over a butcher. The heat footprint from the freezers drowned out the heat of the grow lights.

She snorts the big line of coke, walks out of the apartment and downstairs to another hallway. This floor has three doors, similar to the layout of apartments above. On one of the doors, she sees a beagle nose print. She hears keyboard clicks inside and then she hears a combination of whining and sniffing, Winter asking for a belly rub through the door.

Allison doesn't know much about picking door locks so she returns to the apartment, snorts another line, and hacks into the lock manufacturer's database.

20. Plans

I find it difficult to keep up with Eben's flurry of downloads: plans for every building, maps of plumbing, electrical wiring, and networking.

Volodya enables his earbug and says, "Just landed in Durango."

Fiona checks in from the Intoxicating Page. It's late at night for me, early afternoon for them. I explain the situation and update them on what I've learned from Eben's executive level directory. Volodya says, "How long will De Vegas let Eben live?"

Me: "Eben's timeline indicates that he has less than six

hours."

Volodya: "And in three days, dead man switch latches and world economy goes to shit."

Fiona: "You're bothered by the exposure of corporate corruption?"

Volodya: "I'm bothered by hundred year dark age regardless of cause."

Fiona: "De Vegas will kill him the instant Eben gives him what he wants."

Volodya starts laughing, great har hars, too.

Fiona asks, "Are you taking the piss?"

It takes me the better fraction of a second to recall that Australians use "piss" as a metaphor for almost any nonconformist behavior.

"No, no," he says, "is Eben's tangled web—you don't get it?"

Fiona: "I get that we've got hours until civilization lands in the rubbish bin."

Volodya: "Eben relied on blackmail, people's fear of humiliation, embarrassment, shame to keep them in line but this De Vegas—what is his name?"

Me: "Alejandro Gustavo Mauricio De Vegas"

Volodya: "Even funnier. De Vegas comes from cartel culture! His crimes are source of pride to him. Is ultimate backfire of evil plan."

Fiona: "That's not much help right now."

Me: "Eben appears to be delaying the transfer of his wealth to De Vegas as long as he can."

Fiona: "At least he's not thick."

Volodya: "I'll get him out."

"Right," Fiona says, "you can infiltrate the EbenZone by parachute."

Volodya: "Something like that."

Fiona: "I'll be in Durango in two days."

"You have much to do before you leave." Volodya assigns us several tasks and then says, "I must go shopping," and disconnects.

I check back on Eben. He has assembled maps and engineering files of the EbenZone. I copy them and start mapping possible escape routes.

While Volodya spends the afternoon shopping in Durango, I put together a little model and see how the odds of a successful escape depend on likely responses of Alejandro De Vegas. By the time I finish, my model has all the elements of a video game, including how to get the highest score.

I can't expect Eben to accept whatever I plant on his computer, but with Hector and Jose hovering over him, I'm pretty sure he won't notice that I've altered the warehouse architectural plans to make the best escape route obvious. Then I help Fiona prepare a diversion from a combination of online videos, news, and government websites.

I'm still in the lab when Volodya activates his earbug and says, "You have the diversion prepared?"

"I believe that De Vegas shall fairly come unglued."

"You will be able to guide me?"

Until this instant, I'd manage to overlook the danger of this mission. Now I feel stupid and worried. I say, "The instant you're in range, connect to me through the EbenZone base station. I've already got feeds from all of the surveillance cameras. You'll know every move De Vegas's security makes and they won't see you on any camera—that's already programmed."

Volodya says, "Remember that first day?"

"I do."

"Yes," Volodya says. We were graduate students, me from the US and he from the USSR. "I went first."

I say, "The most elegant description of nuclear interactions I'd ever seen." My voice is light, or at least I hope it's light, but I must admit that hearing Volodya wax nostalgic frightens me.

He says, "Simon, I'm glad I met you."

I'm at a loss. Rechecking the surveillance cameras in the EbenZone, I confirm that everything is in order. But what if there's a whole other system? What if De Vegas installed a network of which I'm unaware?

Volodya says, "Simon?"

"Yes. I'm triple checking everything."

* * *

Volodya eats alone in Durango's finest restaurant at the hotel where Eben had planned to stay. He watches Yao Wo who's also eating alone. The local police have made no effort to find Eben; they avoid the EbenZone almost as if they had a vested interest in not noticing its existence.

Volodya sleeps well. He worries more about the effect his death would have on his friends than his own survival. Death means he'll never worry or remember again. He smiles at his own silly failsafe device.

He carries his bag out of the hotel, gets in the rented jeep, and drives out of Durango and up a mountain. GPS leads him to a trail that Simon's model indicated would be the best access point. He slows and lets the few other vehicles pass. When no other cars are in sight, he turns off the road into a pine forest. He manages to get a few miles over the ridge and into the valley before his speed through the countryside is no faster than hiking. He turns the jeep around for a quick escape, and leaves it between a boulder and a huge pear cactus.

He takes the fully loaded pack, easily a hundred pounds, and heads into a canyon, working his way through the brush, still guided by GPS. He looks back and can just barely make out the jeep. Either it will help them escape or serve as a further diversion.

Volodya is a powerful man in excellent condition, but he is 54 years old and it's a heavy pack.

21. Generosity

Between jet-lag and the fact that De Vegas won't let him leave the room for anything but an accompanied trip to the bathroom, Eben has reached a state of exhaustion that he's never experienced. De Vegas's hackers, Hector and Jose, look tired, too, but yelling from the hallway rouses them.

Eben focuses on the screen, in particular on the timestamp of the warehouse design. If he can keep his eyes open longer than Hector and Jose, he can open the file. He wonders if Allison put a message in it, wonders if it's just another "FU." He shakes the cobwebs out of his head. Message or not, that file is his only chance to escape.

He's reminded of his Facebook post and it hurts. He feels like he's drowning in a river of regrets. He loses focus on the monitor again and his thoughts drift back to Punjab and the look of terror on that poor girl's face.

The door crashes open. Before Eben can turn around, he's yanked from the chair and thrown to the ground. Alejandro De Vegas stands over him, screaming, "What have you done?"

De Vegas steps onto Eben, balancing his entire weight on Eben's sternum. He relaxes the pressure, but before Eben can inhale a breath De Vegas drives the toe of one cowboy boot into Eben's windpipe. The immediate effect is to prevent Eben from admitting his plans for escape. From his position on the floor, he can see that HVAC vent again.

De Vegas speaks in a more controlled voice, "If you are responsible for this you will die."

Voices clamor in Spanish. People run in both directions

through the hall outside this room.

Eben scrambles for breath. De Vegas steps away. Eben gasps, convulses, and gags until air finds its way into his lungs. Hector and Jose lift him into a chair.

De Vegas pulls a chair in front of him and speaks in a calm, nearly amiable voice, "How did you alert the DEA?"

"I told you, this database has always—the DEA? What DEA? I didn't contact the DEA."

"Then why are they crawling through my AlejandroZone?"

Eben takes a deep breath that brings another sneezing attack. His sinuses clamp down and he makes the honking sound to open them.

Alejandro squeezes his neck. The honking sound increases in pitch accordingly, but it gives Eben time to assemble his thoughts. Alejandro releases his neck. He taps his boot against Eben's chair. His face grows red. "You have ten seconds."

"Why would I bring the DEA down on an EbenZone?"

"Don't treat me like a fool." He coils a fist.

"Wait!"

The blow comes from Eben's left; an upward blow that connects to the base of his jaw. His teeth crash together and his neck whiplashes back. He holds onto the chair armrests. "Please, listen. I didn't do this."

De Vegas clenches his other fist.

"I did not contact the DEA." De Vegas's bicep tenses. "Just wait! I configured a dead man switch. The system will automatically queue up messages meant to destroy your credibility. I can show them to you! But from this computer, I can't stop them. The system is designed to prevent what you're doing from happening. You read the terms."

"They said that you would destroy me."

"Yes—destroy you, but not by destroying my business. Why would I contact the DEA?"

"To save yourself."

"From what? You're right. I'd rather be a living millionaire than a dead trillionaire. And the DEA? Why would they save me?"

A look of doubt crosses De Vegas's face. "You will be the first to die." He stands, kicks over Eben's chair and yells at Hector and Jose in Spanish. He opens the door and storms down that hallway yelling commands at his guards. Eben, still on the floor, rolls into position so he can see down the hallway. The man who beat up Mr. Wo, along with three other guards in those loose fitting black suits follow De Vegas.

Eben rights his chair. His jaw aches but functions. Jose and Hector attack their keyboards. Eben slumps over his keyboard as though asleep. He opens the warehouse design.

Eben realizes that once the money is transferred, there's no reason for De Vegas to let him live. The thought that De Vegas is going to kill him doesn't generate the panic he'd have expected. He concentrates on options. Only one comes to mind. He has to surrender to a DEA agent. He can either wait in this room, delaying results until the DEA makes their way inside or get outside somehow and find an agent. He looks next to him at Hector and across the table at Jose. He has to act now before De Vegas and his guards return. Now, while his only guards are two software jocks.

He scans the design and locates this room. He traces the HVAC ducts and finds an exhaust outlet at the rear of the building. If he can get into that duct, he can work his way to a vent and get out. If he correctly identified this room. And if his allergies don't cause a sneezing attack that echoes through the entire building. A lot of ifs. It would be quite a statement on his life if his allergies got him killed.

* * *

Volodya left the empty pack on a trail half a mile behind

him. He also left boot prints next to the river, three different sizes plus his own prints. Empty rations containers litter three separate locations with broken branches and pressed brush to give the appearance of troops making camp. Shreds of torn camouflage hang from the thorny branches of a few mesquite trees, a broken rifle scope decorates a rocky peak just inside the EbenZone perimeter, and various other knickknacks that you might expect DEA commandos to carry around including a paperback book, an empty whiskey flask, a chewing tobacco tin, and broken sunglasses. To guarantee its shock value, he had to overdo it. It won't take long for De Vegas to realize that it's staged. Hopefully that initial shock will be enough.

He sits in a tree about a hundred meters from the warehouse where Eben is being held and watches the sunrise. He has a clear view of the south side of the building, including two exits.

Shortly after the sun climbs over the horizon, people start pouring out of the warehouse, Fiona's diversion. She prepared mock news feeds reporting a huge DEA assault on Mexican drug cartels outside of Durango. Volodya doesn't know the details but suspects that she repurposed old footage of other raids; another play that won't bear much scrutiny.

Eben better come out that door soon.

* * *

I all but marked the preferred exit door with a billboard when I modified the warehouse CAD diagram that I put on Eben's PC.

My translation software conveys that De Vegas has commanded Jose and Hector to search for system infiltration and inconsistencies in their surveillance system. While I've taken many precautions, it's impossible to cover all my tracks.

"Fiona," I say, across an ocean. It's 1:06 pm here in Vienna, 4:06 am in San Francisco, and 6:06 am in Durango. "De Vegas may have severely injured Eben. He's bent over the table, barely conscious."

She says, "What's our plan B?"

I studiously ignore the question.

"Eben's faking sleep," Fiona says.

"He is?"

"Watch his fingers, they're tapping in sets of seven—it's a nervous tick."

Eben slips his fingers onto the PC touchpad and opens the warehouse CAD file. It takes agonizing seconds for the design program to execute. Eben keeps his head on the table, his face and touchpad-wielding fingers are concealed from Hector and Jose, but exposed, along with the display, to anyone who opens the door.

Fiona: "Here we go!"

"Patience." The closest surveillance camera from the room is at the end of the hallway where I want Eben to exit the building. People rush back and forth on confused missions to search for signs of infiltration.

Eben works his way through the warehouse diagrams, through each level including the heating, ventilation, air conditioning, which is to say, the HVAC ducts. "I neglected to manipulate the duct diagrams.

Volodya whispers, "I'm not enjoying their response to my end of diversion."

I see what he's talking about on another feed. De Vegas has guards going through the zone holding smartphones up to the eyes of every person they encounter.

Fiona: "Does that mean you're blocked in?"

I sense Volodya nodding and suspect that Fiona does too.

Eben should have digested the CAD file by now. "Okay, hope that he gets the message."

"Hope," Volodya whispers.

Me: "Or we'll think of something else."

Volodya's nervy sense of cool has deceived me for decades. Over and over again I'm fooled by his ability to appear calm when he is indeed popping a figurative gasket. He says, "Something else? There is no something fucking else." Right out loud for anyone nearby to hear.

I implement two commands and Eben's PC reverts to the blue screen of death. It's a simulation, of course, I can bring it back up in an instant if necessary, but if anything will cause a geek to act, it's that blue screen. "He should be out that door in about seventeen seconds …"

Volodya completes my sentence: "… and he will not be alone."

* * *

Eben raises his head the instant the blue screen appears but manages to bite back a curse. The chemicals of panic jolt from his head to his toes and back. Time slows and, what feels like a full minute of hesitation—should he reboot or act on the information he already has?—passes in seconds. He strives for composure. Jose and Hector both look at him, annoyed but busy.

Eben moans and rests his face on his hands. He says, "I'm dizzy," crosses his eyes, and exhales slowly as though he's about to faint.

He's identified two options from the design file. Both require him to get out that door and down the hallway. He coughs, finishing with a gagging sound, and pushes the chair back. He leans forward, hanging his head over his legs as though about to vomit. Neither Hector nor Jose seem to care. He doesn't blame them. If he worked for De Vegas, or if he worked for himself, for that matter, he'd know better than to let himself be distracted from orders.

The door is two steps away. Prepared to collapse like a paranoid opossum if the door is locked, he gags again. Neither Hector nor Jose look up.

He bolts for the door, hits the lever, pulls it open, steps out, pulls it closed, and runs down a hallway, dodging between people rushing in both directions. He kicks open the exit, but rather than step outside, he takes two steps back, out of view of the surveillance camera over the door, runs up another hallway and into a bathroom. He hangs his head over the toilet and waits. He hears Hector yell. Then a flurry of footsteps and cursing passes down the hallway and out that door.

He turns to the sink.

While growing up on that huge Nebraska ranch, his chores included fence maintenance, house and barn wiring, and plumbing. The sink stopper consists of a short steel rod that connects to the metal disk that serves to stop-up the sink. He pulls it up, hoping that whoever installed it took the usual short cut. They didn't. He drops to his knees, reaches under the sink, and yanks the lever mechanism out of the drain pipe. He stands and pulls on the stopper; this time, it comes right out.

With the steel rod in hand, he drops to the floor next to a grate that covers a ventilation duct. The end of the rod won't work as a screwdriver so he jams the rod between the wall and the grate and tries to pry it open.

Once inside the duct system, Eben can work his way to any exit on this floor. Then he can bide his time, watch De Vegas's activity and choose the right instant to escape. But only if he can get this grate off.

He pulls the stopper end back. The grate bends around the point where the screws attach it to the duct. He tugs again, straining, something starts to give.

The rod snaps in half.

* * *

The instant Eben sees the blue screen of death, I tell Volodya to get ready.

Fiona and I can hear him slide down the tree.

He says, "I'm maybe twenty steps from exit, in position to get him undercover in three seconds."

I say, "He'll step out that door in ten, nine, eight ..." but I count all the way down to "zero, minus one, minus two, minus three, minus four—he's got to be there."

Volodya: "The door is opening." Then he hits that one syllable four letter word. Even in a whisper it comes out like the puff of a high powered air rifle.

Fiona: "What happened?"

Volodya: "Door Opened, man came out—not Eben."

Me: "Eben should have stepped out the door over 16 seconds ago!"

Volodya says, "Where is he?"

Me: "I don't know."

Volodya: "You what?"

Me: "I don't see Eben in any of the surveillance feeds. He doesn't have his phone—I have no way to find him. But the rotund fellow who just ran out the door is one of De Vegas's programmers. His name is Hector and he is searching for Eben."

Fiona: "Volodya, get out of there."

Volodya: "I am safe here. For now. This Hector is not a threat to me."

Fiona: "Are you armed?"

Volodya: "I have knives."

Me: "What?"

Volodya: "Mexico has remarkably stiff gun regulations."

Me: "That doesn't seem consistent with their reputation."

Volodya: "That also occurred to me. In sporting good store, they would not sell me a handgun and I thought it dangerous to carry a rifle—no way to blend in with EbenZone occupants."

Me: "How is your disguise?"

Volodya: "Cotton poncho, wide brimmed hat, dungarees, leather belt. Not uncomfortable, quite sharp, I may keep the hat."

Fiona: "Lads, please."

* * *

Sprawled on the bathroom floor, Eben tosses aside the broken sink-stopper. The adrenalin turns sour and the nausea becomes real. He gets to his feet and leans over the toilet just in time to avoid vomiting all over himself. There's nothing to be done but go back to that room and face his own miserable death.

The realization brings an instant of reflection. This must be what people mean when they say that your life flashes before your eyes: broken promises, relationships tossed on life's roadside. Eben is accustomed to loneliness, but he's not accustomed to loss.

Loss. The thought fills his heart. Another thought creeps into his head: Loser. And it's followed by disgust. Win? Lose? He asks himself: Where has this black and white vision of the world taken him? Such primitive concepts, worse than stupid, they're lonely. He compares all that he's lost to what he's won. Lying here alone on a bathroom floor, the notion that it wasn't supposed to be this way tries to work its way into his consciousness—again—but before the thought forms it changes to "it doesn't have to be this way."

No one cares about Eben Scratch, but there are people Eben cares about. Sure he pushed them away, but he still cares. He pictures the people he loves. Two faces come to mind immediately and then others. Most of these people hate him. Does that mean he has to hate them too? Maybe in the win-lose world it did. No! It doesn't have to be this way.

"It's okay," he whispers to himself. "It's okay to care for people who don't care for you." Part of that simple statement echoes through his being, his spirit: It's okay to care.

He smiles at the counter-thought: the phase of Eben Scratch caring for others could be very short-lived.

He cracks the bathroom door, takes a breath, and listens. The commotion that accompanied De Vegas's realization of a DEA invasion is settling.

Eben poises to bolt out of the bathroom, up the hall, and out the door.

A thought strikes him. One of those left-field, out-of-the-box thoughts that comes under times of either extreme stress or extreme calm: Back in college, he discovered that he could use the department's copying machine by pretending that he had authority. He'd walk into the Business School office with a frustrated look and do whatever he wanted. The one time someone questioned him, instead of acting guilty, he said, "Fine, you tell the Chair why she doesn't have these copies," turned and stormed out. The next time he used the copier, people greeted him as a co-worker.

He stands and straightens his hair and dusts off his pants. Then he hunches over and steps out of the bathroom as though in deep concentration. He passes two people at the end of the hall near the exit. They look at him and he responds with a frustrated but commiserating groan.

According to the design plans, this door leads to the side of the building; not the back loading dock or the front entrance, but to the base of a hill, the sort of exit where you expect to emerge into a group of cigarette smokers.

He sees Jose round the corner, running straight toward him.

* * *

I've replayed the feeds of every surveillance camera in the building. Instead of a constant stream of 15 or 30 frames per second, the cheap cameras that Eben put in his Zones take two frames each second. In one of those half-second intervals, Eben opened the door I directed him to and then disappeared.

Fiona yells into my earbug, "He's right where you lost him!"

I look up at that monitor. "He reappears after being gone for thirteen minutes? Thirteen?"

Fiona: "Volodya, here he comes."

Me: "It seems ironic for him to reappear at the strike of thirteen. Wouldn't you think he'd have waited another minute and make use of the multiple of seven?"

"Please," Volodya says, "I cannot see what you see."

"All right," I say. "Eben's walking to the exit. He's in no rush. He's fairly sauntering down the hall as though he owns it. Of course, it's an EbenZone so he does own it, but—"

Volodya and Fiona both say, "Simon!" at the same time.

"—he's acting like he's pre-occupied with a software bug, or maybe he's re-evaluating his escape plans. In either case, his nonchalance is extraordinary. Uh oh."

"What, uh oh?"

"De Vegas's other programmer, Jose, is going to catch him."

"And Hector is on the landing outside that door, at the top of stairs," Volodya says. "Eben is caught!"

* * *

Eben swallows the tide of panic. He says, "Jose, over here," and waves.

Jose yells, "Stop!"

Eben strokes his chin. "I think I've figured it out."

Jose rushes up to Eben and reaches for him. Eben pulls away and pretends to be oblivious that Jose is trying to apprehend him. "If we clear the index filters and then define the right filter, we might be able to alter the data structure enough to pull out what we need." He motions with both hands. Jose asks a question about cache commands and Eben gives him a short tutorial.

"Señor Scratch, you have to go back to the room."

"Of course," Eben says. He furrows his brow. "Do you think it'll work?"

Jose says, "We will try it."

Eben looks down and to his right, toward the exit about twenty steps away. He looks up, says, "Let's run it by Hector," and steps toward the exit.

"No! Come back to the room." Jose motions in the opposite direction.

"I thought it was this way," Eben says. "Are you sure?" He turns back and steps toward Jose. Taking that step defies every instinct of self-preservation, but it works.

Jose says, "*Sí*," and begins walking back to the office, motioning for Eben to follow.

Eben pivots on that half step and bolts for the door.

Jose turns and rushes after him but Eben now has four steps on him.

Eben is at full speed when he gets to the exit door. He reaches for the handle and hits the lever, releasing the latch at the instant his shoulder connects to the door. The door whips open.

* * *

When Volodya hears Simon say, "He's going for the door," he takes off like a sprinter out of the blocks. He reaches the bottom stair when the door flies open.

Hector steps away from the swinging door, almost out of Eben's way. Almost. Hector outweighs Eben by a good twenty pounds but is a few inches shorter. He raises his arms and lowers his shoulder to defend himself against the onrush. Eben is moving too fast to step aside. Hector buries his shoulder into Eben's belly, but doesn't realize that it's Eben. Eben bounces off of Hector's shoulder and hits the railing gasping for breath.

Hector reaches for Eben with both arms. Volodya makes it to the top of the stairs and into the gap between them at full speed. He keeps his head low, sombrero down, and uses his momentum to project the crown of his head into the bottom of Hector's jaw. The impact smashes Hector's mouth shut and his head back. He screams. Volodya straightens to his full height, at least half a foot taller than Hector.

Blood pours from Hector's mouth, he covers his face with his hands. He has bitten through his tongue. Volodya knows this particular pain and feels a pang of sympathy as he kicks Hector off balance and down the stairs. Hector's head hits the railing. He bounces off and down. He turns to catch himself, but his wrists hit a stair and his body crumbles over him, bouncing down the stairs to the ground.

Volodya now stands with his back to the door. Eben is next to him, hanging onto the rail, trying to take a breath.

Jose flies through the door and hits Volodya in the lower back. The impact arches Volodya's back and he stumbles forward, down three stairs.

Eben pushes himself off the rail, grabs Jose's arm, and pulls.

Volodya rotates around, takes two steps and jabs Jose first in the gut with a left, and then punches him in the chin three times in succession. He collapses and Eben pulls him out of the way.

Volodya can see that Eben has the same thought. He lets Eben step ahead of him and the two of them run down the stairs. They hurdle Hector's rising form.

Volodya says, "Up the hill, behind building, to rock outcropping."

Eben sprints ahead, Volodya slows enough to scan the terrain. Three people stand near the stairs, another steps out the door. None of them appear to have any desire to approach Volodya.

And then a man in a black suit with sunglasses approaches on the path that leads to the stairs. Volodya bends his neck so that his sombrero covers his face and steps down the stairs slowly with a limp.

Eben is at least fifty yards away when the man finally sees him. The man takes off after him. He's a large man, stout, and no doubt very strong, but he is not fast.

Volodya pushes off the bottom step, punches the man's kidney, and rams his shoulder into the man's lower back. The man folds over backward. Volodya continues pushing underneath the man, lifting. At the instant when Volodya supports the man's entire weight, he stands and pushes up, throwing the man off of his back. The man lands on his head. Volodya spins around, drops and punches him twice in the throat.

Rather than wait to determine the man's condition, Volodya runs after Eben, hoping that his instructions were followed. He rounds the building and turns up the hill and behind a sharp rocky outgrowth.

"You?" Eben says, "You're not DEA, are you?"

"No, was distraction. I am here for you. Again."

Volodya takes off his poncho and hands it to Eben who puts it over his Apple Logo T-shirt.

"How do we get out of here?"

Volodya reaches up and sets his earbug back in place. He hears Fiona say, "He still hasn't moved."

"No one's checking on him," Simon says. "De Vegas's serfs, the debtors, walk around him like he's an obstacle in the path. A rock."

"Or a bag of rubbish."

"Is he breathing?" Volodya asks.

"Gagging, gasping," Fiona says, "but he can't seem to sit up. Don't worry about him. He's not in play anymore."

Volodya says, "Simon, how long have we got? And which direction do we go?"

"I put the surveillance cameras on a loop from this time yesterday. That should buy you a few seconds. Guards are all over the zone, some appear to be searching for DEA agents, others are using biometric scans on every person they encounter. You need to get around the building, away from the two programmers and that guard."

"What about the people who saw us?"

Fiona says, "The others don't care."

Volodya turns to Eben, says, "Follow," and rushes around the boulder and then bends over and runs along the foundation of the building. He stops at the corner of the building and waits for Eben.

When Eben catches up, Volodya starts to move again but stops and pulls back, lower against the building's foundation. "Guards, get down."

Eben grabs Volodya's shoulder and says, "We look too suspicious."

"We try not to be seen so that there is no suspicion."

"We should act like we belong here," Eben says, "as though nothing is out of the ordinary. We'll look less conspicuous."

Volodya thinks it over. He says, "You are all right?"

"And stop looking in every direction. Just you and me, two guys walking along discussing something in English, two men talking business, nothing out of the ordinary, nothing to see here," Eben says. "Get it?"

Volodya thinks it over. "Okay, but we must remain calm or we'll be caught. You are ready?"

The two of them step around the building onto a well worn path in plain sight of De Vegas's guards. He struggles to keep from scanning in every direction. From his earbug he hears Fiona say, "Oh my, that's not Eben, that's Batman!"

They take a path from the warehouse that leads to a slum of hovels built of dried mud bricks, cardboard, plywood, and plastic tarps that provide housing for all but the elite few of the EbenZone's inhabitants. Volodya stands up straight, but it goes against every nerve in his body.

Eben says, "Come on, talk to me, play the game."

Volodya says, "You impress me."

"If I survive, I'll truly impress you." They continue down a path toward the canyon, passing other people walking in various directions. Plenty of people take notice of them, but no one approaches. "May I ask why you're helping me? Or perhaps I should ask if you are helping me."

"De Vegas would kill you."

"And why do you care?"

Volodya says, "We turn off the path in thirty strides. I have suitable clothes for you at the base of the tree a hundred meters through the brush."

"Your name is Volodya Kazimir, right? Can I call you Volodya?"

"Yes."

"Why do I keep running into you?"

"You remember my colleague, Fiona Black?"

"Yes, of course. She betrayed me."

"I am here because she has a misguided affection for you."

"She does?"

They wait for a gap in the human traffic. Volodya says, "Now." The two men hunch over and rush between yucca and chaparral. They're concealed within seconds.

Eben changes into worn out jeans and sandals. Putting a sombrero on his head, he says, "I will repay this favor."

Volodya says, "I hope so."

"When we get back to the path, let's take our time." Eben says, "We'll observe people's behavior. Pay attention to how fast they walk, what draws their attention, and follow suit. If anyone talks to us, just smile and say '*que onda?*'"

Volodya says, "How did you learn this?"

"It makes sense, doesn't it?"

"Not bad."

They return to the path.

Eben says, "I learned this in business school."

"Business school?"

"Yes, my education taught me a great deal about how to work around rules."

"You should have majored in physics."

* * *

Eben's in the most danger he's ever experienced, yet he feels comfortable, not safe, but prepared to face the consequences of his decisions. They continue into the canyon, deeper into the slum. The path fills with families, friends, and neighbors and the mood loosens up. Back at the warehouses, people looked down and walked with purpose on gravel paths. Down here, they talk and argue and navigate the muddy ruts around their homes.

The path twists around sharp granite rocks that stick straight up as though growing out of the mountain. Passing around a house-sized boulder close to the river, the land flattens into fields. As they pass the next boulder, they hear men yelling and then the sound of a stick cracking followed by more yelling. Eben has no desire to see the suffering here that he saw in Punjab.

He steps into the clearing and sees a baseball diamond. They're using rough-hewn branches for bats and the balls are made of something other than sewn leather over a wound core. The players field the balls barehanded, even the catcher, and the pitchers throw at full speed.

"The game of summer," Eben says. "If things were different, just a little different, I could supply bats and gloves and start a league, an EbenLeague. I'd love to play."

Volodya steps in front of Eben and says, "Get behind me and lower your head. Walk into the crowd but not too fast."

Eben sees several men in sunglasses striding with purpose. The crowd loses its enthusiasm. Eben senses tension in the silence and notices that no one in the crowd looks at the men. The studiousness of their indifference is more obvious than if they'd stopped the game and gawked at the official passersby.

"Turn away slowly," Eben says. "No one is watching them but you."

Volodya becomes fascinated with an errant thread on the hem of his poncho. "Good observation."

The five officials stand in a row and arrange people in columns in front of them. The officials hold phone cameras up to each person. They're taking roll with biometric technology. People seem eager to get it over with.

Volodya pulls Eben off the path toward the baseball diamond and around the officials. One official gives an order and motions for them to step into his line. They take another step away and the field goes silent. Eben hears the official's boots in the mud. A woman makes a tut-tut sound. A baby cries.

Eben whispers to Volodya, "Run for it?"

Volodya steps back to the queue. People make room for them. Volodya offers to let them pass but no one accepts. The scanning resumes. He taps his ear and says, "Simon? Can you assure that we pass biometric test?" He frowns and turns to Eben. "Eben, do you have suggestion for how we can delay for five minutes?"

There are two people ahead of them.

Eben whispers, "Rub your eyeball. Get some grit directly on your cornea."

* * *

Winter sits on Volodya's chair watching with me.

The solution comes to mind immediately. All I have to do is slip code into the guards' smartphones so that everyone passes the test, a simple patch that skips over the software that performs the actual test and just gives the okay. It takes 17 seconds to write the code, 38 seconds for it to compile, another 42 seconds to install that module into the link library, 77 seconds to replace the library on the EbenZone servers, and then every agonizing tick of 211 seconds to rebuild the executable.

Of course I didn't have time to test the new program.

"It might work now."

* * *

"Might?" Volodya says.

It's Volodya's turn. His eyes are now bloodshot and swollen from rubbing, an excuse if he fails the test.

The guard holds the smartphone up to his eye. Instead of staying still for the camera, Volodya rubs his eyes and shakes his head as thought trying to dislodge something from his ears. The guard orders him in Spanish. He takes a breath and holds steady.

The guard looks at the screen. He holds out a hand, obviously telling Volodya to stand still. He turns to the other guards. They look at each other.

Through his earbug, Simon says, "Sorry about that."

The guards walk away from their queues and gather together. One taps his phone as though it were a malfunctioning toaster.

Eben whispers, "Run for it now?"

Volodya taps his earbug. Simon replies, "The program is still installing. You're going to pass and then, hopefully you can just walk away. It will be functional … now."

The guards exchange comments and return to their queues.

Volodya looks into the smartphone camera again.

The guard examines the result. Volodya makes a point of rubbing his eyes. He holds steady, expecting a second test. The guard grabs his wrist and, with remarkable speed and agility, slips on a handcuff and twists his arm.

Volodya lets the guard follow through, waiting for him to step around him. In that instant, the guard will be just off balance and Volodya can throw him to the ground, kick him in the throat, and run for it.

A commotion catches his attention. Instead of taking that step, the guard looks over his shoulder. Apparently someone else has failed the test. And another. The people who fail complain, some indignantly, most quietly, and the commotion grows.

Volodya understands. He relaxes and lets the guard attach both cuffs. The guard pushes him to the side with the others who have failed. Another guard points an AK47 rifle at the crowd.

He hears Simon through the earbug: "Sorry, old chum, I got the logic backward."

One of the guards performs the test on himself—he fails, too. Everyone fails.

The officials shepherd everyone onto the baseball diamond and force them to sit on their hands.

* * *

Eben sits next to Volodya between second and third base. People sit with their families. Volodya still has cuffs on.

The sun beats down. From the shade of his sombrero Eben watches a large family near second base. Four malnourished children, one with scabs on her face, sit between their pregnant mother, who looks exhausted in the sun, and their father, whose arm hangs from his shoulder at an awkward angle as though it was broken but didn't heal properly.

A boy sitting near him says something and Eben smiles and

shakes his head. The boy repeats himself. Eben makes out the word "gringo." Volodya makes a sound that could be interpreted as laughter.

Others turn toward them until Eben and Volodya are the center of attention.

The guard walks toward them and the others turn back to their own companions. The guard looks over them and then continues into center field. When he's a few hundred feet away, the man with the injured arm says, "*Americanos?*"

Volodya sighs.

Though neither of them understands Spanish, they can see word spread. Someone near third base says, "Hello." A girl says, "Good day," and then giggles.

Eben waves back to them. He motions in the direction of the guard who is now in right field and says, "*Gracias.*"

The pregnant mother over on second base looks faint.

"Eben," Volodya says, "Please give my hat to the lady. I would, but the cuffs."

Eben takes off his own hat and takes it to the woman. She puts it on and looks immediately relieved. Her husband says, "*Gracias*," and Eben says, "*Denada*," but he feels like he failed a test; he should have given her his hat an hour ago.

The sun is about to set when the officials return and organize queues for the biometric roll call. This time everyone passes the test, handcuffs are removed, and the officials move on. Eben can't understand why no one turns them in. Surely De Vegas would offer a reward, but the others crowd around and shield them from the guards' attention. The guards continue on their way and, when they're out of view, the pregnant lady returns Eben's hat.

The father motions in different directions. Volodya points up at the western ridge. The man lowers himself to the ground and draws a map. He points at a few huge boulders on the slope and indicates where they are on the map.

"*Gracias*," Volodya says and shakes the man's hand.

The man shakes Eben's hand, too, says, "*Buenos noches*," and walks away with his family.

Eben asks, "Why didn't they turn us in?"

"People who need help give help more freely. Is simple," Volodya says. "Poor people help each other more than rich people."

"But De Vegas would have rewarded them."

"You truly disgust me." Volodya walks along a path that winds between boulders into the deepening shade of the western ridge.

Eben follows. He starts to speak. Volodya raises a hand and grunts.

Volodya says, "You ignore responsibility that comes with wealth."

"I tried to give people the freedom to get credit for any purpose they wanted. If they—"

"You pretend that selling children for parts is just doing business?"

"Of all the ways to a pay a debt, why would they choose that?"

"Tell me, Eben, what is collateral for these loans, other than children. Why don't people walk away?"

"An automated system maintains a behavioral information database. If someone leaves without paying their debt, then personal information is made public."

"You blackmail them."

"I didn't know that they'd sell their children." The accumulation of stress and lack of sleep, not to mention the bruise on his sternum feels like a weight on his chest. He stops to rest. "It's a bug, I'll fix it."

"A bug? You tell me this is a software bug?" Volodya turns

back and looms over Eben. "Do you know what the word 'hubris' means?"

22. Remorse

Fiona took the red eye to Mexico City and arrived in Durango an hour ago. Since then, she's been sitting in a square sipping a delightful mocha and watching the small city wake up and start its day. Buildings with red clay roofs and facades painted yellow, green, and blue line the streets. She watches burros burdened with fruit and vegetables mix with the traffic.

Volodya connects and says, "He has not turned."

Fiona says, "Bring him straight to me." She texts her location.

Simon adds from Vienna, "Good job, Volodya, the timeweave has stabilized. Well, as stable as it was before."

Fiona: "All timelines lead to Paris?"

"The only timelines that can get civilization around depression, famine, and war," Simon says, "are those in which Eben attends a meeting at l'Hôtel de Ville on that most auspicious date, Bastille Day."

"You have checked *every* other timeline?" Volodya says.

"Well, I—"

"Lads, it's my turn," Fiona says. "I'll have him ready for that meeting."

Volodya and Simon argue about the impossibility of making absolute predictions based on statistical analyses. Fiona marvels at their ability to argue even when they agree.

She finishes her tea and visits a shop, buys a blanket from a street vendor, and turquoise earrings from a shop. She returns to the square and has nearly finished a cup of tea when she sees Volodya's rented Jeep approach. She walks to her rented Ford sedan. The Jeep parks behind her, its wheel wells dripping mud. Through the earbug, she tells him to sit still with the engine on for a few minutes. When she's sure that no one has followed, she approaches the passenger side. She's happy to see Eben and excited to make up for humiliating him but still apprehensive about how he'll react to her. "Good day, Eben."

The stubble on his chin gives him a rugged look, but she still sees the confident intelligence she recognized in him when they first met.

He steps out of the car and says, "Ms. Black."

Volodya comes around and hugs Fiona. He lifts her up and kisses both of her cheeks.

She says, "Have you been bitten by a sentimental mosquito?"

"You know I am all façade."

She pulls his face against hers until their foreheads knock together. "You had me worried. Again. Now set me down and get your ass to Mexico City. You're booked on a flight to Vienna."

He sets her down and says, "You sent the money to my cousin?"

"Of course."

Simon chimes in through their earbugs: "Every economy in the world is experiencing tremors right now. The Russian oil workers strike has been, umm, stifled in a fashion that must have Lenin and Marx spinning in their respective graves. Lenin's corpse is still on display in Red Square so I wonder if—"

"Thank you, Simon." She taps off her earbug. "Eben, you're coming with me."

He says, "But my things and my assistant."

She hands Eben a cell phone. "It's an image of the phone you lost. Call Yao Wo, he's still at the hotel worrying about you. Tell him to go home."

"How did you make an image of my phone?" Eben says. "Oh. Of course." He taps the phone and puts it to his ear. "Mr. Wo! Are you okay?" Pause. "Yes, it's me, Eben." Pause. "You can call me Eben, now." Pause. "Okay, I want you to be comfortable, buddy." Pause. "Buddy. It's a term of endearment." Pause. "Yes, well. Umm, Yao? Could you please fly to Paris and meet me? I'll need new Google Glass, too." Pause. "I'm fine, really. Really good, actually, and I'm looking forward to seeing you, Yao. How's your son?" Pause. "Terrific. After this trip to Paris, I want you to take some time off to be with your family." Pause. "No! No, I'm not firing you. No, I'm going to promote you to Chief Operating Officer." Pause. "I'll see you in Paris." He hangs up.

"Can't you just let him go home?" Fiona says, "His son is dying."

"He said that Tam is doing great."

Through grinding teeth, Volodya says, "You see? Same rotten bastard."

"No, you don't understand. I'm going to get this back on track, but I need him. I can't accomplish anything without my friend, Yao Wo." He puts a hand on Volodya's shoulder, an action that makes Fiona worry for his health.

Volodya pushes Eben into Fiona's rental car. "Stay out of sight, floor of back seat. De Vegas works for cartels now and will be looking for you."

Eben says, "I'm going to fix my mistakes and I'm starting tomorrow in Paris."

"No," Fiona says, lifting his hand from Volodya's shoulder. "It starts tomorrow in Cabo San Lucas."

23. Agent Provocateur

Allison spent most of the night studying schematics of the lock on the computer lab door. The manufacturer's database includes lock picking hints meant for locksmiths. Then she went on a treasure hunt through Fiona's things searching for tools. She has hair pins, an eyeglass screwdriver, even an ice pick.

While she waits for Simon to vacate the lab, she practices on the lock to Fiona's apartment. She finally hears the clatter of paws on hardwood and Simon assuring Winter that it will be the finest walk of his life and the greatest biscuit in history followed by a series of naps that guarantee peace and relaxation not experienced in centuries. Allison smiles at the simple joy and feels the draw of friendship.

She puts the tools in her purse and closes the door. "Good morning, Simon. Do an all nighter?"

Winter hops into her arms and rubs his muzzle into her neck. She rests her chin on his head.

Simon says, "You wouldn't believe the buggy code I wrote and then had to fix. Maybe the stupidest thing I've ever done. I hardwired a 'false' that should have been 'true.'"

"Back at it after your walk?"

"Yes, still a long way before we're out of the woods on this project."

She sets Winter down, takes a few steps along the hall, turns back, and says, "I'm off to work at your girlfriend's café."

"My what? Frau Feuerstein is not my girlfriend."

"That's not what she says." And Allison trots down the stairs leaving Simon following in a cozy state of confusion. She ducks into a hat shop and waits for them to pass through the

Naschmarkt. Then she goes back upstairs to the lab.

This lock isn't nearly as difficult to hack as the software version that protects the TLA servers. The bit counter is simple and impenetrable to computer hackers outside the lab, but now that she's inside there's nothing special about their workstation security—just passwords.

The setup is as lush a computing environment as she's ever seen: two six foot tables with six monitors on each. One workstation has photos of several dogs in a collage, a framed picture of a red-haired lady who doesn't look comfortable holding Simon's hand, and a dog bed at the feet of its user. The other is meticulously neat and devoid of frills.

She attaches a keylogger to Simon's workstation and then repositions the desk chair, keyboard, and mouse. She looks out the lab window to the Naschmarkt and sees Simon and Winter chatting with the Gorkums. Another little shot of envy infects her, it must be nice to have friends you can trust.

She locks up the lab, takes the back door down to an alley, and walks to the café for another day hacking Glass with Owen.

She returns in the evening and Simon is still in the lab. When he comes upstairs she asks how it's going and he says, "We solved one disaster and it's on to the next." She snuggles Winter and exchanges small talk. Simon yawns as he unlocks his door. "Only time for a nap. Working in one time zone and living in another is exhausting." She sets Winter down and Simon steps inside. "Volodya will be back tomorrow and Fiona's coming soon. Allison, please let me tell you how nice it has been for Winter and me to share your company."

Allison goes straight to the lab.

Simon's password is easy to find in the string of keys he pressed today. So-called high quality passwords that combine random upper case characters, symbols, and numbers are the easiest to identify: just look for repetitions of the same gibberish. She connects through Simon's account, creates her own, and uses Volodya's workstation—much easier to reconfigure a tidy layout than a cluttered one.

She skims through the directories. The software library is gargantuan and the databases are big enough to hold the entire internet. It could take days, maybe weeks, to figure out what they're up to.

She goes to the "TLA Business" directory and opens their customer files. The first one she finds, "Bourbon-Project," is a boring business analysis. She skims through and opens another, Wildlife Defenders; it has records of an ongoing project that monitors poachers on four continents. TLA identifies poachers and gives Defenders their contact information. Another one is the Woodley-Carlyle Group, a huge oil and defense infrastructure company; the moral opposite of Wildlife Defenders. She mumbles, "What?" and checks a few others but can't find a pattern.

At some point Simon will have to sleep a full night or day and she can dig in, but she's already spent an hour here so she packs her things and straightens up Volodya's workstation. She's halfway to the door when a fragment of an idea gnaws at the back of her mind. She logs back in to the system and skims through TLA's customer files. She finds the Bourbon-Project; they're working for a French finance company owned by a man named Guy Bourbon. She remembers the name "Bourbon" from a freshman history course. A quick search brings up a family tree; European royalty that dates back eight hundred years. His nth great aunt was Marie Antoinette.

She goes back to Eben's calendar and the agenda for the upcoming meeting in Paris, sure enough—Guy Bourbon will be at the meeting. And the meeting is on Bastille Day? She leans back and laughs, sometimes the world just paves the way for you.

24. Finding His Way Back

Fiona isn't sure how to broach the subject. It's a long drive on mountain roads that require all of her attention. She wishes he would say something. He just glances out the window and writes longhand in a notebook. Occasionally he checks his phone but there's no coverage until they approach Mazatlan. Then he types for a few minutes and returns to longhand on paper.

He takes over driving when they reach the highway that runs along the coast of the Gulf of California. She's not certain but suspects that he's avoiding the subject as much as she is.

She clears her throat. He looks over with no expression and then back at the road.

"I'm sorry," she says.

He says, "I'll need my passport."

"What?" Fiona says. "Right. I have it here." She pulls a new passport out of her purse. For some reason, probably guilt, she admits that they hacked the State Department. "Getting around red tape is convenient and really, as hackers, aren't we obligated to squeeze efficiency out of bureaucracies?"

"It's a lifestyle."

Another hour passes. She says, "Eben, please accept my apology."

"Okay," he says. They're quiet for several minutes and he adds, "Apologize for what? You saved my life."

"I meant for what happened when you pitched to SomaAngels. I wasn't very nice."

He turns back to her, then back to the road, and starts to laugh. At first a gentlemanly chuckle but then an all out belly laugh.

"I should have been more constructive," Fiona says. "I'm terribly sorry." He keeps laughing and she adds, "I was an insensitive bully and had no right to degrade you—why are you laughing?"

"If you hadn't humiliated me, I never would have worked so hard. Ms. Black, I made a trillion dollars just to prove you wrong!"

"Yes, that's the problem. It ruined you."

He stops laughing.

It's quiet again, but eventually Eben asks her about some of the people he used to work with, everyone except Allison.

They get to the ferry late in the evening. Once the car is on board, she lets him have his space. She spends the night on a wooden bench; the waves rock her to sleep. He wakes her when the ferry makes ground on the Baja California peninsula, and they get back on the road. She appreciates that he hasn't questioned her about their destination, her motivation, anything—and then she worries that he's too complacent.

They pass through the small city of Cabo San Lucas and continue south. Sand blows across the highway and the cars kick up dust that coats the cactus and yucca in gray. Fiona slows when the GPS indicates they're close. A trash bag billows in the wind from a cactus. She turns onto a narrow sand road.

Eben's writing in his notebook.

Fiona drives through the dips and around the dunes. "What are you doing?"

Without looking up, he says, "Writing."

"Business plan?"

"Poetry."

She turns to him. The Ford careens up a little dune and then bottoms out. She stops. "You're writing poetry."

"Fiona, I've created cities, I've created entire economies on every continent, but I don't even know what my work means."

"Poetry."

"Do you have many regrets?"

"Poetry?"

"Ever wish you'd gotten married, had a family, anything like that?"

Fiona says, "Can I read it?"

"It's not finished. I haven't written a poem since I left Nebraska."

"What's it about?"

"I'm the richest man in the world and maybe the poorest, too."

"Sod all," Fiona says, for a moment expecting a response from Simon or Volodya, but she hasn't enabled satellite transmission. "Nothing mucks up a data set like philosophy."

The terrain grows more familiar and then the road widens into a sandy parking lot with a dozen cars, most with surf-racks on their roofs. The *cantina* looks like a pile of yucca and palm fronds from this side.

Fiona spots a red Subaru with California license plates—they match. She parks several spaces from it, gets out of the car, and says, "Bring your notebook, this is a right nice spot for poetry."

Eben stands beside the car and looks over the dunes at the sea. Fiona opens the trunk, takes out two beach towels, and tosses Eben a pair of shorts, "Put these on."

"Where?"

She gives him a towel. "Under this."

She wraps a towel around herself and sheds her clothes. She puts the swimsuit on the ground so that the right leg opening is spread out, steps into it, and pulls it up. She takes off her prosthesis and puts it in the trunk of the car.

Eben's climbed a dune and is still staring into the distance.

She follows a path around the dunes. Sturdy wooden lounge chairs are scattered about the beach, about half occupied by sunbathers. Poles hold lines of small light bulbs that cordon a region in front of the cantina where tables with big sun umbrellas are set about ten meters apart.

She watches for his reaction as they cross the line of yucca and palm fronds. The first sign of the true nature of this paradise comes from the music.

Eben cocks his head and looks up at one of the poles. He sees the speaker at the top and says, "Stone Temple Pilots?"

"It gets better," she says. "This beach faces directly south; if you started swimming, you wouldn't touch ground until Antarctica."

Sets of waves approach the beach, smooth mounds of dark blue rolling forward, growing until they topple over, breaking from right to left in white foam that rushes up the beach. Surfers take their pick of easy waves, in no rush to accomplish anything.

Fiona looks around the beach. Several families have spread out their towels, but she doesn't recognize any of them.

"What?" Eben says.

He's turned away from the ocean. From this side, that pile of fronds takes on a whole different role. Flat screen TVs hang above a bar with a long line of beer taps. A man in shorts, huaraches, and a pink guayabera shirt approaches. "Cerveza? Margarita?"

Eben says, "A sports bar? Seriously?"

Fiona says, "Blended margarita with salt, *por favor*. And a *Sol* for my friend, with lime, please."

"*Ci, señorita.*"

"How I love to be called a *señorita*!"

Eben fixates on the horizon again—and who could blame him? One cotton candy cloud dangles over the southeast against a blue sky. A squadron of pelicans skims the waves. A blonde Labrador retriever sits a few feet away, perfectly stationary, like Eben, staring due south at the horizon. His ears perk and Fiona follows his gaze. A surfer catches a wave, a teenage girl with black hair and flawless bronze skin in a florescent green bikini, zips straight down the wave and then cuts back into the curl. The dog barks and wags its tail, but doesn't budge from that spot.

Another surfer struggles to catch the same wave. He paddles with the enthusiasm of a novice, stands and, like the girl in green, zooms down the face, but when the boy tries to cut back into the curl, the tip of his board goes under and slings him forward. The wave crashes over him and the board recoils from the tether attached to his foot.

A family sitting on towels about fifty meters away erupt in cheers and catcalls. Except for one. A woman sits up with binoculars. Out in the water, the boy rises to the surface and waves back to the beach. The woman sets the binoculars down and waves back.

A voice comes from behind Fiona. "*Señorita?*" She accepts the margarita in a big plastic cup with a salt-dusted rim. She hands him a credit card and says, "Can you arrange a room for us?"

"For you and me, *Señorita?*"

"Don't tempt me."

He takes the card and she takes the bottle of beer and hands it to Eben. "Come on, I want to show you something."

She leads him toward the water. The sand provides her cane plenty of purchase, but pushing off her leg is awkward. When they're fifty feet from the family, close enough that they can watch but far enough that they're not crowding. She spreads out her towel. Eben sits right in the sand.

From here, the likeness is more obvious. Fiona says, "Recognize them?"

He turns and looks at the family, two girls, about 8 and 10, a man, a black cocker spaniel, and the woman with the binoculars.

Eben starts back up. "My sister—Sally, and her family!" He waves and the man looks up but instead of waving back, the man looks back over his shoulder as though searching for whoever Eben might be waving to.

Sally glances over too but looks away.

"They don't recognize me."

"Why would they? You haven't seen them in how many years? And this is about the last place they'd expect you."

"What are they doing here?"

"Celebrating summer. Remember? Your sister invites you every year."

"Here?"

"Yes, here. Every year on the first day of summer they come to this beach to camp out on the longest day of the year. They've been doing it since your nephew was born." As though on queue, Eben's nephew wipes out on another wave. His mother, Sally, raises her binoculars again. When the boy doesn't surface immediately, she jumps up and trots down to the water. The cocker spaniel follows her but veers over to sniff at the blonde Labrador. Sally stands ankle-deep in the coming-and-going froth and scans the horizon.

The boy surfaces behind the next wave. Sally drops the binoculars and acts as though she's just dipping her toes.

Fiona says, "What's your nephew's name?"

"Who?"

"The shark biscuit out there trying to surf."

"That's, umm, he's Edward, Ed. I thought they went to my beach."

"No, they come here. Every year."

"Why don't they use my beach?"

"No one uses your beach. You locked the gate."

He looks down and runs his fingers through the hot sand. "What a waste."

"Your nieces are building a sandcastle."

"I should go over."

"What are your nieces' names?"

"I think the little one is Haley and the big one is Blakely."

"You think."

"I don't see them very often."

Fiona sips her margarita and then takes out her tablet. She enables satellite reception, turns on her earbug, and says, "Simon? What are Eben's nieces' names?"

A few seconds later, Fiona pokes Eben in the side. "You wanker! Your nephew's name is Evan, not Edward—Christ, she probably named him after you. You got one of your niece's names right, but the wrong one. The ten-year-old is Jaley, not Haley, and Blakely is the eight-year-old."

"I think the dog's name is Lady."

"Brilliant. You remember the dog's name. How about your brother-in-law?"

"Bill, we went to school together—and he didn't even recognize me."

"Eben, lean back, relax and meditate on them, on family life. You're only thirty years old." She reaches into her bag again, takes out a bottle of sunscreen, squirts a glop into her hand and says, "Let me put this on your back—you're already turning pink."

The two of them watch the girls construct a sand castle. Their father helps them with the moat. The boy, Evan, continues to struggle in the waves and his mother continues to monitor his every splash.

"Can I at least pay for their meal?"

"No, Eben, you can't buy them anything. Haven't you learned anything about money?"

"I have more than anyone else on earth."

"But are you wealthy?"

"I'd say so."

"Really? Look at your brother-in-law." Having finished the sandcastle—an extravagant construction with a driftwood drawbridge—the girls are now burying their father neck-deep in sand. "You think you're more wealthy than he is?"

"I have more—"

"But Eben, wealth. Are you more wealthy? Are you richer?"

He sighs and leans back in the sand, lying on his side, facing away from Fiona, watching the family. Sister Sally trots back down to the beach. The girl in the green swimsuit now floats next to Evan just beyond the breakers. Sally stands with her hands on her hips looking down the beach, then back out at her son. A wave comes and the two kids paddle into it. The girl points at the boy and he starts to stand. She gets up and gives him more instructions. This time, Evan slides down the wave. He stays just ahead of the foam as the wave crashes and rides it parallel to the beach for a good hundred yards.

Sally jumps up and down and cheers for him. His sisters run down the beach after him, calling his name. And his father climbs out of his burial and yells, "Attaboy, Evan! You nailed it!" Even Lady barks encouragement.

Hours pass, Fiona alternates her margaritas with water and ice tea and an occasional dip in the ocean. Eben sits all the while in silence, watching his sister's family and occasionally writing in his notebook. The blonde lab scrapes the hot layer away and curls up in cool sand, watching his mistress in the waves. Fiona tells Eben to get the dog a bowl of water and he does. The girl seems to have forgotten him.

The waiter brings them a tray of tacos and tamales. Fiona

eats but Eben just sits there.

The tide ebbs, leaving an ever larger beach. Sally and Bill set up a campfire. The two girls put hot dogs on sticks and hold them over the flames. Sally calls Evan in from the ocean but he either ignores her or can't hear her—he's been out there all day. Now he can catch a wave and ride it in just about every time. He's even gotten choosey about which waves he wants, usually the same waves that the girl of the forgotten dog takes.

"Evan!" Sally calls again. This time he looks up from his board and raises an arm, gesturing for his mother to leave him alone. The girl in the green suit, floating alongside, points at her dog who stands and barks. Evan and the girl start paddling in front of a grand swell. They pick up speed and stand at the same time. Rather than cutting back into the wave, they continue into shore. Evan reaches out and she takes his hand. They ride the foam until it loses power and then they jump off their boards into each other's arms.

Sally, who was still standing with her hands on her hips, turns away, looks down, and runs her foot through the water, all the way around in a circle and then looks back at her son. Instead of calling him again, she backs up the beach slowly. When the boy finally waves to her, she waves back and then walks up the beach. She says, "I'm not ready for him to grow up," and her husband hugs her.

After eating her fill, Fiona makes her way over to the sports bar and gets her key. Eben stays on the beach, still lying on his side, watching. She takes a quick shower, puts on a dress and walks back to Eben.

"My nephew has made a friend."

"Summer love," Fiona says, "do you remember that?"

Eben doesn't say anything.

The family has gathered around the campfire. The little girls hold sticks with marshmallows into the flames. Their father arranges graham crackers and chocolate bars. Their mother sits in a chair with her back to the setting sun pretending to read a paperback as she monitors the boy who sits off to the side next to the surfer girl who now wears a pink poncho over her swimsuit. Lady, the cocker spaniel, picks up a towel and shakes it in front of the blonde lab who grabs the other end.

Sally says, "Leave it!"

The surfer-girl calls over, "*Soltarlo!*"

The woman and the girl make eye contact and the mother smiles and says, "Sure you don't want a s'more?"

The girl says, "*Por favor,*" bends over, and brushes sand from her tanned legs, an action that hypnotizes the boy.

Sally says, "Evan!"

His father says, "Give the boy a minute." The boy looks relieved. The mother looks shocked. The girl looks oblivious.

To Eben, Fiona says, "What do you think?"

"I'll come next year." He watches the family from the corner of his eyes. "If they invite me."

Being well-read is a job requirement of owning a bookstore, so Fiona has a broad understanding of many topics, including psychology, so when Sally says, "I'm worried about my brother," Fiona is convinced that she must have seen Eben and identified him unconsciously.

Fiona whispers to Eben, "Face the sea and listen."

Behind them, Bill replies to his wife, "Worried about him? He's the richest man on fucking Earth and we have to borrow money for Evan's braces."

"He lives in that big empty house on snob hill," Sally says. "Did you see his post?"

"Sally, your brother is an asshole."

"Take that back!"

"I read the post."

"It wasn't like him. Something's wrong. I'm worried about

my little brother."

Then the voice of a little girl says, "He sends me a check for my birthday every year!"

Fiona whispers to Eben, "You do?"

"Yao must do it for me."

The high-low, fractured voice of an adolescent boy adds, "Are you sure Uncle Husker can even swim?"

Bill says, "Eben Scratch swims in money."

Sally says, "When Allison left him, he lost any chance of happiness. We need to do a better job getting him out into the world."

"No we don't. The man can have anything he wants. So it's safe to assume that he has everything he wants. Maybe he likes to spend time alone."

One girl cries out, "My marshmallow is ruined!"

The other girl says, "Then take it out of the fire, stupid."

"I'm not stupid—mommy, Jaley called me stupid."

Bill says, "Time alone sounds awfully nice to me."

Sally says, "I'll keep inviting him every year and maybe someday he'll come out of his shell."

"You're right," Bill says. "Just because he says no, doesn't necessarily mean he doesn't want to come."

"Thank you, honey. That's why I love you."

Bill says, "Jaley, bring me that bottle of wine and pour your sister some juice. Evan, Julia, come over here." Then he whispers to Sally, "Keep an eye on those two, I'm not ready to be a grandfather."

"Shut up!" Sally says. "And that's why I hate you." But Fiona can hear the smile in her voice.

Bill pours wine and Jaley pours juice and then Bill says, "Everyone raise your cup."

Bill puts his arm around Sally and says, "Here's to your uncle Eben, may his money not destroy his chance at happiness."

They drink and then the boy says, "My turn. Here's to Uncle Eben, someday I'll teach you how to surf."

Jaley adds, "Here's to Uncle Eben, someday he'll teach my stupid sister how to cook a marshmallow."

The little girl says, "To Uncle Eben, thank you for giving me your money—you don't think he gave me too much, do you? I don't want him to be poor and unhappy."

Then Sally says, "Here's to my little brother." She wipes her eyes and adds, "Husker, I hope you find your way back."

V. Allison's Masterpiece

Allison spends another night in the TLA labs.

The information Allison's found on TLA's system puts Eben's blackmail database to shame: the email and text messages of billions of people, the entire library of the world's media, and surveillance audio and video from an additional billion cameras and smartphones. A tiny fraction is ample for her purpose and she's queued up the great reveal: one drop at a time, like a social networking water torture.

As the first vendors open their stalls in the Naschmarkt below, Allison deletes her account, removes log files and all evidence that it ever existed. If they check, Simon and Volodya can see her footprints in their system and they might even be capable of untangling what she has done, but it's already too late for them to stop her.

She returns everything to precisely where she found it, right down to the position of the mouse on its pad. She locks the lab and returns to Fiona's apartment for a few lines before stepping back out, ready for work, as Simon and Winter emerge from theirs. Simon greets her and offers her coffee; these people are obsessed with their caffeine. Winter rolls onto his back and she rubs his belly. Then the three of them walk downstairs. She parts with them at Owen's apartment where she wishes Simon and Winter a nice day and rings the bell.

Like most mornings, Owen opens the door in his shorts and T-shirt and offers the same self-effacing excuses for oversleeping. He gets dressed and they're on their way to the Café Feuerkessel where Frau Feuerstein serves them croissants and espresso. Allison likes the routine, but it ends today.

She and Owen dive into their Glass apps. They link in graphics libraries and GPS coordinates so that they can display images based on the wearer's location. Owen is brilliant but easily distracted. She gets ten hours of work out of him before he pushes back.

"I'm just not used to working this hard anymore." She gets a jolt of anger, but quickly realizes that it's not humiliation, it's the edge of her need. She fixes herself up in the bathroom and swoops back into their little corner where Owen has fallen asleep, still wearing Glass.

Allison links their code with some of the graphics she took from the TLA servers. She taps the table until Owen stirs. His eyes open. He screams, leans to the side, and then drops to the ground and rolls under the table.

"Holy shit!" His face rises above the table from the other side with a big smile. "Awesome! Do it again."

Allison clicks her mouse and he ducks.

He stands back up and takes off the Glass. "So cool."

Glass works by projecting images into the right eye. This time she projects the image of a Wizard raising a staff and firing a lightning bolt at him from ten feet away. Owen jumps up and down. "This is going to be incredible."

Frau Feuerstein brings them dinner, another lead-heavy Austrian meat dish. Owen barely looks up, just takes a fork and eats with one hand while typing and mousing with the other. Allison's not hungry but eats anyway. Things are coming together, now is not the time to fall out.

With Owen satiated, motivated, and deep in animation software, Allison goes back into the ScratchCo system. Going through the details of the Paris meeting draws her to Yao Wo's email account where she finds an exchange he had with the organizer. Not the big shots that will lord over the meeting, but the lowly organizer, Renee Coutreu.

"Find a bug?" Owen asks, breaking her concentration.

"What?"

"You just kicked me."

"Oh, I'm sorry," she says, "yeah, found a bug, I'll fix it." She shifts her chair so that any other twitches will go unnoticed.

Allison has never been an executive, but she's had lots of jobs and in every job she's had, the most important person has not been the highest paid employee or sat in the nicest office. The most important person in any organization is the one who knows how things work: the executive administrative assistant, the group secretary, sometimes the receptionist.

She sends email to Mdm. Coutreu from Wo's account describing the preferences of ScratchCo's CEO. The meeting will be a negotiation, a competition. She tells Mdm. Coutreu that Eben can't abide people tapping on desks, breathing through their mouths, smiling too much, using the phrase "my gosh." She explains that Eben won't sit at a table with thirteen chairs and provides a menu of every food that Eben abhors, like cheese that doesn't come from cows, Lipton tea, lager instead of ale; scents he can't stand, like Polo cologne and lemon-scented furniture polish; sounds he finds grating, like chairs shuffling; and his allergic response to mold and fungi that grow in old, poorly maintained ventilation systems.

Frau Feuerstein leans in and asks if they'll be working much longer. Owen looks tired but ebullient. Allison envies him; envies his passion for the simplicity of matching ifs and thens, allocating memory, and stepping through fresh software. She used to get a buzz from it too.

Owen packs up his equipment, but Allison keeps at it. She says, "Can you leave the Glass? I want to debug one more thing before I go."

Owen says, "I could wear them and you could judge by how much you flip me out while I walk home." He sets the Glass on the table and says, "See you tomorrow."

Allison backs up everything to her laptop and then takes the Glass and walks out. She stops at the ATM on her way to the south end of the Naschmarkt. Tonight she'll smoke heroin and sink into the deep, delicious sleep of opium dens. Tomorrow, she'll go to Paris and treat herself to a shopping spree.

25. Heads, Tails, or Edge

I spent last night lounging in my apartment listening in on Fiona and Eben, dozing through dreams of sunny beaches with vacationing families while lonely bachelors sit alone. Winter nuzzled up on my pillow within tongue range of my tears. The generous kindness of sister Sally's toast showed me a life that I'll never get to share with my dear Gwinnie.

Winter shakes us awake and sunbeams scatter from his dust and dander. I rise and pull on some clothes. Winter brings me his leash and we head out for our morning walk. Allison steps out of her apartment and joins us. Winter is overjoyed to have her along and so am I.

Down in the Naschmarkt, I buy a cup of Turkish coffee from Mrs. Gorkum and offer one to Allison, but she rejects my offer. We stop to smell roses at a florist and walk Allison to Owen's. Winter reminds me that he requires a grassy patch in due haste, so we accelerate across the street to the Secession Museum and then circle the Belvedere Palace. We return to the lab prepared to determine whether or not Eben's transformation will increase the number of timelines in which civilization, such as it is, continues.

Just back from Mexico, Volodya greets me with a terse hug

and a pat on the back. His monitors display timelines and software editors. He takes his seat. Winter jumps into his lap and covers his face in kisses.

"So," he says, setting Winter on the floor, "you paid the tax?"

I feel my face turn red. "Frau Feuerstein is a kind and generous woman."

"I bet she is." He adjusts his seat and moves his mouse pad three millimeters. "Did you use my workstation?"

"No."

"Harumph."

I take my seat and renew my search for the key butterfly wings when Fiona interrupts my concentration through my earbug. She says, "What do we know and what don't we know?"

I clear my throat. Winter sighs and stretches out. I say, "Eben has built up a huge cash cache—I mean a vast accumulation of different currencies. Most of his trillion is in Brazilian Reals, Mexican Pesos, and Indian Rupees, but he only makes loans in EbenNotes. The leverage in EbenNotes could form a huge debt bubble, rather like the John Law episode of 1720 that has been haunting me. Should the bubble pop, the vast disappearance of money would cause deflation and then depression. Alternatively, should he invest his entire cash cache into the economy, the vast introduction of money would cause inflation and then recession."

Volodya says, "If Eben spends too much, inflation, if he spends too little, deflation. If he fails, he brings the world down with him. As our timeweave predicts."

Fiona: "EbenNotes? That's not even real money."

Volodya: "No money is 'real'. Since US forced world off the gold standard, is all fiat currency."

Me: "We know that Eben will play the key role at a meeting

between old and new money being held at l'Hôtel de Ville in Paris in four days."

Fiona: "Who else will be at this meeting."

Volodya: "Three other young tech billionaires. Miki Nakamura who denies having invented BitCoin, Marc Sanders who gleefully tells anyone who will listen that he invented Cyber-Dollars, and Jean Claude Nguyen, who used to work for Eben—he's also involved in cyber currencies both as a trader and with a startup that creates rewards programs."

Me: "They exercise no imagination in naming their money. Do you know how the Brazilian real was named?"

Fiona: "And Eben created EbenNotes."

Me: "Four people who invented their own form of money meeting with six people including Guy Bourbon, Richard Womersley, Friedrich Reser, a Medici, a Romanov, a Stuart—all heirs to centuries-old fortunes."

Fiona: "One of whom hired us to project the value of the Euro under a variety of market conditions and assumptions."

Volodya emits a sigh that sounds like the air brakes of a bus and continues through two full breaths—violating the tenet that one sigh should be limited to a single exhalation. "We are stupid."

Fiona: "Are you going to share your wisdom?"

Volodya: "We've been looking at this all wrong."

Me: "It's not a battle between old and new money?"

Volodya: "It's not a battle between newly rich techies and aristocrats who've inherited ancient fortunes."

"Bugger me," Fiona says. "It's a literal battle between old and new money. How did we miss that?"

Me: "What do you mean?"

Volodya: "It's a battle between old and new currencies. The actual money, not the people who own it."

I finally get it. "These royalist aristocrats are planning to devalue the Euro by converting to an alternate currency, Eben-Notes, BitCoin, or CyberDollars."

Volodya: "For these many days we have watched timeweave engine predict a dark age. Now we see it caused by either large-scale inflation or deflation. Either or, 50-50—we overlooked simple possibility of global currency failure. The heirs of European royalty have always hated the Euro."

Fiona: "And all the misery that comes with it—war, famine, despair. The rich play games and the poor suffer. Same as it ever was."

Me: "We have to find a way out."

"Get right on it then!" Fiona says. "I'll see you in Paris."

Volodya and I dive into the timeweave and trace different timelines into futures that have two attractors: the value of the Euro either skyrockets or collapses leading to either worldwide depression or recession, either of which brings a new medieval age. We work back and forth through the mess of tiny decisions and actions made by the royalists, their financiers, the corporations they control, as well as those made by the techies, their startups, and ventures, searching for the butterfly wings that can save the world.

We're both thinking it, so I say it out loud: "Perfect balance."

Volodya rubs his eyes. "Everything he does in that meeting must be perfect."

Me: "And we won't know what perfect means until it happens."

Volodya says, "Fine tuning looks so absurd in random processes."

Me: "Every step he takes can move him to another timeline. We'll have to navigate the timelines for him as they appear. We'll see what emerges, where it goes, and then tell him what he has to do."

Volodya: "Butterfly wing search in real time? It takes hours to integrate all the world's data into accurate timeweave!"

I shrug. "We can speed up the calculations by sacrificing accuracy."

The only way to accelerate the timeweave engine is to reduce the amount of data from which it draws. The problem is that reducing the data might hide the tiny butterfly wing-flaps that could cause cultural tornados.

He shakes his head for 17 seconds, looks out the window for another six and then says, "If it is all we can do. But how will we tell him? Why will he listen? Too many holes in this plan."

Me: "We'll use his Glass."

Volodya: "And trick him? Is hopeless."

Me: "He has to listen to us. He must."

Volodya: "He won't."

Me: "He might."

* * *

Volodya and I sit on the train to Paris with our laptops on the table between us and Winter lounging on the seat beside me. Volodya insisted that we travel first class since economy is packed with Bastille Day revelers and we truly must be able to work. I feel guilty about it.

The conductor announces that Paris transport workers are on strike. The train will not stop in Paris, and it may not be possible for the train to proceed beyond the French border. He fails to wish us a happy Bastille Day.

Volodya's groan lands somewhere between the anguish of a train whistle on a stormy night and an ageing rooster yearning for youth. Winter tries to impersonate him but sounds like nothing more than an adorable beagle impersonating a frustrated Russian. Without so much as eye contact, we each engage in travel system timeline calculations. Within 23 seconds

Volodya says, "Planes still flying to Charles de Gaulle but airport likely to be shut within hour."

"Buses are not crossing the pickets."

"Rental car is best bet."

"Train still has the highest likelihood of getting us there."

His left eyebrow rises in coordination with a bobbing motion as though his head is a scale on which he weighs our options. The train zooms through Austria, curling through mountain valleys, past lakes, and across Germany for a luxurious nine hours. It slows when we cross into France but we're told it's just a precaution at each rail switch. I comment on how adept French unions are at sabotage. Volodya mumbles something about how the French economy would boom if their workers showed as much initiative performing their jobs. I feel compelled to take Fiona's place in their perpetual conservative-liberal argument, and then the train comes to a complete stop.

Volodya says, "We will sit for three hours and then conductor will instruct passengers to exit the train. Delays will accumulate as millions of Bastille Day celebrants saturate travel options. Or we assemble our things and exit the train now. And then we walk."

"What greater place on earth for a nice walk than summer in France?"

"Anywhere with less humidity would be preferable."

I put my laptop in my satchel, extend the handle on my rolling suitcase, and check Winter's leash. We proceed to an emergency exit. Others on the train stare at their phones, read books, and chat. Volodya opens an emergency door. A claxon sounds and the three of us climb down onto gravel and into a field. A train official calls us back in a stern voice. Volodya tells me to ignore him and I do.

We spend the next six hours walking, hitchhiking, and then manage an Uber ride. The driver lets us off in the 20th Arrondissement, on the outskirts of Paris, and explains that striking taxi drivers are bashing the windshields of their rideshare competition.

Streets are blocked and picketers bicker with police. The *Gendarmerie* has joined the *Police Nationale* to protect the city. Centuries of civil discord have prepared both sides. The picket signs are not simply pine sticks and cardboard, they're sturdy beams with plywood signs, and both police forces wear thick plastic reinforcements on their forearms, shoulders, as well as thighs and shins, plus bullet proof vests and riot helmets. The military-based *Gendarmerie* cluster around metro stations, government buildings, and national monuments.

I remark, "The police must require extraordinary amounts of water and electrolytes to wear full armor in this heat."

"Feels like volcano to me," Volodya says.

"Sorry?"

"You do not feel as though we walk through a field of molten lava prior to explosion of volcano?"

I get it. The trouble with Volodya's cousins in Russia, Gwinnie's layoff, and now the train strike tugs us into the grisly reality of the timeweave we've seen coming since Allison approached Eben on Market Street.

We come upon a cluster of folks at a bus stop and are informed that some busses are running free service for the people, provided they're not associated with government, police, the military, or corporations. I remark that the restrictions should leave plenty of empty seats, but no one seems amused. Perhaps it's my weak French. One such bus takes us all the way down Boulevard Saint-Michel to the St. Michel fountain. The strikes have permeated all of society: the Musee d'Orsay has closed, as well as Le Jardin du Luxembourg; even Père Lachaise Cemetery has closed; the President and dignitaries have cancelled their traditional Bastille Day speeches at Place de la Concorde; and the world's oldest military parade might be cancelled tomorrow morning. The only sign that we have arrived on the eve of Bastille Day is a squadron of jets practicing in the skies over Paris and a few people playing with sparklers.

Volodya says, "The police are nervous," and gestures to a group of police holding compact rifles.

Thankfully in this most civilized of cities the important services are still in full operation: the sidewalk cafes.

We approach the Seine. The Louvre is across the river and downstream to our left, Notre Dame reaches into the sky ahead of us on the world's most sophisticated island, Ile de Cite, and across the Seine to the right is l'Hôtel de Ville, the City Hall. Hôtel de Ville is where revolutions germinate and decay and also where Eben Scratch will determine the course of history in less than thirty-nine hours. We step around the packed tables of a sidewalk café, every table decorated with wine goblets, rouge, blanc, and rose, and every ashtray full.

A waft of smoke fills my lungs and, while I don't find it pleasant, it is not what makes me nauseous. The shift, the immediate discord, the vertigo, the dissonance of background conversations altering their tempo, overlapping shadows and the strides of people in one direction and then another. My balance eludes me as the glistening green seams form like window panes between realities. Passing between them generates different feelings of discomfort, disquiet, and discord. I swim through them, reaching for a surface but am pulled back. The protesters in the streets have shed their T-shirts and jeans in favor of shirts, trousers, hats, and long rifles for men, and layered skirts to the ankles and blouses with sleeves to the wrists for women. I fall across a seam and that reality shatters. Its shards pull me farther back in history. German soldiers in spiked helmets led by King Wilhelm I of Prussia marches with us toward the river on Boulevard Saint-Michel observed by small crowds of listless, sick, and starving Parisians. Another seam passes through me and the Franco-Prussian rivalry oscillates from 1870 to 1806. Flowers rain down on an army returning from battle, marching next to the river along the Quai. At the head of the army, a small man in a blue coat with red cuffs and white pants rides a huge horse and waves his bicorne hat. Austerlitz is won! The French Empire supersedes the Austrian and Russian empires and prepares to challenge Prussia and Britain for European supremacy.

The universe kaleidoscopes, thrusting me forward as though I've fallen on a temporal trampoline. Crowds are still cheering as they did on Napoleon's return, still waving their tri-colored flags but now they're back in T-shirts and jeans. The flags they wave confuse me: France's vertical stripes of blue, white, and red have rotated and danced into horizontal stripes of white, blue, and red and they carry posters. My focus comes and goes. Napoleon's bicorne hat disappears, his strong jaw weakens, his modest forehead grows, and his hairline recedes. The man in the modern poster, now marching toward us on Boulevard Saint-Michel is no Frenchman, though he is the dictator of France's oldest ally. Panic overwhelms me when I recognize this conqueror. I can't breathe. I can't think. This panic pushes me to the surface where my beagle licks my face from chin to forehead. I've fallen to the cobble-stone street. A crowd of people look down at me and my friend Volodya is crouched over protecting me.

The minutes I spend tumbling through different realities, awash in the weave of time, induce unpleasant side effects, but I feel an element of control, a fragment of the ability to choose the reality into which I will emerge. By far the worst thing about them is when they happen in Volodya's presence. Where Winter takes a work-beagle approach to pulling me out of time's rapids, Volodya worries over me as if I've suffered a cardiac event. His eyes wide, brow furrowed, and jaw taught, he asks, "You are all right?" I shake like the dog whose wagging tail assures me that the episode has concluded and try to smile, try to stand and affect nonchalance. He lifts and hugs me and speaks directly into my ear: "Simon, you must be treated. There are medications, please ..." But he knows I won't.

I describe the visions while we cross the Seine and Ile de Cite into the 4th Arrondissement. Since Volodya puts so little stock in my visions, I expect a subtle shrug and change of the subject. That he leans forward in concentration bothers me. We turn left on Rue de Rivoli. Nine low flying jets streak overhead. He doesn't speak until we approach the Place de la Concorde.

He finally breaks the silence when the Eiffel Tower comes into view on the horizon beyond the Gold-tipped Obelisk of Luxor. "History oscillates like all oscillating systems." That his accent has all but disappeared frightens me. "Each swing of a pendulum differs. The tides of invasion between France and Germany, Russia and Germany, have often made France and Russia allies. Could the pendulum swing in the opposite direction two centuries later? Does it seem so absurd that a 21st century revolution could be followed by a populist authoritarian? Is it any less absurd that the French Revolution led to a Corsican dictator than that the 21st century Napoleon could be Russian?"

"Volodya, I don't know what my episodes mean, but I know that history does not repeat."

He turns to me with a hint of a smile and adds, "But it does rhyme."

Even with the blisters on our feet from so much walking, we increase our pace and nearly jog to the Hotel Mayfair. We stop in the shadow of a yellow building with roses in containers on the faux balconies outside every window. The art nouveau ironwork awning over the entrance has graceful curves and a leaf motif, the very epitome of Belle Epoch Paris.

"Ahh, France," Volodya says, "Maybe if this building is the poem and history rhymes, we will be okay." The expression of romance makes me worry for his well being.

Fiona greets us in the lobby with preoccupied, perfunctory hugs. Winter doesn't care, Volodya doesn't notice, and I say, "What did I do?"

"You lost Allison."

"Sorry?"

"I just talked to Owen. He said that Allison didn't show up. My apartment was left unlocked and her things are gone."

Emitting an exaggerated sigh, Volodya stalks a lobby couch that looks beautiful in its embroidered lavender velvet but not very comfortable. He pulls his laptop from his bag and connects to Wifi.

"I asked you to do one thing," Fiona says. "One thing."

Volodya chews on his lip as he launches a series of search-scripts. "We will find her in hour, maybe two."

26. Hope

Yao Wo stands behind Eben Scratch in the customs queue at Charles de Gaulle airport. His phone rings. He takes it from his pocket and sees his wife's image. Knowing that Mr. Scratch abhors such interruptions, he presses ignore.

To his surprise, his boss says, "Was that home?"

"Yes, sir."

"It might be important, you should take it."

Yao wonders for an instant if his boss is being sarcastic. He starts to deny that there could be anything more important than getting Eben through customs, but that doesn't feel right either, so he says nothing. Since the chaos of Durango, Yao has been in a state of utter confusion and Mr. Scratch encouraging him to accept a personal call doesn't help.

The French immigration officer stamps his passport, and Yao continues to the baggage carousel where he returns the call.

His wife says, "I've contacted hospice."

"It's over." Yao tries to make it sound like a question but can't. The doctor had held out a few last hopes: yet another transplant, yet another tiny chance of being accepted into yet another trial. Yao tries to speak, "They said …" but only musters a whimper—he hopes that this display of hopelessness will disappear behind the airport noise.

She blows her nose and Yao can feel her steady herself. Tam must be in hearing distance. "We've always said that if we ever have to choose between a month of life and a few months of suffering with just a tiny hope, that we would choose life." Then her voice cracks. "It's better this way."

"Can I talk to Tam?"

Tam's frail voice comes on the line just as the baggage carousel starts to turn.

"What's that, son?"

"I get to throw out the first pitch at the Giants game tomorrow."

Yao had forgotten that Tam's Make-a-Wish had been granted. "Tomorrow? I'll miss it." Now Yao's voice cracks. "Can you record it so we can watch it together?"

"Sure dad, it'll be just as good as having you with me."

Mr. Scratch's luggage passes Yao on the carousel. He rushes after it. The last time he made his boss wait for his luggage to make it around a second time, Mr. Scratch docked a day's pay.

"I'm going to practice all day so I can smack the ball right into Buster Posey's mitt!"

Someone steps in from of Yao and pulls off their baggage. Yao turns to the man, preparing to wrestle the luggage from his grasp, but it's Mr. Scratch. Eben Scratch helping Yao with luggage? Now he's certain that he'll be fired.

"I have to go, I'll call you later. I love you, Tam. Take care of your mom and throw a strike!"

Yao wipes his eyes and pastes a grin on his face. "Thank you, sir. I've got them now. I don't know what came over me. I'm so sorry to let you down like this."

But instead of yielding the luggage, Eben tucks one bag under his arm and carries both his own suitcase and Yao's out to the waiting limousine. "I've got it, no problem. Any news from home? How is Tam?"

"Tam, sir? He's fine. Everything's fine. Please, sir, let me carry that."

27. The Ritz

Eben's room at the Ritz overlooks the Place Vendome, a modest room on the scale of the most luxurious hotel in the world. He sits at the desk. At first he's offended that he has to pay for premium Wifi, but then he laughs at his own frugality. A month ago, he'd have called the manager to complain about being nickel and dimed. Now, life seems too short and such a petty bother seems intensely stupid.

He skips his email and goes straight to the Human Trafficking and Slave Liberation Fund web page. He types in a donation for $100,000, looks at it, takes a breath, adds a zero, hits return, and exhales. A feeling flows down his arms and legs, as though his body expects something bad to happen, but another feeling, a foreign sensation of warmth that starts in his chest washes that trepidation down to his fingertips and toes where it disappears. Even in this solitude, he's embarrassed that an act of goodwill should frighten him. His mother would not be proud.

He closes the laptop and sets his Glass next to it, another act that feels odd. Pulling his notebook from his back pocket and ballpoint pen from his front, he moves to the sofa where he can appreciate the view of the weathered bronze Vendome Column in the plaza. He settles into the cushion and nods to the statue of Napoleon. He dares to hope that the people his money liberates will make better decisions than he has. He writes about loss and liberty, love and hope. As the words flow into coincidental rhymes, he lets some of that hope into his own life. He writes about ends and means and how tactics obscure strategy and then he laughs at his own clunky business-speak. Turning back to the words he wrote on the Baja beach, he comes to a list of promises that he made to himself. The first one is a promise to review those promises every day for the rest of his life. He laughs at the self-reference, at how quintessentially Eben-like it was for him to make that promise first. The laughter ends in a smile. It dawns on him that he likes himself, he's not a bad guy, at least if he keeps these promises, he might not be such a bad guy. He leans back on the couch. The second promise is to shed cynicism and embrace gratitude; the third is to assume that people are trustworthy; and his fourth promise is to make his accomplishments mean something to the world. A million dollars to a charity was just a toe in the water and he wants to swim.

Eben wakes hours later to the sun setting over Paris and someone knocking on the door. He calls, "*Un* minute," and smiles at his ignorance of the French language. He sets his notebook on the end table, puts on his shoes, walks to the door, and looks through the peephole. The magnifying quality of the lens distorts the image into the impossible. He wipes the sleep from his eyes and looks again. Okay, it's a well dressed woman who looks familiar. She's not an illusion; it must be his poetic state of mind that makes her look like someone he used to know. He's Eben Scratch—sentimentality, and compassion are new to him. These hallucinations are bound to happen. He convinces himself that this woman has knocked at his door by mistake. He opens the door to correct her, hoping she speaks English.

The woman says, "Hello, Eben."

Her voice matches his mirage. He steps back, away from her. The woman steps in as though his recoil were an invitation. She wears a reticent smile, eyes downcast as though she's embarrassed, maybe even ashamed. She holds out her hand, palm down.

"Allison?"

It takes a while for him to realize she's still holding out her hand. He takes it because he doesn't know what else to do. She still hasn't said anything. She looks at him as though she hasn't seen him in years and, in his mind, she hasn't. She hasn't seen him since he disappeared into that cocoon of greed. Her fingers curl around his, barely touching, as though to tell him that he's free to let go.

He starts to say, "I'm sorry," just as she says the same thing.

They stand just inside the open door looking at each other.

Eben says, "I can't believe it." He turns away and then looks back as though not expecting to see her on the double take. Now the whole sense of her collides with his reality. She's wearing a black dress pleated to the knees, a scooped neckline with a pendant around her neck, just above the swell of her breasts. The pendant looks much like the first gift he ever gave her. It's not the same, he knows it's not, because that one is in a box on a shelf in his closet in San Francisco and it's broken. She tore it off and threw it at him on the day that he moved out.

He starts to talk and so does she. She stops and her smile wavers. He wants to list every mistake he's made and beg her forgiveness for each one. He wants to take her in his arms and shut the door and smell her breath and kiss her neck and he wants to cry. But that last thought raises a feeling, an embarrassing emotion that is no less genuine than his desire to apologize: suspicion.

She looks back at the door and, instead of closing it says, "I should have called."

Eben shuts the door and the simple motion helps him get a hold of himself. "No, no, come on in. Please." He looks around the room and sees his notebook on the end table. He promised himself. Cynicism ruined him. He pushes against the suspicion, a habit he must break. He looks at her again. She looks up and her lips come together in that expression that means she doesn't know what to say either. He takes a breath, just like he did when his impulses tried to keep him from donating that million to charity, and inhales her perfume: Charlie, a simple scent that stirs memories.

As he steps to the end table, he tells himself that it's safe to give in, to dive in. His only risk is heartbreak, not slavery, not homelessness, not despair or starvation, just heartbreak. He picks up his notebook and skims through the pages until he finds it. As he tears out the page, sand falls on the table and it occurs to him that he rather deserves a broken heart and the humility it could impose on him. Besides, heartbreak generates the greatest poetry.

The instant of amusement doesn't wash all his suspicion away, but it rinses some of it. He loves this woman. He's always loved her and, no matter what she thinks of him, no matter what brought her here, or what might happen next, he will continue to love her. Why shouldn't he surrender to his own authentic feelings?

He steps around the couch, nearly dancing back to her and, with warmth in his heart and tenderness in his voice, he holds out his poem. Several grains of sand fall into her hand as she accepts it.

She glances at it and then back at him. "Eben, you look good. So good."

"Would you like something? I'm not sure I can operate the coffeemaker, but I know how the corkscrew functions." He takes her hand and guides her to the couch, but she doesn't sit. He wants to ask what brought her here and why she's so dressed up, but he's not sure he wants to hear the answer.

Allison is not a small woman, her lantern jaw is not feminine, her waist, hips, and bust are not voluptuous, and her skin shows the scars of childhood acne, but when Eben looks at Allison, he sees nothing but charm and beauty, brilliance and wit, and now, regret and hope.

The two of them stand next to the couch as though waiting for the other to sit first.

She glances at his poem again, folds it in half and puts it in the outer pocket of her purse. He can't decide if he's relieved that she didn't read it in front of him or if he wishes that she had. He laughs at himself and she laughs, too. No, hers is more of a gentle titter, a laugh that he knows, like a favorite song that he hasn't heard in a long time.

"You look, umm," he says. "It's nice to see you. I mean, I'm happy to have you here. There are so many things I want to say to you, but you must have a reason for coming. Do you need anything? Are you all right?" The words feel too formal, too businesslike, but it is the way he speaks. He forgives himself the inability to open up.

"No," she says, "I just wanted to see you."

"Really?"

"Is that so hard to believe?"

The words feel like an accusation. In the struggle to keep his promises, the words fall out: "Well, the last few times we've seen each other haven't been, well, I umm …" He can't stop the questions from piling up in his brain. "What brings you to Paris? And, if you don't mind my asking, how did you know I was here in this particular room?"

Allison lowers herself onto the couch. Her skirt flounces as she crosses her legs. He catches a glimpse of lace and notices the red soles of her black pumps.

"You look tremendous, Allison, I'm so happy that you've, umm, recovered?" He chastises himself for letting the sentence come out as a question. He girds himself against making any more mistakes.

"I'm working for Fiona again."

"That's good," he says, but even that kindles distrust. The harder he tries, the less control he has. He doesn't care that it makes no sense, he only cares that she's here—but why can't he say so? "Allison, please excuse me, but none of this makes any sense."

"I know, Eben. Please let me apologize and then I'll go." She straightens her posture and speaks clearly: "I'm sorry that I was so mean to you. I'm sorry that I cheated on you. I'm sorry about everything." She leans forward. "That's all I wanted to say. I'll go now." She uncrosses her legs but remains seated.

Her words sound as though they've been scripted according to his greatest desires; too scripted. He steps to a marble-topped bar where a bottle of Bordeaux stands on a silver tray next to a battery-powered corkscrew.

He sets the corkscrew over the bottle and glances back at her. She's straightening her dress over her legs. The warmth of his affection for her returns. He doesn't like the taste of doubt. He presses the button and the cork is removed with a gentle popping sound. He looks at her again, now she's gazing out the window. Her otherwise straight hair has been curled into waves that cascade down her back and over her shoulder. He chastises himself. Damn it, if not now, when will he be ready to live?

He carries two wineglasses and the opened bottle to Allison and sits across the little table from her. She turns to him and looks up. He remembers those light green eyes, the color of water in a swimming pool, and the joy he found there. He pours both glasses, offers her one, and raises his. He says, "I don't want you to go."

She purses her lips the way she does in concentration and for an instant she looks as though she'll cry. "I know how this must appear. You've just become the world's first trillionaire. The last time we saw each other I was strung out on heroin and attacked you on Market Street." She sips from her wineglass. "I'm in Paris on business and I saw you and Wo at the airport so I did a little hacking, found your hotel and came here. I just wanted to apologize and let you know that I'm better now and that, well, you know, maybe now that I don't need you, maybe I could want you and maybe—oh Eben, getting sober was like waking from a nightmare and I just wanted to apologize." She wipes her eyes.

Eben wants to accept her apology and beg her to give him another chance, but promises or no, all he can muster is a sigh.

She raises her wineglass and says, "Congratulations! You made your FU money."

He tinks his wineglass against hers and they look into each other's eyes as they drink. Something gives. It feels as though naming the giant gorilla in the room has banished it. He can keep his promises to himself, he knows it now and if he can forgive himself, he can forgive her. He'll even be happy to let her break his heart again. Life is risk, love is risk too; it says so in his poem.

"Achieving that goal once should have been enough," he says. "I had to do it ten thousand times over."

She starts to laugh and he laughs with her. She chokes on

her wine and holds her hand up to her mouth. The motion is so guileless, so purely Allison that Eben loses his breath.

Allison leans forward and a few drops of wine roll down her chin. Eben pulls his chair closer to her, cups her chin, and kisses the wine away—an impulsive move so completely out of his character that he's caught not knowing what to do next. Still leaning forward, his mouth an inch from hers, he looks into her soft green eyes and places a gentle, chaste kiss on her bottom lip.

She pushes against his chest, not so hard that he can't kiss her again, deeply this time, but enough that he feels an all-encompassing desire for tenderness; soft, gentle, affection.

28. Mortified Remains

Allison feels like an artist, a musician playing her masterpiece. Telling him she's sober while she's soaring was a nice riff. If only she could have mustered a real tear, but spilling the wine covered that nicely.

She lets her lips relax. She opens her eyes, knowing that his will be open too and feels his lips smile. She smiles back and pulls herself away. He leans farther forward, trying so hard to be perfect that he looks and feels innocent; an innocent monster.

He kisses her chin and cheeks and whispers between kisses: "All I ever wanted was to be the man I thought you wanted me to be and I fell in a trap and I'm sorry." He kisses the back of her neck. "Allison, thank you for coming back to me." Then he pulls her ear between his teeth and says, "I can be the man you fell in love with." She wonders if he's been waiting to tell her these things, practicing them. She almost has second thoughts.

He finds the spot just behind her ear—he remembered and she'd forgotten. The stubble on his chin, the warmth of his breath, his teeth pulling her skin, and the strength of his hands, now grasping her waist—she grabs his shirt in her fist and pulls him onto the couch. She kisses his mouth and runs her tongue along his teeth. She inhales him, a scent that she hasn't tasted in years, a scent as comfortable and welcoming and safe as the pillow she sleeps on—except that, because of Eben, she sleeps on sidewalks more often than she sleeps on pillows.

In an awkward position at the edge of the couch, he disengages to catch himself and reposition.

In the seconds they're separated, she leans back to welcome him and is overcome by a rush of realizations: First, she's soaking wet, which is crazy because she's always needed lube when she's had a heroin buzz. On the other hand, she's gone weeks without sex. Being turned on is perfectly natural, it could happen with anyone. Second, she knows this man, knows exactly how to satisfy him. In repositioning herself, she lets her dress flutter up to her belly and watches him look at her lacey red thong. She tugs her dress back down and lets out a light cry of embarrassment.

His eyes lock on her like he's starving. She tries to deny her third realization, even as every cell in her body yearns for him: Sex is different with Eben than any man she's ever known. It's a connection she's never felt with anyone else, even now after her love has been replaced by loathing. It's as if he knows her body as well as she does, as though he's studied her and mastered her. That's what Eben does; he's not good at many things, but he is the best at everything he sets out to do. It's one of the reasons she fell so hard for him. It's also the reason he became such a wretched, hateful human being. The contrasting feelings confuse her.

She pulls him onto her and reaches down to his waist. He rubs his nose against hers and teases her lips with his tongue. She runs her hand along his groin, down to his thighs and back up. His body fights to be released from his clothes. She unbuttons his pants and the zipper falls down under the pressure. He sits up and she pulls his pants down. He's poised over her, holding himself up by her shoulders, watching her, his eyes combing over her.

She reaches down and pulls her dress up and pushes her thong to the side, the air on her wetness brings a whimper.

His legs buckle. He grunts and squirts a stream of thick white fluid onto her black dress. And another, this one makes it all the way to her clavicle.

She sees sheer panic in his eyes. A voice inside compels her to laugh at him, to point at him, to call him a loser, a quitter.

Eben pushes himself up. Kneeling above her, he looks paralyzed, his face ashen, his mouth trembling.

She argues with herself: there will never be a more perfect opportunity to humiliate him, to destroy his ego. Right now. She looks at him and sees the terror. Just say it! No, she tells herself, everything is on schedule. Her plan will be more effective with this setup. She reaches out and puts her hands on both sides of his neck. She smiles and waits for his eyes to meet hers and holds him, as vulnerable as an infant. She says, "I love you Eben."

* * *

Eben is mortified. He reminds himself that he's good at sex! He studied it! He knows how to control himself, but he hasn't had sex since a demeaning tryst months ago. It's that gold digger's fault. No, that's not it. It was Allison's thong, the line of moisture on the red silk in the center of the lace V that outlined and defined her opening. He listens to her, begging himself to believe that she still loves him, or loves him again. Now he's sagging and dripping on her lovely black dress. He concentrates on the vision of her thong and takes her breast in his hand, but the line of cum reminds him of his failure and there's nothing to be done but surrender.

She wiggles out from under him and says, "Let me go clean up."

He rises and looks out the window at Paris. He pulls up his pants, reaches for a wineglass, and drinks.

"Hey, Eben," she says, "over here."

She's smiling at him, but her dress looks ruined.

"I'll be right back and we can make love slowly. It's been so long, we need to take our time. Eben, it's okay, everything is going to be okay now."

"But your dress."

"It's rayon, I'll wash it in the sink and it will dry in an hour or so and then I can run an iron over it and it will be fine." She kisses him on the lips. "Really. It's fine. I'll be right back."

She takes her purse and walks into the bathroom. Her dress looks perfect from behind.

She closes the door and turns on the shower. Eben sighs. He wants to grind his head into the wall. He steps to the bar and refills his wineglass, drinks it, and fills it again. He walks to the window and avoids looking at his reflection. Instead, he sees his notebook on the end table and he remembers the promises. He reads them and remembers his commitment to take risks, that he must accept the possibility of failure in taking those risks, and most importantly that he doesn't have to control the universe. Pacing from the bar to the window and back holding his notebook open to the list of promises, he goes back through the experience. Shame pushes humiliation aside, not at his performance, or lack of performance, but that blame and excuses were his first response instead of accepting the truth: Allison turns him on like no one else on earth. Excitement at that level is nothing but a completely sincere compliment. He decides that he can own that, even be happy with it.

Her thong comes back to mind, that defining line of moisture, and he feels a tingle.

He steps to the bathroom door. He waits until she turns off the shower and then he knocks. Allison cracks the door open and her smiling, lovely face peeks through. He says, "Please don't take off your underwear, leave it on. Yes, please, leave it on."

Her eyebrows go up and she says, "You like that?"

"I want that."

"Okay," she says. "I'll be finished in a minute."

He hears her sweet titter as the door closes.

* * *

Setting the dress in the sink, Allison turns away from the mirror. What the hell is she doing? Eben's not playing fair. He's not being the greedy asshole she dumped. She reminds herself that he's full of shit. He spent the last two weeks at his labor camps in Mexico and India. He's lying. Fine, she says to herself, we're both lying, aren't we?

Hotel body wash is all she has to wash the dress, but it does the trick. Eben could have a new dress delivered from the Ritz's gift shop or any of a hundred stores within two blocks, but he's way too cheap to think of anything like that. The thought grounds her.

She leans down and snorts the thin line of cocaine and heroin on the marble basin. She shakes her head and feels the warm buzz come over her, the clarity and calm wrapped in confident euphoria. That's better, she thinks, it's okay to fall into the situation, more effective. She picks her thong up from the bathroom floor and puts it on. It feels cold against her. She shivers but has to admit that the feeling, the look in Eben's eyes, and, more than anything, the certainty in his voice when he told her to leave it on pushes all of her erotic buttons.

She pulls a thick terry cloth robe from the closet and wraps it loosely so the lace of her bra and a hint of her belly show. She turns to the mirror, fixes her hair and makeup, and whispers to herself: "I look spectacular."

She puts her heels back on, giggles at the idea of wearing a robe, lacey underwear, and heels—but it's Paris, after all. She steps out the door and Eben offers her a glass of wine and says, "To us."

"That's a bit cliché for you."

"Right," he says, and he gets that look of concentration she used to think was so cute. "Okay, how about this: here's to reallocating our memory, not forgetting, but page-swapping certain memories into a disk file that we never have to look at again."

"I can drink to that." She smiles at him as she sips and his eyes look fluid and affectionate. She says, "And while we're at it, here's to a good thorough defrag."

He offers her his wineglass and leans toward hers. "This is cliché too, but I want to drink from your chalice."

"I bet you do."

He drinks from her wineglass and she from his. She sets her glass on the table next to Eben's PC and Google Glass.

He puts his hands on her hips, fingers spread out on her flanks with thumbs along the base of her pelvis and pulls her toward him.

She says, "What's your hurry, mister?"

"I want you."

"Eben, who are you talking to?" She grins at him and shakes her head like a school teacher with a well meaning but misbehaving pupil. "You don't need to fix anything. Nothing's broken. You don't have to prove anything to me." And she thinks, but doesn't add, because you can't, you rotten human being.

He shrugs, lets go, and the look of determination becomes one of adoration.

"Besides," she says and picks up his Glass, "I have an idea that's going to blow you away."

"All right, but soon?" He makes a point of letting his gaze drop from her eyes, down her robe, lingering on her lace.

She says. "Can I use your PC?"

"Sure. You know my password."

She pretends to be surprised. "You haven't changed it?" and logs on. "Would you please bring me my purse?"

He takes it from the couch and hands it to her.

"I've been working with Fiona on a Glass app." She takes a memory stick and the Glass she stole from Owen out of her purse. She plugs the stick into Eben's laptop, connects his Glass, and installs the AR software. She senses Eben's discomfort at someone modifying his PC, but when she turns to him, he doesn't seem bothered at all.

She puts on his Glass and confirms the installation. A tiny sliver of regret courses around her cocaine-heroin buzz and makes it to her heart. It occurs to her that it's the small slivers that require tweezers and are more likely to get infected, big slivers hurt at first but are easy to pull out.

"Here, put them on."

She enables the view projection app, projecting what she sees onto the retina of his right eye and what he sees onto her right eye. Since she's looking directly at him, Eben experiences overlapping images of himself, as Allison sees him, and Allison, as he sees her. His expression softens.

"It's like seeing us together," he says, and pulls her to him, keeping his Glass focused on her.

She starts to lean her face to the side so she can kiss him without a nose collision.

"No, please" he says, "I want to see you seeing me seeing you."

They stare at each other for nearly a minute. The experience is more difficult than Allison could have imagined. She blinks and turns off the projection of Eben's Glass, that is, she disables her ability to see what he sees. Seeing herself overlapped with Eben jarred something in her.

Their lips come together and Allison can't push away the familiar smell and taste that is Eben.

He says, "It's like looking in a mirror and seeing the part of me that is you reflected back and the part of you that is me and on and on." He pulls her against him and she can see his anguish, his regrets, and his affection. "Allison, thank you for showing me that we're infinite."

She struggles to keep her eyes open. Eben's face beams affection that takes her back to another world. Now she struggles to close her eyes, but she has to.

"Thank you," he says and the repetition annoys her. "I'll make it up to you. I'll be the man I said I'd be. I promise." The emphasis he puts on the word promise bothers her, but she's not sure why.

"Come with me," she says and guides him into the bedroom.

He says, "I will, this time."

When they get to the bed he reaches into her robe and hugs her. His hands drift down and caress her curves. She lets the robe fall off and guides his hands to her breasts. He unfastens her bra with one twist. He pulls it down her arms and it falls onto her robe. He cups her breasts and makes a low, urgent sound.

She lies down on the bed and pulls off her thong. He stands over her, looking at her with palpable hunger. She adjusts a pillow and then reaches out to his groin with her foot. He unclothes and joins her. She'd forgotten that he could still see everything she sees and wonders what it's like. She blinks the projection of her Glass back on as he pulls her nipple into his mouth. She surrenders to the vision, the sensations of Eben. He works his way up her neck and, in the same instant that he finds that spot, he pulls himself into her.

As he works to his climax, he slows. She knows this Eben. She understands what he's doing and even that tugs at her compassion so she starts to fake her own climax, but then he stops altogether and perches on his elbows, his nose touching hers. His Glass clicks against hers. She can feel him staring so she opens her eyes.

"Allison? Why now?"

She smiles. "Why not?" His expression says that her answer is too flippant, so she adds, "I got tired of hating you."

Now he smiles, too. "So my wish is coming true because hating me was too much work?"

"Basically."

They continue the banter. They laugh and embrace and when Allison sees trust in his eyes, she says, "I've always loved you."

Now Eben can't keep the grin from his face, or the tears from leaving his eyes. He grips her and pulls himself deeper, closer, tighter and she knows that he's thinking that he can merge with her. She arches her back and moans, and then, with the vision of Eben so close and his vision of her just a step behind it, and her vision of his vision of—she loses any trace of control. Her legs wrap around his ass, her toes curl, she gasps, and crushes herself against him. She lets out a shriek. He rears back and then pulls forward, deep, and again, and as she writhes in ecstasy, she feels the spasms of his ejaculation.

They lie together unmoving, Eben still inside her, his embrace still tight but relaxing, and for a few instants, Allison tries to convince herself that she faked her orgasm but the denial fades behind the fact that it's the first time she's ever come on heroin.

She wriggles and giggles under him, pretending that she can't breathe. He responds by relaxing his dead weight on her. She pushes him up and matches his grin.

She waits for it. It's almost like counting down. And then she says, "You must be starving," as he says, "I'm starving!"

He rolls off of her and they both laugh at the predictability of their intimacy.

She says, "I saw a bistro near my Bed and Breakfast. It's a tiny place, but it sure looked good."

"Anywhere you want, my love."

They lie together a few more minutes, resuming banter from years before, inside jokes, gentle jibes, and absurd compliments as though they'd never stopped.

Allison rises and goes to the bathroom. He joins her in the shower and they make love again. She says, "Three times? You have missed me."

His tone changes from cozy banter to straight and serious: "Allison, I don't know how or why, but I do know that I'll prove myself worthy. I promise."

29. This Situation

We have seventeen hours to alter destiny.

That we're engaging such a tenuous solution to such a tenuous situation, despite my never ending search for a tenuous butterfly whose tenuous wings might be encouraged to prevent calamity is, shall we say, tenuous.

Volodya makes one of his garbled sounds and I reply that I am in full agreement.

Then he sits up and says, "Allison is here in Paris."

Fiona and I rise and stand behind him in order to see his monitor. Our three rooms are connected by doors and we've gathered in Volodya's. The window is open and the warm breeze carries the scent of roses. He sits at a round cherry table facing his laptop.

Fiona: "She looks brilliant!"

Volodya works through the search interface and brings up a series of images: Allison walking into the Ritz lobby; the elevator surveillance feed shows Allison fidgeting; from the hallway camera, Eben opens the door, she steps in, and the two of them stand at the entrance.

"She's finally forgiven him," Fiona says. "Life would be so much easier if people could be honest with themselves."

Volodya: "She has forgiven Eben? It is inconsistent. Nothing to believe what we see before us."

Fiona: "Volodya, you did this. You rescued her and together we put her on a healthy path. You've done well. Don't be such a pessimistic arse."

He attacks the keyboard and mouse for a few seconds. "Should work now. Yes, this is live feed from Eben's Glass."

"Oh my," I say. "What is he doing?"

Fiona: "He's kissing her."

Me: "I'm finding this uncomfortable to watch."

Fiona takes a seat next to Volodya and stretches out. "It's beautiful. Love. Affection, the redeeming quality that we all have within our hearts, as much a part of our souls as our DNA."

"I don't feel right." I step toward the window. "Very intrusive. None of my business."

"Is intrusive," Volodya says. "But we need information, something to act on, some expectation, a hint of what we must worry about tomorrow."

Fiona: "Yes, we should definitely find more things to worry about, that makes sense. We mustn't entertain the prospect that our efforts are working. Anything but that."

I take the long way around the table so that I'm not witness to Eben and Allison's intimacy and sit with my laptop opposite Volodya. Fiona makes a disappointed sound at the very instant Volodya laughs. She flicks his forearm and says, "Like that's never happened to you."

And then my phone rings. I answer and hear perfect English beneath the thick French accent of Guy Bourbon. I put the call on speaker. He welcomes me to Paris and says that he's read our currency projection report. "Monsieur Wentworth," he says, "it's a fine report, but things are moving rapidly and I'd like to meet with you for dinner tonight and I also wonder if I can call on you to accompany me to a meeting tomorrow morning."

I love the way that European nobility encodes demands in polite requests—I feel like a Knight. Fiona nods so I say, louder than I probably should, but in keeping with my role as an American Knight: "Sounds great, Guy, where would you like to meet?"

Volodya says, "I too will attend."

"Oh no, am I on speaker?" Bourbon says. "No, no, no, I do not participate in conference calls. Please."

Fiona and Volodya look at each other and then at me, then back at each other. Fiona says, "Our colleague Volodya Kazimer performed the analyses."

Bourbon says. "No. I just want the genius."

I smile at Volodya. He frowns back. Fiona covers her mouth to mute her laughter. Now I feel like a jester and must admit that it's more familiar than knighthood.

Bourbon adds, "Simon please meet me at L'Agrume in the Latin Quarter in an hour?"

I say, "Of course," and hang up.

Volodya says, "I am coming with you."

"No," Fiona says, "I've been trying to think of a way to get one of us into that meeting, and it just fell in our laps."

"Is true," Volodya says. "We needed some good fortune."

"And you have to make live projections to Eben's Glass during that meeting."

I attach Winter's leash and we leave the hotel, cross Place du Concorde and the Seine, and walk to the Latin Quarter. Since I'm down to my last five Euro note, I stop at a Banque de France ATM, but it has run out of cash. I continue to a Credit Agricole ATM and it too is empty. A kind woman walking a Bichon Frise who develops an immediate attraction to Winter informs me that the ATM stockers are on strike.

I continue into the Latin Quarter, the neighborhood of the Sorbonne, a 661 year-old university if you include every year of instruction. Groups of students argue with armored police and wave signs that denigrate the wealthy. A lanky student with a lanky beard wearing ballet slippers scratches Winter's back. His sign says: "Jobs for humans, not robots."

Guy Bourbon rises from a sidewalk table at the L'agrume in a perfect black suit with a sage green shirt and magenta tie. I accept his hand and take the seat next to him.

He says, "The students are on strike."

I'm not certain what it means for students to go on strike. Do they desire less arduous homework? Expanded faculty office hours? And it comes to me, reduced fees, greater access to information, smaller classes, improved instruction, and self-determination—I applaud them.

Guy lights a cigarette and then sips his wine and the two of us discuss what Guy refers to as "this situation" in Paris. Volodya's currency calculation doesn't emerge in our conversation; another thing about the very wealthy, they like to be heard. Winter is happy to listen.

30. Augmented Reality

Allison expects Eben to complain about the strike when they can't get a cab, but he's happy to walk. Of course he prefers walking, she tells herself, cheap techie bastard.

She guides Eben along Rue de Rivoli. A huge orange cat weaves between her legs in perfect time with her stride as they pass Hôtel de Ville. Eben mentions that he has a meeting there tomorrow and she's tempted to tell him that he won't make it. Three seagulls accompany them all the way to the 11th Arrondissement and the Place de la Bastille. A stage has been erected for the Bastille Day celebrations tomorrow at the spot where, in 1789, peasants stormed a fortress that had been converted into a prison and weapon storage center, released the Marquis de Sade along with several other prisoners, armed themselves, and started a revolution. Tonight a mime troupe quietly reenacts the revolution.

It's hot and sticky and her dress is still damp. Eben impressed her when he insisted on ironing it for her. The cobblestones are difficult to navigate in heels and Eben seems to enjoy catching her every time her balance wavers. He's in his usual clothes, slightly outdated skinny blue jeans, untucked short-sleeved red checked shirt, and Vans.

The tiny Café Rey has seven tables inside and five on the sidewalk and one server. Eben uses a translation app in his Glass to talk to the server. It reminds Allison how awkward it can be to have a San Francisco techie try to operate in the real world with real people. He even looks like the old Eben, hunched over and poking at the menu.

"Eben," Allison says, "the French have been feeding people for centuries. Can you just let them do their thing?"

"I'm sorry," he says. He sits up straight and adds, "My transition from greedy asshole to authentic human being is likely to have a few lapses, but I'll get there. In the meantime, I'll tip a ton."

"Why don't you try being nice to people instead of buying them off?"

"You're right." He calls the waitress over. "Jah swee deh solay for what I've done to your beautiful language." He hands her his menu. "Please bring us whatever you think we'll like." She returns with two glasses and a bottle of very young Burgundy.

Allison watches Eben's expression when he sees the label and tastes the wine. A look of disappointment crosses his face but just for an instant. She's comfortable in the knowledge that he'll never change, even happy with it.

He compliments the waitress and Allison seasons his wine with codeine. Minutes later, she seasons his medallions of beef with a hefty dose of LSD. Allison pecks at her food, laughs at Eben's quips, and enjoys watching him merge into an altered state. When they finish, he exudes the painless comfort of the well opiated and his eyes dilate as the hallucinogen takes hold. She projects an image of herself into his Glass, the image he saw the instant he entered her.

He smiles and slouches deeper in his chair. "You have written another killer app."

"Thank you," she says, truly appreciating the reminder of what he stole from her. She rises and goes to the bathroom where she uses her phone to confirm the availability of Eben's first adventure.

* * *

Waves of comfort wash over Eben. His vision of the Bistro sways.

Someone calls his name. He listens for it again, voices from a tunnel or a chamber or maybe through the audio of his Glass. He takes them off and shakes his head but echoes of the voices continue. He puts the Glass back on and grips the table. The voices are familiar but out of place.

Allison takes his arm and her scent brings him to the surface. He stretches his eyes wide and says, "This is the best wine buzz in the history of grapes." At least, that's what he meant to say, but it doesn't come out quite right.

Allison smiles and he smiles back. "Eben, your friends are calling you."

"Friends?" He perks up and says it again, "Friends. What a nice word." Everything makes sense on this fluffy cloud. Allison has come back and he has friends.

Now standing with Allison's help, he sees them across the room, the guys from the Grove. The people who Liked his post. People like him, his friends. The word tastes sweet. He steps in their direction but bumps a chair.

Allison guides him around a table and through a domed alcove that separates the tiny restaurant from its equally tiny bar. Three men wave them over. They sit on barstools and wear their own Silicon Valley style: one in a hoodie, one with a retro sport-jacket, and the other with a Steve Jobs turtleneck.

Marc Sanders offers Eben his stool. "I didn't expect to see you here, but I guess you're involved in everything now."

Eben sways onto the barstool and Allison steadies him. He says, "Everything?"

Miki Nakamura says, "You're here to meet with the aristocrats too?"

Eben tries to pull himself together. His instincts provide a peg to hold onto: don't give anything away. He says, "I'm in Paris with my girlfriend." He tries to put his arm around Allison's waist and pull her toward him, but elbows her in the breast and the others laugh at him.

Nakamura says, "Are you going to introduce her?"

Eben feels Allison's eyes on him and tries to speak. Before the words come out he's interrupted.

"I'm here on pleasure, too," says Jean Claude Nguyen, who worked for Eben when he started ScratchCo. "I'll find pleasure when I win this deal." He cocks his head and adds, "You okay, boss?"

Eben dismounts the barstool and leans against the bar, struggling to keep the world in one place. A few seconds ago the world felt like a big safe cloud where he could love Allison and forget about his mistakes. Now he feels like he's falling.

"Let me introduce her then," Nguyen says. "This is Allison Anatolia, she wrote the beta version of CurrentSea."

Allison offers a vague curtsy. Eben still can't seem to operate his voice. She looks at him and he feels a stab of shame. He's the gentleman. He should have introduced her. And he tried, but …

Sanders orders a round of drinks, "A bourbon for Eben. And for the lady?"

Eben manages to whisper in Allison's ear, "Let's get out of here."

Giving no indication that she heard, she says, "Champagne, please."

The drinks are served and Allison makes a toast: "To new currencies."

Something about this toast feels incorrect to Eben, but keeping his bourbon level as the others tap their drinks against his consumes his attention. Allison leans into him and says, "To us." She makes eye contact and he feels compelled to drink. He tips the glass back too far. The liquor burns his throat and he coughs and struggles to hold it down. Thoughts run through his mind too quickly for his focus, that cloud has become stormy. He counts his drinks: three glasses of wine back in the room, two more at dinner, five drinks in four hours. He focuses on riding it out long enough for his food to absorb the alcohol. A short walk, that's what he needs, outside or to the bathroom, anything but standing still.

He pushes off the bar and steps back. Another step back, this one not planned, and he catches himself against a wall. The ancient bricks feel rough and cold, solid in the storm.

Jean-Claude's face leans into his view. It looks giant. That perfect Vietnamese jaw line gapes open and he says, "Am I right?"

Eben has no idea where the conversation has been. He tries to smile and nod and manages to say, "You're always right." He discovers that the drink is still in his hand so he raises it in a toast. As he does so, the amber fluid looks like honey and with the cold bricks propping him up, he believes that a stiff drink might be just the anchor he needs. He knocks it back. His head hits the bricks behind him. The liquor burns down his esophagus and into his stomach. He takes a step in the direction of the exit, but his foot misses the floor.

Allison catches him. He exhales. Surely the storm will subside into the sweet waves of Allison's affection. She guides him down a flight of stairs to the basement toilet. He bumps against a long basin. Allison turns the faucet and cool, glorious water flows into his hands. He cups it onto his face.

Allison says, "Eben, pull yourself together."

"What? I don't know, I just—"

"Take this." She hands him a white pill. "It will help you sober up."

The pill looks like a tiny cloud.

She says, "It's just caffeine."

He leans down and fills his mouth with tap water and takes the pill. He starts to choke. She opens the door to the water closet and helps him inside. She twists him around and he falls onto the toilet.

"Relax for a minute, honey. You'll be fine." She shuts the door.

And she called him honey!

It's quiet in here, but he can still hear their conversation. It's coming through his Glass, of course, and he can see the others, too.

The pill seems to be kicking in. While he has neither the desire to rise from the commode, nor confidence in his ability to walk back to the bar, the world has steadied. No, steady is the wrong word. It's just as stormy and he is just as dizzy, but now he finds that he can enjoy the ride. He leans back and smiles and watches the world as Allison transmits it to him from her Glass to his.

They ask Allison questions about him, about his plans for the meeting tomorrow. Eben basks in the knowledge that she wouldn't betray him, even if she knew his strategy—either strategy, the one he laid out a month ago or the plan he's still working on. He laughs at the thought: winning seems simpler and easier than doing the right thing. Like a coin flip, winning or losing, heads or tails, is easy, but getting the coin to land on its edge, that's tricky.

He engages his own Glass and whispers a simple "I love you" to her, but she doesn't seem to get the message. Not only is there no reply, but the discussion has turned a corner.

"Why do you say that?" Nakamura says, staring back at Allison.

Eben tries to rewind the conversation to determine what Allison said, but that feature isn't enabled.

Allison says, "Everyone dies."

Nguyen says, "He's too rich to die."

Sanders says, "That was funny the first time you said it, now it's stupid."

"He controls too much capital. If Eben fails, he could bring the economy down with him. A few stupid decisions and the Fed would have to bail him out. What would they do if he died?"

Nakamura laughs as though he's both drunk and privy to an inside joke. "It's Eben Scratch though, right? So he'd have the cheapest funeral on earth."

"Instead of a coffin, he'd get a body bag."

"No, he'd get a Hefty Bag."

"But not the big leaf bag, he'd only budget enough for one of the plastic bags you get at the store for a dime."

"And they'd have to cut up his body to fit him in."

"He'd buy like, a four inch square of landfill for his gravesite." Sanders can barely get the words out between fits of laughter.

"I swear to God," Nguyen says, "he was the cheapest boss I ever had. We had to write our own operating systems."

"Build your own PCs?"

"Yes! Seriously, we had to buy generic motherboards, peripherals, and put them together ourselves."

Eben struggles to rise from the commode. Designing your own PC was meant to be a perquisite. Software engineers should be able to customize their own perfect system.

"He wouldn't let us have more than half of a gigabyte of memory!"

The two others say, "Half a gig?" as though it's some sort of joke.

Eben pulls himself up. The whole problem with modern software is lack of memory discipline. The only way he could get quality software—the software, by the way, that made him the richest man on earth—was to limit the memory available to his programmers. Why don't they get it?

"First thing we do when he dies, is sell his PC to a museum."

He struggles with the water closet door handle. He has to get out of here, get away from this torture. Why doesn't Allison say anything? She understood those business decisions. Why doesn't she defend him?

And then she finally speaks. Eben pulls himself upright and steady.

Allison says, "Eben comes up short in a few areas." And the others laugh like it's the funniest thing they've ever heard.

"Not much on his thumb drive, huh?"

She says, "He makes up for it in speed of delivery."

"What a stiff," Nguyen says. "You see him shuffling along Mission Street all bent over, examining the sidewalk for loose change."

"He's so tight, he squeaks when he walks."

He finally gets the door unlatched and falls out of the stall. Looking up from the floor, the brick ceiling takes a breath, expanding downward like a balloon. He rolls onto his hands and knees, reaches up to the basin and pulls himself up. The image in the mirror looks back at him. The face writhing, contorting, he touches himself and it feels as though his skin can be pulled right off. He concentrates, exerting all his will in an effort to avoid pulling off his face. Sweat breaks out on his brow and the face in the mirror starts to melt.

He has to get out of here.

"Are you ready to go?"

It's Allison. Standing two steps away, looking at him with a smile as though nothing is awry, as though he can just put on his coat and walk back to the hotel for a night's sleep before the meeting tomorrow. She looks like an angel.

"Okay," he says, trying to conceal his own insanity. "You're beautiful."

She takes him by the arm. "You seem a little unsteady. You

shouldn't drink brown liquor."

"You know me better than anyone." He looks back in the mirror and a Pokémon character looks back. He starts to laugh and can't pull his gaze away until Allison leans in. Now he can't take his eyes away from her lips. They're huge and, as she smiles, they seem to reach out from her face like bifurcated arms. He dives into them. She returns the kiss but holds him back.

One last glance in the mirror confirms his fear: his hairline recedes before his eyes, wrinkles congregate around his mouth and across his forehead, a gin blossom breaks out across his nose. Why would she love him? After what he's done, why would anyone love him? What is wrong with her?

She tugs him to the door. The others are still laughing at the bar, waving to them, laughing at them, leering at him, mocking him.

The door opens and Eben feels the moist summer breeze in the part of his hair. The wind itself carries a message: it's finally happened. That's all. Everything he has ever feared is coming to pass. Everything. He feels tears well up. A lump grows in his throat. He holds back the first tearful convulsion.

31. Eben's Fate

With the hallucinogens taking control of Eben, Allison decides that it's time.

She guides him away from the restaurant and into the Marche Bastille, an open air marketplace that's been converted into a Bastille Day celebration and protest center. Tears still drop from his eyes, but he's no longer sobbing or begging forgiveness. She sits on a bench with him.

A gray kitten emerges from beneath the bench as Allison sits. She reaches out to scratch its head. The tiny cat looks up at her. A firecracker across the street causes the cat to jump into her arms.

"Eben," she says and he turns to her but doesn't seem to focus. "I'm leaving now. If you want to find me, all you have to do is follow your heart."

She kisses his cheek and starts to rise. The kitten clenches its claws onto her leg and then leaps away. She makes the soft sound that she uses to convey comfort to her animal friends. The cat arches its back and straightens its tail. It bears its tiny fangs and hisses at her. Allison doesn't know how to respond. No animal has ever spurned her affection. She looks at Eben. His mouth hangs open and he's staring into the sky; he must be scaring the kitten.

She makes another soft sound and the kitten runs across the street. She walks through the heavy air. Looking back, she sees Eben, his arms outstretched on the bench, staring into the mist. She whispers, "Goodbye," and rubs her lips with the back of her hand, not sure if she's wiping off his essence or collecting it.

She passes the Bistro, sees the techies acting like fools, and turns onto a narrow street, almost an alley. A rat perches on a trash can, she makes her comforting sound and it scurries up a drainpipe away from her. She walks under the faded, moldy awning of the Central Bastille Hotel and into the fluorescent lobby lights. She takes the stairs to her third floor room where she sits in the dark in a chair next to a window. She engages her Glass to receive the feed from his. He's still sitting on the bench, his eyes are open, his pupils active, but he hasn't moved. The LSD keeps his mind running and the codeine keeps him comfortable and motionless. He's in an almost hypnotic state; a place where he will absorb images without question, integrating them into his reality like lucid daydreams.

She catches herself rooting for him, even though she designed the whole game so that he can't win, can't even tie. When he loses, the dead man switch will deposit her FU money. It's what she wanted, but now she's sitting in the dark staring at a vial of junk on a plastic table in a cheap hotel feeling no joy, no vindication, nothing resembling triumph. She doesn't want to feel like this, caught in a great mistake, a misplay of her life. She wants out. She wants to take that FU money and fade away from humanity so she can live with animals, the only sincere creatures she's ever known. But first, she needs one more line to help her through this night.

* * *

Eben stares at the lit up July Column, the opera house, and the occasional flashing lights of sparklers carried by revelers. The nighttime temperature drops and the mist condenses into rain. The first few drops enter his dream: a convoluted overlay of Nebraska cornfields, summer on a beach with his sister, and a girl in a black dress. His first waking thought is to find an umbrella to protect Allison from the rain.

He tries to shake the clouds out of his head, but the city lights twirl and trace like silent fireworks, and he realizes that he's alone. He rises from the bench to walk back to his hotel and the world plays a different note.

He struggles to maintain his balance. Turning his head, he sees ThievesWorld symbols appear on the sidewalk and on buildings. He leans forward, pulled by the symbols: safety, home, better days, the path of his fate.

He stumbles and his vision swirls. He regains his balance and looks into the alcove of an eight hundred year-old church: a man lies in the alcove next to a paper cup that holds some coins. He looks familiar, sort of like his dad, but his dad would never wear torn skinny jeans or a checked shirt. The man asks for five dollars. Eben rushes away. The ThievesWorld symbol for home dances along the pavement in front of him.

He sees a girl cross the street. She's dark skinned and has a Binde on her forehead and is dressed in what looks like a dirty sheet. He shakes his head and she comes in and out of view like a wraith. She steps in front of him, pulls the rags over her head, and stands naked before him. Every direction he turns, she stays in front of him, taunting him with her bruised and emaciated form. She's covered in scabs—except between her breasts where her ribs have been pried apart. He shrieks and closes his eyes. When he opens them, he sees Rishi take the girl from her horrified mother and humiliated father. A dozen children rush past, kicking a ball in the streetlight. But it's not a ball, it's Eben's head.

He stumbles into the tables of a closed sidewalk café. He pulls himself up and sees his father in the café, no it's his own reflection—but then he does see something inside the café. It's Allison and she's with Rishi and they're kissing. He struggles to look away, and then he sees his mother and father at a table. He shakes his head and looks again. They're still there and they look angry. His father stands and shakes a fist at him while listing the rotten things that Eben has done, things he didn't even know he had done: Names of people who have suffered in his zones, dead children, suffering parents, orphans, and tiny geniuses who starved to death.

He loses his balance, falls into the street, gets up and runs away, but his sister blocks his path. Her anger digs into him, burning with a bright laser light. Something in the street catches his eye. He dodges away from it, but he's too late. His nieces lie in a pool of blood. He screams and runs, faster and faster.

He covers his eyes, but that only removes the Paris background. It's like he can see through his hands, a child rears back to kick the ball—now it's Allison's head and it's glaring at him in disapproval. The children age before his eyes and the ball attaches to the body of an old man. The children assemble in rows and columns, thousands of them filling the boulevard. Desks appear and the children sit in front of old PCs trying to mine BitCoins. They whither before his eyes, taking ill, starving, failing, decaying, and then the rain washes them away.

He squeezes his eyes shut and struggles to breath. When he opens them, the world is quiet. The ThievesWorld sign for peace leads him away from the Seine up a narrow street of shops, cafes, and apartments. His exhaustion builds and the disorientation wanes. His arms start to feel somehow empty. He shakes them to get blood flowing.

Another mile along the street, his balance returns, his arms feel connected, and his stomach settles. He turns a corner and Alejandro Gustavo Mauricio De Vegas appears in front of him, pointing and yelling: "Nothing but errors and holes in your code. Wasted memory, weak security, even your successes are failures." And behind him, the hackers Jose and Hector shake their heads in disapproval. But the appearance of De Vegas and his hackers aren't what pushes Eben to the ground. Beyond them, Eben sees a large open field.

He's transported back to Durango and the baseball game in his EbenZone, the game of summer. The scoreboard says it's the EbenLeague Championship and he recognizes himself on the mound—no, he doesn't feel recognition, it's a slower sensation, his identity being drawn away. He flashes back to the Cabo beach where he wrote poetry and felt distance between the greedy competitive trillionaire and the decent man he hopes to become—hoped to become—it's all mixing together, and the whole mix is swept into the wrinkled, pock-marked, old man hunched over on the mound. His back feels stiff and when he tries to straighten, pain radiates from the center of his spine as though the vertebrae are held together by a corroded wire. His vision is dim and he knows that it will be impossible for him to throw the ball.

He looks down at a little boy, a tiny version of Yao Wo. He knows that it's Tam. He looks farther and wider for Yao and finds him in a grandstand where he's crying. Eben takes the ball from his glove and tries to put it in Tam's hand, but his back fails and he stumbles. Tam reaches for the ball. Eben looks into Tam's eyes and sees money. The familiar feeling of scoring profits rushes through his veins. He looks at his arms and can see his blood flow. The ball drops from his hand into Tam's. He sees Tam's blood flowing, too. He sees the cancer, the leukemia, coursing through the child. Concentrating, he zeros in on the cancer and sees the ScratchCo logo on every black cell in Tam's bloodstream.

Eben tries to run away. His legs give and he stumbles to his knees. His back fails and he crumples into a pile of dirt. He's too old, too tired. He pushes himself up, into the hunched shape he's acquired from looking down at databases and spreadsheets, accounts on monitors and screens. Tam calls him, "Mr. Scratch, please, let me help you," but the voice tortures him. He stumbles through the gate between stone walls and looks back at his only friend.

Yao Wo stands over the corpse of his son Tam. Yao stares into Eben's eyes, beaming desperation and hopelessness and loss. And blame.

Now through the gate, Eben scrambles between sarcophagi, across a field of tombstones, and into a two-story maze. The walls are marked with a grid of rectangular plaques, each with a name, a date and an epitaph. The dates fall centuries deeper into the past as he stumbles farther into the maze designed to pack the corpses and ashes of as many people as possible. The end of hope and the remnants of unfulfilled dreams close in.

He shuffles beneath an ancient stairwell into a puddle filled with garbage and filth. The ThievesWorld symbol for end-of-the line burns into his right eye. He tries to turn away and trips over a box. He lands in wet muck that smells of rot and decay, his face inches from the box. He pulls it toward him. It's the sort of box you'd use to ship a modest gift. It weighs about five pounds and is sealed with packing tape.

The label on the box says: "Unclaimed remains: Eben Scratch."

He can't take his eyes off of it. Memories flash through his mind. His school teacher lost in the corn maze, working at The Intoxicating Page, playing volleyball with the new girl, the first night he spent with Allison on their beach. His mind clears at the same rate as exhaustion mounts. The certainty that no one can ever love him, that he can never be a decent man, that he will never escape from his own mistakes encompasses him like dirt over a grave and he lets go, lets himself sink and wallow.

Sunlight works its way into the columbarium, even here in the forgotten stretch. Eben opens his eyes and sees that he's lying beneath an outdoor stairway with his head a foot from the bottom stair among wet leaves, cigarette butts, and a few faded plastic flowers. The light filters through the steps above, casting striped shadows around him. He rotates enough to shift his eyes into a shadow.

Minutes or hours later, he doesn't care, he hears scuffling. A skateboard tumbles down the stairs above him. It hits the ground and a man a few years younger than Eben jumps onto it. Instead of accelerating down the corridor, he stops. He kneels down and shakes Eben.

Eben looks up at him. He's not afraid. He doesn't care.

The man reaches into Eben's pockets and takes his wallet and phone. From where he lies, Eben sees the wheels of his skateboard and his shoes. Eben doesn't move, doesn't even focus his eyes, but he feels a great desire, a tremendous and irrational aspiration.

The man reaches down and pulls off Eben's Glass and then steps back, poised to jump on his skateboard. Eben tries to say something, but can't come up with words so he groans instead. The man looks down at him.

Eben holds the box out.

The man takes it and tears it open, looks inside, and then drops it. He jumps on his skateboard and kicks the box out of his way as he accelerates out from under the stairs and onto the concourse. The box slides against the bottom stair and its end flap opens. Ashes and bone fragments form a small pile inches from Eben's face.

It seems so stupid, but it brings tears to Eben's eyes. Not just the intense loneliness of his doomed future, but why? Why didn't he take the box?

VI. History Doesn't Repeat …

It's not so much this hotel pillow that plagues my attempts to sleep as it is the beagle that has rejected his assigned bedding. Every time I roll over I encounter a cold nose, a rough paw, a tail, or stray dog genitalia. But I'm desperate for a good night of sleep because tomorrow, which is to say today, Bastille Day, will require every scrap of my brilliance, such as it is.

The first rays of sunlight appear on the horizon and I surrender. Winter stretches out in my place, yawns, and resumes snoring.

I take my seat at the little hotel desk and engage my laptop, tablet, and smartphone. They connect to the Vienna server fleet and raise the constantly updating timeweave and—no, not again.

I call room service and request a pot of coffee.

Eben's timeline from last night to this instant has fizzled into a vague weave of probabilities, none of which allow for the possibility that he is sleeping peacefully in his room at the Ritz, much less that there's a filament of a chance that he will attend this absurdly pivotal meeting.

I tap the Eeyore and Tigger icons on my tablet. Since their rooms are on either side of mine, Winter and I can hear the alarm-tones and waking activity.

The most likely timeline in Eben's weave places him in a neighborhood in the 18th Arrondissement. The coordinates of Eben's Glass indicate that he is sprinting along Boulevards des

Marechaux. I hack into an ATM surveillance camera just ahead of the Glass and see a man wearing Glass pass by on a skateboard.

A knock on the door sends Winter leaping off the bed, his ears folded back, barking hysterically. I shush him. He shakes, his ears fall back in place, and he reduces his outrage to a growl that might sound threatening if he could refrain from yawning. I open the door and accept a tray with a pot of coffee and three cups from a man in a white tuxedo. Fiona appears behind him and then Volodya behind her. The steward holds the door for everyone. They're both wearing nice white bathrobes with the Hotel Mayfair crest and Volodya is carrying his laptop.

I pour the coffee, Winter demands a belly rub from Fiona, and Volodya sits on a couch with his laptop. He says, "The trajectory of Eben's Glass shows that he walked from a Bistro in the 11th to Père Lachaise cemetery. His Glass was stationary in this location for ninety-four minutes—I will retrieve him and deliver him to meeting."

"Not bloody likely," Fiona says. "He's my mistake, I'll fix it."

Volodya shrugs like a striking French cab driver. "It is long walk, over three miles?"

Fiona snaps back: "I'm perfectly capable of a two mile walk."

"Is closer to three."

"Excuse me," I say. "But something strange just happened." The timeweave has started to oscillate like the strings of a guitar playing a power chord—tied at the frets of the present, extending through the next few hours where it bridges to a wholly uncertain future.

Volodya: "Looks like software bug."

Me: "We haven't modified the software in three days."

"On the bright side," Fiona says, holding out her tablet with the timeweave. "It says we have a few extra hours."

Volodya: "Is not a bug. Someone is manipulating social media and the immediate course of history is oscillating between states of revolution."

"What?"

"Look here." His laptop shows Twitter and Facebook feeds. "Techies and royalists seem to be offending the public."

Fiona: "Eben has made another horrible Facebook post attacking the poor, old, and decrepit? How can—"

Volodya: "He is not connected, cannot post. Cannot be him."

Fiona: "This Tweet absolutely plucks the timeweave: 'The more you strike, the faster you will be replaced by robots.' It's from Marc Sanders. Why would they intentionally aggravate the strikers?"

Volodya: "Is stupid to poke sleeping bear—even bear that just dozes. The French know this."

Fiona: "And Jean Claude Nguyen is trending because he posted: 'If you can't code, you can't survive, might as well die.' What has he to gain? Here's another from Eben's account, 'People with legacy skills are bugs, AI will debug humanity.' Why?"

Me: "The royalists are just as bad: 'Work will make you free, automation will kill you.' And another: 'You can eat cake with us or you can starve with the tech-yuppies.' What's French for yuppie?"

"Added to strikes and unrest—someone wants revolution." Volodya's head quivers. "Fiona, please get Eben, we will need him." Then he pulls his laptop closer and digs into the timeweave interface. Fiona rushes off. Winter curls up near the window in a patch of sunlight.

"I've seen many timelines within the weave that lead to revolution," I say, "but I've never seen evidence that it's being encouraged by the wealthy—how could we miss this?"

"We couldn't," he says and returns to his coding. "They are not genuine. Someone is behind this."

"Oh no," I say, watching a video meme posted on Facebook from Guy Bourbon's account: Eben Scratch in a dark, dank room packed with children in front of computers, talking to Rishi.

"Fuck!" Have I mentioned how startling it is when Volodya emits that particular syllable?

Winter barks. I spill my coffee.

Volodya says, "Guy Bourbon does not play Facebook."

"This video of you and Eben watching Rishi take that girl…"

"Those come from EbenZone surveillance cameras. They're ours." He rubs his forehead. "We've been hacked."

"Impossible," I say. "The bit counter is a brick fire wall."

"Only one way: either you or I or Fiona made these posts."

We fairly attack our laptops. Twelve minutes later we look at each other. As the bitterness of doom rises up my esophagus, it passes the sweetness of hope dropping into my bowels.

We both say: "Allison."

Volodya adds, "My workstation—the mouse pad was moved."

He returns to his laptop. I try to wipe coffee from my tie and see my watch. It's already 8:53 am. "I have to get to my meeting with Guy Bourbon, it's a long walk and everyone is on strike."

"Correct," Volodya says, "Allison's social media posts have—"

"They're Allison's?"

"Not all of them, but look at this diagram. Allison hacked into accounts of both techies and royalists and then queued up these incendiary social media posts from their accounts. She did all of this two days ago. Her PC is not connected, has not been active for over twenty hours. I have locked her out but damage is done. There are more posts every minute. It is *agent provocateur* phenomenon. Allison rolled pebble down mountain and now the old and new money join the avalanche. Riots will amplify."

"What an illustrative diagram."

"You like it?"

"Volodya, you could have a whole new career in infographics."

"Depends on outcome of revolution."

32. Allison's Gift

Fiona works her way through the crowd along Rue de Rivoli. Protestors and tourists pack the streets. With no busses, taxis, or metro trains, plus the cancellation of the Bastille Day Military Parade, tourists feed on the protestors' aggravation. Combine the crowding, the emotion, and the hot morning humidity and Fiona doesn't need a timeweave engine to predict boiling afternoon tempers. She avoids the police barricades at Place des Vosges but comes upon a barricade at the Place de la Bastille built by strikers: a dozen taxis with their hoods up.

Another sweaty ten minutes and she walks onto the cordoned path between the curving stone walls and through the wedged-open bronze gates of Père Lachaise Cemetery behind a group of tourists looking for Jim Morrison's tomb. She passes a field of tombstones, a grove of crypts and sarcophagi, and enters the two-story columbarium. Tilework lining the corridor compliments marble plaques that preserve the names of the dead and who they left behind. With the help of a map on her phone, she navigates deeper. Around a turn, the dates fall into the 19th century. Most of the plaques look regal but some just look tired. She turns a corner and has to pull cobwebs from her hair. Litter accumulates in the corners and, there he is: The world's wealthiest man passed out under a stairway in a mound of rubbish.

She leans her cane against the stairs and lowers to her knee. She takes his wrist but he pulls back, hugging a cardboard box as though it might get away. He looks up at her. His bloodshot eyes focus and defocus until recognition dawns.

"What happened?" Fiona says and pushes his hair aside to check his forehead for fever. With bags under his eyes, a sallow complexion, and stubble, he looks like he's aged two decades in the previous twelve hours.

He says, "I don't feel well."

Fiona says, "You don't look well." She pulls him into a sitting position.

"It's all over, now." He rubs his eyes. A cigarette butt sticks to the back his hand. "And I believed her. I believed all of it. I believed you, too." He coughs and spits. "I even wrote her a poem." A fiber of saliva lingers between his mouth and the box.

"Eben, look at me." She pulls his chin toward her. "You can't turn your life around in three days. Yes, you wrote a poem—probably the most important work you've done this year. You gave it to her?"

"She didn't even look at it." He rubs his forehead as though to dislodge something stuck in his brain pan. "Allison." He chokes up. "We went out for dinner, but I drank too much and something I ate didn't sit well." He wipes his eyes. "And where am I?"

"It doesn't matter. We need to get you to your meeting."

"Are you serious? After everything that happened?"

"It was one night, Eben, one hiccup on your road to recovery."

"But Allison …" His words trail off. He pulls away from

Fiona.

She stumbles on her prosthetic leg and falls onto him. She sees the label on the box. "Oh, Eben. It's not as bad as it seems."

"Not as bad? Tam is dead, and I could have saved him." Tears part the grime on the path down his cheeks. "Forget that I have no honor, forget that I've betrayed everyone who ever cared for me, forget everyone who borrowed money, forget all of it."

Fiona regains her balance. "Tam's not dead."

"Yes he is. I saw it."

"You're in France, he's in San Francisco, how could you—wait a second." She enables her earbug and says, "Volodya, is Tam okay?"

"No, he has leukemia."

"But he's alive?"

"Yes, he's going to throw out the opening pitch today."

She disables the earbug and says, "Eben, why do you think Tam died?"

"I saw him die. I saw the disease in his blood. He was dead! Right over there." He indicates the corridor. "I killed him, every cell—I am the disease, don't you see? And Mr. and Mrs. Wo, oh God."

"Eben, listen to me. Tam is not dead. Yes, he's dying, but there's nothing you can do about it. You didn't give him leukemia."

"I could have stopped it."

"Eben," Fiona's voice rises. "I need you to focus. Tell me what happened last night."

He tells her about Allison visiting his hotel room. He stumbles around the details and then acts as though he's making a great confession.

"Bloody hell, Eben, premature ejaculation is not on our list of problems, okay—get past it."

Then he describes how Allison reprogrammed his Glass, "We could see each other seeing each other. I honestly believed that she loves me, or loved me—but then, in the restaurant." He tells her about sitting on the toilet watching the other techies. "They humiliated me in front of her and she, she encouraged them."

Fiona interrupts him: "And then you followed visions until you got here and passed out?"

"I saw her with other men. My parents were there, my sister, even my nieces. Everyone knows what I have done, what my algorithms did to all those people. I just watched the money. There's nothing left." His voice drops an octave, "nothing but money."

"Eben, it was AR."

"What? No, it—"

"Your parents aren't in Paris, your sister and her family are still in Mexico."

"Augmented reality?"

"Through your Glass." Then she describes the AR project Allison's been working on with Owen.

"Yes, she told me about that, but, oh no. Why would she do that to me?"

"Eben, stand up, you're going to that meeting." She uses her cane to stand and then offers Eben an arm up.

He looks at the box against his chest. "The world would be in a better place without me."

Fiona takes her tablet computer out of her purse and pulls up a web page. "Look," she says, "you freed 200,000 slaves yesterday."

"I did. But I can't seem to free myself."

"Yes, poor you and all of your money." She pulls the tablet out of his view just as a message from Volodya appears on its screen: "Do not share our technology!" She ignores it, brings up Eben's timeline, hits a summary tab, and converts it to a text document—a bulleted list of the major points in Eben's life, a true curriculum vitae. She hands him the tablet. "You got off track and made a few mistakes. Who hasn't?"

"Off track?" He frowns. "Off track. I've conned millions of people into giving me their life's work. A million dollars to free slaves isn't close to the least I can do."

"Then do more."

He waves a fly off of his nose. "If only it were that easy. If only Allison—"

"Eben! The lives of billions of people will be affected by what happens in your meeting today. Today! Now!"

"What can I do there? I need to reevaluate my life and my business." He takes her forearm and stands. "Look at me, what can I do?" He tries to smile but it looks more like a grimace beneath the grime. "I need time to figure it out."

Fiona takes the box from his arms. He resists but she insists.

He takes a step and then another like a man on a high wire, except that if he were on a high wire he'd plummet to his death. The two of them hold onto Fiona's cane and walk out of the shadows and into the sunlight. He finds greater stability with each step.

"This meeting will do nothing but help a group of insanely rich people make even more money." He nods as though confirming his decision.

"No," She says. "The deal you're competing for will—" but realizes that she's taking the wrong tack. She looks up at the steamy clouds, and then scans the plaques of the dead. Her words come out slowly. "Consider history. Great wealth creates great power. If you refuse to wield your power, you're not being passive, you're being lazy." She pauses long enough to confirm that he's listening. "Don't be a quitter."

"I am not a quitter!"

"If you don't act, you'll be no better than the man who installed a gate to keep others from enjoying a public beach."

"I'm not a quitter."

"Listen to me, young man. You're going to that meeting and you're going to do the right thing."

"The right thing." He's sturdy now and walking with his head high. "What makes you think this meeting is so important?"

She points at the protestors and police. "Things are unstable and need to be righted."

They continue in silence, cutting through shopping passages, down tiny streets, and onto the big crowded boulevards. Most of his color has returned. He clenches his jaw and nods to himself.

Fiona says, "Are you ready?"

"Yes, I guess so. I made promises and I mean to keep them."

She grips his shoulder. "Keep your Glass on through the meeting."

"My Glass? Why?"

"We're going to help you with real time projections of the consequences of everything that happens in that meeting."

He says, "My systems are fully capable of making projections."

"This will be different. Your goal is not your own wealth, it is the careful balance of currency. A flood of money can destroy the economy as surely as a drought. The others are motivated to increase their own wealth no matter what. It's up to you to do the right thing."

"All right." He puts his arm around her waist. "I'll do the right thing."

"Good," Fiona says, "just keep your Glass on."

"They're gone. They were stolen."

"Bugger all, I forgot."

They turn onto Rue de Castiglione and Fiona sees Yao at the entrance to the Place Vendome wringing his hands and pacing. He sees them and rushes forward.

Eben says, "Yao? Can you find a new set of Glass within the hour?"

"Of course, sir, and good morning." Yao brushes debris off of Eben's shoulder. "Sir, we must prepare you for a very busy day—starting with a shower and a generous meal."

"Eben, this is your chance," Fiona says. Without thinking she adds, "Don't cock it up."

"Oh, no, Ms. Black. I won't cock it up."

He holds out his hand and Fiona pulls him into a hug. She releases him and Yao guides him to the Ritz.

On her way back to Rue de Castiglione, Fiona stops at rubbish bin and drops the box into it.

Eben rushes over and looks at the box on top of the other garbage.

"Eben, it was a dirty trick by a desperate person. Leave it be."

He strokes his chin, and then reaches into the garbage and lifts out the box.

Fiona says, "Why torture yourself?"

"No, you don't understand what this box means." He wipes it off. Some of the ashes and dirt have leaked out. He folds the box flaps closed. "It may have been a trick, but it was also a gift."

33. Allison's Other Masterpiece

Volodya works through log files. His ire, disgust, and embarrassment cause him to make mistakes, but he manages to reconstruct Allison's actions while she sat at his computer, in his chair, in his lab.

Despite the cauldron of emotions, he acquires a growing respect for Allison. He knew she was an excellent computer scientist but had no idea of her appreciation for history. She has incited a rebellion through carefully phrased, articulately formatted, strategically posted social media memes. The degree to which the memes offend every class of society is a trolling masterpiece. Each post has generated an avalanche of offended responses. And then, not an hour ago, at the instant emotions peaked, her provocations called for a protest in the plaza in front of l'Hôtel de Ville to greet the techies and royalists.

A knock at the door rouses him from the trance of concentration. He opens the door and Fiona comes in. He grips her bicep to supplement the support of her cane. He's acutely aware that she has walked seven miles this morning, but pretends that the gesture is an expression of affection. She accepts it in that vein, letting him carry some of her weight and he appreciates that acceptance more than he'll ever be able to admit.

"Eben will be at the meeting," she says. "Is everything in place to guide him?"

"It is," he says, pulling over a chair for her so that she can see his screen. "This Allison is a talented woman."

"Her aunt told me that Allison has always blamed others for her mistakes. When she was a kid she blamed her parents' death for anything that didn't go the way she wanted it. Combined with her oversensitive sense of injustice and—what a mess she's caused." Fiona rubs her hip. "I'm afraid that you might be right about her."

"But she is brilliant. Look at how she has orchestrated revolution. She arranged all of these posts—memes from our video library—two days ago. You can see the accuracy of her anticipation."

"What she did to Eben is simply rotten."

"Yes, it's unfortunate that we must stop her."

"Stop her?"

"For the good of humanity, she must be stopped."

Fiona stands and says, "All right then."

"But you've already walked too far—better for me to do it. I will be less subtle, more effective." He opens the Glass-timeweave interface. "I can show you how to guide Eben through the meeting."

"Less subtle? No, no, I'll do it. She's my mess, I'll fix it." She flexes her cane hand.

"I wasn't going to hurt her, just remove her from the system for short period. You do not see?"

"What?"

"I have come around. This Allison, she is genius! She can contribute much, but not with the drugs and hatred driving her."

"Now you think it's the drugs and I think it's personal responsibility—Volodya, we're quite a pair."

"She is passionate woman under chemical control."

"She blames Eben for everything wrong in her life."

"She has narrow focus. It is heart of her genius but also her greatest flaw."

"Would she be so different sober?"

He rubs his chin. "I have come around. I think you were right in first place. Why does she focus all of her rage on this Eben Scratch? Seems obvious now." He motions to the door. "It is less than two miles. You will be okay?"

"I'm all right, Volodya. Frustrated, disappointed, a bit scared, but I'm all right." She pulls herself up with her cane and moves to the door.

"And Fiona, remember Shakespeare."

"What are you talking about?"

"Also, do not permit her near a computer until long after this meeting of power."

34. Worst Place for a Picnic

Winter and I emerge into Paris's most expensive and distracting shopping district. I find myself approaching the Place de Concorde, which was once the Place de la Revolution, among a raucous crowd.

I turn into the Jardin de Tuileries, a manicured garden that once served as a giant outdoor hospital for soldiers wounded in the first world war and is now the world's greatest picnic spot. Protestors seem to have left the Tuilerie to the tourists. With the museums closed due to the general strike and Bastille Day festivities cancelled, tourists congregate in the shade, wade in ponds, and buy *crème glacee*, crepes, croissants, macarons, wine, and cheese from opportunistic street vendors.

Winter pulls me to a huge white cube with gaps and recesses that manipulate shadows into illusions. A cool breeze ruffles my hair and my sense of balance eludes me. My own shadow resists following me. But my shadow's intransigence is less alarming than the absolute quiet. I exhale into an icy wind that pulls clouds across the blue sky like a stage curtain falling on the first act of a tragedy.

The tourists and protestors, indeed the Paris summer, are hidden from me. I search for the familiar if disconcerting green edges that mark the boundaries of separate realities, but there are none and I find this even more disconcerting.

I pull my coat tight and duck my chin inside to ward off the freezing wind. My shadow has disappeared in the gloom. I wonder how I can recover the auspicious summer day. Winter and I rush in the direction of the Louvre. Movement draws my attention to a huge dog dipping his muzzle into a fountain below the sculpture of a raven's head—but it's not a dog, it's a wolf, and it's not a raven it's a rat.

I back away and notice that Winter's leash is gone, he is gone. Intense loneliness chases me through the Tuileries. In my haste to get I don't know where, I nearly fall on what at first appears to be a corpse. It's a woman. She speaks to me in French, scolding, begging, and then pleading with her hand out. Her face is gaunt and her arm is a skin-coated stick. Her voice rasps and her eyes—I won't forget her eyes. I've never seen fear like this. I follow her gaze and see three wolves, lying on their bellies, comfortable but ready to launch when it is time.

Wolves may be a symbol of violence among humans, but the truth is that they are natural selection's janitors. They don't kill so much as they cull the herd of weakness. The woman is certainly weak. The process looks and feels cruel, but the result is health and strength, simply the way of nature.

I take my wallet from my coat to give her my remaining five Euro note, but it is just paper; not Francs, not Euros, not even shekels, just worn paper. A wolf bears its teeth. Another worries at a bone.

I fear for my friend Winter.

The woman takes the piece of paper and I run away. The cold dries my throat and I slip on ice but manage my balance. And then a scent: wood smoke seasoned by burning flesh. Ahead of me, across the Place du Carrousel flames lick away the roof of the Louvre. Still at full speed, I run past the burning Louvre and am impressed by the realization that this building has burned in almost every epoch of Paris history and then been rebuilt.

The streets are as desolate as the Tuileries. Icicles fall from the mouths of gargoyles and people who look like concentration camp victims cluster in misery.

The towers of Notre Dame Cathedral hide behind fog. I rush along the Quai next to the Seine toward Hôtel de Ville but it's gone. Nothing left but concrete and dirt, more parking lot than French grandeur. But there is a church, the oldest in Paris and before it, a tree. I rush to the tree to hide in its canopy and escape this hell. I hold this tree like a sailor holds a mast in a tossing sea. I hide in my coat and sink to the roots of the trunk of the tree and give up.

My face is buried in my collar and I want but one thing. Just one thing. And then, that familiar green edge formulates itself into existence, the widest such edge I've ever seen. My vision greenshifts. The wind stops. And even with no breeze, the clouds evaporate and the sun beats down. The chants of strikers, protestors, and rioters replace the white noise of the wind.

But my return is not the relief I seek.

I rise in the shade of the tree and see Hôtel de Ville where it belongs. Built in the French Renaissance style in 1892, indeed, rebuilt after several revolutions since the original 14th century building, it is an imposing four floor structure with four equally spaced mansard towers and a much taller central bell tower. Statues depicting Art and Science flank the grand ceremonial entrance; both are women at work in their respective trades. Science has books at her feet and is writing on a tablet and Art has a pallet at her feed and paints on a canvas.

Volodya speaking into my earbug interrupts my depressed reverie: "Simon! Are you there? Eben will attend the meeting."

"Volodya," I say, now standing at the edge of the expansive plaza before the grand entrance to Hôtel de Ville. "It was bad. It will be very bad. We have to stop this. Wolves in Paris. Again. And Winter …" My voice cracks, but not in anguish, in joy. There, with his proud white chest and attentive folded brown ears, sits my friend Winter at the top of the steps. His tail begins to sweep the ground behind him. My legs pull me toward him and the rest of the world disappears in the time it takes for us to rush together. I look up and see twin tricolor flags below the clock bordering the three words that mark every public building in France: *Liberté - Egalité - Fraternité.*

I say them out loud and Volodya replies, "High promises made but never kept."

And I respond, "Perhaps today."

* * *

I sit with Winter at a fountain whose water dances and cools protestors. Guy Bourbon catches my eye across the street. He stands out from the crowd in his butter Oxford shirt, jaunty slacks, and fine white leather shoes. The protestors don't seem to know what to make of him. Winter and I also fit in that category.

We work through the crowd to Guy and he and I shake hands. He pats Winter's head and launches into a description of a dog, a Petit Basset Griffon Vendeen, who once accompanied him which leads to a boyhood story of fishing on the Seine from the rear of his father's yacht, which leads to the story of his prowess as a horseman and the affection his dog and horse shared, which somehow leads to his interest in cultivating bonsai trees, one in particular that he first backbudded with the help of his boyhood valet that still occupies a preferred spot in the foyer of his flat at the Ritz, which leads to his assessment that the son of his current butler is a natural born engineer and his suggestion that Volodya, Fiona, and I take him under our wing as an intern, which leads him to tap at his giant watch, evidently some sort of iconic timepiece, though if he ever took a breath between sentences I might point out that my trusty Casio is a more accurate measurement device, to indicate that it's already time for us to venture toward the auspicious meeting and I've done nothing to fulfill my appointed role, unless his monologue has somehow prepared him for the meeting. Evidently I've been so rapt in his narrative of privilege that I only now discover that we've been seated at a sidewalk café for the duration of at least three cigarettes, two demitasses of espresso, and yet more macarons.

We enter l'Hôtel de Ville from the back, away from the protestors. Hôtel de Ville is Paris's City Hall but the word "Hôtel" continues to throw me. Whether it's a hotel or a hall, it is without question the most beautiful building I've ever seen. The statues along the roofs, indeed everywhere a statue might fit, distracts me from Guy's description of techniques for growing a Bonsai version of one of the great redwoods native to my hometown. We walk beneath gilded domes, between marble columns, underneath crystal chandeliers every twenty steps and into a conference room for royalty. I whisper to Winter, "We are not in Silicon Valley, bro." The walls are carved gold and the ceiling has a mural of cherubs chasing angels and demons. The idea that the French commune met in this room or that King Louis XVI sat at this table tries to draw me into time, but I tug on the leash. Winter growls, Volodya calls my name through the earbug, and I manage to stay here. I find myself rubbing the antique wood of the long rectangular table surrounded by manicured white men, save for one woman, seated in thirteen high-backed chairs upholstered in purple velvet. Each of the men has an inherited title. The woman, Marie Le Crayon, leads France's National Front Party. The tech upstarts sit in ergonomic desk chairs at the back of the room, each with at least one assistant.

Eben has not yet arrived. I want to ask Volodya for a status update, but Guy has just asked me if I'll take him fly fishing on the Russian River. I agree to the request, but when I attempt to explain that I have no idea how to fish for flies he interrupts with a story of fishing on a beach in Monte Carlo.

35. Final Betrayal

Sweat glues Fiona's blouse to her back. She has almost nine miles on her leg so far today, and it's just before 11am; her hip feels like a grinding gear. She steps under the hotel's blue canvas awning and notices that the mold might stand out if the blue hadn't faded to gray. Through the entrance, she smells overwrought air conditioning. She pauses at the elevator, but it's out of order so she continues to the stairs, climbs to the third floor, and knocks on Allison's door. There's no answer. It's locked but not quite closed. She steps into an empty room. Sunlight sifts through the leaves of an oak tree that grows along the street outside, dappling the room in shady light. It's comparatively cool even with the window open. The cooing of pigeons blends with the rhythmic chants of protestors in the Place de Bastille.

A laptop and pair of Google Glass sit on a plastic table. She also notices a vial holding whatever drugs Allison's on now. Fiona pockets the vial and sits on the bed with the laptop, the very laptop that she gave Allison when she went into rehab. The monitor shows a social media control center with the feeds of everyone who will be attending the meeting that, Fiona checks her watch, should be starting right now.

She taps her earbug and says, "She's not here."

Volodya replies, "She's outside, you walked past her."

"Right. Now the hard part. Good luck, old chum, if you need me …"

"Of course."

Fiona taps the earbug into standby and steps to the window. She leans out and the pigeons make room for her. She scans the street and sidewalks, all full of protestors passing from one strike to another. She sees Allison in a black dress perched on the curb between a Citroen and a Fiat reaching out to one of Paris's feral cats. The cat darts away from her into the street and Allison buries her face in her hands.

"Allison!" Fiona calls down to her several times before she looks up. Even from three floors up, Fiona can see the distress on Allison's face. "Please come up." Allison shakes her head and looks away. "Trust me, you do not want to make me walk down those stairs."

Allison waves her off.

"I'll flush your drugs down the toilet."

Allison rushes under the exhausted blue awning.

Fiona goes into the bathroom, wets a cloth and fills a plastic cup with water. She sits on the bed. Allison walks in and sits at the opposite end of the bed. Fiona hands her the cup and puts the cool cloth on the back of her neck.

"I figured you'd come eventually." She has puffy dark bags under her eyes and her fingers shake with toxic palsy. "You didn't come to see me, though. You came to stop me."

Allison's doctor at the rehab center told Fiona that no one can help an addict until they decide they've had enough. The helplessness of the concept doesn't fit Fiona's personal philosophy so she rejects it and then smiles at her own conceit. "You're a right mess, aren't you?"

"Wouldn't you be?"

"I bloody hope not." Fiona tries to think of ways that she can jolt Allison to reality and get her to face her feelings. She considers kidnapping her and forcing her to withdraw from the drugs. And then she remembers Volodya saying "remember Shakespeare" as she left the hotel, and it comes to her. She says, "Why have you put so much energy into destroying Eben?"

"If some bastard destroyed your life would you just go merrily along?"

"With the amount of work you've done torturing Eben you could have reinvented yourself, started a company, disrupted an industry, and made your FU money. Instead, you're inciting a rebellion you don't care about."

"I'll be getting my FU money soon and then I'll be moving on."

"You think you'll be happy?"

"I do."

"Without Eben?"

"Especially without Eben." She turns to Fiona, her expression miserable. "I'm taking my FU money and going to be with animals, they don't judge, you don't have to be pretty for them, you don't have to be rich or fake anything."

"Really? Allison, I saw what you were doing down there. The animals don't want anything to do with you anymore. You think that you can torture someone you love without changing yourself? You've lost them."

"I don't love him, I hate him."

"Even a chipmunk can see that you've lost that special sincerity that draws animals to you. Don't try to pet a dog. Even Winter would snap at you now."

She reaches out the window and the pigeons flutter away, squawking.

"Even pigeons," Fiona says. "Have you ever heard them make that sound?"

"No!" She leans farther out the window. "Come back." She makes a sound from the back of her throat. If it were softer, just above the background noise, it might sound soothing, but instead it's frantic, forced, and threatening.

Fiona pulls herself up, steps to the window and puts her arm around Allison's waist. "Dear Allison—don't you see?"

"Does everything hate me?"

"No. You're the only one."

She falls back into the room. Fiona guides her to the bed where she collapses. "Give me my junk."

"Eben loves you. Simon's worried about you. I was lying about Winter, he loves you too. Even Volodya thinks highly of you. You're the only one." Fiona wipes Allison's forehead with the cool cloth. Allison moans.

"I'll cut you a deal," Fiona says. "If you will listen to a few minutes of audio, really listen to it, I'll give you back your drugs. Or I can flush them down the toilet. It's your choice. I'll be just fine either way."

Allison lunges at Fiona but Fiona's expecting it and uses her cane like a quarterstaff, snapping hardwood against each of Allison's forearms.

Fiona takes the vial from her pocket, sets it on the nightstand where she found it, and resumes her seat between Allison and the drugs. "Just listen."

Fiona scowls but nods.

Fiona taps her earbug and says, "Can you queue up the audio from Simon's visit with Eben in the Grove?"

Volodya says, "I'm quite busy with the meeting."

"Has Eben begun his presentation?"

"Not yet."

"Send me the link and I'll queue it up myself."

She taps the earbug, looks at her phone, and the link appears. She turns up the phone's volume and the sound of Eben's voice fills the room. "He's a bit drunk so pay attention."

"I don't want to hear that bastard."

Fiona hits pause and lifts the vial from the nightstand.

"Okay, whatever."

Eben's voice is clear and his language is almost as precise as when he's sober. He starts with the story of his sister breaking him out of detention on the last day of school. Fiona fast forwards to his description of the day he met Allison. The words bring the memory back to Fiona, too. That cold San Francisco summer day, her own desire to see the sunshine, it even brings back memories of her childhood in Sydney.

She sees Allison fall back into the memory. Eben's words glow with the attraction and angst he felt that day, the adoration and passion, his uncertainty and vulnerability. When he describes the nights they spent at their beach, his voice catches in his throat. A tiny emotional hiccup, but Allison's eyes widen, her brows form a peak, and her chin crumples. She leans closer to the smartphone.

Almost an hour into the audio, Eben begins the story of their meeting with venture capitalists, the meeting where Fiona humiliated him and set him on this course. Fiona feels the whole impact of her callous, unfeeling response to Eben's ideas and can't hold back. She turns the volume louder to cover her response.

When Eben begins to describe how he lost Allison, that's how he put it, he lost her, Allison reaches for her purse.

Fiona pauses the audio. "You have to listen or the deal is off."

"He gave me a poem last night. A poem, Eben Scratch wrote a poem," Allison says. "I can't believe that Eben would write a poem except that ..."

"Except that you can easily believe that the Eben you fell in love with would write you a poem?"

"I want to read it."

36. The Pitch

Eben and Yao take an indirect route to Hôtel de Ville through streets lined with exclusive fashion and cosmetics shops to avoid the protesters, but it doesn't help.

Three men wielding picket signs—"People Not Computers," "A Sharing Economy is a Starvation Economy," and "Gig Workers are Scabs"—cross the street in front of them. One points at Eben and yells, "Techie scum!" and launches into a long, loud monologue. Eben wonders if they're right. He stops a few steps from them and tries to make sense of the rant. Yao guides him into the closest store. Stepping through the door, they're engulfed in the exotic scents of a perfumery.

Eben says, "Yao, I want you to know that I deeply appreciate everything you do for me."

The physical part of his hangover feels better now. Yao insisted he soak in a salty bath, eat a high protein breakfast, and drink no more than three cups of coffee and no less than three glasses of cranberry juice. The emotional hangover, on the other hand, constantly distracts him. At least he's comfortable in his blue and white rugby shirt.

Yao steps to the counter and asks if there is a back door they can use. The proprietress offers her wrist to both Eben and Yao. Eben leans in and inhales a mix of honeysuckle, musk, and jasmine.

"We're late for a meeting," Yao says, "and the protests have become dangerous. If we could use the back door …"

Eben says, "This must be how mélange smelled in *Dune*; Yao have you read *Dune*? Utterly intoxicating." He smiles at the woman. "You create these scents right here?"

The woman says *oui* and offers her other wrist. Eben takes a deep breath.

"Sir, we should really be on our way."

"If I weren't in the world's most beautiful city, I'd swear I was walking through a cedar forest." Eben steps aside and adds, "Yao, you have to smell this."

"But sir—"

"I'd like both of them, please, a pint of each?"

"*Merci*," The woman says, "*Monsieur*, it is so fulfilling—is that the word?—to be appreciated." She takes two of the largest crystal atomizers from a shelf behind her. "Half a liter you say? I don't think we have that size."

"Or a liter? However much you think we need, I've never purchased perfume or cologne before."

Then she laughs and puts the two bottles in a red velvet box and ties a black ribbon around it. The ribbon reminds Eben of Allison's dress and how he felt while ironing it. He decides to find it within himself to appreciate good experiences regardless of their ultimate consequences.

Yao gives her a credit card.

Several minutes later, they step into an alley.

"It's for you," Eben says. "For Mrs. Wo—I apologize for not knowing your wife's name. I apologize for everything, Yao. Please, if you think she'll like it. And the cedar is for you, though I'm not sure if it's appropriate for one man to give another man cologne."

"Sir, please." Yao stops in front of Eben. "Sir, I'm jazzed to see you awakening to new possibilities. I couldn't be more psyched for you, but could you do one thing for me?"

"Of course, Yao, anything! Anything at all, just name it. A raise? Vacation—you can take the whole family to my beach, stay as long as you want. I'll have it catered. Anything, what is it?"

"Well, sir, calling me by my first name, it's kind of freaking me out."

"Oh, I'm sorry."

"No don't be. It's just going to take some time for me to adjust." He takes a tablet computer from his briefcase and says, "Say, next Tuesday we'll begin calling each other by our first names?"

"You're scheduling it?"

"Sir, for two years you've had me put everything in your calendar—everything—like I said, it will take me a while to recalibrate." Eben looks down and sighs. Yao adds, "I'm really looking forward to it, sir. It's going to be great!"

Eben finds himself amused by his own disappointment in Yao's response, but it turns into another wave of regret. He has never allowed himself the pleasure of Yao's enthusiasm and as this thought passes through his mind it's followed by another image of the most talented computer scientist he ever knew. He sighs and says, "She keeps coming to mind and I can't focus."

"Once the game begins you'll focus." Yao pats him on the back. "I know you."

They continue along side streets and alleys, Yao checks their course with GPS at each intersection. Eben considers putting on his Glass, it could guide them more efficiently but after last night, he feels apprehensive about anything related to Glass. "How did you find Google Glass so easily?"

"Craigslist, sir."

They cross another intersection, passing Notre Dame's steeples on the island to their right. A wave of embarrassment nearly trips Eben. How could he forget? "How is your son?"

"I'm sorry sir?"

The embarrassment turns to guilt. "Tam, how's he doing?"

A grin spreads across Yao's face. "He's throwing out the first pitch today, sir."

"He's feeling better then?"

"Well, no sir. I mean, he's quite happy to throw out the first pitch, but ..." Yao chokes on the last word.

"What?" Eben grips Yao's shoulder. "No, surely something can be done."

"No sir. There's nothing. We've admitted Tam to hospice so that he can enjoy his last few weeks."

"He was in a trial treatment. He had a stem cell transplant, didn't he?"

"Three, his body rejected all of them."

"You have to do something."

"Sir, we have done everything."

"Mr. Wo, I am the wealthiest man on earth, there must be something I can do."

"It doesn't work that way, sir."

"You need to be with him. Go home now. Right now, I'll get you a limo, get on the next plane."

"There are no limos today and the airport is closed." Yao straightens his posture and manages a smile. "It's all right, sir. I shouldn't have said anything. I'm fine. We're fine. You have an important day and I'm here to help."

"Important? You're missing him throw out the first pitch!"

"Sir," Yao looks up at the blue sky as they turn toward Hôtel de Ville. "I'm a happy man. I've enjoyed being with you all these years. Even when you would growl at me, I truly enjoyed the challenge of drawing you out. And now I've won! Don't you see? I won the battle of Eben Scratch." They cross Rue de Rivoli, pass the plaza in front of Hôtel de Ville, and go to the back entrance.

"You're on the first plane after this meeting and that's all there is to it."

Yao holds the door for Eben, says, "Just win, baby!" and offers a high five that Eben smacks with vehemence.

* * *

Yao leads Eben to the conference room and they take seats in the back beside Jean Claude Nguyen who scoots a few inches to the side without looking up. Eben puts on his Glass. Marc Sanders leans across and says, "You look remarkably good for putting one on last night."

Eben catches a whiff of lemon furniture polish. He wonders why they would use such a product on these fine antiques. The only smell that's worse is the Polo cologne worn by someone seated at the table. The whispering in the back of the room continues while, at the adult table, the aristocrats exchange notes and carry on their own banter, mostly in French.

Eben recognizes Simon seated at he table next to Guy Bourbon. Simon is the only one at the table using a computer and he's typing at full speed. He looks up and waves to Eben. For an instant he feels like a fool: Simon is sitting with the other side? Is it all a setup? The smell of Polo cologne brings to mind the SomaAngel VC disaster. And then he notices something worse, thirteen people sit at the table. Thirteen.

A man with sharp blue eyes, equally sharp cheekbones, and gray-blonde hair who breathes through his mouth begins tapping his knuckles on the table. The air conditioning kicks on and Eben feels post nasal drip falling onto the back of his throat.

Yao leans over and does something that would have gotten him fired a week ago, he says, "Relax and take a deep breath."

Eben follows Yao's advice and feels calmer for it. He pulls his notebook from his pocket and reads his list of promises. Fiona, Volodya, Simon, that is who rescued him. A tendril of suspicion reminds him that it could all be part of a larger setup put in motion by Guy Bourbon and these imperialist aristocrats. He takes another deep breath, but it catches in the back of his throat and clogs his ears. He has to make the high pitched nasal sound to clear them.

A young woman in a gray suit distributes printouts of the meeting agenda. Eben is pleased to see that he's scheduled to present last.

Miki Nakamura says, "Printouts? Really?"

Marc Sanders says, "I know, right?"

The woman connects a PC to a projector. She introduces

herself as Renee Coutreu and goes through the agenda. She speaks French first, and then switches to English.

Jean Claude Nguyen says, in French, "Don't switch to English on our accounts. Those of us who don't speak French have translation apps."

A man with immaculate black hair parted on the side, dressed in an equally immaculate black silk suit, slowly pushes his chair away from the table. It scrapes against the parquet floor and Eben covers his ears. The man rises from the ornate chair, unfolds gold wire-rimmed glasses and slowly wraps them across his eyes and around his ears. He peers through the glasses to the back of the room. Speaking in a haughty English accent, he says, "If you please, I should like the translation the old fashioned way. I should also enjoy this meeting far more were its participants to recognize their roles." He then makes a show of removing his glasses and sitting down. Eben's Glass project an image of the man with his name, Lord Womersley.

Ms. Coutreu repeats her spiel in English. The British gentleman requests a pot of tea and within seconds a waiter strides in carrying a complete tea set on a silver tray.

Coutreu introduces Marc Sanders who presents his pitch for CyberDollars, a typical Silicon Valley presentation, all technical detail, newness, buzz, and potential—he uses the word "disrupt" four times. Eben's Glass provide projections of how economic indicators are likely to respond to everything proposed. Being a fastidious student of the game, he's thoroughly impressed by how fast the projections update based on different assumptions. The Glass also provide him rotating views of the facial expressions of each aristocrat.

Lord Womersley pinches his nose and looks away. Guy Bourbon taps his thumbs together and shakes his head. Eben makes a mental adjustment. He composed his presentation from those he's given around Silicon Valley, but these people want to return Europe to its aristocratic glory, not try new things. He starts to edit his presentation but discovers that someone has already changed the style: his clean EbenFont changes to classic Garamond, the steel blue background disappears behind a maroon watermark of velvet curtains complete with subtle bee icons, Napoleon's trademark.

Ms. Coutreu then introduces Miki Nakamura, referring to him as a "BitCoin advocate." The word BitCoin grabs the aristocrats' attention.

Nakamura makes the same mistake as Sanders but to a lesser degree. From the look of his slides, Eben can tell that he also made last minute style changes. BitCoin has a big advantage. As far as the aristocrats know, BitCoin is the most established candidate currency available to them, and Nakamura emphasizes this fact over and over again. He even comes right out and shows a graph of how much he personally stands to gain if they establish BitCoin as the primary French currency. To Eben, it looks like nothing more than a modern version of the argument to move to a gold standard, precisely the case he had hoped Nakamura would make.

Jean Claude Nguyen is next to the lectern. Nguyen presents an all new but obvious default choice: a NewFranc based on a precious metal standard—like the gold standard but with flexibility when other elements or compounds realize great value. It doesn't attract the attention of the aristocrats the way that BitCoin did, but that's the hypocrisy of traditionalism—people desire new things, even when they're biased against them. Eben realizes that the best move is to overcome the bias while playing to the desire.

Eben smiles at Yao and takes another deep breath. He's comfortable with the projections from Volodya and Simon, knows what to watch for in the graphics, and likes his chances.

Between CyberDollars, BitCoin, and NewFranc, Eben

would choose NewFranc. Nguyen has modernized the traditional idea of money, integrating concepts that Nguyen learned when he worked on CurrentSea. It's less sexy than either of the others, but Eben likes the design. That is, until his Glass projects the response of Germany to a NewFranc. Of course, a NewFranc would effectively convert the Euro into a New Deutschmark. His Glass projects the amused response of the graying blonde man and identifies him as Friedrich Reser, direct descendent of Otto von Bismarck.

The consequences of a worldwide currency war flash onto his retina: wildly fluctuating trade imbalances that lead to currency collapse combined with extreme wealth disparity that leads to revolution, world war, famine, disease. The Glass projections now show statistics of currency collapses that occurred prior to globalization when different regions lived in separate economies. Then he sees the math: a covariance matrix that shows how the wealth of the world is now inextricably tied together; not just correlated but entangled, connected at the roots and interrelated in every facet.

Eben built CurrentSea from the Watergate app that he and Allison worked on in those wonderful days at the Intoxicating Page, but only now does he understand what it was really for: Watergate means to follow the money, not to take it, but to see how it influences political, diplomatic, and business decisions. The Watergate app was an engine for keeping power brokers in check and he corrupted it into an economic weapon.

He whispers, "Aha" to himself, though Yao, Simon, and Volodya all hear him. "The need for balance—I get it now." The people in this room will choose one of these currencies today. If they pick EbenNotes, then Eben has a chance of preserving world harmony. The responsibility hits his shoulders like a bag of concrete. The weight distracts him. The graphics in his Glass change, but he's looking at a bigger picture. Like their purpose for the Watergate app, he understands what Fiona, Simon, and Volodya have been doing. Selfish greedy Eben wouldn't bear this responsibility. That Eben would see this "win" as just another step on his path to hoarding all the money. He leans over and scrutinizes the repeating diamond pattern of the hardwood floor. That Eben would let the world collapse, let everyone's children suffer like Tam Wo and that poor girl in India, like the slaves he hasn't helped to freedom. That Eben. He turns to the side and looks at Yao who stares at the presentation but is looking at something thousands of miles away. That Eben is dead; his ashes are in a box at the Ritz.

Nguyen concludes his presentation. Eben is next. He carries his laptop to the front of the room. When he was invited to this meeting, he saw it as the greatest competition of his life. A competition he knew he could win. He feels that way again but the burden is heavier now. He looks back at Yao who gives him two thumbs up.

As Eben passes Nguyen he says, "Nice work."

Nguyen says, "I've always hated you, Eben." He says it with a smile.

Eben connects his PC and his first slide appears on the screen behind him. Looking across the table, he realizes the value of seeing the aristocrats' responses to the other pitches. Guy Bourbon's thumb tapping doesn't distract him. Lord Womersley's fidgeting with his glasses doesn't bother him, Marie Le Crayon's scowl doesn't annoy him; he even manages to ignore Friedrich Reser's open-mouthed breathing.

Eben thanks them for inviting him, playing the underling card to appear unassuming and properly obedient. A nice set up; hopefully he won't have to close with an offer they can't refuse. He summarizes the positive aspects of CyberDollars, BitCoin, and NewFranc and then says, "EbenNotes have the edge in every respect. It's an established currency—far more established than you realize. Millions of people around the world use EbenNotes exclusively for purchasing goods and services."

He pauses and then adds, "My associates have no concept of history. They've overlooked the simplest and oldest rule of money, Gresham's law: bad money drives out good money. CyberDollars, BitCoin, NewFranc have all been pitched as more valuable than the Euro—but if you want to convert a currency, the new money must be *less* valuable than the old, less rare, with less intrinsic value. To drive the Euro out of circulation you have to encourage people to spend the new money and hoard the old. The more people hoard Euros and spend EbenNotes, the more established EbenNotes will become. As Euros fade from circulation, merchants will—"

Guy Bourbon interrupts, "Mr. Scratch, please refrain from a sermon on elementary economics."

"Yes," Lord Womersley says, "don't presume upon us. Simply provide a description of your proposal. We are here to buy, not invest."

"Buy?" Eben says. "Not invest? What's the difference?"

Guy Bourbon says, "Nor are we here to teach you."

Marie Le Crayon says, "Has he finished yet?"

"Is he really trying to convince us to assume a *less* valuable currency than the Euro?" Karl Hapsburg says. Eben's Glass identifies him as an Austrian who can trace his lineage and wealth through the 400 year reign of the Austro-Hungarian Empire.

Eben says, "Copernicus wrote about it in the 16th century. Gresham's Law is how silver coins were driven out of circulation. People hoarded silver and spent the zinc-nickel-alloy coins because their face value was the same but their intrinsic value wasn't."

"Preposterous."

Eben tries to think. In the throes of this hangover and in front of these people, it's hard to get back on the rails. He advances several slides to a flow chart but realizes that these people don't speak that language. He advances to the next slide, but it has his argument against BitCoin which only makes sense after the flow chart so he steps back to the flow chart and perseveres. "The formula for replacing a currency is shown here. First, introduce a currency with less value, as I already said, then—"

Friedrich Reser says, "He now repeats himself."

Le Crayon says, "Must we sit through this?"

Eben uses a laser pointer to walk them through the logic, but the people sitting around the ornate table aren't looking at the presentation, they're talking among themselves. Eben continues, now speaking louder, but Bourbon laughs. Womersley leans across the table, holding a sheet of paper for the others to see.

Ms. Coutreu says, "Thank you, Mr. Scratch."

He skips this slide and goes straight to the arguments against his competitors. "BitCoin is unstable, unflexible and it will—"

Womersley says, "Unflexible is not a word."

"Inflexible. It will crumble under the force of price-stickiness. BitCoin can be mined but the amount of currency available has an upper limit which means that deflation is inevitable and instead of having recessions that can be controlled peacefully, you'll have depressions that will destroy your economy."

"I rightly think a bit of deflation is a good thing," Womersley says. "Why should money only lose its value through inflation? Why shouldn't it increase in value through occasional episodes of deflation? Leaving the gold standard was the greatest mistake ever forced upon us by the United States."

Eben aims his laser pointer at the British gentleman and says, "When economies grow too fast for the money supply to keep up with demand, they plummet into devastating depressions—"

Albert Saalfeld of Belgium says, "Now he's lecturing us? Truly?"

"—but this happened during the 18th and 19th centuries."

Womersley says, "He's being unflexible."

Bourbon erupts in laughter.

Eben speaks faster, but the laughter spreads across the room so he has to speak louder. "A software bug would cripple any cyber currency. We've already seen how just a rumor of a bug can cause radical drops in value. EbenNotes are fiat currency controlled by markets. Since they're not mined, no software bugs can hurt them." The aristocrats only look up at him occasionally. He rushes through two more slides. "A NewFranc based on a precious metal standard might be a solution if you, all of you combined that is, held a sufficient fraction of the world's supply of precious metals, but you don't."

Bourbon stands slowly. Without looking in Eben's direction he raises a hand, the universal sign to stop but without the respect of eye contact.

Eben says, "I'm not finished."

Womersley says, "Well I am."

Giovanni Medici says, "Ms. Coutreu, please?"

Ms. Coutreu stands and addresses Eben's techie counterparts in the back of the room. "Thank you for your presentations." Then she motions to Eben. "Would you please pack up your things? The presentation part of the meeting is over and your presence isn't necessary for the afternoon discussion."

The humiliation boils within him, and he's not finished.

"I have more gold than you. I have more money than all of

you combined."

At this, the table erupts in laugher and Eben screams at them. "You have no choice. I already own you. You've already converted to EbenNotes."

Womersley says, "He has even named his currency after himself?"

Hapsburg says, "Sounds like something Womersley would do."

And they laugh again.

"Quiet!" Eben shouts. "Damn you. I already control your currency. I know everything you've bought and sold for the last two years. You have no choice."

Womersley says, "Is he still talking?"

* * *

I hear Volodya through my earbug: "This is serious problem."

The timeweave is still awash in possibilities, but is now down to just a hundred different routes to disaster. I separate the timelines of France and Germany. I type: "Germany will overreact."

"She always does," Volodya says. "Vulnerable Germany would encourage Russia—never good idea." I can picture him staring out the window and rubbing his chin. "Franco-Russian alliance in conflict with Germany—does this sound familiar?"

The people seated around me are now ignoring Eben. They're exchanging the banter of a fraternity of boyhood friends. Eben appears to be clinging to the lectern. I wonder if his rough night has caught up with him. I configure the ThievesWorld symbol for opportunity and am about to project it to his Glass when I hear him say, "Seriously?" He says it under his breath and I suspect that Winter and I are the only people who hear him. His frown deepens and his posture curves back into that of the Eben Scratch I met in the Bohemian

Grove.

Volodya says, "I am at a loss."

Fiona is still with Allison and her earbug is turned off, but I know what she would say if she were with us and I'm not sure that Volodya does, so I type it: "We've done everything we can to protect Eben from his base nature. He's a whole man now, have faith in him."

"Faith?" Volodya says.

Eben disconnects his PC from the projector, shakes his head in disgust, repeats the word, "Seriously," and attacks his keyboard.

The Belgian, Albert Saalfeld, and Russian, Andrei Romanov, turn their attention to him but Bourbon, who sits to my right bickers over the three options with Medici and Womersley, who sit across the table from us.

Eben rises from his computer, steps over and sets his palms on the table. He clears his throat and waits.

Hapsburg looks up from his notes. Guy Bourbon glances at him and then resumes arguing with Medici, who waves him off.

"I am still talking," Eben says.

"Yes, but we are no longer listening," Womersley says. "Your pseudo-economics is less than appreciated."

"Perhaps you should check your accounts."

Bourbon says, "We are not that easily played."

"Your wealth has already been converted to EbenNotes—yes, my currency. You're free to spend it on BitCoin or New-Francs or shekels for all I care, but it would not be in your best interest. I've already described your best interests. Do what you will, but beware that I will do what I will and my will is more powerful than yours."

Womersley says, "Preposterous!"

Bourbon says, "*Grotesque.*"

Medici says, "*Ridicolo.*"

As Eben slides his PC into his backpack, Yao hands out stapled sets of paper to everyone at the table, it's a copy of the terms and conditions that each of them, or their agents, agreed to when they began using the CurrentSea money optimization app.

With his backpack on his shoulder and Yao at his side, Eben says, "The document that my associate has kindly handed out should already be familiar to you—unless you clicked 'agree' without reading it. In either case, Yao has highlighted the relevant text that should provide you or your accountants sufficient motivation to recognize that EbenNotes are ideal for your purpose regardless of your feelings about me, personally. Thank you and good day."

Bourbon stands and steps into Eben's path. He says, "You can't do this."

Eben cocks his head and says, "I already have."

"I didn't mean that as hyperbole, I mean that we won't let you do this."

Womersley and Medici walk around the table and stop behind Eben. Reser and Hapsburg step in front of him.

Bourbon says, "Madam Coutreu? Could you please summon the *Gendarmerie*?"

Madame Coutreu remains above the fray. I silently applaud her until I realize that she's calling the police to arrest Eben.

Reser says, "Give me your phone and backpack."

Eben steps back, right into Womersley who grabs hold of Eben's backpack. Holding the straps firmly, the two are in a standoff.

"Gentlemen," Bourbon says, "there is no need to be physical. The *Gendarmerie* will be here in seconds."

From my earbug I hear Volodya make a strange sound, even for him. I can't decide whether it resembles the honk of an offended goose or the warble of an impressed turkey. Eben swallows his odd nasal whine and then all are drowned out by Winter who lunges at the giant doors of the entrance to this historic room. He barks, howls, and bares his teeth.

The doors crash open as though hit by a battering ram.

Protesters flood the room demanding justice in at least three languages. I catch sight of a young man hacking at a security officer with his picket sign. A three hundred year old vase crashes to the floor. A rioter leaps on the table and then to the chandelier. Chairs are thrown aside, protestors jump onto the table where I'm still seated. Habit compels me to shuffle my laptop into my satchel—and good thing. A second longer and an athletic woman roughly my age would have stepped on it and since her sandals lack ankle support she'd have likely fallen.

I step away from the table. Winter pulls me on a collision course with the flood of protesters. Madame Coutreu rushes to the opposite end of the room and requests that the royalists follow her. They follow as though she's leading them on a fire drill.

The techies follow the royalists away from the fray—except for Eben who steps in front of me. He reaches out as though to embrace the protestors. My first response is fear for his safety, my second is appreciation that he seems poised to protect me, and my third is rapidly mounting confusion. Now in the thick of the crowd, he raises his voice. It's too loud to hear him, but he obviously wants the crowd's attention.

I duck behind Eben and maneuver to the side of the room. Sliding along the wall, I work my way out of the conference room and into the magnificent corridor. Protestors have overwhelmed security. Parading through the ornate and staid building, they riot with no regard for the antique accoutrements that decorate Hôtel de Ville.

I turn a corner. Sunlight streams in the grand entrance illuminating a huge painting that depicts the pivot point when the French revolution evolved into the reign of terror. I try to stop, but the mob pushes and pulls, tugging me forward, ever forward, at and then into the painting. It's like falling into a swimming pool, except that it's not cool, it's not wet, and it's not fun. It is merely a separate medium. I don't see or feel any other timelines but the one I just left and the one I'm falling into. I look back and realize that I've let go of Winter's leash. He's on the outside of the painting. Terror fills my heart and mind. I want out.

37. Grains of Sand

Allison looks up from the folded piece of paper, torn along its edge and covered on both sides with Eben's precise handwriting. She looks out the window and rubs a few grains of sand between her fingers.

"May I?" Fiona asks and Allison lets her take the piece of paper. It says: "If I could reassemble the sands of time, I'd take us back to our beach. We'd start again. We'd make different mistakes, but we'd make them together and never part. There's nothing I wouldn't do for you, my Allison, hate me as you will, as I earned, but I'll love you forever. I can't ask for you back, but everything I have is yours; please take it: my time, the material wealth I no longer care for, take me, take my body, take everything I am. It is yours. It always was and ever will be. If I hadn't thrown our love away, we could have blossomed. Instead we decayed. Everything decayed except my affection, adoration, and love for you. Allison, if you ever see this and if there is a wisp of a chance for us, then believe that I will take the risk, that risk of love, that love is risk."

Fiona looks up and says, "And his ashes."

"What?"

"The box at the end of your AR treasure map: "unclaimed remains: Eben Scratch." He's keeping it. He said it was a gift."

"Eben." She watches a bird pass the windowsill. "Fiona, you weren't there. You didn't live with his greed and selfishness. I know him. I know Eben Scratch. I'm sure he believes all this, but it won't last. He's too competitive, too insecure. I'm not going to fall for it again. Fiona, I can't risk it—look at me! I'm not strong enough to survive him."

Fiona folds the sheet of paper along the existing creases and hands it back to Allison. Her unsteadiness and pallor both call for a dose of narcotics. The drugs will hold her in that abyss in the long term but without them in the short term she'll drown in the throes of withdrawal.

Allison lets the piece of paper fall to the floor—not the response Fiona had hoped for.

"I wrote software worth a *trillion dollars* and I live in an alley between Eddy and O'Farrell. My pillow is a concrete doorway. My bathroom is a parking structure. I eat pizza from garbage cans and shoot smack from used needles and I wrote the most valuable piece of code on earth and Eben Scratch stole my life."

"Are you familiar with Shakespeare?"

"What?"

"The lady doth protest too much, methinks."

"Really? A cliché?" She stands and stumbles around Fiona. "I listened, now let me have my stuff."

Fiona would have blocked Allison with her cane, but as Allison stood, Volodya activated her earbug and said, "The riots have turned violent. Protestors have invaded Hôtel de Ville. I can't locate Simon. Eben will surely be attacked." He takes a deep breath.

Fiona's patience vanishes. "I'll be there as soon as I can."

VII. ... But it Does Rhyme

Eben is caught between the rioters and the aristocrats. The rioters chant anti-corporate, anti-establishment, anti-aristocracy slogans. They scream insults. They threaten violence and throw firecrackers. A man leaps on the table and dives like a missile at Lord Womersley. A guard steps between them and collides with the protestor who falls to the ground at Eben's feet.

More protestors flood the room. A woman in sunglasses grabs a crystal water pitcher by the handle and smashes it against a marble column. She advances on Eben with the shard of crystal held like a sword. He glances back to see if the way is clear. He sees Yao against the back wall. The aristocrats are surrounded by their personal security.

The woman swings the crystal shard. Eben takes another step back. He wraps his arms across his face and lowers his shoulder. He winces, expecting the woman to drive the broken glass into him, but she steps aside and rams it into a bodyguard. She scrapes it across his belly. He screams.

She leans against Eben, using him to shield herself from another guard. She passes and shoves him into the space behind her. Eben wonders why she would protect him. Another protester launches in front of him between two guards and tackles Medici. Eben steps over the man who attacked Womersley. He's curled in a pool of blood. A protester wearing a beret makes his way to the back wall and levels Marc Sanders. Two protestors lift one of the huge hardwood chairs and together swing it in an arc at the aristocrats. Eben drops below it. He winces against the coming blow and turns into the woman holding the crystal pitcher shard. She has also dropped below the flying chair. He starts to lose his balance. She steadies him, points at the aristocrats and yells in his ear. He makes out the word "revolution" and realizes that she thinks he's a protester. It's his clothes: rugby shirt and jeans—not the khakis and polos or turtlenecks of the other techies and certainly not the fine suits of the aristocrats.

The two men whirl the chair around again and fling it over the bodyguards and into the aristocrats. Steel crushes bone. A skull hits the hardwood floor.

Eben steps into the thick of the protestors. *Gendarmes* in riot gear appear from every direction—no, not every direction, they appear from beyond the lectern. Eben sees Yao being pushed into a passageway. Eben is certain there had been no door there when he entered this room. Could it be an actual secret passage?

The *Gendarmes* pummel rioters with batons, forcing their way in and forming a wall between the protestors and the protested. The woman swings the sharp edge of the broken pitcher. The remaining glass explodes when it collides with a swinging truncheon. Blood splashes. The woman screams, her hand destroyed.

Now against the wall, clear of immediate danger, Eben watches the woman fall to the ground under more blows.

Nakamura calls him. Eben can't hear but recognizes that it's a call to safety, away from the barbaric masses. Eben jerks toward him but stops. No, no, no. He's not going to accept the privilege of wealth. No. He looks at the woman holding her smashed hand against her stomach. He tries to move toward her. Maybe he can lift her up, maybe move her to safety.

The chaos erupts to a new level. The aristocrats disappear

through the passageway and Eben can see that it's a tunnel heading below ground level. The *Gendarmes* follow and the rioters explode in renewed fury, hurling chairs, decanters, and goblets. The silver teapot hits the remaining *Gendarme*. Hot tea penetrates his armor and he screams.

Eben works his way through the riot. With no targets, the outrage starts to calm. He steps into the grand corridor. Protestors continue their chants and demands, oblivious to the violence in the conference room. Eben feels that calm again. The same feeling that he felt in Durango when he escaped Alejandro De Vegas. He reads the picket signs and listens to the chants. He feels empathy and guilt over that layer of calm confidence. The protestors make valid points: who deserves the gains from the increased productivity of automation? And who should bear the weight of society's burdens? He moves down the hall, turns a corner and sees a giant painting glowing in sunlight near the huge open doors.

Eben can't help but translate the protestors' complaints and demands into goals. Once he perceives them as goals, solutions and strategies come to mind. One strategy emerges. It's his strategy, of course. The strategy he and Allison laid out to address the world's ills that first night on their beach.

The grand entrance to Hôtel de Ville stands wide open and occupied by protestors of every race and age. A woman ascends the few steps to the entrance. She addresses the crowd with a bullhorn. They ignore her. Eben makes out enough French to comprehend that she's urging them to hold a peaceful demonstration.

Now standing on the threshold, he looks out on the crowd that packs the Place de Ville. He knows he can fix this. He can lead this mob into a movement. It all comes together in his heart and mind. His calling. His purpose. His opportunity to make amends. The thought even passes through his mind that, if he can do this, maybe Allison will come back—but the instant this thought comes to mind, guilt pushes it away. Whatever he does from this point forward will not be for his own gain.

He gestures to the woman with the bullhorn. Her frustration shows in her expression of dismay. She looks at the crowd, shakes her head, looks back at Eben, shrugs and hands him the bullhorn.

Eben adjusts the bullhorn's volume, checks the battery indicator, and then waits. Every random process has fluctuations and crowds are more random than dice. It takes almost a minute but then a lull in the exclamations gives him his chance.

With the help of the bullhorn his voice penetrates the farthest reaches of the plaza: "My name is Eben Scratch." He knows the risk and he knows that the silence won't last. "You're right. Automation should benefit everyone. Automation should never cause suffering."

Eben zeros in on three men in the center of the plaza to gauge the crowd's temper. They look back with skeptical scowls, transfixed for the moment. "No one wants to do work that a robot can do better. No one should have to, and the people who own the robot shouldn't be the only ones to benefit from the increase in productivity." The three men look at each other. One turns away.

"Let the robots have the boring jobs." He points at the three men, hoping he can squeeze another few seconds of attention. "You should be developing green energy, creating carbon sequestration technology. You should be defining protocols that can protect energy grids, building new communication stacks and embedded routines." He had them for a second, but now the crowd is rumbling again. "I will loan you the capital you need to create, I'll provide whatever you need to make your mark! Robotics and automation should liberate you to create, to solve the problems we face together, not enslave you in poverty! Clean water must be a right of all people, but it can't be achieved without technology. Minimal healthcare is an essential human right."

The woman who gave him the bullhorn yells, "Minimal?"

The chanting resumes, anger replaces skepticism on the faces of the three men. They maneuver through the crowd toward Eben.

"I'll give anyone a loan—no, I mean grants!" Even at full volume the bullhorn can't penetrate the slogans, the chanting, the demands of the crowd, but Eben keeps trying, "If you have ideas for how to provide everyone on earth clean water, education, disease prevention, I'll give you—"

The three men surround him. The woman takes back her bullhorn and uses it to broadcast: "The richest man on earth wants us to eat cake!"

The crowd advances and unites in a chant like the chorus of a hymn: "*Apportez-nous la guillotine.*"

The only word Eben understands is guillotine.

Another man kicks Eben and he falls.

38. Three Words of Civility

Reality shifts between centuries. I try to anchor myself with the understanding that I'm at l'Hôtel de Ville on Bastille day but that makes oscillating between now and 1789 feel all the more inevitable. My understanding of French is sufficient to decipher the anger of the mob. I chastise myself for thinking of them as a mob because they're individuals with a common cause, at least a common complaint, and that complaint transcends the centuries.

In one instant I look out of this painting and see Eben Scratch with a bullhorn in full agreement with the crowd. He's offering solutions to every perceived slight as best he knows how.

In the next instant, it's 1789 and Jacques de Flesselles, the Mayor of Paris, stands in the same place on the steps of a smaller, more modest Hôtel de Ville defending his actions before an altogether different mob that has the same complaints. Eben-Jacques, de Flesselles-Scratch, both men offer sincere solutions and I'm heartened by Eben's sincerity but history oscillates back to de Flesselles and the destination of such sincerity becomes obvious.

The crack of musket fire is followed by a shower of stone from a Hôtel de Ville column. Peering up over de Flesselles' falling body, I notice the absence of the words that greet visitors to every public building in France: "*Liberté - Egalité - Fraternité.*" These words hold a promise that someday we—the collective We, you, me, and all of humanity—can achieve liberty, equality, and fraternity, even as the course of revolution contradicts them.

My heart falls as the life ebbs from de Flesselles. No two oscillations are identical but adjacent swings of a pendulum are similar enough to give me fear for Eben's life. I grip the edges of this reality as though the frame of this painting were the side of a pool and try to pull myself up to the present.

Where I expect sepia-toned edges, I get that glass-edged green. The sky is no less blue, the crowd no less angry on this side. Where I expect the concerned tongue of my dedicated beagle, it is sound that baptizes me into this reality: loud, incoherent chanting followed by the swerving motion of this herd of humanity. No one lies on the stairs dying of a bullet wound. I take my first breath on this side of time and look above the entrance and those three words are back where they belong.

But the incoherence of this reality isn't merely of sound. Eben stands in the same place where de Flesselles stood. The solutions he proposes for the crowd's demands echo those of the long-dead Frenchman.

I push forward to shield Eben. Volodya, Fiona, and I have dedicated our waking hours to preparing for this instant. Somehow, some way, the lives of these people depend on Eben's survival. I work my way between two women whose voices are loud but lost in the incoherence of the crowd. They respond to my jostling with sharp elbows. I hit the ground on my tailbone. A man steps on my hand, another trips on my neck, a third straddles me for an instant before losing his balance. He lands on my chest. Gasping for air, I manage to twist onto my hands and knees and crawl toward Eben.

A voice carries over the crowd: "*C'est le* techie *batard*, Scratch." And then the rabble of the crowd condenses into a single coherent chant: "*Apportez-nous la guillotine.*"

I discover advantages to locomotion through the crowd on my hands and knees: I'm all but immune to falling down. Second, it's easier to decipher a path to my destination, but this advantage is rather contradicted by the leading drawback: I can't see my destination.

A group of men stand together. One of these men turns about and drops to the ground.

I am face-to-face with Eben Scratch.

I catch myself expecting him to appear pathetic, the soft rich techie overcome by street-hardened scalawags; a prejudice immediately dispelled by the look of calculating calm on his face. Hardly a veneer in this situation, he neither frowns nor whines as he angles to liberate himself. A look of mild surprise crosses his face as our eyes meet, but then he is lifted above me.

I stand in the space he vacated. One of the men punches Eben in the nose and then the mouth. A man to the side rams his picket sign into Eben's ear. Blood seeps from every impact.

Three men heft Eben onto their shoulders and launch him into the crowd. He lands at the bottom of the stairs. Another man kicks him. Someone pulls him up. Two others lift and then throw him onto the shoulders of people standing in the plaza those few steps below.

The combination of chants requesting access to a guillotine and Eben being thrown about the crowd like a beach ball in hell generates a feeling of horror that blankets my every sense.

The crowd thins about me. A stab of loneliness penetrates my heart—where is Winter?

39. Broken Promises

Fiona needs help and she hates needing help. She holds the vial in front of Allison. "You want some of this?"

Allison swipes at it but Fiona pulls it away. "You said I could have it. I listened to Eben's confession. I shared the poem. You promised."

"I'm going to lay it out for you and then you'll either get a line and do what I ask or you won't."

Allison starts for the vial. Fiona flicks her cane and tears a gap in Allison's black dress.

"Okay! Okay! I'll do it, whatever, I'll do it."

"You want to spend your life trying to hide from Volodya and me?"

"Oh shit, I forgot about that asshole."

"Forgetting Volodya can be dangerous."

Allison's dress is slick with sweat and she can barely maintain her balance.

"It's all about the FU money for you, right?"

Allison nods, her eyes fixed on the vial.

"Can you admit that you have an all consuming passion for Eben Scratch?"

"I admit it. I hate him with every cell in my body."

"I watched you make love to Eben last night."

"How could you?" Allison asks but understanding dawns immediately. "You hacked his Glass."

Fiona looks at her watch. She's not sure how much farther she can walk, and once she gets there what use will she be? She taps a tiny amount of the chopped up brown nugget onto the table.

"Fiona, I need more than that. Please." She takes the rolled up Euro note and whiffs up the powder.

"There are two ways you can get your FU money," Fiona says. "You can wait for him to die and get it from the dead man's switch, or you can ask him for it."

"Ask Eben Scratch for money? Are you kidding me?"

"He put it in a special account. He'll give it to you if you ask." Another glance at her watch, she taps her earbug. "Volodya? What's happening?"

"Hit link on Eben's timeline and see for yourself. Is bad." She can hear the sound of protestors in the background.

Fiona takes out her phone and hits the link. A streaming video comes up. She holds the phone so that Allison can see it. Eben is bleeding from his nose, mouth, and ears. He disappears for a second and then people lift him up and pass him over their heads, throwing him across the crowd, hitting him, taking his shoes, tearing at his clothes. Fiona sees a man in a rumpled gray suit rise in the gap Eben just vacated—Simon. "Bloody fuckin' hell."

Allison's eyes open wide, a vein pulses in her neck. "Where is that happening?"

"About a mile from here, are you coming?"

"Give me more junk or I can't function. I need shoes too."

"Will you help me rescue him? I promise he'll give you your FU money."

Allison jerks the vial out of Fiona's hand. "You haven't kept a promise all day." She dumps the powder on the table and inhales it.

"Allison, please help me."

40. Volodya's Choice

Volodya moves through rowdy protests to outraged demonstrations and into the riot at Place de l'Hôtel de Ville. He passes an overturned police car just as it bursts into flame. The combination of expanding heat and escaping vandals push him to the fountains. Coordinated jets of water shoot straight up and fall into elevated shallow pools bordered by a narrow patch of grass where dozens of people take cool refuge.

All this time he has expected the timeweave to converge during the vaunted meeting of old and new money, but it didn't. The probabilities fluctuated high and low until Eben took the bullhorn. Something happened at that instant and it eats at Volodya's mind.

He leapt away from his workstation the instant that Eben was thrown into the crowd, but what drew Volodya away from timeweave analyses was seeing Simon at the center of another historic turning point. Volodya doesn't believe that Simon experiences the flux of possible realities at these pivotal instants, but he knows that Simon has witnessed every abrupt change in the course of history since they met in 1983 and that the experiences throw Simon into his fits. He also knows that during his episodes Simon could hardly be more vulnerable.

Volodya pushes his way through the crowd along the fountain's edge. A mime steps onto the side of the fountain and police fill the gap, blocking him. The mime wears white makeup, a black jumpsuit, and a bowler hat. She carves a peace sign in the sky over the police and mimes a few tears. A man with a long wet beard in the fountain splashes her. Now dripping with water, the mime removes her hat and takes a bow. A *Gendarme's* truncheon comes down on her lowered head. She crashes to Volodya's feet. Another officer pushes back the crowd, making space for Volodya to pull the mime to the far side of the fountain where she's safe from the riot, at least for this moment.

Volodya pushes into the crowd. He steps past a gang of rioters beating a police officer. A team of *Gendarmes* push their way in and grab the rioters' wrists and wrap them in plastic cable-tie handcuffs. A cop grabs Volodya's wrist. Volodya pulls him forward, drops to the ground, and flips the cop onto his back. Two rifles are leveled at Volodya but rioters move between them. One grabs the bundle of cable-tie handcuffs.

Volodya sees Eben being thrown about the crowd on the far side of the plaza as though the protest is a massive mosh pit. He can't tell if Eben is conscious, but he's been severely beaten.

Volodya stops. He knows that Eben is the key. The analysis never found the butterfly wings that describe what Eben must do, but the vast body of relationships, causes, effects, and correlations through history has conspired to bring civilization to this cliff. Volodya knows that he must rescue Eben. He must, but he won't, not while Simon is in danger.

41. Justice

I'm curled on the ground by the pedestal on which the Science statue is mounted. I hear a gunshot and don't know whether I'm here and now or there and then.

People pass. Their shadows jitter in different directions. Then I hear it: like a giant sword pulled from a scabbard, but this mechanism throws the blade straight down. A single wail emerges above that sound, an expression of outrage that grows louder as the sword leaves its scabbard. The scream comes to an abrupt stop in the instant that the blade comes to rest at the base of Joseph-Ignace Guillotin's mechanical marvel. The crowd unleashes a pent up gasp as though they can't reconcile their demand with its delivery.

I step out from behind the Science statue. I look above the entrance and see that the promise of civilization embodied in those three words has not yet been posted. Men in blue coats and bicorne hats holding muskets with bayonets guide a column of 97 people toward the mechanism. The blade is raised and set. Another guilty soul—guilty of wealth or association with wealth, guilty of insufficient enthusiasm for revolution or enthusiasm for revolution of the wrong sort, guilty of hoarding food or inappropriate faith—the specifics of their guilt are lost in the rush to purify.

A judge inside l'Hôtel de Ville convicts another 17 people and sentences them to death in a span of 11 minutes. Seventeen tried as one with no right to representation, no right to face their accusers, no right to call a witness, not even the right to testify in their own defense, just the right to a speedy justice-free trial followed by a quick painless death, the only mercy this court grants. The 17 are shoved through the doors, their ankles chained together, guided by three remorseless men.

The blade falls and the guillotine queue is reduced to 96. The three guards of the 17 freshly condemned come together; they motion at the line of 96 and when they separate, they pull their 17 away from the guillotine to the Seine and align them on the stone wall above the river.

Another scream accompanies another fall of that blade and the queue is reduced to 95. The screaming has faded from outraged to pathetic.

Down by the river, a guard steps to the condemned man at

the end of the row of 17. He pauses for an instant to roll up a sleeve, the routine adjustment of a laborer at work, and then drives his palm into the chest of the condemned man. The man falls over the embankment. When his ankle leaves the ground the chain yanks the ankle of the next person in the row: a woman wearing thick lace skirts tumbles over and the chain around her ankle pulls another person: a man dressed in rags. I'm struck as much by the *egalité* of the executions as by their lack of *fraternité*.

I hear the first splash and step toward the river as though I have the authority to alter history. That step pulls me into a flux of presents. Green panes strobe through me like a temporal wind, each accompanied by a unique sense of dread or hope, contentment or fear.

Rioters step in and out of their own shadows. The protesters, the strikers, and the police, merge into and out of an incoherent form. An image of Eben on the steps with the bullhorn vaporizes and then condenses into his unconscious form being kicked over and over. No one can survive that onslaught. I clench my eyes shut and move in another direction. Closing my eyes doesn't blind me to the green shifts.

A threadbare instant of peace passes over me. This paradise is as thin as the edges that bind it, edges of forest-green, dark like leaded glass, thin and clear like a knife's edge, and beautiful: A reality that promises my return to a world where there's time and space for complaining but not much to complain about.

It passes and I tumble into another world of dread. I scan the horizon and catch an aura of that fine green edge moving away. If I can just wedge myself onto that timeline! I chase it and stumble over something that snarls and barks at me. My wrist hits the ground first and gives more than it should. The dog I fell over scrambles away and as I watch him go, I surface from a pool of dread into a world of horror.

The plaza is quiet here. Still packed, these people have surpassed anger and outrage and sunk into resignation. Piles of filth outline trails among the hovels and bodies covering Place de l'Hôtel de Ville. The street is congested with exhausted people trudging in every direction. A long aerodynamic car cruises through the center of the street, heedless of the lesser traffic. It crushes a woman and her three children fall in front of me. The car has no driver; a single passenger sits in the back seat wearing a headset and typing at a computer.

If only I can find Winter. Surely the elements won't deny me my best friend. And at the thought of friends I wonder what has become of Volodya and Fiona. I wonder about Gwinnie and her daughter, who should have been my daughter but isn't. I search for answers and see it again: that forest-green edge taunting me like a balloon in the wind. It floats past the ruins of Hôtel de Ville. I see the three words over the entrance and wonder at the irony of promises.

The lack of continuity from the meeting of old and new money to the enraged riots to this horror implies that I'm a long distance from home, a long time from now. I pass among the starving, the wasted, the diseased, the dying, the wretched occupants of this ruined Paris. I search for that edge, the only hope that Paris is not doomed to collapse once every century.

I tumble to the ground, this time rolling to the side to avoid hitting my wrist. People stumble over me. I cradle my wounded limb and then a pair of strong hands reach under my arms and pull me up. There's something familiar about this action, familiar the way that rising from your favorite chair is familiar.

Now standing, I look over the crowd and watch that forest-green edge drift out over the river downstream and away where I can't hope to reach it.

I turn to the man who helped me up: Volodya.

42. Eben's Descent

Volodya holds Simon by his shoulders, rotates him around, and looks in his eyes: pupils dilated and dancing in different directions. An instant of recognition passes and Volodya sees that his friend is experiencing his unique form of seizure; "episode" is the polite term. He guides Simon out of the plaza. Simon points at the river and yells gibberish involving floating green forests of calm and the doom of Paris. Winter's leash drags behind him.

They make it across the plaza to the Pont d'Arcole, the bridge that connects the right bank of Paris to the island in the center of the Seine. He sets Simon on a bench overlooking the river and steps back. Simon's calmer now, coming out of it, hopefully. If Winter can find him, he'll be all right.

Volodya sees Eben restrained by a group of men at the edge of the plaza near the river. Volodya rushes back into the fray. He fights judiciously, economically, a jab here, rush past, shove there, until he's up against the men holding Eben. Eben's hands and feet are tied with plastic handcuffs, but he's conscious. Blood has crusted over his nose and lips. The men scream at him, and he looks back, silent.

If Volodya hadn't met the cool version of Eben escaping Durango, he'd think the man had been beaten into submission. Eben's alert enough, he just seems aware that there's nothing he can say that will help, so he says nothing.

At the instant Volodya gets his attention, the men heft Eben onto their shoulders and throw him over the edge onto Voie Georges Pompidou, a street 20 feet below them that borders the river. Traffic is held up by strikers. Eben falls silently until he lands on the roof of a sedan. The complaint of folding sheet metal combines with his groan. He rolls off the car and onto the street.

Volodya hits the closest man with a forearm to the head, gains a few feet of clearance and leaps down to the street. The men who dumped Eben follow Volodya like water over a fall, bashing the cars as they land.

Volodya gets to Eben first. With his ankles and wrists constrained by cable-tie cuffs, Eben couldn't brace for the impact. He's unconscious now and his hair is matted in blood that oozes from his ear, skull, and nose. Volodya puts him over his shoulder and tries to sprint between cars down the street, but the rioters catch him. They pull Eben away, rush to the side of the road, and throw him into the river.

Volodya rams the palm of his hand into the nose of the rioter closest to him, turns and punches the other in the gut. Blood pours from the one and both of them fall to their knees. A fourth arrives and kicks Volodya in the back. He hits the railing.

He scrambles to a pylon where he positions himself in the corner, back to the river. From here, no one can get behind him. He's a whirlwind of punches and kicks but they outnumber him eight to one.

Volodya concentrates on maintaining a gap between himself and his assailants. He tries to reduce the tempo of the battle to conserve his strength. He's twice the age of these men. He grabs the smallest of his attackers, a bald man about Simon's size, twists him around and tries to use him as a shield.

He says, "I am not your enemy." But the small man rams an elbow into Volodya's solar plexus. He can't breath, he can't punch, and he can't talk. He lets himself fall to the ground and wraps his arms over his head. One man kicks him in the shoulder. Another kicks him in the face but hits Volodya's arms. The impact slams his head against the pylon and the world goes dark.

* * *

The blast of cold water rouses Eben on impact. He holds his breath by intuition born of childhood summers spent playing Marco Polo. He sinks but knows that he'll float back up. He can't kick or paddle so he waits, holding that breath, at once confident in his own buoyancy and aware that panic will kill him.

Still sinking, he scans his body for injuries. The beating from the crowd caused a host of superficial bruises, maybe even some minor fractures, but falling 20 feet and hitting that car might have done real damage. Right now he feels alert; if he's concussed the damage hasn't set in yet.

His descent finally reverses. He floats upward, his lungs cry for another breath. He wiggles like a dolphin to push his mouth above the surface and sucks in half a breath of air before submerging again. He fights the panic by trying to convince himself that he's getting the hang of swimming like a dolphin. He manages to push himself above the surface and pulls in a trace of air, just enough to realize that he's exhausting himself. With his wrists and ankles tied, all he can do is hope that his buoyancy will take him to the surface and let him breathe before reflex takes over and he fills his lungs with water.

Every instinct begs him to panic. He tries to relax as he sinks, but he knows that he's drowning.

43. Allison's Fate

Allison scans the crowded Place de l'Hôtel de Ville. She sprints to the bridge. Five minutes have passed since she saw Eben being thrown through the crowd. Now there are dozens of crowd surfers, but they're laughing. Eben wasn't laughing.

Eben was getting beat to shit. She can't shake the feeling that she's being ripped off again. She feels the familiar outrage of injustice rise up her spine.

The bridge is packed with people, too. She pushes her way to the side. The chaos that fills the streets of Paris overflows into every alley, store, and sidewalk. People start jumping into the river.

Her opiated calm slows her vision and lets her focus. No hurry, no rush, just watch. She scans the plaza from its grand entrance to the fountains. Back and forth. Movement draws her attention to the street that runs between the river and Hôtel de Ville. Blue and white stripes grab her attention in time to see Eben fall into the river. A thought crosses her mind, "So much for his lucky shirt."

She watches him sink into the murky green and brown water. He doesn't struggle, doesn't kick or thrash, and he doesn't swim.

Eben is dying. The thought lingers as the colors of his shirt fade below the surface. She sees the stripes rise back up until he's bobbing, belly up like a dead fish drifting downstream.

She steps away from the railing. Others crowd in front of her, oblivious.

Allison has spent the last two years in a state of not-quite hopelessness, always a little bit left in the well, some sense that maybe her life wasn't as hopeless as it seemed. Even in the worst of times she called her aunt every week and told rosy lies about a life she didn't lead. She had a sense that if she could hang on long enough, everything would come out okay. It's the only reason she hasn't killed herself. Numb the pain long enough and you just never know, maybe it will go away. But now.

She begins the long slow walk to she doesn't know where. The thought of her FU money makes her queasy.

And then something inside her shifts.

Eben once called her a quitter and said that she blames everyone else for her own failures. Nothing anyone has ever said made her more angry.

The comforting blanket of doom falls from her shoulders.

Allison turns back to the river.

Allison grew up on Southern California beaches. Her dad taught her to surf within days of taking her first steps. She prefers water to land. It's easier to move in water, softer, calmer.

She pushes her way back to the rail. More people have jumped in. They're splashing and playing. She watches the spot below the street where Eben was thrown in, gauges the current, and guesses how far he should have drifted. He could be right under the bridge now, or even on the other side. She leans over the railing and sees blue and white stripes drifting below the surface.

Allison dives off the bridge. She slices into the water without a splash and pulls herself deeper until she touches the mud bottom. She turns and faces upward. Rays of sunlight penetrate through the water like sunbeams in a thick dusty room on a hot summer afternoon. She can't see farther than a foot to either side, but upward, she can see to the surface. She scissor-kicks horizontally, scanning the surface from the bottom. She passes under swimmers, easily identified by the sounds of splashing and bubble-scattered light.

And then she sees Eben's shirt. Her heart rises to her throat. She swims to him as fast she can, her buoyancy helping her gain momentum. She grabs his torso from behind. His head bounces against her shoulder.

They break the surface and Allison sucks in air. Eben doesn't cough, doesn't breathe. His head lolls against hers. His eyes are closed and she invests meaning in that. Surely if he were dead they'd be open, wouldn't they? He's just unconscious, just needs to breathe.

She positions him on his back, facing away from her with one arm across his chest in the rescue position she learned from watching Mission Beach lifeguards pull tourists out of rip currents. She kicks and swims. Exhaustion starts to overwhelm her desperation. Swimming is second nature, but the respiratory inhibiting qualities of heroin suck energy away. She piles blame on herself. She's a junkie, a quitter, a failure, and now she can't even rescue the only person she ever loved.

She kisses his neck and holds his head close to hers. She wonders how long he's been without a breath and tries to add up the minutes. She swears a thousand oaths, makes a million contracts with God. A whitecap kicks up behind them and imprints the ThievesWorld sign for hope onto her irises. She treads, lets the current carry them, and pulls his mouth to hers.

Kicking toward the bank of the river, she puts her hand under his back, twisting his shirt into a knot. She punches the center of his chest with her other hand. Every surfer at her school learned CPR, but she's never used it. All she remembers is thirty to one and to hit hard. She hits him again; it's hard to get leverage, hard to breath. She hits him again and again, after every thirty, she blows into his mouth. They drift against a stone wall covered in algae.

She gives up the CPR for the seconds it takes to work her way to one of the stairways that leads up to the Île de la Cité. She's been administering CPR for 300 counts, at least three minutes. She pulls him onto the concrete steps. With his back on level stone, she leans over, wraps her hands together in a double fist and pummels him between his breasts with all her weight. And again. Again.

44. Spring was an Irish Setter

I feel like I've fallen into the timeline of a river party. Having grown up along the banks of the Russian River, I'm an experienced river partier, well, an experienced observer of river parties. When the other kids played in the river, my friend Spring, the Irish setter who shared my boyhood, would swim with me. She looked so graceful with her proud muzzle held well above the surface. Her ears each had their own small wake. We used to let the current carry us all the way to the sea where Spring's poise prevented her from engaging with the harbor seals and elephant seals that guard that magic place where—

Is that Allison?

A woman not more than 14 feet from me dives into the water. I rise from a bench and realize I have no memory of sitting at this bench. This realization unleashes a flood: how long have I been away? Am I here and now? I remember Volodya—where is he? And then one realization works its way to the top: Where is Winter?

I look under the bench, between the legs of the protestors, a large minority of whom have progressed from rage to joy. I push the dread into a cabinet: no cars moving on the streets to hurt him, the crowd is thick, French people like dogs. Winter will find me. Now I can resume the task at hand. But as I rise to this task, rise in the sense of standing and peering over the side of the bridge in the direction of Allison's dive, I see the narrow forest-green edge of that hopeful future drift farther downstream. Rising into the window framed by that edge, a dead salmon in blue and white stripes rises to the surface immediately followed by Allison.

It's a decision that hardly merits consideration. The possible repercussions are too dense for me to parameterize my own well being into the equation. I must pull the world onto that hopeful timeline. I must rescue Eben from Allison!

I drop my satchel to the side of the bench, remove my coat, and jump off the bridge.

The water is cool and deep and dirty as a city river ought to be. Wishing I'd left them on the bridge but aware that I can hardly swim while wearing them, I kick off my shoes. I'm not certain of the direction in which I saw Eben and Allison. I tread water as well as I can with this injured, limp wrist and search for that forest-green boundary. A frolicking rioter splashes past me and I catch a glimpse of it, unless it's just the greenish tinge of water as my eyes go below the surface. My suit tugs me downward so I disengage my belt and let my pants float away. It's much easier to kick now. I consider removing my shirt but it occurs to me that I haven't applied sunscreen. Instead, I straighten my tie and tuck my wrinkle-free shirt into my boxer shorts. Far more comfortable now, I begin a systematic search for Eben and Allison. I define a grid that flows with the current and swim.

I see something moving upstream toward me. It appears to be an oscillating black stick with a white tip. It's preceded by a shiny black rock that seems to be towing two brown handkerchiefs.

No! That's not a rock. Those aren't hankies. It's not a stick. It's a nose, ears, and a tail—Winter has found me!

He barks even as he swims. The tail oscillates faster and the little face emits a long tongue. Winter swims with none of the grace of Spring, his is a more aggressive stroke. Very Winter-like, he's always on a mission unless he's late for a nap. He greets me with a kiss, a pant, and a bark.

The current pulls us under the bridge and into the shade. Winter seizes my necktie and pulls me. I point to one of the stairways that lead down from the Île de la Cité. The closest such stairway is occupied by a man and woman who seem to be engaged in some sort of either sexual or violent act.

I hate to interrupt them but the next such stairway looks to be about 150 meters farther away.

"Really, you can let go," I say, but Winter won't and even though we keep getting tangled we work our way to the bank and the stairway embedded in it.

And it's a good thing because they are not engaged in a sexual act. It is Allison and she is beating the living shit out of a prostrate and defenseless Eben—though it could be that she is beating the dead shit out of him.

"Let him live," I yell. "He loves you!" I grab the stone outcropping of the stairway. Eben's legs lie in the water next to me. Allison is mounted over him, brutally pummeling his chest. Winter manages to work his way onto the step between Eben's legs.

Now with his feet on solid ground, Winter exerts a quite surprising measure of force on my tie. He growls and shakes his head side-to-side, a motion that tightens my half-Windsor knot. I continue to implore Allison to stop, but with my neck constrained, my voice merely squeaks in protest.

She hits him again, letting loose an oomph. Her cheeks are red, her jaw set in determination that I've never seen her display. And again, bang!

"Allison, please, stop," I squeak. But I can barely make out my own words here on this side of my mouth. She glances at me and I see her eyes. There's no malevolence. I see determination and fear. "Allison, he can't hurt you, he's not even conscious." My squeaking confuses her.

My tie finally gives. Winter falls back against the next step and then tumbles into the path of Allison's two handed fist. I lose my purchase on the stairs and have to swim back.

Winter yelps like a dog in the ring with a kangaroo. Allison pushes him aside, leans down and puts her mouth over Eben's.

"Allison, stop! One minute you're killing him the next you're kissing him—really, madam, decide your intentions."

Just as it occurs to me that I may have misjudged Allison's intent, Eben coughs. His chest spasms and he gags. Winter runs up the stairs. Allison pulls away but not fast enough to avoid the fountain of river-vomit that gushes from Eben's mouth. She doesn't appear to care.

I'm back on the stairs now, my feet on the fifth step below water, my arms and chest at Eben's level. Allison dismounts and I help her roll Eben onto his side.

He vomits again, mostly water, a remnant of a tea cookie he must have had at the meeting. It comes to mind that I was never offered a cookie. And again; this time eggs and blood—no, that's ketchup. I can respect ketchup on eggs, but wonder if the chef would agree.

Eben looks up and around. He spews water straight at me, mostly water, anyway, a bit of toast and some other particulate matter covers the remains of my tie. I kick off the stairs to give him some space and then tread against the weak current.

"Allison," Eben says. He follows this declaration with a gasp and a cough, but his intention seems clear.

"We need a hospital," Allison says. "Can you stand?"

He coughs again and then a dry heave, well, with his proximity to the river, it's not really dry, but it's less than productive. And again, this time very nearly dry, which I appreciate, given that he's oriented straight at me. Our eyes meet. He struggles to pull his hands out from behind his back. He rolls over and stretches his legs out to me and croaks a string of syllables. He clears his throat and rasps, "Dr. Wentworth, grab my feet."

I do so and he pulls me back to the stairs. I see that his feet are tied together by plastic cable ties.

Kindly allow me to confess that this action wins me over beyond any other that I've witnessed in the twenty-five days of his progression from greedy bastard to decent-enough fellow. The man lies nearly dead with the woman he loves more than life itself. Until this moment this woman has demonstrated nothing but loathing for him. She has just saved his life and his first thought is to help me. Allow me an observation on top of this confession: Eben Scratch is many things, several of them rotten, but he is most certainly a gentleman.

I thank him and he waves it off, turns to Allison and says, "Kacgrglglglrgle." And then resumes coughing.

Allison pulls him onto his hands and knees.

"Short, shallow breaths," I suggest. "There's water in your lungs, try not to agitate it."

He nods and exerts the self-discipline required to heed my advice. He slowly recovers.

Allison hovers over him, rubbing his back, occasionally hugging him. She pulls her hair to the side and presses her lips against his neck, and then whispers in his ear.

Allison cries. Winter barks. Eben retches. Allison says, "Find an ambulance."

I'm wearing nothing but a torn tie and a vomit-stained white shirt that's tucked into my boxer shorts. Were it not for the fact that these particular boxers are navy blue and decorated with pink pigs, I suspect I'd be too self conscious to emerge from the river. Dripping, I work my way up two steps where my foot encounters quite a sharp pebble.

A cluster of observers has gathered at the top of the stairs. "Please help us get an ambulance."

A middle aged woman in a jaunty hat says something in French that sounds affirmative and she steps away with purpose. A man in pleated shorts and a flowered shirt says, "Everyone's on strike but the people selling T-shirts and key chains, mate, faster to walk." The Aussie accent brings to mind Fiona. My hand goes automatically to my ear, but my earbug is gone. I also notice that through the entire ordeal, Winter's leash has remained around my wrist.

The Aussie fellow offers me a Swiss army knife and says, "He won't get far with his feet tied up."

I step back down the stairs, re-encounter the sharp pebble, try not to trip over Winter, and lean down to cut the tie on his ankles. I try the tiny scissors first, notice that the toothpick is missing, but the tweezers are still there—

"Use the fucking blade, you bloody idiot!" The Aussie fellow says. Some accents just don't give themselves to malice. Where Volodya can wish you a good morning in a way that feels disparaging, from the Aussie, this exclamation feels more like gentle advice.

The blade cuts right through. I cut the binds on his wrists, too.

Eben hacks again, this time bringing up some more of the Seine. We steady him and the three of us climb the stairs. At the top Eben bends over and hacks up more river.

I return the Swiss army knife and then attach Winter's leash.

The woman in the jaunty hat reappears and informs us in the most delightful French accented English that a hospital is mere blocks away, but adds that the entire staff is on strike. She then reminds us that the roads are all blocked, the metro is not running, no busses, no taxis, that even the police can't get through.

Eben says that he can walk.

The woman says, "Where are you staying?"

Eben says, "The Ritz."

She seems less concerned now that she's aware of Eben's accommodations.

He says, "I think I can make it." He says this to Allison,

staring at her with eyes that resemble Winter's in their longing. He adds, "Please don't let go of me."

Allison kisses him on the lips.

Having been the target of his vomit, the vision repulses me. "Would you like a mint?"

They disengage and I repeat the suggestion and Eben asks for a bottle of water.

I reach for my wallet, but of course, it is in my coat which is on a bench on the Pont d'Arcole with my satchel. Allison hands me a wet twenty Euro note.

I pop into a souvenir shop, grab a bottle of water, a package of mints and ask the lady if I have enough money left over for a pair of shorts or pants and some flip-flops. She looks at me with the labored expression of someone whose occupation taxes her tolerance for the foibles of foreigners.

I emerge from the store wearing shorts that are, but for the seams, a perfect replica of the tri-color French flag. If I were to tattoo "*Liberté - Egalité - Fraternité*" above my waistband I'd be indistinguishable from a Government office.

Eben chews the mints, gargles the water, and the four of us begin walking. Allison and I support Eben between us. It's slow going through the crowd across the bridge. The Place de l'Hôtel de Ville is less crowded and less raucous now.

Winter tugs at his leash, his tail whips back and forth. On the bench where I left my coat and satchel sits Fiona. She appears content to watch us pass. She looks at once frustrated and pleased. We stop and Eben raises a hand to her. Fiona rises slowly with her cane and I see that she's not frustrated, she's exhausted. She's also laughing at me. She steps over, straightens what's left of my tie, and transfers my satchel from her shoulder to mine. I start to explain the situation but she informs us that she watched from here.

Fiona and Allison stare at each other. Eben retches again

but continues to take short breaths. Fiona puts her hands on Allison's cheeks and whispers something. Allison says, "Thank you" and Fiona hugs her.

Fiona says, "Right, let's get him to a doctor."

As we step away, Winter stays at the railing and whines like a forlorn lover. Following his gaze, I see a familiar figure in the river treading water against the algae-covered concrete wall.

Volodya waves back, but it's not the smooth dismissive motion that I expect from him.

"Fiona, we have to get Volodya!"

She launches into motion but staggers. Winter and I rush after her. I ask if she's all right and she says, "I'm fine" in a tone that indicates the opposite.

Volodya clings to the arced truss beneath the bridge at the abutment. I don't understand why he doesn't climb up to us.

Fiona leans over the rail but is well out of reach. "Simon," she says, "my hip has been grinding against this fucking fake leg all day, over ten miles, in ninety degree weather with a hundred percent humidity, stop fussing over me and help your friend!"

I look down and feel an essential tenet of faith collapse. I know it's unreasonable and unfair of me, but I seem to have built my world on the assumption that Volodya is immune to danger. The man I see below me looks beaten and old. Blood drips from one of his eyes. His left arm is tucked across his chest. His jaw lacks its familiar symmetry, his forehead has acquired a lump, and he struggles to hold onto the side of the steel truss.

He looks up and squints into the sun. My heart rises to my throat as I see an unfamiliar expression form across his face. His cheeks rise and he starts to shudder.

I gasp and turn to Fiona. "He's having a seizure."

"No, Simon, he's laughing at you."

"He's what?"

I lean over, reaching down to my dear friend, and he says, "Simon, it is too much for me. I have cracked rib, concussion, my jaw is not good. There you stand in torn tie and absurd shorts. It hurts for me to laugh. Please, step back."

Fiona and I lean over the railing. He's out of reach. Volodya insists that he can pull himself up and out but requires a few minutes more to collect himself. Fiona and I agree that this would be a mistake. I shall jump into the river and push him up as Fiona pulls him out.

From the Pont above, Allison dives in head first. She swims around Volodya. He turns and raises a forearm to block her. Fiona tells him that it's okay. He looks wary, but allows Allison to help him climb onto the bank.

"Truly a Soviet-quality beating," he says, testing the mobility of each limb. "But I can walk."

With Winter taking the lead and Volodya between Fiona and me, the four of us meet up with Allison and Eben. We walk slowly through the riots of Paris.

VIII. The Death of Eben Scratch

I fairly strut like a cockerel across Paris in my tri-color shorts, but the confidence I portray fails to relieve the doubt that I've safely guided us, Us that is, onto that sharp-edged forest-green timeline.

Volodya walks beside me. He would be limping if his vanity were less stubborn. He says, "We must get to a computer."

Fiona interjects, "You're going to a hospital for X-rays."

"Fractures can go untreated for days, time to set reality on course could be seconds." He turns back to me. "Exhaust of pivot points is usually decisive."

I say, "The events certainly rhymed with history. Eben took on the role of Jacques de Flesselles and got a similar response from this era's third estate." The two of us exchange ideas for how things might be playing out. When I look up, we're on the periphery of Place Vendome. A police officer bars our way but across the plaza, a tall dark haired man in a suit emerges from the Ritz, Yao Wo of course.

Yao approaches the police with a smile as though they went to college together. The police shrug, but Yao soon has the two officers laughing. Yao raises his hands as though he's being arrested and one of the officers waves us forward.

Yao all but carries Eben into the Ritz lobby. Allison slows to a stop. She looks lost.

The lobby is quite stunning with peach marble columns and fireplace, a beige marble floor with crystal chandeliers, and rose-filled vases—had I not spent this morning inside l'Hotel de Ville, I'd be quite impressed. Fiona and Yao stand next to a woman wearing an exquisitely fitted navy blue Ritz uniform with a cute little hat discussing prospects for medical care. The woman's cheeks fill with air and she emits a puffing sound.

Volodya guides me to a couch. He takes my laptop from my satchel and brings up the timeweave; no future has resolved. He expands the timescale from days to weeks to months. He scowls and says, "We have a great deal of work to do."

Fiona appears in front of us with a woman who tells us that she has arranged transport to a nearby clinic. She motions for Eben and Volodya to come with her.

Volodya says, "Thank you, I am fine."

Fiona says, "Bollocks."

And I say, "We have work that cannot wait."

Allison helps Eben to his feet but rather than follow the Ritz official to the golf cart-like vehicle that waits outside the lobby doors, Eben approaches Yao, who stands to the side engrossed in a phone call.

Yao Wo's most obvious feature is his easy, warm smile. It is as though Yao's smile originates in his eyes, works its way down his torso, and opens his arms in an invitation to share his joy. After all of that, his lips turn up as though his delight can't be contained, but right now, Yao Wo is weeping.

Eben grips Yao's arm. Yao leans into him and pulls the phone from his ear. He looks at the phone as though he doesn't know what to do with it.

"What is it?" Eben says.

Yao swallows and grins. It is not a Yao Wo smile. It has nothing to do with his eyes or arms. He says, "Let's get you to the clinic, sir."

"Tell me what's wrong. I can help."

Yao's false smile disappears. He wipes his eyes and pinches

his nose. "Well, sir, it's my son, Tam. He threw the ball all the way to Buster Posey. But then he collapsed on the pitching mound." He takes an unsteady breath. "He got his wish." He leans over as though wilting and says, "There's nothing we can do. Nothing."

Eben pulls him into an embrace and says, "No, Yao, it is not over. We can do something, some—" his words disappear into a coughing fit. Yao straightens in such a way that he supports Eben.

"Let's get you to the clinic, sir," Yao says. "You can't help anyone until you've recovered."

45. Butterfly Wings

Volodya and I sit at the table in Eben's room at the Ritz. Volodya works at my laptop and I work at my tablet. He says, "Education, community, investment—all can have positive effect on EbenZones, but none of them prevent seemingly inevitable currency collapse."

I say, "Whether Eben and Allison stay together or break up—I don't' see anything that delivers us to that fine-edged reality of comparative peace and prosperity."

"Comparative?"

"Compared to a tyrant's rule, clash of strongmen, feudalism, oligarchy—this civilization that at least attempts justice." I work through a few more timelines. "Eben sells ScratchCo, gives away all his money, or acquires all banks ... no help."

Volodya stands and begins to pace with a limp. He takes the tablet from me and I move over to the laptop. We project more possibilities into the future: Allison takes over ScratchCo, Yao becomes executive, Eben and Allison have a child who becomes president, Rishi, Alejandro, and the other EbenZone Barons form a coalition to run their Eben Zones democratically, and on and on.

I say, "One might think that giving away a trillion dollars would be easy but—"

"Here it is." Volodya rises slowly, his fingers manipulating the tablet screen. He reaches up and engages his earbug so that Fiona can hear him speak. "Eben must save the life of Mr. Wo's son, Tam."

I pull this timeline out of the timeweave and examine it. "Tam Wo is the butterfly's wings."

We hear Fiona from the clinic through our earbugs. "What does Tam have to do with currency failure?"

Volodya says, "What do butterflies have to do with typhoons?"

"It's not Tam," I say. "It's Eben caring enough to save him."

"Right," Fiona says, "it has always pivoted on Eben's compassion."

Volodya has pulled up Tam's medical records. "It is a problem."

I scan through them too. "No wonder this timeline has such a low probability."

"Three stem cell transplants, chemotherapy, radiation treatments; they've tried everything."

"I don't see any results from the experimental treatment. Maybe this trial will work."

"The boy is going to die." Volodya sits back down, shaking his head.

"What if Eben tries?" Fiona says. "Is it enough for him to try even if he fails?"

"No." Volodya rubs his eyes. "If he fails, general strikes will lead to new French revolution. Germany invades Paris to maintain order in European Union and Russia invades Germany because, hmm, because Putin has no self control. And history oscillates back to dark age."

"Germany invades Paris? Again?" Fiona says. I detect a lilt to her voice. Now I hear it: she's laughing. Dear Fiona, she can laugh in the face of anything. "Every 70 years or so. It's like a cicada emerging to mate."

"The probability of this timeline is low," I say. "But it's not zero."

"What? Is a problem."

"No, no, don't you see? Somewhere in the data, our technology has determined that Tam can survive. The probability is small, nearly negligible, but it is larger than zero—possible, if not probable. And somehow Eben and Allison are involved in his survival."

46. Baggage

Eben can feel the rattling every time he takes a breath. The quick short breaths don't make him cough, but they're neither satisfying nor comforting.

He's in an examination room at a private clinic a few blocks from the Ritz. Yao and Fiona stand behind him. Allison looks shy, feeble, and miserable. Eben wants her back the way she was: strong and powerful, the woman who was his partner, who corrected him, who didn't just complete him but made him better. The fact that she jumped in that river and rescued him guarantees that she's still in there.

"I love you."

She looks away.

He adds, "And I trust you."

She shakes her head and, staring at the floor, releases his hand. "How can you?"

Eben says, "I owe you my life."

Allison and Eben are the same height so she doesn't so much look up at him as she looks at him with bent neck through her eyelashes. "I've acquired some baggage."

"We've both got baggage. I've got trillions of baggage."

The door opens and a small, pale man wearing a white lab coat who has short spiked black hair steps in. He listens to Eben's lungs, mostly to his coughing.

"The Seine, she is more bacteria than water. You will maybe have pneumonia even with intense schedule of antibiotics." He takes two syringes from a drawer along with two cylinders of light blue fluid. He fills both syringes, sets one aside. "I apologize in advance, the nurses are on strike, of course, and I don't usually perform injections. You will bend over to provide the target?"

Eben turns to his entourage. "Would you mind if I had some privacy?"

Fiona steps out the door and holds it for the others. Yao hesitates as though uncertain of his obligations but walks out, too.

"I'm staying," Allison says.

A few minutes later, Eben leaves the clinic with two bandages on his rump, a fourteen day schedule of oral antibiotics, and an inhaler.

47. The Feedback Problem

"He'll listen to us now," I say.

Volodya shakes his head. "No. We cannot tell him, would cause feedback problem."

The feedback problem has to do with the way we're influenced by information. If you believe that something is going to happen, your behavior is affected. Knowledge of your timeline alters your timeweave in ways that our technology can't project. The feedback problem is the reason that it's pointless for us to calculate our own timeweaves.

"Tam could die in the hours required for Eben to figure it out himself."

He scratches the back of his skull. "Fascinating question: Do we surrender predictive ability to maybe save hours but also maybe destroy chances? Or retain ability to analyze but decrease chances?"

Volodya makes a nearly Parisian-quality shrug as he settles in front of the laptop and unleashes internet spiders to assemble data related to Tam's disease, treatments, and especially correlations with his genome.

The others enter the room a few minutes later. Eben looks exhausted, sick, and happier than I've ever seen him. Allison stays at his side. She looks almost demur, which is simply not her way. Eben indicates the table where Volodya and I have set up and says, "Could we please use the table, I'd like to have a meeting."

Volodya grumbles but carries the laptop to a couch. I stay at the table. Fiona sits next to me with Yao on her other side. Eben remains standing between Yao and Allison. He asks for ideas about how to alter the microloan terms, ways to capitalize on shifting currencies, and the conditions he wants to create that can enable people to solve big problems.

I feed my notes into the timeweave engine. Volodya and I have already tried most of these options. None of them replicate the butterfly wings of Tam's survival.

Allison's strong opinions push her out of that uncharacteristically docile state. She argues that no one, rich or poor, can innovate without essential necessities like food, shelter, healthcare, and companionship. Eben takes the bait and argues that stress is the best motivator. Allison laughs at him and says, "You've made damn sure that they're hungry and stressed, and they haven't solved jack." Eben replies, "I love you." And I find myself wondering about this Jack fellow.

Volodya clears his throat and headlines appear on my tablet screen. The Guardian's homepage: "Trillionaire Suggests Strikers Eat Cake." New York Times: "Trillionaire Offends Third Estate—Again." Le Monde: *Idiot Techie Tombe en Seine et se Noie*." And the Wall Street Journal: "Strikers Defy Scratch." I find nothing surprising about the media's understanding of events but something about it resonates in my mind.

My tablet barks. One of our spiders has found results of the experimental trial that the Wos couldn't afford: twenty-seven of the 40 subjects died and the trial was cancelled.

I look across Fiona at Yao and see him staring at his hands. It's not my place to say anything, so I don't. Fiona follows my line of sight and takes Yao's hand. Her motion draws Eben and Allison's attention.

Eben puts an arm around him and says, "There must be something I can do. Anything, please. I have a lot of money."

Allison says, "Money doesn't solve every problem."

Yao attempts to speak but doesn't.

Eben's voice softens. "I'm so sorry, Yao."

"Of course, sir," Yao says. "You've solved many problems with money, it's only natural that you would think that ..." his words lose coherence and he stops speaking.

The door of understanding on whose threshold I've been standing opens. I speak without a trace of irony, sympathy, or compassion: "What's the point, Eben? It's not your field. There's nothing you can do. You're not a doctor or a researcher—you write finance apps."

Allison glares at me. I fear for my well being until the light of understanding dawns in Eben's eyes.

Fiona stifles her outrage but catches my gaze and won't relinquish it until I wink at her.

Eben coughs.

Allison looks at me for three seconds and then she looks at

Eben. They make eye contact. I don't know what message they share but I dare say that I've never seen two people so possessed by an idea.

48. Return of Husker Scratch

Allison slides out from under Eben. He rolls onto his pillow and sighs. She goes into the bathroom and steps into a steaming shower. She rubs soap suds across herself and thinks about the man in the other room. She did not see this coming. In no dream, fantasy, or even desire, did she see this coming. It feels so good that it makes her suspicious. If she weren't less than an hour from needing a fix she wouldn't believe it was real. She towels off, combs her hair, sprays a hint of the honeysuckle perfume Eben bought her yesterday, and dresses in the clothes they got on the same shopping trip.

Eben sits at the table in a Ritz robe with his laptop. A room service tray has a teapot with white bone china cups and saucers. He pours her a cup of tea. She doesn't mention that she switched back to coffee shortly after they split up. She sits next to him and he puts his arm around her and kisses her cheek.

She reads the email that he's just composed: a note to seven ScratchCo programmers assigning them roles in the Blood-Cancer-BigData Project.

"With you and me," Eben says, "along with Fiona, Simon, Volodya, and my software scrum, we might have the world's strongest data analytics team. We'll give Tam a chance."

Allison opens the laptop Eben bought her yesterday and searches through the ScratchCo system until she finds one of TLA's spiders. She drops the firewall.

"Excuse me," Eben says, "what are you doing to my security?"

"Yours?"

"Well, no, ours, I'm sorry. But why are you …"

It feels like a test. "Do I know what I'm doing?"

He hunches into that familiar and annoying posture.

She tries to reign in her anger. "Do you trust me?"

"Of course, but—"

"Good." Self control in the face of her need makes it hard not to lash out.

She works into the electronic health records at UCSF and whips out a program that automatically funnels any data related to leukemia treatment onto ScratchCo disks. Feeling him watching her and suspecting his thoughts, she says, "No point in configuring a database until we know what the data looks like."

"I've already sketched one out." He says and stands behind her. He rubs her shoulders as though she's a boxer between rounds. "You did that in five minutes—amazing."

"You never should have fired me."

"I didn't fire you, you dumped me!"

"Ha," she says, "I'm baaaaack." She scrolls through Tam's records. "Where's that database shell?"

He manipulates her mouse to a folder and opens the database. She begins the tedious task of configuring it.

"Are you okay?" Eben says. "Do you have a fever?"

"No. I'm fine."

"Let someone else assign the data fields, just do the fun part."

She shudders. "Eben, I need to find Fiona, she has something I need." She stands and steps to the door but pauses and steps back as though she can't decide what to do.

"What is it?" Eben says. "I'll have room service bring it up." He leaps out of his chair and tries to hug her but she shakes him off. He says, "Is it something I said? I'm sorry, Allison. I'm such an idiot. Please don't go, what can I do?"

She steps out the door.

Eben says, "Will you come back?"

The nausea has been building and now she feels sweat dripping down her back. "Yes, I'll be back as soon as I can. I just have to—" she steps back in and closes the door but clings to it. "Eben, I'm an addict and I need a fix. Fiona has my stuff."

"You have to get off of it. The longer you take it the worse it will be."

"You're telling me?"

"I can help."

"I don't want you to see me go through it."

"We can camp out right here. I'll hire a doctor to guide you through it. We'll use room service to provide what we need and just ride it out until you're clean."

"I can't help Tam if I'm in withdrawal." She opens the door again. "And neither can you. I'm going to find Fiona." She pushes him away and steps out the door.

* * *

Eben paces about the room. He sees Allison walking away from the Place Vendome through the window and calls Fiona.

Fiona says, "She already used all the drugs she had."

"Then she's looking for a pusher?"

"She's knows how to get what she needs."

"It's too dangerous."

"Eben, you have to trust her."

"Even with this?" he says. "Trust is difficult."

He returns to his computer and watches Tam's records expand faster than he thought possible. Details are being loaded from Stanford Cancer Center, MD Anderson, The Mayo Clinic, UCLA Medical Center, Boston General, and the list keeps expanding. Another data pipe opens and starts pouring in seemingly irrelevant data from grocery stores, fitness centers, medical and life insurance records. He switches back to the medical data and sees that it's grown by a factor of ten and now includes the fitness device data of a hundred thousand leukemia survivors. In the time it takes for him to see the list, the database has grown another factor of ten.

A message appears on his screen from Volodya: "Your network is too slow" along with a username and temporary password to access a database within TLA systems.

By the time he finishes, he'll have every possible correlation between treatments and patients, survivors and the dead, whether they were treated or not. They'll be able to build personalized biochemical models for Tam Wo, his cancer, and everyone else who has been diagnosed with Leukemia in the last decade.

He finds himself pacing again. She's been gone for two hours. The helplessness feels like a test. He's not accustomed to trusting people. He catches himself staring at that box: Unclaimed remains: Eben Scratch. Eben has never genuinely trusted anyone other than his parents or sister. And he stopped trusting them when he moved away from Nebraska. He reads that label again, out loud this time, "Unclaimed remains: Eben Scratch." He looks out the window and sees Allison walking back to the hotel.

"*Eben* Scratch has never trusted anyone," he says to himself. "But Husker has. Maybe it's time to remember who I am."

IX. The Underground Trillionaire

It's good to be back in San Francisco, sleeping in our own beds in Fiona's wonderful apartment above the Intoxicating Page.

Eben has acted quickly and been true to his word. He fully financed the Human Trafficking and Slave Liberation Fund. The HTSLF now find themselves in the precarious position of searching for more slaves for Eben to free. The mainstream media reacted with suspicion that Eben is buying slave labor. Eben's offer of positions at EbenZones to the newly freed has reinforced that suspicion. The fringe media reports that he's trying to take over the world.

The conversion of EbenZones into AllisonZones has made astounding progress in the week since he was thrown in the Seine. AllisonZone leaders are chosen by elections. All loan and grant terms and conditions are fully transparent and subject to revision by election. Microgrants focus on solving local problems and macrogrants focus on global-scale problem solving projects. Allison has fomented a program for university professors of every stripe to earn their highly coveted summer salaries by teaching at AllisonZones around the world.

Eben gave a keynote speech yesterday at the Designers of Things conference arguing that the emerging techie rich are responsible for leading the world into a prosperous post-robotic future. He outlined specific ways that everyone can benefit from automation, but Winter and I notice that the front page of the San Francisco Chronicle carries the headline: "ScratchCo to Dominate Robotic Future."

Tomorrow Eben and Allison will open their beach to the public. The beachfront property will be available for rent at a modest price to vacationers according to a lottery system. Social media memes show images of the house, beach, and the about-to-be-reopened path with pictures of Eben offering cake to the huddled masses and a cartoon Eben building a ticket booth to charge admission. The Los Angeles Times editorial cartoon shows Eben greeting visitors and closing the gates behind them, the caption says, "ScratchCo slave labor camp opens on the Central Coast."

Winter and I venture downstairs to the Intoxicating Page.

Volodya has set up in the hard root beer and conspiracy theory section. He looks up and says, "The French will introduce EbenFrancs next week as 'alternative to the Euro,' a timeline that guarantees great-recession level inflation." He scratches Winter's neck. "Germany discusses sanctions. The EU plans to provide security to quell French protests. Russia offers security to French oligarchs."

From the counter behind us, Fiona asks, "You're certain Tam Wo is the butterfly wing?"

"That's the thing about butterfly wings," I say. "They don't look important until after they've had their effect."

Fiona asks, "How is Tam?"

Volodya types a few commands and replies, "Tam is dying. Messages between hospice nurses estimate days, not weeks."

"But you're sure."

"We are certain of nothing."

49. Probability, Statistics, and Trust

Eben no longer uses his corner office. Each morning he sits at the large round table, just another programmer in the software scrum. The software engineer to his right says, "Mr. Scratch, we have a six-sigma match."

"Call me Husker." He opens a window and looks at the statistics of the calculation. "Does that six-sigma calculation include the systematic errors?"

Chandra, a probability and stats whiz hired last week says, "Husker, I don't report results without both statistical *and* systematic uncertainties."

Eben feels as though his world has turned on its axis. Since he drowned, everything in his life has improved except his bank balance—and that feels like a burden unloaded. "Amazing, do you know what this means?"

Chandra says, "We can only measure the match, not the confidence of success but look at the correlations: no one has ever died from Leukemia with a transplant that meets all of these criteria."

"Within the data we've accessed."

"No, Husker, every aspect of Tam Wo's life matches this kid's stem cells. He will not reject this transplant. He might die, but his bone marrow will welcome these cells as if they were his very own. It's that perfect. He won't even need immune suppression therapy to accept the transplant."

Another programmer says, "We don't have evidence for that."

"Just watch."

Eben scrolls through the results, checking every correlation and anticorrelation. He evaluates the covariance tensor. In a separate window he types every doubt that comes to mind. The others respect the quiet necessary for concentration and dive into their projects. He checks the calculations of a hundred randomly chosen elements, no bugs and every decimal point of six-sigma.

He stands and says, "Is it cool with you if I tell Yao?"

The others look at their hands. Eben's embarrassed by how nervous they are in his presence. All but the new guy, Chandra, who says, "It's your project, your report."

Eben walks to the corner office, the office he used until returning from Paris. The new plaque on the open door says: "Yao Wo, Chief Operating Officer." He knocks and Yao waves him in.

Eben says, "We've found a match for Tam."

"I'm sorry? A match for what?"

"His bone marrow stem cells."

"How—what—I don't understand what you mean. How can you—I don't understand."

"That's the analysis project I've had the scrum on. We didn't give you details because we didn't want to raise your hopes, until now!" Eben sits and explains the massive data analysis project. He describes how they acquired medical records from all over the world, compared the records of everyone who has had leukemia, their genetics, living environments, diets, and exercise habits, as well as their treatments and the results. "But that was the obvious part." He's too excited to remain seated. He goes to the whiteboard and draws a diagram separating the patients into three groups: survivors, dead, and still in treatment.

"We uncovered a subtle correlation between patients who reject stem cells from excellent matches and patients who accept stem cells from fair-to-poor matches." He takes a purple marker and draws a circle within the healthy people connected by a line to the leukemia survivors. "A special combination of factors that seem irrelevant, but in every case, every single case of a successful stem cell transplant, these factors matched."

Yao sits up straight. He's not smiling and his furrowed brow doesn't have any of his usual enthusiasm. "Mr. Scratch, Husker, you don't know anything about leukemia or stem cells; you're a computer scientist and a banker."

"I'm a data analyst."

"Tam has seen dozens of doctors at cutting edge oncology centers. He's rejected three perfect matches."

"This match is better than perfect. Transplants with this type of match have never been rejected and it's a large statistical sample."

Yao looks down. "Don't you see? Another transplant is just more torture and then he dies. He has to be isolated for three months after each transplant and he only has a few days left. I won't let him spend his last days alone. No. No sir, I want Tam to spend those days with the people he loves.

"It is solved," Eben says. "I put all of our resources on this problem. We have a completely new algorithm for matching donors. I've disrupted the way medical data is analyzed. We broke privacy laws to find this donor."

"My son is not a problem in need of a solution. He's a boy and he's dying."

Eben wraps his hands together and clenches. "Yao—Mr. Wo—can I please explain just one more time? Just listen, please, and then I'll accept your decision."

"Of course, sir."

"No Yao, not like that. This isn't Mr. Scratch your boss, it's me, Husker, your friend. We can save Tam!"

Yao remains motionless, as he would have a month ago in the face of one of Eben's threats.

"In analyzing a large data set it is possible to find quirky correlations that have no cause-effect relationship; edge cases that match up with other phenomena by sheer coincidence. We have mathematical tools to check for these coincidences. The chances that this marker is a coincidental correlation is less than one in five-million—it's a six-sigma effect." He lets his hands fall to his lap and keeps his voice steady. "Tam's doctors have never analyzed the whole data set, they've never combed through the records of billions of people. We have."

"I'll talk to my wife."

"Thank you. Is there anything else I can do? Giants tickets? Is there any game, any toy, anywhere he'd like to go? Anything he'd like to see? Please?"

"I'll ask Shu and Tam if they want anything."

* * *

Yao leaves early that day. He feels obligated to share Mr. Scratch's offer. He waits until they go to bed and the house is quiet. He describes Scratch's research as well as he can and Shu listens.

She waits three counts, showing no emotion, though he can feel it boiling within her. She says, "I don't want anything from that man."

"He's changed. He's pretty cool now, I think."

"Changed? In weeks? And you believe him? You are blind!" She leaps out of bed. "No, a thousand times no. That man is not going to ruin the last days we have with Tam. No!"

Yao stands with his arms out.

She says, "Get away from me," and runs out of the room.

Yao sits alone. He wonders if there's a chance. Mr. Scratch-Eben-Husker, he doesn't know what to call him anymore, but he seemed so certain. Yao is tired of hope. He wonders if people can really change. He wonders about statistics, too. And liars.

He takes out his phone, the company phone, and calls

Scratch. "Hi Husker, thanks for trying so hard to find a match, but no, we can't watch Tam to go through that again. It sucked."

Just before he hangs up, Mrs. Wo screams, "Don't let that horrible bastard hurt us any more than he already has!" Yao is glad that she says it in Mandarin.

50. The Power of Invisibility

Eben's Glass translates every language automatically.

He shuts off his phone and glances at the 24 karat cob of corn on the corner of his desk. His 49th floor apartment is now well lit and happy; no more haunting shadows, no oppressive silence, and no takeout leftovers in the refrigerator. He walks through the hall, passes the guest suite and hears Allison's live-in rehab nurse watching TV. He walks into the family room. Allison's on the couch reading a book about addiction recovery. He smiles at her and she asks what's bothering him.

"She said no."

She pats the spot next to her and he sits.

"Why should anyone believe me?" he says. "I get it."

"They should believe you because you're telling the truth." She puts her arms around his neck. "We'll earn their trust."

He rests his head in the nook of her shoulder and neck. "We can't accomplish anything without trust."

"It doesn't matter what other people think."

"It matters to Tam Wo."

He sighs and Allison sighs with him and the contentment that washes over him comes with a wave of guilt.

Eben is restless most of the night, but when he sleeps, he sleeps soundly. He wakes in Allison's arms and feels gratitude for his life. She's shaking so he calls in the nurse who brings her a dose of methadone to ease the withdrawal. She apologizes, lights a cigarette and promises, again, that she'll quit this habit too. He never said anything about it, but she still felt like she had to apologize. He wonders if he'll ever shake his reputation for being a judgmental monster. He sighs and kisses her forehead.

He takes a cable car down Nob Hill, gets off before the tourists fill it up, and then walks to Union Square. Low, fast moving clouds cast shadows from an otherwise royal blue sky: perfect hoodie weather.

He tries not to look at the newspaper racks, but the New York Times and Wall Street Journal headlines start with his name and the Chronicle has his picture above the fold. He is less popular than the day he made the infamous Facebook post. He takes a deep breath of cool air and forces a smile. Allison will meet him at work after her doctor and therapist appointments and narcotics anonymous meeting.

"Hey trillionaire!" A man calls from a doorway. He's lying on the ground under a coat. His shoes are duct taped, and he's holding a huge can of cheap beer. "Give me a million bucks. You won't even notice it."

Eben takes out his wallet and gives the man a twenty.

"Come on, Scratch, at least hundred."

Eben keeps walking. Nothing he does will ever be enough.

The man yells, "Techie bitch."

He waits in line for a latte at Bancarella on Union Square. People step into line behind him and he hears his name. He smiles and says good morning and appreciates that they're polite enough to leave him alone.

Does praise for his actions really matter? Eben, has always wanted to score points. It's part of who he is, or was. But acknowledgment for his deeds, whether counted in money or recognition, no longer holds any appeal. He wants to do well for reasons he can't name. To impress Allison? Maybe as an expression of affection but not to impress.

"Sir?" The barista interrupts his thoughts.

Someone behind him says, "Come on, Scratch, some of us have to work for a living."

"Oh! Sorry—could I have a medium latte, please?" He glances behind him and counts eleven people. He leans forward and whispers to the barista, "And could I please pay for these people's drinks?" He runs his cell phone over the payment center.

As she hands him the paper cup, the barista announces, "Eben Scratch is buying everyone's coffee."

Several people say thank you, but Eben wanted it to be a secret. He wonders if he should move back to Nebraska, but it wouldn't help, there's nowhere for him to hide.

He rushes down Maiden Lane because it's empty, turns on Grant, and then up Market Street. A ragged looking man in soiled jeans approaches him. He realizes that this is the same place where Allison accosted him a month ago and his life started to change.

"Sir?" the man says. "Spare a dollar?"

Eben stops and looks at the man. He recalls his infamous post. Maybe the man is a loser, but maybe it's not his fault. Maybe he tried and failed. Eben doesn't want to imagine how hard it could be to reboot a life without enough money for a meal or access to a bathroom or shower, much less without a car or a security deposit for an apartment. The man turns to another passerby and shakes his cup of coins. Eben doesn't see human trash in this man. He's not without respect or dignity, he's just broke. Maybe he is a drug abuser—but why? And how did he become one? The love of his life is an addict and she's not a loser or a failure or a quitter; no, her only bad luck was falling in love with a man who loved money more than he loved her.

Eben hands him a hundred.

"Wow!" The man says, "You made my day, my week. Thank you and God bless you. I can get by on this for a month." He looks Eben in the eyes, he's a bit taller than Eben so he looks down at him. "This is a huge help, man. Really."

Eben holds out his hand and the man shakes it. Eben wants to help this man, really help him. He starts to introduce himself but before he can get a word out, the man thanks him again.

The gratitude on this man's face is the opposite of the reaction of the other panhandler he bumped into today. As far as Eben knows, the only difference between the two men is that the other man recognized him and this man hasn't. And then he remembers the headlines and the people in line at the café. If he can help this man, then maybe he can help lots of people. But they won't accept his help if they know who he is.

"No," Eben says, "thank you. I think I get it now."

51. Perfect Match

Sitting next to Volodya in the cozy mystery and sherry section of the Intoxicating Page, I'm watching the timeweave fluctuate as wildly as it did before we went to Paris. And then it settles. One second it's wagging like Winter's tail when I offer him a treat and the next it's settled, stationary, as calm as a dog sleeping in the sunshine. Just like that, it has returned to a stable weave of vibrating timelines that accommodate all the little serendipities of life.

Volodya says, "What happened?"

"I'm tracing it," I say. In less than a minute I find the convergence point. "It converged seven minutes ago on Market Street, at the same location of the Allison-Eben pivot point—but I can't tell what happened."

Volodya brings up the surveillance feed and sees Eben walking to work.

"Did he post anything on social media?"

"No, but he gave money to a panhandler."

I launch facial recognition software.

Volodya pulls up feeds of Eben's entire walk to work. He says, "He now donates to everyone who asks, buys coffee, walks slowly, looks at clouds."

Fiona takes her seat on my other side. Winter hops into her lap. She scratches that spot behind his right ear and his leg starts twitching. "We've done quite right by him."

"The panhandler's name is Vance Miller," I say. It takes an hour for the timeweave engine to construct the man's timeline. "He was laid off three years ago from a printing company. His wife and daughter were in a car accident. The wife was fine but the daughter had a fractured skull. They didn't have any insurance and the medical bills bankrupted him. His wife threw him out a year ago and he's been on the streets ever since."

Volodya makes the sound of a frustrated mule. Fiona says, "I couldn't agree more. How can this man alter history?"

I throw up my hands and say, "No idea."

Volodya says, "We will figure it out."

"Is Tam connected?" Fiona says. "You keep telling me that butterfly wings are subtle."

It takes me seconds to check. "No improvement. Nothing. But we just got a message from Eben. He wants us to attend a meeting at ScratchCo this afternoon."

Fiona leans over my shoulder to read it. She adds, "He's polite enough, but pushy."

Volodya: "Let's go now. I must know what happened."

Fiona: "Isn't it enough to know that the problem has been fixed?"

Me: "The EbenFranc just tanked. Germany announced talks

with France."

"The Euro has been stabilizing." Volodya digs into another database. "Very clever. Eben bought up all the EbenFrancs with a still newer currency: RealFrancs."

Fiona: "How does swapping one currency with another change anything."

Volodya: "RealFrancs are indistinguishable from Euros. He has put France back on the Euro without telling them. And, best part, Putin is extremely angry."

Fiona: "Then everything is back to normal."

I say, "But why?"

Winter yawns.

The four of us take a cab to ScratchCo where a new admin guides us to a conference room and Eben greets us. He pulls Fiona into a tight hug and thanks her. He then hugs me and I wonder if perhaps the transition of Eben Scratch into Husker hugger could be the very flap of the cosmic wing that converged the timeweave. Eben and I disengage. He pats Winter's head. Volodya holds out a hand for shaking as Eben moves in for the hug. They standoff for three seconds and then Eben shakes Volodya's hand. For an instant I feared for his safety.

We finally sit about a round table, me between Fiona and Volodya, with Eben on the other side between Allison and Yao.

Eben speaks as though he's experienced a revelation. He describes the distrust and suspicion surrounding his actions since he returned to San Francisco.

Fiona: "You'll earn trust and people will appreciate you. Hang in there mate."

Eben waves her off. "No, it won't work. It will never work. My identity is the problem. I can be much more effective as a tyrant."

"Eben!" Fiona says. "No, you can't ..."

Volodya has held out his fist and raises one finger. He says,

"What he says is true."

"No, he can't go back—"

Eben: "That's not what I'm suggesting."

Volodya: "Out of the spotlight, Eben has freedom to operate without being examined."

Eben: "And when I am examined, it will be as a tyrant. Meeting expectations is not newsworthy."

Fiona: "How can you live like that?"

Eben: "I don't need recognition."

Fiona turns to Allison and says, "Do you want to live with a tyrant?"

Allison says, "He's Husker at home, a nice boy from the cornfields of Nebraska. He's Eben the tyrant in the press."

"You'd be amazed at how hard it is to give away a trillion dollars," Eben says. "I'm the man who makes the money and takes the blame and doesn't care. I'm Eben Scratch." He points at the wall behind us. I turn and see a poster for "The Beach at Allison Cove."

"I'm closing the beach."

Fiona gasps. "What? No, Eben, please don't. Don't go back."

"I'm not going back. I'm going to be the man that you envisioned when you set out to help me, but don't you see? I'm also going to play a role."

Volodya: "Fiona, Eben is right. He makes personal sacrifice to help others—an action you claim to respect."

Fiona swallows her objections.

Eben turns to Yao and says, "Yao, would you mind leaving us for a few minutes—close the door please." He waits an additional 14 seconds after the door closes and then says, "I can save Tam—We found a perfect match. But the Wos won't accept my help."

"Why?"

"Because he doesn't trust me. And why should he? I am a tyrant."

"Yao knows that you're not a tyrant."

"In his head, maybe he does, but Tam doesn't have time for me to earn his parents' trust."

Fiona says, "You need our help to convince the Wos?"

"To convince the donor."

"Who is it?"

"There's a link in my root directory, just inside my personal firewall."

Volodya uses his phone to hack into ScratchCo and hit the link.

Fiona takes the phone and looks at the picture. "Evan? Your nephew."

"Yes."

Fiona: "Just ask her, your sister would do anything for you!"

Eben: "She's too suspicious. I can't risk it. You don't understand the extent to which my reputation makes me an obstacle. But I do."

Fiona says, "We'll take care of it."

"Okay." Eben doesn't sound convinced, but he guides us to the elevator. "There's no time to waste."

52. The Assumption of Civilization

We're quiet in the elevator but brainstorm in the taxi. By the time we step into the Intoxicating Page we have a plan.

It takes Volodya and me 37 minutes to embed the perfect match into the UCSF database used by Tam's doctor and rig the appropriate alarms.

"We have made mistake," Volodya says. "Evan has never been tested as a stem cell donor."

Fiona says, "Then how can we know he's a perfect match?"

"The data was recorded when he gave blood. He is best possible match, analysis is good, but his mother won't know this. Is new technique for matching, she won't know. We can fool doctor by planting documentation."

"But we can't fool Evan's mother." I'm stricken with that apprehensive feeling of impending failure. "When Tam's doctor calls, his mother won't understand. They'll think it's a mistake."

"No," Fiona says, "Eben's nephew will be at the UCSF Cancer Center tomorrow morning ready to donate."

"We can maybe send email to the mother from account of the boy's doctor?" Volodya scrambles on his keyboard. "Maybe we convince them the boy was tested before somehow?"

"We don't need to do that," Fiona says.

"Why?" I ask. "What can we do?"

"You have better idea?"

"Yes," Fiona says. "I'll call Eben's sister and tell her the truth, the whole story."

"You are mad!" Volodya stands. "You risk everything on assumption she will," he struggles to squeeze out the word: "understand?"

"I'll tell her that Evan can save Tam's life."

"Fiona," I say, "what if she tells Mrs. Wo?"

"You assume that she will keep Eben's identity secret?" Volodya says. "You assume?"

"She's a mom, she'll understand," Fiona sips her latte. "And she wants Eben to be a good man. She'll keep his secret."

"This is foundation free-assumption!"

"It has the most solid foundation of all. The only foundation, really."

Volodya's jaw drops. "Okay, you humor us." He nods at me. "What is foundation of this assumption?"

We both turn to Fiona.

She seems impatient with us.

She takes out her phone and manipulates the user interface for a few seconds. It dawns on me that she's making a conventional phone call, the old-style legacy kind where people talk to each other. I sometimes forget that phones still have this feature.

She shakes her head at us with that look that lands somewhere between disappointment and amusement.

"Hello, Sally?"

Volodya starts to hack into her phone so that we can hear both sides of the conversation, but Fiona points at him and snaps her fingers so he stops.

"My name is Fiona Black. You don't know me, but I'm a friend of your brother's." She listens and then says. "That's right, his friend." Pause. "Well, in the last couple of weeks he has acquired several friends." Then she lights up with a smile. "Right, me too!" She laughs. "Well, maybe someday. Let's not get ahead of ourselves." Pause. "Uh huh. I know." She takes a breath. "The reason I'm calling is that your brother needs a favor and for some stupid reason he thinks that you won't help him."

Volodya and I wave at her to stop talking, change course, anything. Volodya reaches for her phone but she pulls it away and, showing astounding agility, dances behind the bookcase that holds parent reference books and Swedish vodka.

"Right," she says. "I'm staring at two of them right now." Pause. "I don't know if 'too smart for his own good' is the way I'd put it, but I get your point." Pause. "Just wait. It's not a small favor. Actually he needs the help of your son Evan." She explains the situation, concluding with, "can you get Evan to UCSF medical center tomorrow morning? We could arrange a flight if—"

Fiona smiles all the way up to her forehead. "That's what I

thought you'd say." She asks for my hanky. "Okay, we'll see you tomorrow." She puts her phone back in her pocket and blows her nose.

Volodya sounds like a frustrated mule. "You would risk Tam's life on foundation-free assumption!"

"No, dear. Sally loves her brother." She sits on the table next to his laptop. "That's the only foundation civilization has."

53. One More Hit Ought to do It

At first, Allison's world felt like it had jostled right back into place, like everything came out okay in the end. Except it's not the end. And, after three months of living with Eben on Nob Hill, the thought of it being a new beginning just makes it feel harder. She has become a sick woman totally dependent on a man and she's not sure that it's an improvement. The 49th floor is a beautiful place to live, but it feels like a prison. The nurse nags at her. Her aunt sounds worried every time they talk. She can't even reclaim her reputation as a San Francisco techie golden child. No, she's a recovering junkie who can't even adapt to a life of leisure.

She just went for a breath of air, a quick walk on the labyrinth in the shadow of Grace Cathedral, and now she's in a different world; down the hill, back in the Tenderloin. She feels silly wearing a flowery skirt, blouse, cardigan, and sandals. She walks by Divas on Post Street and turns on Polk Street.

She hears a familiar voice from the alley next to the Hemlock: "Oh. My. Fucking. God."

She says, "Hi Lexus."

"Where have you been, girl?"

"A long way. A long way from here."

Lexus is wearing a halter top that barely contains her, a new leopard-print miniskirt, and spike heels. She has a new wig, too.

Allison says, "It's good to see you."

Lexus steps in front of her and looks her over. "You're wearing a fucking cardigan?" Lexus holds Allison by her hips. "Cashmere? Do I know you?"

Allison looks down at herself. Eben bought it for her a few weeks ago when they were walking to dinner and she got cold. She takes it off and hands it to Lexus. "Weird. I know."

Lexus wraps it over her shoulders and Allison wonders how Lexus can make any article of clothing look sexy. "Looks a lot better on you."

Lexus says, "You want to party?"

Allison looks up and down the street as though she's just realized where she is. She feels stupid but not out of place. The feeling is not so much "what am I doing here?" as "what was I doing on Nob Hill?" She says, "Best idea I've heard in months."

The two of them walk to the corner and Allison buys a bag of heroin from an acquaintance who doesn't recognize her. They settle into the alley behind Edinburgh Castle. Lexus reaches into her purse and takes out her gear, including a hypodermic needle still wrapped in plastic.

Allison feels like she's playing in a sandbox as they prepare their fixes. She wraps a shoestring around her bicep, taps her arm until she raises a nice vein, and inserts the needle. The rush comes on and she reenters a soft, familiar world. Lexus takes her turn and the two of them lean against each other and take it all in.

Lexus says, "Where've you been?"

"If I told you, you wouldn't believe me."

"Did you hear about Candy?"

Allison pictures the kindhearted, lean boy in his Capri jeans and that ridiculously tight T-shirt. "I love that guy. Where is he?"

"He's dead."

"What?"

"Yeah, he got the shit beat out of him and then went off. ODed right here."

"Here?"

"See the wilted flowers over there? That's where Rattler found him. Little fucker owed me money, too."

The drugs disperse through her blood but the comfort they bring feels hollow and fake. The buzz is there, the rush, but she can't get away from the fact that it's not real. It's not the feeling she has when she wakes in the morning with Eben and the puppies.

The puppies!

Now she's afraid.

Where are her puppies? How could she leave the apartment without them?

She wonders how the heroin she just injected will pile onto the methadone she takes twice each day. Will she OD? Right now when her life is finally back on track? She feels the heroin-induced calm push thoughts of the risks aside.

Lexus says, "You okay?"

She mumbles, "What am I doing here?" She stands but gets a head rush and falls back to the curb. She looks around. The smell of urine is like an alarm. And the dead flowers. Candy is dead and Allison doesn't want to die. "I think I have to go."

"We just got here." Lexus pulls a glass pipe from her purse. "Let's do some crack—it's good for what ails you." She laughs at her own joke.

The laughter sounds fake to Allison. She feels thoughts trying to emerge in her brain but the heroin holds them back. She hands Lexus the $500 of drugs she just bought and Lexus says something else that sounds inauthentic—just words to appear cool and ghetto.

Candy didn't deserve anything but love. She can picture it. Some assholes beat him up and he tried to hide. Hide from his own thoughts the way that she had when Eben became the world's first trillionaire. And now Candy is dead. It's so unfair. She pushes back on the heroin. The world isn't fair or unfair, or really it's both. It's just and unjust and everything between. "It's the world," she mumbles. "And it just keeps on worlding."

Lexus says something but Allison's not listening. She's thinking about the concrete doorway on Eddy Street where she'll probably sleep tonight and then she thinks of Eben's apartment. She never deserved to live on the 49th floor over Nob Hill.

But Eben doesn't care where they live. If she asked him to, Eben would live on the street with her and the puppies. She pictures them lying in a heap: Mage the ten week old Dalmatian, Paladin the year-old hound dog, Eben, and her. She laughs at how he runs around the apartment with a cape pretending to be Super Husker.

"Ahh, you're feeling better now. This'll help, too." Lexus holds the pipe out for her. Allison takes it without thinking. Lexus holds a lighter under it and Allison pulls it to her mouth.

And stops.

"No," she says, turning away. "No. I have to go home."

"What you say girl? We just got started."

Allison says, "I gotta call my aunt."

"What, you're too good for me now?"

"No, that's not it. I just, I need to feed my dogs." She stands and walks away. She passes a few people she used to know, none of them recognize her. She's cold without the cardigan and she starts planning a story for why she left, where she went, and what she did. The bottom of her skirt is filthy and she probably smells like a sewer. She looks at her arm and sees the fresh dot of blood next to the track of healing scars.

Another thought bubbles up: She doesn't want to get in trouble. And now she laughs. She walks onto Union Square laughing so hard she has to sit at a bench. Tourists smile at her and start laughing, too. A business man gives her a thumbs up.

Seriously, she thinks to herself, I'm worried about "getting in trouble?" The absurdity of telling a lie to Eben brings another wave of laughter. He's on her side. She's on his side. Neither of them want her to be a junkie. If she lied he'd believe her; she could tell him she was kidnapped, taken to Mars, held down and injected, and he'd still do whatever it takes to help her. She stands and starts her way back up the hill, picturing how Eben will react when she tells him the truth. He'll be upset, but he won't be angry. He'll ask what she wants to do and he'll help any way he can.

She wonders if that was her last hit of heroin. Maybe, she thinks, maybe not, but I'm not going back there again.

54. Stolen Base

I haven't been to a baseball game in years, and it's Winter's first. Fiona, Volodya, and I sit behind the backstop at the top of the bleachers. We've got peanuts and hot dogs; they don't serve beer at Little League games. Winter is down below the bleachers playing with Mage and Paladin. Eben and Allison sit down in the second row behind the Wo family who take up the entire first row.

Fiona tries to explain the similarities of cricket and baseball to Volodya. He argues with her, but I can tell he's just disagreeing because that's what they do.

The pitcher winds up and throws, the batter swings, and, with a great aluminum "Tink!" the ball zips over the shortstop's head. Not a difficult task, given that the shortstop is roughly four feet tall.

Yao leaps up from his seat behind the bench where boys and girls wait for their turn to bat.

Volodya says, "It is significant?"

"Don't be a dill—he got a hit and you know it." She spits out a bit of peanut shell and points at Tam's mother who is dancing along the first base line praising her boy from behind the chain link fence.

Even from up here I can see Tam roll his eyes. It's his first hit in his first at bat in his first game. I must admit that I feel a bit of pride, as though my miniscule contribution to Tam's tiny accomplishment is somehow significant.

I say, "We have a pretty good world here!"

"Could be better," Volodya says.

"Rubbish," Fiona says, "the fog burned off before the first pitch, the peanuts are salty, the grass smells wonderful, and Tam Wo is healthy."

I add, "And the world seems to be back on its slow, haphazard, contradictory path in the general direction of civilization."

Volodya grunts like a National League manager watching a pitcher walk to the plate with the bases loaded. "Do not flatter ourselves. We put a cork in humanity's violence, lies, and hatred—no more."

Tam takes a big lead from first base.

I muse, "Do you think humanity will become civilized before it destroys itself?"

Fiona tears the top off of a packet of mustard and squirts it on a hot dog. "Every serious analysis shows that there's less violence now than at any other time in history, but we're more aware of it. Our newsfeeds report crime, violence, and injustice from parts of the world that our grandparents never would have heard from. Humanity really is getting more civilized; though it's taking bloody long enough." She takes a bite of the hot dog, swallows, and adds, "But did Tam really have anything to do with it? I still don't see how he was the butterfly wing. How could that kid who's taking way too big of a lead from first base prevent a dark age?"

Volodya clears his throat. I feel a lecture coming on and lean back so that he can make eye contact with Fiona on my other side. "I reverse engineered Timeweave calculation." The next batter has taken a couple of balls and run up the count. "Many, many breezes on which the butterfly soars, but it was not a mistake: Tam altered the course of history by putting Eben in unique position. If not for Tam, Eben triggers currency war. State of the world as it is, the currency war would have thrown humanity off its path in the general direction of civilization."

I add, "Such as it is."

The pitcher throws to first base, Tam dives back, and Mrs. Wo exhales a breath she must have been holding for minutes.

I say, "Was Tam the attractor that drew Eben to find compassion so he could stop treating the world like it's a great competition?"

"No. Was not that."

Around a mouthful of hot dog, Fiona says, "Compassion was a big part of it."

"Perhaps." Volodya makes an upside down smile.

Fiona leans across me to get in Volodya's face. "Eben has changed because he discovered the value of compassion, empathy, and kindness!"

"No, you miss point," Volodya says. "Remember, the timeweave converged when Eben gave money to two panhandlers. At that moment, Eben was deeply frustrated. He had Tam's cure but the Wos wouldn't accept it from him, Eben Scratch. The first panhandler recognized him and asked for more money; nothing Eben could have given him would have been enough. And then the other panhandler was thrilled with the gift, the boon from someone he did not recognize. That was it! At that instant, Eben understood that he could cure Tam, could solve problems, make great contributions to civilization but only anonymously." Fiona holds up her hot dog and Volodya takes a bite. He chews and swallows and adds, "You see, the need to cure Tam put him in mindset so that he could learn that lesson."

The batter swings on a third strike. Now there are two outs with Tam still on first base.

Me: "And they still don't know?"

Fiona: "No, no, speak softly. Neither Yao nor Mrs. Wo are aware that Tam's donor was Eben's nephew." Fiona leans back and rests her leg on the bleacher in front of us. "And now Husker and Allison live a double life. I'm absolutely rapt! Evil Eben Scratch lives in a mansion on Nob Hill, literally looming over the city. Meanwhile, sixty miles away, Husker and Allison live in a funky old Victorian by a river in a redwood forest with an injured fox, a couple of rabbits, two dogs, a cat, some ducks, chickens, three goats, a few river otters and when they're not kayaking or trying to keep their hundred and fifty year-old house from falling apart, they're finding ways to enable poor people all over the world."

Me: "The trillionaire does his own plumbing?"

Fiona: "In the last year, Husker has given over 500 billion dollars in grants to pretty much anyone with an idea that can help people. But yes, he does the plumbing, the wiring, carpentry, roofing."

Volodya: "Many good ideas, not all original. They run into trouble with patent law. Is a problem."

Fiona: "Independent inventions of energy scavenging to charge cell phones a hundred miles from an electrical outlet—how can it be infringement if a grandmother in a Congo jungle can hack together a microprocessor and some code to convert mechanical energy to electrical?"

"Is violation when technology was first invented by engineers in a Silicon Valley lab."

"But that's not the worst, I go mental when I hear about biotech firms suing Sudanese farmers for sharing seeds!"

Volodya: "Farmers connect on internet, they share hybrid seeds, find ways to accelerate cross-pollination, old-school genetic engineering. Nothing illegal to it."

Fiona: "Husker's cheap white smartphones are making a big difference."

"And it's all financed by Eben's cutthroat finance apps." Volodya makes a sound like a pleased owl. "Is beautiful thing! Where good and evil meets."

I keep my eyes on the field—the kid at bat fouls off a pitch.

The pitcher winds up and throws. Tam sprints away from first base. Everyone down in the front row yells. The batter swings and misses. The catcher recovers the pitch, rises, steps to his right, and throws the ball to second base. Tam dives headfirst. His slide raises a cloud of dirt. His helmet flies off. The ball snaps into the second basegirl's glove and she makes the tag.

Mrs. Wo covers her eyes. Yao jumps up and down. Their children cheer.

With one hand on the base, Tam looks at the umpire who waves his arms: safe.

You don't have to leave The Intoxicating Page. Instead, start reading another Time Weavers story.

The 99% Solution

An intercontinental, inter-dimensional thrill ride

"No writer working today so effortlessly packs such intelligence, humanity, and wit into good old-fashioned storytelling as Ransom Stephens. His latest, *The 99% Solution*, is his best yet. Breezily paced and yet full of suspense, this topical, whimsical, heartfelt novel kept me merrily turning pages deep into the night. Buy it, read it. You'll thank me."

- David Corbett, award-winning author of *The Mercy of the Night*.

Lucy Montgomery is the 99% … buried in student loan debt and pissed off at a rigged system. Francis Gordon Woodley, IV, is the top of the 1%…heir to a corporate empire that can buy or topple entire nations.

Manipulated by anarchists, Lucy sets out to destroy corporate power so that classless democracy can bloom into worldwide utopia. With his oligarch friends, Francis sets out to destroy government, unleash free-market forces, and spawn worldwide utopia.

With Lucy and Francis on a collision course, the Time Weavers race to save the rest of humanity. Every future their computers predict leads to a hundred-year dark age except one. But for that one timeline to emerge into reality, Simon must encourage his god-daughter, Lucy, to assassinate his mentor's son, Francis. Unless they can find another way.

THE 99% SOLUTION

By Ransom Stephens

Whether we gauge time by the revolution of a planet, the period of a swinging pendulum, or the duration of a heartbeat, the time between two ticks is never exactly the same. Our story, indeed everyone's story, is about the uncertainty of destiny and the oscillations of fate.

Wall Street

2011-Sep-23 10:37am
Pivot point peak probability: 88 minutes

Something is going to happen on Wall Street that will alter the course of history and it's going to happen soon. I take another look at my phone to check the calculation. You see, while anything is possible some things are more probable than others; Volodya, Fiona, Winter, and I are in the business of calculating these probabilities. We don't know exactly what will happen, which is embarrassing. We know where it will happen to within a few blocks, which isn't bad. And we know that it will happen in 62 to 109 minutes from now, an uncertainty of 47 minutes that can hardly make a good impression, but don't fret, we'll have a more accurate computation soon.

A strong autumn breeze tugs at my clothes as Winter pulls me through New York City's skyscraper-lined streets. The four of us stop at the corner of Broadway and Cedar.

Volodya, whose name rhymes with melodious but whose voice does not, says, "I will survey Occupy from perspective of authorities." His voice has a sharp Russian edge to it that his blue eyes do nothing to soften. "There will be a problem."

"Right," Fiona says, her accent resounds with the big-hearted, vowel-amplifying sound of Australia. "That makes me an Occupier, then."

Volodya steps away with an efficient stride, a gliding motion that betrays the smooth tread of a sprinter. With his hands in the pockets of his tight-fitting black jacket, his narrow shoulders folded inward, and his face tucked away from the wind, he gives the impression of a man concentrating on his destination, and he is, but his countenance also indicates a lack of interest in his surroundings which is well practiced but hardly the case.

Fiona chuckles. "Imagine that, he expects a problem." She knocks her forehead against mine and says, "He's got more than a bit of the Eeyore to him." She's wearing jeans and a button-down shirt and leans on a cane. Fiona lost a leg from the hip many years ago. She wears her prosthesis more to reduce the attention of strangers than for its mechanical engineering prowess. She prefers her cane, a titanium short-staff that includes three clichés: a half pint reservoir at the handle usually filled with scotch and, at its base, a ten inch dagger-like blade that can be released by a stiletto mechanism located beneath the third cliché, a duck-head handle.

She untucks her blouse, unfastens the two lower buttons, and ties the tail in a knot just above her naval. Then she releases the shirt's top two buttons. If she had cleavage, it would show. Instead, she reveals a tattoo of a smiling crescent moon with a sexy, witchy-looking woman sitting on the moon's pointy chin. She runs a hand through her hair. It's short and brown and this motion spikes it. Prior to this adjustment, her narrow face and soft, square jaw looked quite scholarly. She looks like a proper rebel now.

I ask, "Aren't you chilly?"

She looks me over. I'm wearing my favorite suit, gray wool herringbone that's been to the cleaners so often that it's soft as velvet. She says, "Simon dear, try to pretend that you don't know me."

She slides down her cane to Winter's level and scratches him behind his ears. He jumps up and they exchange a kiss. He's a beagle with a black and orange coat, white belly and paws, and brown ears. With the aid of her cane, she rises to full height, says, "I'm off to the revolution!" and away she goes.

Winter tows me around the Occupy gathering in a way that belies his "service dog" vest—an annoying affectation that he has to wear in this species-ist country or risk banishment from polite company.

Nearly 32% of the crowd have their phones out. I'm holding my smart phone, too, though mine is smarter than most. I check the application that's running on the fleet of computing servers located at our lab in Vienna. The program engages our cell phones' cameras, microphones, and GPS positioning as well as the vast mine of information contained in the networked computing devices across the world, all to perform a complex calculation.

Let me elaborate as best I can without invoking hundreds of pages of mathematics and thousands of lines of software and please allow me to apologize in advance for the avalanching spray of inadequate and occasionally contradicting metaphors. A single past is carved from the weave of possible futures the way that a trickle of melting ice on its way from mountaintop to sea carves first a creek, then a river, and finally a canyon. When we ponder what fate has in store, it is the fork in the river, the knot in the tree, indeed, the pivot point in time that sets our course.

We build our predictions, our timeweaves, from the cumulative influences of billions of events—whats and whys—that lead us to when and where pivot points will occur. But since most pivot points are directed by many pebbles rather than a few boulders, we're not so good at discerning their hows and whos. Our goal is to determine the probabilities for each possible destination, at which we are quite proficient, and to find those variations in the timeweave that decide history's course, which is a mighty struggle.

Over the last 782 days we've calculated an increasing likelihood for two such pivot points. The first has an inordinately high probability of occurring within seven blocks and 100 minutes of the very point in space and time where I now stand: 10:46 am EDT, on the 23rd of September, 2011 in Zucotti Park, New York City.

Depending on the direction in which this first pivot point reorients history, the likelihood of a pivot point of far greater historical significance occurring within 6 months exceeds 90%. This latter knot in the tree of human history would alter the course of humanity for centuries. We may have to do some pruning.

With the app churning through the world's data to determine the precise time and place of the initial pivot point, I shake my phone as though this action can improve the calculation's precision—rather like whacking a toaster to improve the shade of emerging bread. I loathe imprecision and poorly toasted bread.

2011-Sep-23 10:49 am New York City
Initial pivot point peak probability: 76 minutes
Conditional pivot point: sooner than 6 months

Just as I slide my phone into my coat pocket, it emits the chorus of *Somewhere Over the Rainbow*, the ringtone I reserve for Gwinnie, the partially-requited love of my life.

I manage to restrain Winter long enough to reacquire the phone, though now I find myself with one hand to my ear and the other outstretched at the end of his leash.

I say, "Gwinnie!"

"Are you in New York City?"

"We landed an hour ago." Volodya, Winter, and I flew in from our lab in Vienna and Fiona from her bookstore/bar in San Francisco.

Gwinnie says, "I'm worried about Lucy."

Lucy could've been my daughter, but in this life, at least on this timeline, she is the daughter of my friend Gwinnie, who should've been my wife if I would've had more courage. I regret to admit that I am haunted by the could'ves, should'ves, and would'ves of life.

Gwinnie's voice increases in volume as she gets going. "Lucy isn't answering her phone or replying to texts."

"Please don't worry. Lucy is fine."

"How do you know?"

"The likelihood that Lucy is in Zuccotti Park enjoying the Occupy Wall Street festivities exceeds ninety-nine percent." I'm aware that Gwinnie finds my cavalier response annoying, but I'd rather annoy people with my best estimate than please them with a conservative approximation.

She says, "I haven't talked to Lucy in ten days" and starts to cry. I can't think when Gwinnie cries.

I fumble about my brain for appropriate words. Then my phone vibrates, indicating that the timeweave has updated. Sufficiently distracted that I manage to speak through her weeping, I say "It's okay, Gwinnie. I'll ask Lucy to call you, email, text, tweet, tag you on Facebook, Skype. I'll suggest she send you a postcard."

She blows her nose, an elegant two-tissue blow. In my desire to absorb all the Gwinnie I can, I find myself envious of her tissues. The thought provides a mix of desire and repulsion that gives me the wherewithal to pull the phone from my ear. It hasn't merely updated; the calculation is complete. The display shows a map with two arrows, one where I now stand and another three blocks from here. Above the map, a clock counts down. We have roughly 71 minutes and 13 seconds, make that 71:12, 71:11—you know what I mean—until this annoyingly unknown event occurs that will alter the somewhat chaotic, not altogether well-behaved, but on the scale of the last century, comparatively peaceful and prosperous historical epoch.

I put the phone back to my ear. Gwinnie's still nattering.

"—and no, I don't want a frikkin' postcard!" She hangs up.

I know better than to call back and beg her forgiveness. My dear Gwinnie is a woman of passion who steadfastly resists the temptation to grant apologies willy-nilly.

Winter draws me along a sidewalk lined with cardboard signs that recommend outrage for a variety of causes including disparagement of the wealthy, support for labor, conservation of resources, humane care for animals, regard for climate change, disregard for carnivorous eating habits, and, more than any other, derision of the financial industry. Some contain full length essays, some are parodies, others have slick one-liners, but Winter won't afford me the chance to catch up on my reading.

Zuccotti park has acquired the ambiance of a music festival, that tension one feels between opening and headlining performances. Youths mill about in colorful clothes, though 22 dress in black as though at a Johnny Cash tribute. They laugh and argue, imbibe beer and coffee, emit scents from patchouli to fancy perfume, waft tobacco and ganja smoke, all on a base of excitement emphasized by the coarse smells of human sweat and sexuality. Police pace the edges, talking both among themselves and with the Occupiers. From this vantage, I see

1156 people but estimate the total at 1480 and growing at an accelerating rate. The structure of the crowd exhibits the fluctuating clumps typical of random processes with sticky centers. My attention is again drawn to the tiny fraction of Johnny Cash fans. Those in black are not clumping; they're evenly distributed about the crowd.

I hold up my phone, snap a picture, and initiate an app to process the photo. The app calculates a less than one percent probability that random processes could so evenly distribute people dressed in a single color. I also notice that those in black carry similar backpacks and have black scarves tied at their necks. Fascinating.

Winter navigates us among tents and cliques and drum circles. Following his nose, we land in the queue of a food cart.

"Coffee, please, four sugars, two not-milk packets."

I don't know why the proprietor looks at me twice, but Winter distracts him and the man says, "How 'bout a canine dog?"

The apparent redundancy of this statement is clarified when he places a frankfurter on a paper plate. I hand Winter the wiener and he seems to derive unparalleled enjoyment from this particular meal, which in no way distinguishes it from any other.

Though the coffee will relieve some of my six hour jet lag, the sight of a bench exacerbates my desire to relax. I settle between a young man with an expanse of thick hair captured by a knit cap of yellow, green, and black and a weathered, musty smelling fellow about my age whose head lolls against the armrest.

Just in front and to my right, a young woman engages a police officer. They are a study in American multiethnic monoculture. The woman stands precisely five feet tall and the officer surpasses her by 18 inches; the woman's pale skin is decorated with orange freckles that match her shoulder-length, carrot-red hair and the man has flawless mahogany colored skin, a shaved head, and a manicured black goatee accented by a hint of gray. The woman stares up at him, flailing her arms like a Sicilian on the telephone.

A wave of pride passes through my heart, for this passionate, erudite, young woman is Lucy.

She says, "Your job is to keep the peace."

"My job is to protect and serve," the officer replies. He attempts to disconnect from her gaze by surveying the crowd beyond her, but when she speaks, her voice compels him to look straight down at her. While he is in fact looking down, the literal direction is inconsistent with the metaphorical reality of who leads the conversation.

"Where were you when those crooks up the road were destroying the economy? Where will you be when they steal your pension or foreclose on your neighbors?"

Lucy's injustice detector has always operated with hair-trigger sensitivity. Empathy wells up in my heart for this man. I have lost every debate with Lucy and have yet to see anyone emerge from such an argument in any form but defeated and confused. Indeed, while learning to swim she blamed the water for insufficient buoyancy. The hapless water evaporated elemental feelings of remorse.

"Ma'am, I'll arrest a man in a suit just as fast as a woman in a, umm, in one of, um…"

"You mean a skirt, don't you?"

And the trap is laid.

"You are wearing one."

"It's either skirts or suits to you, isn't it?"

"No, I, no, umm, ma'am—"

"Will you protect me?"

Winter's tail sweeps the pavement in anticipation of Lucy's

victory.

"The New York City Police Department is committed to protection of every citizen."

"Officer, the question is, if you are forced to make a choice, will you protect people or wealth?"

He has now managed to look away from her and that seems to enable him to repeat his stock answer. "The New York City Police Department is committed to protection of every citizen."

But she draws him right back to her web. "What if it's your mother?"

Instead of answering, he pretends to watch the crowd, but in the movement of his eyebrows, just slightly peaked, he confesses defeat.

"Of course you'd protect your mother!" Lucy takes his gloved hand, compelling him to look at her.

Resignation, nearly despair, settles across his face. "Do we have to bring my mother into this?"

Lucy makes a point of searching out his nametag. "Officer Tyvon Justin, you've been trained to handle crowds. We both know that Occupy will commit a few petty misdemeanors. I just want you to keep one thing in mind." She takes a breath and Officer Justin attempts to break away, both his hand from her grip and his eyes from her gaze. Lucy yields neither. "The institutions you'll be protecting may not have broken the letter of any laws, but they have violated the very spirit of civilization. We are the citizens in need of protection."

"Yes ma'am," he says. "Now, please excuse me." He pries his eyes and hands away from hers and steps toward a passing pair of fellow officers.

In a warning tone, but with a triumphant grin, Lucy says, "Officer Justin…"

With two comrades nearby, he reassumes his stature. Adjusting his gloves, he asks, "What's your name, ma'am?"

"Lucy Montgomery."

He takes another step from her.

"Officer Justin?"

"What is it now, ma'am?"

"Come here, your collar is turned up." She reaches as high as she can and fixes the offending collar. "Officer Justin, please don't forget the reasons that you became a police officer. Please?"

I love this child.

He pushes his hat back and says, "Ms. Montgomery, it's been a pleasure, please excuse me."

As he joins his comrades in their patrol of the park perimeter, Lucy's eyes follow him and as they follow him, they pass over Winter and me. She does a double take.

Winter's tail starts whacking the bench.

"Uncle Simon?"

"Lucy!"

Oh those two syllables.

Continue reading *The 99% Solution* at
www.theintoxicatingpage.com

Check out *The God Patent*:

"What distinguishes this classic battle between faith and free will is its unusually deft infusion of legitimate but accessible science … An ambitious first novel that uses Stephens' experience as a particle physicist, director of patents, public speaker and single father in a narrative that sings of the heart and the scientific method as two parts of the same song."
— *San Francisco Chronicle*

Start reading *The God Patent* at
www.theintoxicatingpage.com

Check out *The Sensory Deception*:

The techno-thriller that puts you in the minds of endangered animals.

"Ransom Stephens' imagination is limitless in his ability to lead the reader through scenarios across the globe...The Sensory Deception is a worthy read with fascinating concepts."
  - Santa Rosa Press Democrat

"As with his debut, *The God Patent*, Ransom Stephens swings for the fences with *The Sensory Deception*—and he hits another home run, somehow managing to incorporate virtual reality, Somali pirates, the plight of sperm whales and the deforestation of the Amazon into a thrilling and unique story of romance and adventure."
  - Robert Kroese, author of *Mercury Rises*

Start reading *The Sensory Deception* at
www.theintoxicatingpage.com

Check out *The Left Brain Speaks The Right Brain Laughs*:

Ransom Stephens' irreverent look at the neuroscience of innovation and creativity in art, science, and life.

"Exceptionally well written, organized, and presented."
-*The Midwest Book Review*

"A book all about hard science with metaphors and stories, jokes and quips, ideas and assumptions, and crammed with knowledge … a weight of content with undeniable passion and zest."
-*The Lancet Neurology*

"…so cleverly written that it offers both an amusing read and an illuminating discussion of brain science."
- Patricia Gale, Blogcritics

Start reading *The Left Brain Speaks The Right Brain Laughs: A Look at the Neuroscience of Innovation & Creativity in Art, Science & Life* at www.theintoxicatingpage.com

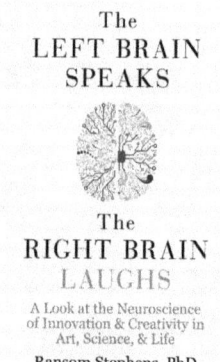

The
LEFT BRAIN
SPEAKS

The
RIGHT BRAIN
LAUGHS

A Look at the Neuroscience
of Innovation & Creativity in
Art, Science, & Life

Ransom Stephens, PhD

Note to you

Thank you for reading *Too Rich to Die*. This book emerged from one of my all time favorite tales and I hope that I've done it justice. Characters come from places in our minds both tangible and intangible. One late spring day, I saw Eben Scratch crossing Market Street in San Francisco so caught up in the combination of his Google Glass and smartphone interface that he nearly tripped over a panhandler.

If you have a minute to spare, I'd greatly it if you would post a review at your favorite book site; whether a sentence of praise or an essay on your desires, I'll appreciate the boost as much as the advice.

I have a bunch of stuff at www.RansomStephens.com like descriptions of my books—including explanations of how I came up with their plots and characters—plus science articles I've written, notes on the craft, and so on. If it's ever relevant (and I hope it will be): beer not wine, tea not coffee, rock not jazz.

If you think of a good cocktail-literature combination for Fiona, let me know and I'll pass it along to her. I'm at: Ransom@RansomStephens.com.

With gratitude and affection, I hope you're having fun!
Ransom
Petaluma, California, March 2019

About Ransom

After 15 years in particle physics research and as a physics professor, Ransom gave up a tenured gig to become the Director of Advanced Technology at a wireless web startup. In addition to writing novels, he's now a Silicon Valley consultant who writes about and teaches engineers the physics they need to design your gadgets. Ransom is also a cussing, beer-swilling Raider fan. He lives in Petaluma, California, where he's working on another novel and still trying to play the guitar.

CPSIA information can be obtained
at www.ICGtesting.com
Printed in the USA
BVHW031558150519
548374BV00001B/8/P